Frankenstein Dreams

Frankenstein Dreams

A Connoisseur's Collection of Victorian Science Fiction

Edited by Michael Sims

BLOOMSBURY

NEW YORK · LONDON · OXFORD · NEW DELHI · SYDNEY

Bloomsbury USA
An imprint of Bloomsbury Publishing Plc

1385 Broadway	50 Bedford Square
New York	London
NY 10018	WC1B 3DP
USA	UK

www.bloomsbury.com

BLOOMSBURY and the Diana logo are trademarks of Bloomsbury
Publishing Plc

First published 2017

ISBN: PB: 978-1-63286-041-5
        ePub: 978-1-63286-042-2

LIBRARY OF CONGRESS CATALOGING-IN-PUBLICATION DATA IS AVAILABLE.

2 4 6 8 10 9 7 5 3 1

Typeset by Westchester Publishing Services
Printed and bound in the U.S.A. by Berryville Graphics Inc.,
Berryville, Virginia

To find out more about our authors and books visit www.bloomsbury.com.
Here you will find extracts, author interviews, details of forthcoming
events, and the option to sign up for our newsletters.

Bloomsbury books may be purchased for business or promotional use.
For information on bulk purchases please contact Macmillan Corporate
and Premium Sales Department at specialmarkets@macmillan.com.

With love to
Helen Derrick,
my cousin
who long ago encouraged me to read and write
and thus enriched my life

I think I will allow my experiment a little more time.

Wardon Allan Curtis, "The Monster of Lake LaMetrie"

Contents

Introduction: That Gulf of Fear

"NOTHING IS SO PAINFUL to the human mind," cries Franken-stein's pitiable monster, "as a great and sudden change."

Published in 1818, Mary Shelley's novel *Frankenstein* was itself a pained response to the great and sudden changes that shook the collective psyche of Western civilization during the nineteenth century. Advances in understanding nature—from the stars to the human body—challenged ancient and cherished assumptions about space and time and even about our lineage as human beings. Every-where readers turned, they encountered evidence that the cosmos was older and more vast than the provincial medieval view whose strictures continued to inhibit study of the world. And as the century aged, the spiritual vertigo from dramatic revelations seemed to increase.

Every new discovery raised questions. In 1781, for example, a German-born musician named William Herschel—a self-taught amateur astronomer—discovered the planet Uranus, and acciden-tally shook loose the last grip that ecclesiastical thinking had on astronomy. The notion of "deep space" soon followed and opened the door to even more devastating concepts such as "deep time," which provided eons for the gradual change of plants and animals.

Even the most passionate fans of natural history, which was an internationally popular recreation during much of the nineteenth century, found the intellectual terrain disconcertingly wobbly. What was our status in the cosmos? Were there really things called galaxies out beyond our local solar system? How can there be both a microscopic world beneath us and a telescopic world above us? Why do we find seashells fossilized on mountaintops? And, after Darwin's *On the Origin of Species* in 1859, people had to ask themselves if it could really be true that we are genetically related to other creatures rather than having been directly crafted from the same clay.

During the nineteenth century, from the era of the pioneer manned balloon flights to the time of the Wright brothers, the conceptual cosmos evolved from a cozy local solar system and a token prehistory to planetary kinship and the beginnings of institutionalized environmentalism. When the century opened, there were few professional scientists and no science courses in schools; church doctrine still dominated "natural philosophy." By the time it ended, the once-reviled Darwin was buried in Westminster Abbey in a state funeral and the Natural History Museum in London had been built as a secular temple to knowledge—with its botanical rather than Ionic columns adorned by apes and lizards instead of gargoyles and saints.

New ways of thinking required new ways of writing, and the writer now considered the founder of science fiction saw the need for fresh metaphors while still a teenager. Mary Shelley confidently declares her position, midway between science and fancy, in her introduction to the 1818 first edition of *Frankenstein; or, The Modern Prometheus*:

The event on which this fiction is founded has been supposed, by Dr. Darwin [Erasmus Darwin, grandfather of Charles], and some of the physiological writers of Germany, as not of impossible occurrence. I shall not be supposed as according the remotest degree of serious faith to such an imagination; yet, in assuming it as the basis of a work of fancy, I have not considered myself as merely weaving a series of supernatural terrors. The event on which the interest of the story depends is exempt from the disadvantages of a mere tale of spectres or enchantment. It was recommended by the novelty of the situations which it developes; and, however impossible as a physical fact, affords a point of view to the imagination for the delineating of human passions more comprehensive and commanding than any which the ordinary relations of existing events can yield.

Shelley's last sentence could serve as a manifesto for fantastic tales in general. Not surprisingly, most critics cite *Frankenstein* as the founding document of the genre that this anthology celebrates. It wasn't named "science fiction" until 1926; Hugo Gernsback used the term when he launched the first magazine devoted to it, *Amazing Stories*. Yet most critics consider modern science fiction to have emerged like Athena from the brow of Zeus in 1816, when Mary Wollstonecraft Godwin (not yet Shelley) woke from a nightmare and began writing *Frankenstein*. The novel was an expression of some of the ancient themes of literature—anguished dread of mortality, the consequences of obsession, and *hubris* and consequent *ate*, the divine retribution that in mythology always follows overweening pride. Young Mary was an unwed, pregnant teenager. She and Percy Bysshe Shelley married later the same year.

Her first novel has lasted, in part, because the central figure quickly strode off the page and into popular culture. Nowadays the cobbled-together, nameless "monster"—long mistakenly known by his creator's name—is familiar to millions who have never read the novel. He is a stock figure in horror movies, a favorite of editorial cartoonists, a cautionary fable about science. Frankenstein and his tormented creation are perfect figures to open a tour of the nineteenth century's troubled dance between science and fiction.

IN SEPTEMBER 1831, THE English poet Samuel Taylor Coleridge attended the British Association meeting at which the word "scientist" was voted in to replace the antique term "natural philosopher."

At the same time, a twenty-two-year-old failed medical student named Charles Darwin was packing his duffel for the *Beagle* voyage and packing his mind with the earthshaking notions of such geologists as James Hutton, who saw a vast prehistory behind our own recent debut. Coleridge also enjoyed the work of the popular scientist Humphry Davy. "I attend Davy's lectures," he declared, "to increase my stock of metaphors."

In doing so the poet took sixty pages of notes such as this: "No difference of Oxygen in cities, Woods, or Sea shore." Coleridge participated in one of Davy's demonstrations of electric shock from a "Leyden Phial," the new chemical battery. Instantly linking the physical spark with theories of vitalism versus materialism, he jotted in his notes, "More's antidote against Atheism." No spark could leap between electrodes more quickly than it could make connections in a writer's mind.

Percy Bysshe Shelley's preoccupation with science dated from the early days of his youth, long before he met young Mary Wollstonecraft Godwin. He devoured every text he could find about astronomy, magnetism, and the recently discovered electrical nature of lightning. His younger sister recalled how he placed her and other children "hand-in-hand round the nursery table to be electrified" with the kind of chemical battery that fascinated Coleridge.

The cross-fertilization occurring between science and literature inspired poetry, drama, sermons—and, yes, science fiction. The stories collected in *Frankenstein Dreams* chronicle how Western civilization responded to the dizzying new discoveries of the nineteenth century. Gravity, time, distance, mortality, sensory limitations, our inability to divine the future—all of these barriers to the human spirit's dreams were tackled through fantastic, entertaining tales that merged ancient human concerns with new revelations and anxieties. Technological innovations and conceptual advances created new lenses through which to view every aspect of the body and nature and society.

The variety of such sparks makes literary taxonomy difficult, but anthologizing is a subjective game. Within the lively pages of this collection, therefore, readers may consider "science fiction" to be loosely defined as tales of the fantastic that exclude the supernatural—no ghosts, no deities, no magic. What may sound like an arbitrary distinction actually demonstrates separate ways of regarding the cosmos. *Homo sapiens* is a restless, curious animal. Whether increasing or reducing heat, converting plant and animal products into clothing, redirecting streams, or constructing tools out of wood and stone, primitive human beings devoted much of their time to manipulating nature. Such attempts included investing the world with spirits and deities whose help required magical intervention—prayer, ritual, sacrifice. The scientific approach that had achieved a new world-view by the nineteenth century, in contrast, regarded nature differently and sought to manipulate it solely by nonmagical means. It is this view of nature that animates most of the stories in *Franken-stein Dreams*, and it proves no less moving or fantastic than earlier viewpoints.

Throughout the century, fantastic concepts permitted writers to explore real-world issues from new perspectives. Among the tales gathered in *Frankenstein Dreams*, Mary Shelley conjures Faustian monsters from the discoveries of Galvani regarding electricity, and explicitly cites Charles Darwin's grandfather Erasmus and his notions of reanimating a corpse. In his 1845 story "The Facts in the Case of M. Valdemar," Edgar Allan Poe explores, in predictably morbid fashion, the theories of Franz Mesmer regarding hypnosis and animal magnetism. Blossoming visions of the human psyche's complexity animate Thomas Wentworth Higginson's disturbing 1877 story "The Monarch of Dreams." Alice W. Fuller, in her pioneer story "A Wife Manufactured to Order" from 1895, cheerfully envisions the shortcomings of the first robot girlfriend. In "The Hall Bedroom," published in 1903, the versatile Mary E. Wilkins Freeman—the only author who appears in each of the four Connoisseur's Collection volumes so far—convincingly portrays a stumble into another dimension.

The great themes of modern science fiction showed up surprisingly early in the dawn of the genre: space travel, time travel, destroyed ecosystems, dystopian societies, and even dangerously independent machines. Trapped within the brief journey of a single lifetime, for example, many imaginative writers envisioned both the past and possible futures. Mary Shelley's own postapocalyptic 1826 novel, *The Last Man*, takes place near the end of the twenty-first century, following the handful of survivors of a terrible plague. It was her ill-fated husband, after all, who described poets as "the mirrors of the gigantic shadows which futurity casts upon the present." Edward Page Mitchell's thoughtful 1881 story "The Clock That Went Backward," reprinted here, is one of the earliest time-travel stories, and influenced many of its more famous successors. Mitchell conjures the frisson of displacement and melancholy that is the hallmark of time-travel stories: the poignant sense of fleeting and irrecoverable time that haunts our linear lives and that H. G. Wells explored in more social terms more than a decade later, in his first "scientific romance," *The Time Machine*.

During the nineteenth century, European writers often chose the less explored (from their point of view) regions of the earth as settings for tales of marvel and wonder. By the mid-Victorian era, imaginary trips to unexplored regions were hugely popular. Arthur Conan Doyle wrote again and again about the American frontier or the Arctic or tropical South America; and finally, in "The Horror of the Heights," which you will find in this volume, he sends his characters exploring in the still unknown regions above the clouds.

Often science fiction uses technological or other nonmagical means to transcend the narrative limitations of more realistic stories, effecting the same plot boost that ghosts or vampires might contribute to another kind of story. Inventors replace witches; chemicals and machines stand in for incantations and curses. This idea emerges from a long history. Hindu and Sanskrit epics, for example, describe the vimana, a flying castle—very much a form of technology, but less invented than conjured. "Sit now upon this square of tapestry," instructs the merchant who tries to sell a flying carpet to Prince Husayn in *One Thousand and One Nights*, "and at thy mere wish and will it shall transport us to the caravanserai wherein thou abidest." Is the carpet thus a vehicle controlled by telepathy? No, it appears to be—and is treated within these magical stories as—an enchanted object, like the talking mirror in *Snow White* or the Wicked Witch's crystal ball in the movie *The Wizard of Oz*.

In this volume, Rudyard Kipling in his story "Wireless" employs the recently invented radio to delve into the past, into the mind of a dead poet. Kipling, who wrote superb ghost stories such as " 'They,' " chose technology instead of spirits to animate this particular plot, but the tale has also been reprinted in collections of the supernatural. Ambrose Bierce, known for brilliant supernatural stories such as "An Occurrence at Owl Creek Bridge," appears in this anthology with four brief news-like accounts of people who suddenly vanish from mundane Earth—perhaps into another dimension. Bierce offers no spooky explanation, but this story too has appeared in collections of the supernatural.

In a rather Darwinian turn, American writer William Henry Rhodes envisions a child born with eyes that focus not upon nearby objects but only upon astronomical distances. This mutation becomes a window onto the cosmos. Rhodes's 1876 story "The Telescopic Eye," which you will find herein, also nicely demonstrates that, ninety years before the plastic masks of *Star Trek*, science fiction writers could envision aliens whose biology differed enormously from that of human beings:

> The Lunarians are not formed at all like ourselves. They are less in height, and altogether of a different appearance. When fully grown, they resemble somewhat a chariot wheel, with four spokes, converging at the center or axle. They have four eyes in the head, which is the axle, so to speak, and all the limbs branch out

directly from the center, like some sea-forms known as "Radiates." They move by turning rapidly like a wheel, and travel as fast as a bird through the air. The children are undeveloped in form, and are perfectly round, like a pumpkin or orange. As they grow older, they seem to drop or absorb the rotundity of the whole body, and finally assume the appearance of a chariot wheel.

SPRINKLED AMONG THE COMPLETE stories herein you will find a handful of excerpts from novels. Each such narrative is self-contained, and its individual introduction to the author and the story will set the context. The works may be too long to include in toto, but their characters and themes have proven so memorable that they demand inclusion. And they earned their fame for a reason, by virtue of shocking new ideas and compelling narrative; every anthologist hopes to send readers back to the originals.

As the selection from his *Strange Case of Doctor Jekyll and Mister Hyde* will demonstrate, Robert Louis Stevenson was another writer who paid considerable attention to the ever-changing science around him. He wove many contemporary issues into his 1886 novella, beginning with well-known case studies of dual personality, but they gained resonance when he mixed in evolutionary fears and the recent notion of the violent criminal as an atavistic reversion to our species' brute past. A dramatic passage from it shows how deeply, in illuminating the duality of conscience and character, Stevenson was tapping into the zeitgeist of his era when he unleashed the primitive id. The tale was published in 1886, the year that Sigmund Freud began his clinical practice in Vienna. Two years later, when Jack the Ripper began to terrorize Whitechapel, the newspapers immediately referred to Mr. Hyde, to the lurking midnight viciousness of humanity.

H. G. Wells, who had studied with the great Victorian scientist and educator Thomas Huxley, horrifically weds the controversial topic of vivisection to Charles Darwin's equally vexed discoveries of a bestial history for humanity. Published in 1896, *The Island of Doctor Moreau* is one of Wells's most provocative and suspenseful novels. Few cautionary fables about Frankensteinian tinkering are more powerful than this grisly account of a mad vivisectionist. Vivisection was a ferociously divisive topic in late Victorian England, having occupied the attention of everyone from Charles Darwin to Lewis Carroll. Dark notions of racial degeneration, the influence of our animal nature on our supposedly nobler side, evolutionary legacies and potential, the dangers of dispassionate scientific tinkering—these and many other issues crowd Wells's tale. Appearing near the end of this anthology, Wells's chapter fittingly concludes the running themes of mortal and evolutionary anxiety, as Wells looks back over his shoulder at Darwin and ahead to the technological and spiritual vertigo he could foresee in the future.

Other unusual choices enliven this anthology. For example, Thomas Hardy's 1882 novel, *Two on a Tower*, is not science fiction, but a brief, self-contained scene from it appears herein because it addresses the kind of science-induced anxiety that pervades science fiction of the nineteenth century—and which continues today—and also preoccupied nineteenth-century literary fiction. It demonstrates the limitations and virtues of realistic fiction in addressing the emotional and intellectual vertigo inspired by revelations of an ever larger and older cosmos.

The barriers around Hardy's naturalistic approach illuminate the virtues of science fiction. Swithin St. Cleeve and Lady Constantine are more alive and convincing than most genre characters, but science fiction writers would have taken them into space for an unclouded gaze out at the stars and back down at Earth. Not one to soften his relentlessly male pages with romance, Jules Verne might have left Lady Constantine behind completely, but he would have made the stars themselves (not to mention the characters' vehicle) as important in his tale as the human beings. In science fiction and fantasy, characters don't merely talk about the borders of perception; they pass through them.

RECOUNTING HIS AMBITIOUS AND merciless life, Victor Frankenstein speaks often about dreams both literal and symbolic—nightmares, daydreams, visions, misconceptions, the past. At one point he states his grand ambition: "My dreams were therefore undisturbed by reality; and I entered with the greatest diligence into the search of the philosopher's stone and the elixir of life. But the latter obtained my most undivided attention: wealth was an inferior object; but what glory would attend the discovery, if I could banish disease from the human frame, and render man invulnerable to any but a violent death."

Later, however, having brought to life the nameless creature who shadows and indicts his creator, Frankenstein dreams about the woman he loves. "I thought I saw Elizabeth, in the bloom of health, walking in the streets of Ingolstadt. Delighted and surprised, I embraced her; but as I imprinted the first kiss on her lips, they became livid with the hue of death; her features appeared to change, and I thought that I held the corpse of my dead mother in my arms; a shroud enveloped her form, and I saw the grave-worms crawling in the folds of her flannel."

Mary Shelley lived in a time of rampant disease and death. The mortal body was not protected by antibiotics; the elderly were not hidden away in nursing homes; corpses were not sterilely embalmed by people who did not know the deceased. Graves were overfilled and the dead might well return with a spring flood. Decline and decay, the themes of Edgar Allan Poe, seem grotesque and morbid to us now, but they were the blunt reality for millennia, and for many people they are still. Shelley literally embodied her themes in a hurting, yearning form, and thus made us feel them on a visceral level. Her novel was not merely an intellectual exercise, and this bodily reality is one reason why the work endures.

Much other science fiction of the Victorian and gaslight eras also confronted the real human body in the real world, not just dreams of travel through space and time. The next to last story in this collection is by the English writer E. Nesbit. She shared both Wells's delight in the pleasures of consciousness and his horror at finding it caged inside a mortal animal body. When she wasn't conjuring marvelous creations such as the ancient, vainglorious bird that cavorts through *The Phoenix and the Carpet* or the cantankerous wish-granting Psammead or sand fairy of *Five Children and It*—or chronicling the less fantastical but no less entertaining Bastable family—Nesbit wrote grim, even grisly, tales of the fantastic. Superstitious, a believer in ghosts, she personifies the visceral torment of embodiment, the always looming proximity of pain and death, that haunted Mary Shelley and her descendants.

In her 1909 story "The Five Senses," Nesbit daydreams about transcending the limits of bodily perception, and in doing so creates a character reminiscent of a twentieth-century superhero. Only a half century later, in the world of Marvel Comics, teenager Peter Parker would be bitten by a radioactive spider and turn himself into Spider-Man; lawyer Matt Murdock would be blinded by an encounter with radioactive material, but in return find his other senses growing fantastically acute, and he would choose to exploit them while masked as Daredevil. Nesbit's character, in contrast, deliberately injects himself with a chemical compound that he has spent years creating. It enhances his senses so that he feels the microscopic roughness of a glass syringe and amplifies the lingering aftertaste of coffee until he can hardly bear its intensity. Nesbit's story appears herein not because her protagonist's elixir was scientifically convincing, but because she employed it with science-fictional intent—a glimpse beyond the possible, but not into the supernatural.

The final clause in the closing sentence of Nesbit's story sums up the primordial fears that surge through this anthology, and thus provide the title and theme of this introduction. In referring to "the depth of that gulf of fear which lies between the quick and the dead," she salutes the monsters of our darker nature conjured over the last two centuries—the merciless tormenter of Ernest Valdemar, the vicious other self of Henry Jekyll, the atavistic beast-men bowing to the merciless Doctor Moreau. And we understand again the common fate inspiring the vision of terror and grief that Victor Frankenstein dreams.

Mary Shelley

(1797–1851)

ONLY A SMALL NUMBER of characters from popular culture achieve global recognition. During the last few hundred years, perhaps only Sherlock Holmes and Frankenstein's monster reached this apogee of popularity prior to the invention of motion pictures. These figures became household names.

The origin of Frankenstein's monster is the key moment in Mary Shelley's revolutionary novel, and the birth of the novel itself is a milestone in the history of literature—and especially in the genre we now call science fiction. The story's genesis brings together Enlightenment science and the Romantic critique thereof; that strutting, womanizing genius Lord Byron, as well as his physician and acolyte, John Polidori; young Mary Godwin's lover and future husband, the poet Percy Bysshe Shelley; and the teenage Mary herself, a young woman of extraordinary intelligence and talent.

The birth of the story is even rich in lush atmosphere worthy of Shelley's novel. Historians often refer to 1816 as the Year without a Summer, because of such dark clouds and low temperatures that winter seemed to linger and take up residence. Wagnerian thunderstorms tormented the heavens. These unusual conditions derived from clouds of ash and other substances that entered the atmosphere during the eruption of Mount Tambora on the Indonesian island of Sumbawa the previous summer and fall.

At Lake Geneva, Switzerland, in June 1816, Byron and Shelley and company were often forced to abandon their boating and hiking plans to spend time indoors. On one such occasion, at the Villa Diodati that Byron was renting on the lakeshore, Godwin and Shelley and Byron and Polidori entertained each other by reading stories from a recent anthology of German ghost stories, *Fantasmagoriana*, edited by a French writer and geographer named Jean-Baptiste Benoît Eyriès. Their enjoyment of this activity inspired Byron to challenge the members of the party to each write a horrific fiction. "Have you thought of a story?" Shelley recalled that she was asked each morning—"and each morning I was forced to reply with a mortifying negative."

Then she suffered through what would come to be one of the most famous nightmares in history:

> I saw the pale student of unhallowed arts kneeling beside the thing he had put together. I saw the hideous phantasm of a man stretched out, and then, on the working of some powerful engine, show signs of life, and stir with an uneasy, half vital motion. Frightful must it be; for supremely frightful would be the effect of any human endeavour to mock the stupendous mechanism of the Creator of the world.

She began writing what she thought would be a short story. But the narrative grew in her imagination, and Percy Shelley encouraged her to follow it as it became a novel. She completed it in May of the following year. In March 1818, the firm of Lackington, Hughes, Harding, Mavor, & Jones published the five-hundred-copy first edition, in a three-volume format, of *Frankenstein; or, the Modern Prometheus*. It was published anonymously. Not until the second edition did Shelley put her name on the title page.

Ordinarily, anthologists choose to reprint an author's final version of a story, but critics and your editor agree that this first incarnation presents a stronger, unadulterated view of Shelley's dark vision. Thus the following excerpt derives from Shelley's 1818 edition. Preferring this edition to the later version is rather like refusing to accept Dickens's surrender to Bulwer-Lytton's suggestion of a sentimental ending to *Great Expectations* and keeping the first or printing both so that readers may choose their own literary adventure. Her revision was published in 1831. In her introduction to it, Shelley explicitly states, "I have changed no portion of the story," and claims that her revisions were limited to matters of style. Actually she greatly altered the spirit and implications of the story. She also saluted the memory of her brief but life-changing romance with Percy Shelley, who had died in a boating accident on the northwestern coast of Italy in 1822.

Reading Bram Stoker's classic vampire novel, *Dracula*, can be chilling, but in retrospect it strikes few philosophical notes and often seems absurd. Shelley's *Frankenstein*, in contrast, reads as tame by our narrative standards but horrific in its implications. The critic Michael Dirda lists some of the themes apparent to an attentive reader: "the persistent interconnection of sex, birth, and death; the mirroring of monster and creator; the conflict between instinctive goodness and the societal creation of the criminal; the power of nature to soften and civilize; the human yearning for sympathy and love."

In her introduction, Shelley employs the term "hideous" again and again. It was apt. Meaning ugly, repulsive, even disgusting, it derived, via Middle English, from an Old French word for fear. The fear of death, but also the fear of embodiment—the terror of an aspiring consciousness chained to a mortal animal—are chords that sound throughout this novel written, we must remember, by a teenage girl. "And now, once again, I bid my hideous progeny go forth and prosper," she writes in her preface. "I have an affection for it, for it was the offspring of happy days, when death and grief were but words, which found no true echo in my heart. Its several pages speak of many a walk, many a drive, and many a conversation, when I was not alone; and my companion was one who, in this world, I shall never see more. But this is for myself; my readers have nothing to do with these associations."

And in the 1831 version of *Frankenstein*, Shelley removed the epigraph that haunted the opening in 1818, from Milton's *Paradise Lost*:

> Did I request thee, Maker, from my clay
> To mould me man? Did I solicit thee
> From darkness to promote me?—

Dreams of Forgotten Alchemists

(from *Frankenstein*)

T HE NEXT MORNING I delivered my letters of introduction and paid a visit to some of the principal professors. Chance—or rather the evil influence, the Angel of Destruction, which asserted omnipotent sway over me from the moment I turned my reluctant steps from my father's door—led me first to M. Krempe, professor of natural philosophy. He was an uncouth man, but deeply imbued in the secrets of his science. He asked me several questions concerning my progress in the different branches of science appertaining to natural philosophy. I replied carelessly, and partly in contempt, mentioned the names of my alchemists as the principal authors I had studied. The professor stared.

"Have you," he said, "really spent your time in studying such nonsense?"

I replied in the affirmative.

"Every minute," continued M. Krempe with warmth, "every instant that you have wasted on those books is utterly and entirely lost. You have burdened your memory with exploded systems and useless names. Good God! In what desert land have you lived, where no one was kind enough to inform you that these fancies which you have so greedily imbibed are a thousand years old and as musty as they are ancient? I little expected, in this enlightened and scientific age, to find a disciple of Albertus Magnus and Paracelsus. My dear sir, you must begin your studies entirely anew."

So saying, he stepped aside and wrote down a list of several books treating of natural philosophy which he desired me to procure, and dismissed me after mentioning that in the beginning of the following week he intended to commence a course of lectures upon natural philosophy in its general relations, and that M. Waldman, a fellow professor, would lecture upon chemistry the alternate days that he omitted.

I returned home not disappointed, for I have said that I had long considered those authors useless whom the professor reprobated; but I returned not at all the more inclined to recur to these studies in any shape. M. Krempe was a little squat man with a gruff voice and a repulsive countenance; the teacher, therefore, did not prepossess me in favour of his pursuits. In rather a too philosophical and connected a strain, perhaps, I have given an account of the conclusions I had come to concerning them in my early years. As a child I had not been content with the results promised by the modern professors of natural science. With a confusion of ideas only to be accounted for by my extreme youth and my want of a guide on such matters, I had retrod the steps of knowledge along the paths of time and exchanged the discoveries of recent inquirers for the dreams of forgotten alchemists. Besides, I had a contempt for the uses of modern natural philosophy. It was very different when the masters of the science sought immortality and power; such views, although futile, were grand; but now the scene was changed. The ambition of the inquirer seemed to limit itself to the annihilation of those visions on which my interest in science was chiefly founded. I was required to exchange chimeras of boundless grandeur for realities of little worth.

Such were my reflections during the first two or three days of my residence at Ingolstadt, which were chiefly spent in becoming acquainted with the localities and the principal residents in my new abode. But as the ensuing week commenced, I thought of the information which M. Krempe had given me concerning the lectures. And although I could not consent to go and hear that little conceited fellow deliver sentences out of a pulpit, I recollected what he had said of M. Waldman, whom I had never seen, as he had hitherto been out of town.

Partly from curiosity and partly from idleness, I went into the lecturing room, which M. Waldman entered shortly after. This professor was very unlike his colleague. He appeared about fifty years of age, but with an aspect expressive of the greatest benevolence; a few grey hairs covered his temples, but those at the back of his head were nearly black. His person was short but remarkably erect and his voice the sweetest I had ever heard. He began his lecture by a recapitulation of the history of chemistry and the various improvements made by different men of learning, pronouncing with fervour the names of the most distinguished discoverers. He then took a cursory view of the present state of the science and explained many of its elementary terms. After having made a few preparatory experiments, he concluded with a panegyric upon modern chemistry, the terms of which I shall never forget:

"The ancient teachers of this science," said he, "promised impossibilities and performed nothing. The modern masters promise very little; they know that metals cannot be transmuted and that the elixir of life is a chimera. But these philosophers, whose hands seem only made to dabble in dirt, and their eyes to pore over the microscope or crucible, have indeed performed miracles. They penetrate into the recesses of nature and show how she works in her hiding-places. They ascend into the heavens; they have discovered how the blood circulates, and the nature of the air we breathe. They have acquired new and almost unlimited powers; they can command the thunders of heaven, mimic the earthquake, and even mock the invisible world with its own shadows."

Such were the professor's words—let me say such the words of the fate—enounced to destroy me. As he went on I felt as if my soul were grappling with a palpable enemy; one by one the various keys were touched which formed the mechanism of my being; chord after chord was sounded, and soon my mind was filled with one thought, one conception, one purpose. So much has been done, exclaimed the soul of Frankenstein—more, far more, will I achieve; treading in the steps already marked, I will pioneer a new way, explore unknown powers, and unfold to the world the deepest mysteries of creation.

I closed not my eyes that night. My internal being was in a state of insurrection and turmoil; I felt that order would hence arise, but I had no power to produce it. By degrees after the morning's dawn, sleep came. I awoke, and my yesternight's thoughts were as a dream. There only remained a resolution to return to my ancient studies and to devote myself to a science for which I believed myself to have a natural talent. On the same day I paid M. Waldman a visit. His manners in private were even more mild and attractive than in public, for there was a certain dignity in his mien during lecture which in his own house was replaced by the greatest affability and kindness. I gave him pretty nearly the same account of my former pursuits as I had given to his fellow professor. He heard with attention the little narration concerning my studies and smiled at the names of Cornelius Agrippa and Paracelsus, but without the contempt that M. Krempe had exhibited. He said that, "These were men to whose indefatigable zeal modern philosophers were indebted for most of the foundations of their knowledge. They had left to us, as an easier task, to give new names and arrange in connected classifications the facts which they in a great degree had been the instruments of bringing to light. The labours of men of genius, however erroneously directed, scarcely ever fail in ultimately turning to the solid advantage of mankind."

I listened to his statement, which was delivered without any presumption or affectation, and then added that his lecture had removed my prejudices against modern chemists; I expressed myself in measured terms, with the modesty and deference due from a youth to his instructor, without letting escape (inexperience in life

would have made me ashamed) any of the enthusiasm which stimulated my intended labours. I requested his advice concerning the
books I ought to procure.

"I am happy," said M. Waldman, "to have gained a disciple; and
if your application equals your ability, I have no doubt of your
success. Chemistry is that branch of natural philosophy in which
the greatest improvements have been and may be made; it is on that
account that I have made it my peculiar study; but at the same
time, I have not neglected the other branches of science. A man
would make but a very sorry chemist if he attended to that department of human knowledge alone. If your wish is to become really
a man of science and not merely a petty experimentalist, I should
advise you to apply to every branch of natural philosophy, including
mathematics."

He then took me into his laboratory and explained to me the
uses of his various machines, instructing me as to who I ought to
procure and promising me the use of his own when I should have
advanced far enough in the science not to derange their mechanism.
He also gave me the list of books which I had requested, and I took
my leave.

Thus ended a day memorable to me; it decided my future destiny.

FROM THIS DAY NATURAL philosophy, and particularly chemistry,
in the most comprehensive sense of the term, became nearly my sole
occupation. I read with ardour those works, so full of genius and
discrimination, which modern inquirers have written on these
subjects. I attended the lectures and cultivated the acquaintance of
the men of science of the university, and I found even in M. Krempe
a great deal of sound sense and real information, combined, it is true,
with a repulsive physiognomy and manners, but not on that account
the less valuable. In M. Waldman I found a true friend. His gentle-
ness was never tinged by dogmatism, and his instructions were given
with an air of frankness and good nature that banished every idea
of pedantry. In a thousand ways he smoothed for me the path of

knowledge and made the most abstruse inquiries clear and facile to my apprehension. My application was at first fluctuating and uncertain; it gained strength as I proceeded and soon became so ardent and eager that the stars often disappeared in the light of morning whilst I was yet engaged in my laboratory.

As I applied so closely, it may be easily conceived that my progress was rapid. My ardour was indeed the astonishment of the students, and my proficiency that of the masters. Professor Krempe often asked me, with a sly smile, how Cornelius Agrippa went on, whilst M. Waldman expressed the most heartfelt exultation in my progress. Two years passed in this manner, during which I paid no visit to Geneva, but was engaged, heart and soul, in the pursuit of some discoveries which I hoped to make. None but those who have experienced them can conceive of the enticements of science. In other studies you go as far as others have gone before you, and there is nothing more to know; but in a scientific pursuit there is continual food for discovery and wonder. A mind of moderate capacity which closely pursues one study must infallibly arrive at great proficiency in that study; and I, who continually sought the attainment of one object of pursuit and was solely wrapped up in this, improved so rapidly that at the end of two years I made some discoveries in the improvement of some chemical instruments, which procured me great esteem and admiration at the university. When I had arrived at this point and had become as well acquainted with the theory and practice of natural philosophy as depended on the lessons of any of the professors at Ingolstadt, my residence there being no longer conducive to my improvements, I thought of returning to my friends and my native town, when an incident happened that protracted my stay.

One of the phenomena which had peculiarly attracted my attention was the structure of the human frame, and, indeed, any animal endued with life. Whence, I often asked myself, did the principle of life proceed? It was a bold question, and one which has ever been considered as a mystery; yet with how many things are we upon the brink of becoming acquainted, if cowardice or carelessness did not restrain our inquiries. I revolved these circumstances in my mind and determined thenceforth to apply myself more particularly to those branches of natural philosophy which relate to physiology. Unless I had been animated by an almost supernatural enthusiasm, my application to this study would have been irksome and almost intolerable. To examine the causes of life, we must first have recourse to death. I became acquainted with the science of anatomy, but this was not sufficient; I must also observe the natural decay and corruption of the human body. In my education my father had taken the greatest precautions that my mind should be impressed with no supernatural horrors. I do not ever remember to have trembled at a tale of superstition or to have feared the apparition of a spirit. Darkness had no effect upon my fancy, and a churchyard was to me merely the receptacle of bodies deprived of life, which, from being the seat of beauty and strength, had become food for the worm. Now I was led to examine the cause and progress of this decay and forced to spend days and nights in vaults and charnel-houses. My attention was fixed upon every object the most insupportable to the delicacy of the human feelings. I saw how the fine form of man was degraded and wasted; I beheld the corruption of death succeed to the blooming cheek of life; I saw how the worm inherited the wonders of the eye and brain. I paused, examining and analysing all the minutiae of causation, as exemplified in the change from life to death, and death to life, until from the midst of this darkness a sudden light broke in upon me—a light so brilliant and wondrous, yet so simple, that while I became dizzy with the immensity of the prospect which it illustrated, I was surprised that among so many men of genius who had directed their inquiries towards the same science, that I alone should be reserved to discover so astonishing a secret.

Remember, I am not recording the vision of a madman. The sun does not more certainly shine in the heavens than that which I now affirm is true. Some miracle might have produced it, yet the stages of the discovery were distinct and probable. After days and nights of incredible labour and fatigue, I succeeded in discovering the cause of generation and life; nay, more, I became myself capable of bestowing animation upon lifeless matter.

The astonishment which I had at first experienced on this discovery soon gave place to delight and rapture. After so much time spent in painful labour, to arrive at once at the summit of my desires was the most gratifying consummation of my toils. But this discovery was so great and overwhelming that all the steps by which I had been progressively led to it were obliterated, and I beheld only the result, what had been the study and desire of the wisest men since the creation of the world was now within my grasp. Not that, like a magic scene, it all opened upon me at once: the information I had obtained was of a nature rather to direct my endeavours so soon as I should point them towards the object of my search than to exhibit that object already accomplished. I was like the Arabian who had been buried with the dead and found a passage to life, aided only by one glimmering and seemingly ineffectual light.

I see by your eagerness and the wonder and hope which your eyes express, my friend, that you expect to be informed of the secret with which I am acquainted; that cannot be; listen patiently until the end of my story, and you will easily perceive why I am reserved upon that subject. I will not lead you on, unguarded and ardent as I then was, to your destruction and infallible misery. Learn from me, if not by my precepts, at least by my example, how dangerous is the acquirement of knowledge and how much happier that man is who believes his native town to be the world, than he who aspires to become greater than his nature will allow.

When I found so astonishing a power placed within my hands, I hesitated a long time concerning the manner in which I should employ it. Although I possessed the capacity of bestowing animation, yet to prepare a frame for the reception of it, with all its intricacies of fibres, muscles, and veins, still remained a work of inconceivable difficulty and labour. I doubted at first whether I should attempt the creation of a being like myself, or one of simpler organization; but my imagination was too much exalted by my first success to permit me to doubt of my ability to give life to an animal as complex and wonderful as man. The materials at present within my command hardly appeared adequate to so arduous an undertaking, but I doubted not that I should ultimately succeed. I prepared myself for a multitude of reverses; my operations might be incessantly baffled, and at last my work be imperfect: yet, when I considered the improvement which every day takes place in science and mechanics, I was encouraged to hope my present attempts would at least lay the foundations of future success. Nor could I consider the magnitude and complexity of my plan as any argument of its impracticability. It was with these feelings that I began the creation of a human being. As the minuteness of the parts formed a great hindrance to my speed, I resolved, contrary to my first intention, to make the being of a gigantic stature, that is to say, about eight feet in height, and proportionably large. After having formed this determination and having spent some months in successfully collecting and arranging my materials, I began.

No one can conceive the variety of feelings which bore me onwards, like a hurricane, in the first enthusiasm of success. Life and death appeared to me ideal bounds, which I should first break through, and pour a torrent of light into our dark world. A new species would bless me as its creator and source; many happy and excellent natures would owe their being to me. No father could claim the gratitude of his child so completely as I should deserve theirs. Pursuing these reflections, I thought that if I could bestow animation upon lifeless matter, I might in process of time (although I now found it impossible) renew life where death had apparently devoted the body to corruption.

These thoughts supported my spirits, while I pursued my undertaking with unremitting ardour. My cheek had grown pale with study, and my person had become emaciated with confinement. Sometimes, on the very brink of certainty, I failed; yet still I clung to the hope which the next day or the next hour might realize. One secret which I alone possessed was the hope to which I had dedicated myself; and the moon gazed on my midnight labours, while, with unrelaxed and breathless eagerness, I pursued nature to her hiding places. Who shall conceive the horrors of my secret toil as I dabbled among the unhallowed damps of the grave or tortured the living animal to animate the lifeless clay? My limbs now tremble, and my eyes swim with the remembrance; but then a resistless, and almost frantic impulse, urged me forward; I seemed to have lost all soul or sensation but for this one pursuit. It was indeed but a passing trance, that only made me feel with renewed acuteness so soon as, the unnatural stimulus ceasing to operate, I had returned to my old habits. I collected bones from charnel houses; and disturbed, with profane fingers, the tremendous secrets of the human frame. In a solitary chamber, or rather cell, at the top of the house, and separated from all the other apartments by a gallery and staircase, I kept my workshop of filthy creation; my eyeballs were starting from their sockets in attending to the details of my employment. The dissecting room and the slaughter-house furnished many of my materials; and often did my human nature turn with loathing from my occupation, whilst, still urged on by an eagerness which perpetually increased, I brought my work near to a conclusion.

The summer months passed while I was thus engaged, heart and soul, in one pursuit. It was a most beautiful season; never did the fields bestow a more plentiful harvest, or the vines yield a more luxuriant vintage: but my eyes were insensible to the charms of nature.

IT WAS ON A dreary night of November, that I beheld the accomplishment of my toils. With an anxiety that almost amounted to agony, I collected the instruments of life around me, that I might infuse a spark of being into the lifeless thing that lay at my feet. It was already one in the morning; the rain pattered dismally against the panes, and my candle was nearly burnt out, when, by the glimmer of the half-extinguished light, I saw the dull yellow eye of the creature open; it breathed hard, and a convulsive motion agitated its limbs.

How can I describe my emotions at this catastrophe, or how delineate the wretch whom with such infinite pains and care I had endeavoured to form? His limbs were in proportion, and I had selected his features as beautiful. Beautiful!—Great God! His yellow skin scarcely covered the work of muscles and arteries beneath; his hair was of a lustrous black, and flowing; his teeth of a pearly whiteness; but these luxuriances only formed a more horrid contrast with his watery eyes, that seemed almost of the same colour as the dun white sockets in which they were set, his shrivelled complexion, and straight black lips.

The different accidents of life are not so changeable as the feelings of human nature. I had worked hard for nearly two years, for the sole purpose of infusing life into an inanimate body. For this I had deprived myself of rest and health. I had desired it with an ardour that far exceeded moderation; but now that I had finished, the beauty of the dream vanished, and breathless horror and disgust filled my heart. Unable to endure the aspect of the being I had created, I rushed out of the room, and continued a long time traversing my bed-chamber, unable to compose my mind to sleep. At length lassitude succeeded to the tumult I had before endured; and I threw myself on the bed in my clothes, endeavouring to seek a few moments of forgetfulness. But it was in vain: I slept indeed, but I was disturbed by the wildest dreams. I thought I saw Elizabeth, in the bloom of health, walking in the streets of Ingolstadt. Delighted and surprised, I embraced her; but as I imprinted the first kiss on her lips, they became livid with the hue of death; her features appeared to change, and I thought that I held the corpse of my dead mother in my arms; a shroud enveloped her form, and I saw the grave-worms crawling in the folds of the flannel. I started from my sleep with horror; a cold dew covered my forehead, my teeth chattered, and every limb became convulsed; when, by the dim and yellow light of the moon, as it forced its way through the window-shutters, I beheld the wretch—the miserable monster whom I had created. He held up the curtain of the bed; and his eyes, if eyes they may be called, were fixed on me. His jaws opened, and he muttered some inarticulate sounds, while a grin wrinkled his cheeks. He might have spoken, but I did not hear; one hand was stretched out, seemingly to detain me, but I escaped, and rushed down stairs. I took refuge in the court-yard belonging to the house which I inhabited; where I remained during the rest of the night, walking up and down in the greatest agitation, listening attentively, catching and fearing each sound as if it were to announce the approach of the demoniacal corpse to which I had so miserably given life.

Oh! no mortal could support the horror of that countenance. A mummy again endued with animation could not be so hideous as that wretch. I had gazed on him while unfinished; he was ugly then; but when those muscles and joints were rendered capable of motion, it became a thing such as even Dante could not have conceived.

I passed the night wretchedly. Sometimes my pulse beat so quickly and hardly, that I felt the palpitation of every artery; at others, I nearly sank to the ground through languor and extreme weakness. Mingled with this horror, I felt the bitterness of disappointment: dreams that had been my food and pleasant rest for so long a space, were now become a hell to me; and the change was so rapid, the overthrow so complete!

IT WAS NEARLY NOON when I arrived at the top of the ascent. For some time I sat upon the rock that overlooks the sea of ice. A mist covered both that and the surrounding mountains. Presently a breeze dissipated the cloud, and I descended upon the glacier. The surface is very uneven, rising like the waves of a troubled sea, descending low, and interspersed by rifts that sink deep. The field of ice is almost a league in width, but I spent nearly two hours in crossing it. The opposite mountain is a bare perpendicular rock. From the side where I now stood Montanvert was exactly opposite, at the distance of a

league; and above it rose Mont Blanc, in awful majesty. I remained
in a recess of the rock, gazing on this wonderful and stupendous
scene. The sea, or rather the vast river of ice, wound among its
dependent mountains, whose aerial summits hung over its recesses.
Their icy and glittering peaks shone in the sunlight over the clouds.
My heart, which was before sorrowful, now swelled with something
like joy; I exclaimed—"Wandering spirits, if indeed ye wander, and
do not rest in your narrow beds, allow me this faint happiness, or
take me, as your companion, away from the joys of life."

As I said this, I suddenly beheld the figure of a man, at some
distance, advancing towards me with superhuman speed. He bounded
over the crevices in the ice, among which I had walked with caution;
his stature, also, as he approached, seemed to exceed that of man. I
was troubled: a mist came over my eyes, and I felt a faintness seize
me; but I was quickly restored by the cold gale of the mountains. I
perceived, as the shape came nearer (sight tremendous and abhorred!)
that it was the wretch whom I had created. I trembled with rage and
horror, resolving to wait his approach, and then close with him in
mortal combat. He approached; his countenance bespoke bitter
anguish, combined with disdain and malignity, while its unearthly
ugliness rendered it almost too horrible for human eyes. But I
scarcely observed this; anger and hatred had at first deprived me of
utterance, and I recovered only to overwhelm him with words
expressive of furious detestation and contempt.

"Devil," I exclaimed, "do you dare approach me? and do not you
fear the fierce vengeance of my arm wreaked on your miserable
head? Begone, vile insect! or rather, stay, that I may trample you to
dust! and, oh! that I could, with the extinction of your miserable
existence, restore those victims whom you have so diabolically
murdered!"

"I expected this reception," said the dæmon. "All men hate the
wretched; how, then, must I be hated, who am miserable beyond
all living things! Yet you, my creator, detest and spurn me, thy
creature, to whom thou art bound by ties only dissoluble by the

annihilation of one of us. You purpose to kill me. How dare you sport thus with life? Do your duty towards me, and I will do mine towards you and the rest of mankind. If you will comply with my conditions, I will leave them and you at peace; but if you refuse, I will glut the maw of death, until it be satiated with the blood of your remaining friends."

"Abhorred monster! fiend that thou art! the tortures of hell are too mild a vengeance for thy crimes. Wretched devil! you reproach me with your creation; come on, then, that I may extinguish the spark which I so negligently bestowed."

My rage was without bounds; I sprang on him, impelled by all the feelings which can arm one being against the existence of another.

He easily eluded me, and said, "Be calm! I entreat you to hear me, before you give vent to your hatred on my devoted head. Have I not suffered enough that you seek to increase my misery? Life, although it may only be an accumulation of anguish, is dear to me, and I will defend it. Remember, thou hast made me more powerful than thyself; my height is superior to thine; my joints more supple. But I will not be tempted to set myself in opposition to thee. I am thy creature, and I will be even mild and docile to my natural lord and king, if thou wilt also perform thy part, the which thou owest me. Oh, Frankenstein, be not equitable to every other, and trample upon me alone, to whom thy justice, and even thy clemency and affection, is most due. Remember that I am thy creature; I ought to be thy Adam; but I am rather the fallen angel, whom thou drivest from joy for no misdeed. Everywhere I see bliss, from which I alone am irrevocably excluded. I was benevolent and good—misery made me a fiend. Make me happy, and I shall again be virtuous."

"Begone! I will not hear you. There can be no community between you and me; we are enemies. Begone, or let us try our strength in a fight, in which one must fall."

"How can I move thee? Will no entreaties cause thee to turn a favourable eye upon thy creature, who implores thy goodness and compassion? Believe me, Frankenstein: I was benevolent; my soul glowed with love and humanity: but am I not alone, miserably alone? You, my creator, abhor me; what hope can I gather from your fellow-creatures, who owe me nothing? they spurn and hate me. The desert mountains and dreary glaciers are my refuge. I have wandered here many days; the caves of ice, which I only do not fear, are a dwelling to me, and the only one which man does not grudge. These bleak skies I had, for they are kinder to me than your fellow-beings. If the multitude of mankind knew of my existence, they would do as you do, and arm themselves for my destruction. Shall I not then hate them who abhor me? I will keep no terms with my enemies. I am miserable, and they shall share my wretchedness. Yet it is in your power to recompense me, and deliver them from an evil which it only remains for you to make so great that not only you and your family, but thousands of others, shall be swallowed up in the whirlwinds of its rage. Let your compassion be moved, and do not disdain me. Listen to my tale: when you have heard that, abandon or commiserate me, as you shall judge that I deserve. But hear me. The guilty are allowed, by human laws, bloody as they are, to speak in their own defence before they are condemned. Listen to me, Frankenstein. You accuse me of murder; and yet you would, with a satisfied conscience, destroy your own creature. Oh, praise the eternal justice of man! Yet I ask you not to spare me: listen to me; and then, if you can, and if you will, destroy the work of your hands."

"Why do you call to my remembrance circumstances of which I shudder to reflect, that I have been the miserable origin and author? Cursed be the day, abhorred devil, in which you first saw light! Cursed (although I curse myself) be the hands that formed you! You have made me wretched beyond expression. You have left me no power to consider whether I am just to you or not. Begone! relieve me from the sight of your detested form."

"Thus I relieve thee, my creator," he said, and placed his hated hands before my eyes, which I flung from me with violence; "thus

I take from thee a sight which you abhor. Still thou canst listen
to me, and grant me thy compassion. By the virtues that I once
possessed, I demand this from you. Hear my tale; it is long and
strange, and the temperature of this place is not fitting to your fine
sensations; come to the hut upon the mountain. The sun is yet
high in the heavens; before it descends to hide itself behind yon
snowy precipices, and illuminate another world, you will have heard
my story, and can decide. On you it rests whether I quit forever
the neighbourhood of man, and lead a harmless life, or become the
scourge of your fellow-creatures, and the author of your own speedy
ruin."

As he said this, he led the way across the ice: I followed. My heart
was full, I did not answer him; but, as I proceeded, I weighed the
various arguments that he had used, and determined at least to listen
to his tale. I was partly urged by curiosity, and compassion confirmed
my resolution. I had hitherto supposed him to be the murderer of
my brother, and I eagerly sought a confirmation or denial of this
opinion. For the first time, also, I felt what the duties of a creator
towards his creature were, and that I ought to render him happy
before I complained of his wickedness. These motives urged me to
comply with his demand. We crossed the ice, therefore, and ascended
the opposite rock. The air was cold, and the rain again began to
descend: we entered the hut, the fiend with an air of exultation, I
with a heavy heart and depressed spirits. But I consented to listen;
and, seating myself by the fire which my odious companion had
lighted, he thus began his tale.

"IT IS WITH CONSIDERABLE difficulty that I remember the original aera of being: all the events of that period appear confused and
indistinct. A strange multiplicity of sensations seized me, and I saw,
felt, heard, and smelt, at the same time; and it was, indeed, a long
time before I learned to distinguish between the operations of my
various senses. By degrees, I remember, a stronger light pressed upon
my nerves, so that I was obliged to shut my eyes. Darkness then

came over me, and troubled me; but hardly had I felt this, when, by opening my eyes, as I now suppose, the light poured in upon me again. I walked, and, I believe, descended; but I presently found a great alteration in my sensations. Before, dark and opaque bodies had surrounded me, impervious to my touch or sight; but I now found that I could wander on at liberty, with no obstacles which I could not either surmount or avoid. The light became more and more oppressive to me; and, the heat wearying me as I walked, I sought a place where I could receive shade. This was the forest near Ingolstadt; and here I lay by the side of a brook resting from my fatigue, until I felt tormented by hunger and thirst. This roused me from my nearly dormant state, and I ate some berries which I found hanging on the trees, or lying on the ground. I slaked my thirst at the brook; and then lying down, was overcome by sleep.

"It was dark when I awoke; I felt cold also, and half-frightened, as it were instinctively, finding myself so desolate. Before I had quitted your apartment, on a sensation of cold, I had covered myself with some clothes; but these were insufficient to secure me from the dews of night. I was a poor, helpless, miserable wretch; I knew, and could distinguish, nothing; but feeling pain invade me on all sides, I sat down and wept.

"Soon a gentle light stole over the heavens, and gave me a sensation of pleasure. I started up, and beheld a radiant form rise from among the trees. I gazed with a kind of wonder. It moved slowly, but it enlightened my path; and I again went out in search of berries. I was still cold, when under one of the trees I found a huge cloak, with which I covered myself, and sat down upon the ground. No distinct ideas occupied my mind; all was confused. I felt light, and hunger, and thirst, and darkness; innumerable sounds rung in my ears, and on all sides various scents saluted me: the only object that I could distinguish was the bright moon, and I fixed my eyes on that with pleasure.

"Several changes of day and night passed, and the orb of night had greatly lessened, when I began to distinguish my sensations from each other. I gradually saw plainly the clear stream that supplied me with drink, and the trees that shaded me with their foliage. I was delighted when I first discovered that a pleasant sound, which often saluted my ears, proceeded from the throats of the little winged animals who had often intercepted the light from my eyes. I began also to observe, with greater accuracy, the forms that surrounded me, and to perceive the boundaries of the radiant roof of light which canopied me. Sometimes I tried to imitate the pleasant songs of the birds, but was unable. Sometimes I wished to express my sensations in my own mode, but the uncouth and inarticulate sounds which broke from me frightened me into silence again.

"The moon had disappeared from the night, and again, with a lessened form, showed itself, while I still remained in the forest. My sensations had, by this time, become distinct, and my mind received every day additional ideas. My eyes became accustomed to the light, and to perceive objects in their right forms; I distinguished the insect from the herb, and, by degrees, one herb from another. I found that the sparrow uttered none but harsh notes, whilst those of the black-bird and thrush were sweet and enticing.

"One day, when I was oppressed by cold, I found a fire which had been left by some wandering beggars, and was overcome with delight at the warmth I experienced from it. In my joy I thrust my hand into the live embers, but quickly drew it out again with a cry of pain. How strange, I thought, that the same cause should produce such opposite effects! I examined the materials of the fire, and to my joy found it to be composed of wood. I quickly collected some branches; but they were wet, and would not burn. I was pained at this, and sat still watching the operation of the fire. The wet wood which I had placed near the heat dried, and itself became inflamed. I reflected on this; and by touching the various branches, I discov-ered the cause, and busied myself in collecting a great quantity of wood, that I might dry it, and have a plentiful supply of fire. When night came on, and brought sleep with it, I was in the greatest fear lest my fire should be extinguished. I covered it carefully with dry wood and leaves, and placed wet branches upon it; and then, spreading my cloak, I lay on the ground, and sunk into sleep.

"It was morning when I awoke, and my first care was to visit the fire. I uncovered it, and a gentle breeze quickly fanned it into a flame. I observed this also, and contrived a fan of branches, which roused the embers when they were nearly extinguished. When night came again, I found, with pleasure, that the fire gave light as well as heat; and that the discovery of this element was useful to me in my food; for I found some of the offals that the travellers had left had been roasted, and tasted much more savoury than the berries I gathered from the trees. I tried, therefore, to dress my food in the same manner, placing it on the live embers. I found that the berries were spoiled by this operation, and the nuts and roots much improved.

"Food, however, became scarce; and I often spent the whole day searching in vain for a few acorns to assuage the pangs of hunger. When I found this, I resolved to quit the place that I had hitherto inhabited, to seek for one where the few wants I experienced would be more easily satisfied. In this emigration, I exceedingly lamented the loss of the fire which I had obtained through accident, and knew not how to reproduce it. I gave several hours to the serious consideration of this difficulty; but I was obliged to relinquish all attempt to supply it; and, wrapping myself up in my cloak, I struck across the wood towards the setting sun."

❋

Richard Adams Locke

(1800–1871)

WHEN FIRST PUBLISHED IN 1835, a series of articles in the New York daily paper the *Sun* appeared under the convincingly dry collective title "Great Astronomical Discoveries Lately Made." The first was published on August 25, a Tuesday, with five more on successive days. Each appeared under the byline of "Sir John Herschel, L.L.D. F.R.S. &c." with the additional information "At the Cape of Good Hope [From Supplement to the Edinburgh Journal of Science]."

John Herschel was a real astronomer, as well as a renowned chemist and all-around scientific polymath—pioneer photographer, restless inventor. He was the son of William Herschel, astronomer and composer, and the nephew of Caroline Herschel, the comet hunter and the first woman to receive the Gold Medal of the Royal Astronomical Society. Recent stories had made the newspaper-reading public aware that John Herschel was indeed at the Cape of Good Hope, near the southernmost tip of Africa, where he was indeed performing astronomical observations.

But he was not the author of the articles, and in fact he did not learn about them until later in the year, when an American showed them to him in Cape Town. The visitor wrote that Herschel read them and exclaimed, "This is a most extraordinary affair! Pray, what does it mean?" After receiving an explanation, Herschel laughingly replied that his actual results at the Cape "would be very humble, in popular estimation, at least," in contrast to the fictional account. Eventually, however, as the factual-sounding stories haunted him over the next few years, Herschel grew understandably tired of the hoax.

The articles were said to be reprinted from the *Edinburgh Journal of Science*. It was a real journal, but one that, as only science-minded readers would have known, had ceased publication a couple of years before the moon articles. The author deftly wove fact and fiction, often lending verisimilitude by citing obscure scientific details, such as the earlier Cape Town observing station of the French astronomer Nicolas-Louis de Lacaille. Thus scientifically literate readers were less likely to immediately dismiss the story as fanciful. Harriet Martineau, the English writer and pioneer sociologist, was traveling in Massachusetts when "Great Astronomical Discoveries Lately Made" began its long reprint life in newspapers. She recorded how quick moon-story believers were to denounce the skepticism of more cautious thinkers.

Technologically savvy readers also realized that the article's claims for Herschel's telescope were impossibly ambitious. In fact, only two years earlier, the *Sun* itself had published an article disproving the alleged claims of German astronomers that with a new powerful telescope they had perceived "cities and regular fortifications in the moon. . . . It is now ascertained that no telescope can be made, in the present state of science or art, which will enable us in the way of further discoveries to 'Pluck bright honor from the pale-faced Moon.'"

But most readers were not technologically or scientifically educated, and what came to be called "the moon hoax" is now considered one of the first media sensations. Despite descriptions of "man-bats" and even the sighting of their temple of worship, the story was widely believed. Records indicate that within a week reprinting of the story had reached one hundred thousand copies— one for every third person in New York at the time. It was some years before the author was identified as Richard Adams Locke, an English-born editor and journalist. The often contentious Edgar Allan Poe complained that the moon articles, whose ingeniousness he admired, derived in part from his own moon-travel story, "Hans Pfaall—A Tale," which had appeared only two months earlier.

The following "account" derives from three of the original articles in the *Sun*.

Man-Bats on the Moon

I N THIS UNUSUAL ADDITION to our Journal, we have the happiness of making known to the British publick, and thence to the whole civilized world, recent discoveries in Astronomy which will build an imperishable monument to the age in which we live, and confer upon the present generation of the human race a proud distinction through all future time. It has been poetically said, that the stars of heaven are the hereditary regalia of man, as the intellectual sovereign of the animal creation. He may now fold the Zodiack around him with a loftier conscientiousness of his mental supremacy.

It is impossible to contemplate any great Astronomical discovery without feelings closely allied to a sensation of awe, and nearly akin to those with which a departed spirit may be supposed to discover the realities of a future state. Bound by the irrevocable laws of nature to the globe on which we live, creatures "close shut up in infinite expanse," it seems like acquiring a fearful supernatural power when any remote mysterious works of the Creator yield tribute to our curiosity. It seems almost a presumptious assumption of powers denied to us by divine will, when man, in the pride and confidence of his skill, steps forth, far beyond the apparently natural boundary of his privileges, and demands the secrets and familiar fellowship of other worlds. We are assured that when the immortal philosopher to whom mankind is indebted for the thrilling wonders now first made known, had at length adjusted his new and stupendous apparatus with the certainty of success, he solemnly paused several hours before he commenced his observations, that he might prepare his own mind for discoveries which he knew would fill the minds of myriads of his fellow-men with astonishment, and secure his name a bright, if not transcendent conjunction with that of his venerable father to all posterity. And well he might pause! From the hour the first human pair opened their eyes to the glories of the blue firmament above them, there has been no accession to human knowledge at all comparable in sublime interest to that which he has been the honored agent in supplying; and we are taught to believe that, when a work, already preparing for the press, in which his discoveries are embodied in detail, shall be laid before the public, they will be found of incomparable importance to some of the grandest operations of civilized life. Well might he pause! He was about to become the sole depository of wondrous secrets which had been hid from the eyes of all men that had lived since the birth of time. He was about to crown himself with a diadem of knowledge which would give him a conscientious pre-eminence above every individual of his species who then lives, or who had lived in the generations that are passed away. He paused ere he broke the seal of the casket which contained it.

To render our enthusiasm intelligible, we will state at once, that by means of a telescope of vast dimensions and an entirely new principle, the younger Herschel, at his observatory in the Southern Hemisphere, has already made the most extraordinary discoveries in every planet of our solar system; has discovered planets in other solar systems; has obtained a distinct view of objects in the moon, fully equal to that which the naked eye commands of terrestrial objects at the distance of a hundred yards; has affirmatively settled the question whether this satellite be inhabited, and by what order of things; has firmly established a new theory of cometary phenomena;

and has solved or corrected nearly every leading problem of mathematical astronomy.

UNTIL THE 10TH OF January, the observations were chiefly directed to the stars in the southern signs, in which, without the aid of the hydro-oxygen reflectors, a countless number of new stars and nebulae were discovered. But we shall defer our correspondent's account of these to future pages for the purpose of no longer withholding from our readers the more generally and highly interesting discoveries which were made in the lunar world. And for this purpose, too, we shall defer Dr. Grant's elaborate mathematical details of the corrections which Sir John Herschel has made in the best tables of the moon's tropical, sidereal, and synodic on which a great part of the established lunar theory depends.

It was about half past nine o'clock on the night of the tenth, the moon having then advanced within four days of her mean liberation, that the astronomer adjusted his instruments for the inspection of her eastern limb. The whole immense power of his telescope was applied and to its focal image about one half of the power of his microscope. On removing the screen of the latter, the field of view was covered throughout its entire area with a beautifully distinct, and even vivid representation of basaltic rock. Its color was a greenish brown, and the width of the columns, as defined by their interstices on the canvass, was invariably twenty-eight inches. No fracture whatever appeared in the mass first presented, but in a few seconds a shelving pile appeared of five or six columns width, which showed their figure to be hexagonal, and their articulations similar to those of the basaltic formation at Staffa. This precipitous shelf was profusely covered with a dark red flower, "precisely similar," says Dr. Grant, "to the Papaver Rhoeas, or rose-poppy of our sublunary cornfields; and this was the first organic production of nature, in a foreign world, ever revealed to the eyes of men."

The rapidity of the moon's ascension, or rather of the earth's diurnal rotation, being nearly equal to five hundred yards in a second, would have effectually prevented the inspection, or even the discovery of objects so minute as these, but for the admirable mechanism which constantly regulates, under the guidance of the sextant, the required altitude of the lens. But its operation was found to be so consummately perfect, that the observers could detain the object upon the field of view for any period they might desire. The specimen of lunar vegetation, however, which they had already seen, had decided a question of too exciting an interest to induce them to retard its exit. It had demonstrated that the moon has an atmosphere constituted similarly to our own, and capable of sustaining organized, and therefore, most probably animal life. The basaltic rocks continued to pass over the inclined canvass plane, through three successive diameters, when a verdant declivity of great beauty appeared, which occupied two more. This was preceded by another mass of nearly the former height, at the base of which they were at length delighted to perceive that novelty, a lunar forest. "The trees," says Dr. Grant, "for a period of ten minutes, were of one unvaried kind, and unlike any I have seen, except the largest kind of yews in the English churchyards, which they in some respects resemble." These were followed by a level green plain, which, as measured by the painted circle on our canvass of forty-nine feet, must have been more than half a mile in breadth; and then appeared as fine a forest of firs, unequivocal firs, as I have ever seen cherished in the bosom of my native mountains. Wearied with the long continuance of these, we greatly reduced the magnifying power of the microscope, without eclipsing either of the reflectors, and immediately perceived that we had been insensibly descending, as it were, a mountainous district of a highly diversified and romantic character, and that we were on the verge of a lake, or inland sea; but of what relative locality or extent, we were yet too greatly magnified to determine. On introducing the feeblest acromatic lens we possessed, we found that the water, whose boundary we had just discovered, answered in general outline to the Mare Nubium of Riccoli, by which we detected that, instead of commencing, as we supposed, on the eastern longitude of the planet, some delay in the elevation of the great lens had thrown us nearly upon the axis of her equator. However, as she was a free country, and we not, as yet, attached to any particular province, and moreover, since we could at any moment occupy our intended position, we again slid our magic lenses to survey the shores of the Mare Nubium. Why Riccoli so termed it, unless in ridicule of Cleomedes, I know not; for fairer shores never angels coasted on a tour of pleasure. A beach of brilliant white sand, girt with wild castellated rocks, apparently of green marble, varied at chasms, occurring every two or three hundred feet, with grotesque blocks of chalk or gypsum, and feathered and festooned at the summit with the clustering foliage of unknown trees, moved along the bright wall of our apartment until we were speechless with admiration. The water, we obtained a view of it, was nearly as blue as that of the deep ocean, and broke in large white billows upon the strand. The action of very high tides was quite manifest upon the face of the cliffs for more than a hundred miles; yet diversified as the scenery was during this and a much greater distance, we perceived no trace of animal existence, notwithstanding we could command at will a perspective or a foreground view of the whole. Mr. Holmes, indeed, pronounced some white objects of a circular form, which we saw at some distance in the interior of a cavern, to be bona fide specimens of a large cornu ammonis; but to me they appeared merely large pebbles, which had been chafed and rolled there by the tides. Our chase of animal life was not yet to be rewarded.

Having continued this close inspection of nearly two hours, during which we passed over a wide tract of country, chiefly of a rugged and apparent volcanic character; and having seen few additional varieties of vegetation, except some species of lichen, which grew everywhere in great abundance, Dr. Herschel proposed that we should take out all our lenses, give a rapid speed to the panorama, and search for some of the principal valleys known to astronomers, as the most likely method to reward our first night's observation with the discovery of animated beings. The lenses being removed,

and the effulgence of our unutterably glorious reflectors left undiminished, we found in accordance with our calculations, that our
field of view comprehended about twenty-five miles of the lunar
surface, with the distinctness both of outline and detail which could
be procured of a terrestrial object at a distance of two and a half
miles; an optical phenomenon which you will find demonstrated
in Note 5. This afforded us the best landscape views we had hitherto obtained, and although the accelerated motion was rather too
great, we enjoyed them with rapture. Several of these famous valleys,
which are bounded by lofty hills of so perfectly conical a form as to
render them less like works of nature than of art, passed the canvass
before we had time to check their flight; but presently a train of
scenery met our eye, of features so entirely novel, that Dr. Herschel
signalled for the lowest convenient gradation of movement. It was
a lofty chain of obelisk-shaped, or very slender pyramids, standing
in irregular groups, each composed of about thirty or forty spires,
every one of which was perfectly square, and as accurately trun-
cated as the finest specimens of Cornish crystal. They were of a faint
lilac hue, and very resplendent. I now thought that we had assuredly
fallen on productions of art; but Dr. Herschel shrewdly remarked,
that if the Lunarians could build thirty or forty miles of such monuments as these, we should ere now have discovered others of a less
equivocal character. He pronounced them quartz formations, of
probably wine-colored amethyst species, and promised us, from these
and other proofs which he had obtained of the powerful action of
laws of crystallization in this planet, a rich field of mineralogical
study. On introducing a lens, his conjecture was fully confirmed;
they were monstrous amethysts, of a diluted claret color, glowing
in the intensest light of the sun! They varied in height from sixty to
ninety feet, though we saw several of a still more incredible altitude.
They were observed in a succession of valleys divided by longitu-
dinal lines of round-breasted hills, covered with verdure and nobly
undulated; but what is most remarkable, the valleys which contained
these stupendous crystals were invariably barren, and covered with

stones of a ferruginous hue, which were probably iron pyrites. We found that some of these curiosities were situated in a district elevated half a mile above the valley of the Mare Foecunditatis, of Mayer and Riccoli; the shores of which soon hove into view. But never was a name more appropriately bestowed, From "Dan to Bersheba" all was barren, barren—the sea-board was entirely composed of chalk and flint, and not a vestige of vegetation could be discovered with our strongest glasses. The whole breadth of the northern extremity of the sea, which was about three hundred miles, having crossed our plane, we entered upon a wild mountainous region abounding with more extensive forests of larger trees than we had seen before— the species of which I have no good analogy to describe. In general contour they resembled our forest oak; but they were much more superb in foliage, having broad glossy leaves like that of the laurel, and tresses of yellow flowers which hung, in the open glades, from the branches to the ground. These mountains passed, we arrived at a region which filled us with utter astonishment. It was an oval valley, surrounded, except at narrow opening towards the south, by hills, red as the purest vermilion, and evidently crystallized; for wherever a precipitous chasm appeared—and these chasms were very frequent, and of immense depth—the perpendicular sections present conglomerated masses of polygon crystals, evenly fitted to each other, and arranged in deep strata, which grew darker in color as they descended to the foundations of the precipices. Innumerable cascades were bursting forth from the breasts of every one of these cliffs, and some so near their summits, and with such great force, as to form arches many yards in diameter. I never was so vividly reminded of Byron's simile, "the tale of the white horse in the Revolution." At the foot of this boundary of hills was a perfect zone of woods surrounding the whole valley, which was about eighteen or twenty miles wide, at its greatest breadth, and about thirty in length. Small collections of trees, of every imaginable kind, were scattered about the whole of the luxuriant area; and here our magnifiers blest our panting hopes with specimens of conscious existence. In the shade of the woods on the south-eastern side, we beheld continuous herds of brown quadrupeds, having all the external characteristics of the bison, but more diminutive than any species of the bos genus in our natural history. Its tail is like that of our bos grunniens; but in its semi-circular horns, the hump on its shoulders, and the depth of its dewlap, and the length of its shaggy hair, it closely resembled the species to which I first compared it. It had, however, one widely distinctive feature, which we afterwards found common to nearly every lunar quadruped we have discovered; namely, a remarkable fleshy appendage over the eyes, crossing the whole breadth of the forehead and united to the ears. We could most distinctly perceive this hairy veil, which was shaped like the upper front outline of a cap known to the ladies as Mary Queen of Scots' cap, lifted and lowered by means of the ears. It immediately occurred to the acute mind of Dr. Herschel, that this was a providential contrivance to protect the eyes of the animal from the extremes of light and darkness to which all the inhabitants of our side of the moon are periodically subjected.

The next animal perceived would be classed on earth as a monster. It was of a bluish lead color, about the size of a goat, with a head and beard like him, and a single horn, slightly inclined forward from the perpendicular. The female was destitute of horn and beard, but had a much longer tail. It was gregarious, and chiefly abounded on the acclivitous glades of the woods. In elegance of symmetry it rivalled the antelope, and like him it seemed an agile sprightly creature, running with great speed, and springing from the green turf with all the unaccountable antics of a young lamb or kitten. This beautiful creature afforded us the most exquisite amusement. The mimicry of its movements upon our white painted canvass was as faithful and luminous as that of animals within a few yards of the camera obscura, when seen pictures upon its tympan. Frequently when attempting to put our fingers upon its beard, it would suddenly bound away into oblivion, as if conscious of our earthly impertinence; but then others would appear, whom we could not prevent from nibbling the herbage, say or do what we would to them.

On examining the centre of this delightful valley, we found a large branching river, abounding with lovely islands, and water-birds of numerous kinds. A species of grey pelican was the most numerous; but a black and white crane, with unreasonably long legs and bill, were also quite common. We watched their pisciverous experiments a long time, in hopes of catching sight of a lunar fish; but although we were not gratified in this respect, we could easily guess the purpose with which they plunged their long necks so deeply beneath the water. Near the upper extremity of one of these islands we obtained a glimpse of a strange amphibious creature, of a spherical form, which rolled with great velocity across the pebbly beach, and was lost sight of in the strong current which set off from this angle of the island. We were compelled, however, to leave this prolific valley unexplored, on account of clouds which were evidently accumulating in the lunar atmosphere, our own being perfectly translucent. But this was itself an interesting discovery, for more distant observers had questioned or denied the existence of any humid atmosphere in this planet.

The moon being now low on her descent, Dr. Herschel inferred that the increasing refrangibility of her rays would prevent any satisfactory protraction of our labors, and our minds being actually fatigued with the excitement of the high enjoyments we had partaken, we mutually agreed to call in the assistants at the lens, and reward their vigilant attention with congratulatory bumpers of the best "East Indian Particular." It was not, however, without regret that we left the splendid valley of the red mountains, which, in compli-ment to the arms of our royal patron, we denominated "the Valley of the Unicorn;" and it may be found in Blunt's map, about midway between the Mare Faecunditatis and the Mare Nectaris.

The nights of the 11th and 12th being cloudy, were unfavorable to observation; but on those of the 13th and 14th further animal discoveries were made of the most exciting interest to every human being. We give them in the graphic language of our accomplished correspondent:—

After a short delay in advancing the observatory upon the levers, and in regulating the lens, we found our object and surveyed it. It was a dark narrow lake seventy miles long, bounded, on the east, north, and west, by red mountains of the same character as those surrounding the Valley of the Unicorn, from which it is distant to the south-west about 160 miles. This lake, like that valley, opens to the south upon a plain not more than ten miles wide, which is here encircled by a truly magnificent amphitheater of the loftiest order of lunar hills. For a semicircle of six miles these hills are riven, from their brow to their base, as perpendicularly as the outer walls of the Colosseum at Rome; but here exhibiting the sublime altitude of at least two thousand feet, in one smooth unbroken surface. How nature disposed of the large mass which she thus prodigally carved out, I know not; but certain it is that there are no fragments of it left upon the plain, which is a declivity without a single prominence except a billowly tract of woodland that runs in many a will vagary of breadth and course to the margin of the lake. The tremendous height and expansion of this perpendicular mountain, with its bright crimson front contrasted with the fringe of forest on its brow, and the verdure of the open plain beneath, filled out canvass with a landscape unsurpassed in unique grandeur by any we had beheld. Our twenty-five miles perspective included this remarkable mountain, the plain, a part of the lake, and the last graduated summits of the range of hills by which the latter is nearly surrounded. We ardently wished that all the world could view a scene so strangely grand, and our pulse beat high with the hope of one day exhibiting it to our countrymen in some part of our native land. But we were at length compelled to destroy our picture, as a while, for the purpose of magnifying

its parts for scientific inspection. Our plain was of course immediately covered with the ruby front of this mighty amphitheater, its tall figures, leaping cascades, and rugged caverns. As its
almost interminable sweep was measured off on the canvass,
we frequently saw long lines of some yellow metal hanging from
the crevices of the horizontal strata in will net-work, or straight
pendant branches. We of course concluded that this was virgin
gold, and we had no assay-master to prove to the contrary. On
searching the plain, over which we had observed the woods
roving in all the shapes of clouds in the sky, we were again
delighted with the discovery of animals. The first observed was
a quadruped with an amazingly long neck, head like a sheep,
bearing two long spiral horns, white as polished ivory, and
standing in a perpendicular parallel to each other. Its body was
like that of a deer, but its fore-legs were most disproportionally
long, and its tail, which was very busy and of a snowy whiteness,
curled high over its rump, and hung two or three feet by its
side. Its colors were bright bay and white in brindled parches,
clearly defined, but of no regular form. It was found only in pairs,
in spaces between the woods, and we had no opportunity of
witnessing its speed or habits. But a few minutes only elapsed
before three specimens of another animal appeared, so well
known to us all that we fairly laughed at the recognition of so
familiar an acquaintance in so distant a land. They were neither
more nor less than three good large sheep, which would not
have disgraced the farms of Leicestershire, or the shambles of
Leanenhall-market. With the utmost scrutiny, we could find
no mark of distinction between these and those of our native
soil; they had not even the appendage over the eyes, which I
have described as common to lunar quadrupeds. Presently they
appeared in great numbers, and on reducing the lenses, we found
them in flocks over a great part of the valley. I need not say how
desirous we were of finding shepherds to these flocks, and even
a man with blue apron and rolled up sleeves would have been

a welcome sight to us, if not to the sheep; but they fed in peace, lords of their own pastures, without either protector or destroyer in human shape.

We at length approached the level opening to the lake, where the valley narrows to a mile in width, and displays scenery on both sides picturesque and romantic beyond the powers of prose description. Imagination, borne on the wings of poetry, could alone gather similes to portray the wild sublimity of this land-scape, where dark behemoth crags stood over the brows of lofty precipices, as if a rampart in the sky; and forests seemed suspended in mid air. On the eastern side there was one soaring crag, crested with trees, which hung over in a curve like three-fourths of a Gothic arch, and being of a rich crimson color, its effect was most strange upon minds unaccustomed to the association of such grandeur with such beauty.

But whilst gazing upon them in a perspective of about half a mile, we were thrilled with astonishment to perceive four successive flocks of large winged creatures, wholly unlike any kind of birds, descend with a slow even motion from the cliffs on the western side, and alight upon the plain. They were first noted by Dr. Herschel, who exclaimed, "Now, gentlemen, my theories against your proofs, which you have often found a pretty even bet, we have here something worth looking at: I was confident that if we ever found beings in human shape, it would be in this longitude, and that they would be provided by their Creator with some extraordinary powers of locomotion: first exchange for my number D." This lens being soon introduced, gave us a fine half-mile distance, and we counted three parties of these creatures, of twelve, none, and fifteen in each, walking erect towards a small wood near the base of the eastern preci-pices. Certainly they were like human beings, for their wings had now disappeared, and their attitude in walking was both erect and dignified. Having observed them at this distance for some minutes, we introduced lens Hz which brought them to

the apparent proximity of eighty yards; the highest clear
magnitude we possessed until the latter end of March, when
we effected an improvement in the gas-burners. About half of
the first party had passed beyond our canvass; but of all the
others we had a perfect distinct and deliberate view. They aver-
aged four feet in height, were covered, except on the face, with
short and glossy copper-colored hair, and had wings composed of
a thin membrane, without hair, lying snugly upon their backs,
from the top of their shoulders to the calves of their legs. The
face, which was of a yellowish flesh color, was a slight improvement upon that of the large orang outang, being more open and
intelligent in its expression, and having a much greater expansion
of forehead. The mouth, however, was very prominent, though
somewhat relieved by a thick beard upon the lower jaw, and by
lips far more human than those of any species of simia genus. In
general symmetry of body and limbs they were infinitely superior
to the orang outang; so much so, that, but for their long wings,
Lieut. Drummond said they would look as well on a parade
ground as some of the old cockney militia! The hair on the head
was a darker color than that of the body, closely curled, but apparently not wooly, and arranged in two curious semicircles over
the temples of the forehead. Their feet could only be seen as they
were alternately lifted in walking; but, from what we could see
of them in so transient a view, they appeared thin, and very protu-
berant at the heel.

Whilst passing across the canvas, and whenever we afterwards
saw them, these creatures were evidently engaged in conversation; their gesticulation, more particularly the varied action of
their hands and arms, appeared impassioned and emphatic. We
hence inferred that they were rational beings, and although not
perhaps of so high an order as others which we discovered the
next month on the shores of the Bay of Rainbows, they were
capable of producing works of art and contrivance. The next
view we obtained of them was still more favorable. It was on the

borders of a little lake, or expanded stream, which we then for the first time perceived running down the valley to a large lake, and having on its eastern margin a small wood.

Some of these creatures had crossed this water and were lying like spread eagles on the skirts of the wood. We could then perceive that they possessed wings of great expansion, and were similar in structure to this of the bat, being a semi-transparent membrane expanded in curvilineal divisions by means of straight radii, united at the back by the dorsal integuments. But what astonished us very much was the circumstance of this membrane being continued, from the shoulders to the legs, united all the way down, though gradually decreasing in width. The wings seemed completely under the command of volition, for those of the creatures whom we saw bathing in the water, spread them instantly to their full width, waved them as ducks do theirs to shake off the water, and then as instantly closed them again in a compact form. Our further observation of the habits of these creatures, who were of both sexes, led to results so very remarkable, that I prefer they should first be laid before the public in Dr. Herschel's own work, where I have reason to know they are fully and faithfully stated, however incredulously they may be received.—★ ★ ★ ★ ★ The three families then almost simultaneously spread their wings, and were lost in the dark confines of the canvass before we had time to breathe from our paralyzing astonishment. We scientifically denominated them as Vespertilio-homo, or man-bat; and they are doubtless innocent and happy creatures, notwithstanding that some of their amusements would but ill comport with our terrestrial notions of decorum. The valley itself we called the Ruby Coloseum, in compliment to its stupendous southern boundary, the six mile sweep of precipices two thousand feet high. And the night, or rather morning, being far advanced, we postponed our tour to Petavius (No. 20), until another opportunity.

We have, of course, faithfully obeyed Dr. Grant's private injunction to omit those highly curious passages in his correspondence which he wished us to suppress, although we do not perceive the force of the reason assigned for it. It is true, the omitted paragraphs contain facts which would be wholly incredible to readers who do not carefully examine the principles and capacity of the instrument with which these marvellous discoveries have been made; but so will nearly all those which he has kindly permitted us to publish; and it was for this reason we considered the explicit description which we have given of the telescope so important a preliminary. From these, however, and other prohibited passages, which will be published by Dr. Herschel, with the certificates of the civil and military authorities of the colony, and of several Episcopal, Wesleyan, and other ministers, who, in the month of March last, were permitted, under the stipulation of temporary secrecy, to visit the laboratory, and become eye-witnesses of the wonders which they were requested to attest, we are confident his forthcoming volumes will be at once the most sublime in science, and the most intense in general interest, that ever issued from the press.

Edgar Allan Poe

(1809–1849)

BORN IN BOSTON IN 1809 to itinerant actors, both of whom died while he was a toddler (the father after abandoning the family), Edgar Poe was then adopted by the Allan family in Richmond, Virginia. He attended various schools in England but was back in Virginia by the age of eleven. In 1826 he enrolled in the University of Virginia and had by the next year accumulated massive gambling debts that inspired him to leave college, move to his family's roots in Baltimore, and join the army. The same year, 1827, he published his first book, *Tamerlane and Other Poems*, and he was off on a legendarily tempestuous career. At the age of twenty-seven, he married his thirteen-year-old cousin, Virginia Clemm. He was reckless with love, money, alcohol, and other drugs, and he died at the age of forty.

Poe wrote in many genres. His stories of criminal pathology, such as "The Black Cat" and "The Tell-Tale Heart," make Dostoyevsky seem tame. His supernatural tales, such as the operatic "The Fall of the House of Usher," have the potent virtue of also inviting nonsupernatural explanations that involve the breakdown of an unreliable narrator's psyche. Poe's poem "The Raven" was hugely popular in his lifetime but flourishes now mostly in parody, as in the version read by James Earl Jones and acted out on a Halloween episode of *The Simpsons*.

As an influential critic, Poe was among the first to celebrate the work of Nathaniel Hawthorne. His restless brain even spawned science-minded essays such as "Eureka: A Prose Poem," a lyrical and insightful tour of a perennial conundrum for astronomers—why the night sky is black if space holds an infinite number of stars. Amid all these writings, Poe also casually founded the genre of detective stories, with the first appearance of the Romantic intellectual hero C. Auguste Dupin, in "The Murders in the Rue Morgue" in 1841—a character who would later serve as the primary fictional inspiration for Sherlock Holmes.

Poe famously proclaimed a manifesto about the writing of short stories, within a review of Hawthorne's collection *Twice-Told Tales*, which appeared in two volumes, in 1837 and 1842. He insisted that the "skilful literary artist's" primary goal in writing a short story must be the contriving of a carefully planned overall emotional effect. Poe himself violated this dictum often, especially in some of his more idea-oriented science fictional tales, such as "Hans Pfaall— A Tale." In "The Facts in the Case of M. Valdemar," he reached his frequent goal of visceral horror by way of the new science of mesmerism. In the hands of Edgar Allan Poe, science's potential was terrifying.

Always fascinated by the many rapid developments in science, Poe also helped found the modern genre of science fiction, influencing descendants from Jules Verne to Ray Bradbury. He was fascinated by the claims of hypnotists. During the last third of the eighteenth century, Franz Mesmer, a German physician with an active scientific imagination, proposed that animals, human beings, and inanimate objects possess what he called "animal magnetism," his description for a transference of energy from one creature or object to another. In the first half of the 1840s, Poe and Hawthorne were thinking about many of the same scientific issues. "Questions as to unsettled points of History, and Mysteries of Nature, to be asked of a mesmerized person," wrote Hawthorne in his diary in 1842. The next year, this aspect of mesmerism was dubbed "hypnosis" by the Scottish scientist James Braid. Nowadays he is often described as the father of hypnotism, but at the time what we would call hypnotic suggestion was still covered under the term "mesmerism." Poe's use of the term clearly refers to hypnosis, although he also mentions a patient's "susceptibility to the magnetic influence."

In 1844 readers encountered the first of three stories in which Poe explored mesmerism. The first, "Mesmeric Revelation," was frequently reprinted—often as a factual account. The New York *New World*, for example, declared, "We *do* believe in the facts of mesmerism, although we have not yet been able to arrive at any theory sufficient to explain them." In 1845 Poe's second tale on this intriguing theme appeared simultaneously in two periodicals, under slightly different titles. "The Facts of M. Valdemar's Case" appeared in the December issue of the Whig magazine the *American Review* (which two months later published Poe's poem "The Raven"). The December 20 issue of the *Broadway Journal*, which Poe himself edited—the sole periodical that he ever owned, and one that survived for only a few months—published the story under the title by which it is now known. It too was often mistaken for an actual case history. The next year, an English practitioner of the more pseudoscientific approach to hypnosis included Poe's story as a case history in his compendium *Early Magnetism in Its Higher Relations to Humanity*. The poet and critic George Edward Woodberry, who established himself in the late nineteenth century as the foremost authority on Poe, insisted that no other story in literature equaled this one "for mere physical disgust and horror."

The Facts in the Case of M. Valdemar

OF COURSE I SHALL not pretend to consider it any matter for wonder, that the extraordinary case of M. Valdemar has excited discussion. It would have been a miracle had it not—especially under the circumstances. Through the desire of all parties concerned, to keep the affair from the public, at least for the present, or until we had farther opportunities for investigation—through our endeavors to effect this—a garbled or exaggerated account made its way into society, and became the source of many unpleasant misrepresentations; and, very naturally, of a great deal of disbelief.

It is now rendered necessary that I give the *facts*—as far as I comprehend them myself. They are, succinctly, these:

My attention, for the last three years, had been repeatedly drawn to the subject of Mesmerism; and, about nine months ago, it occurred to me, quite suddenly, that in the series of experiments made hitherto, there had been a very remarkable and most unaccountable omission:—no person had as yet been mesmerized *in articulo mortis*. It remained to be seen, first, whether, in such condition, there existed in the patient any susceptibility to the magnetic influence; secondly, whether, if any existed, it was impaired or increased by the condition; thirdly, to what extent, or for how long a period, the encroachments of Death might be arrested by the process. There were other points to be ascertained, but these most excited my curiosity—the last in especial, from the immensely important character of its consequences.

In looking around me for some subject by whose means I might test these particulars, I was brought to think of my friend, M. Ernest Valdemar, the well-known compiler of the "Bibliotheca Forensica," and author (under the *nom de plume* of Issachar Marx) of the Polish versions of "Wallenstein" and "Gargantua." M. Valdemar, who has resided principally at Harlem, N.Y., since the year 1839, is (or was) particularly noticeable for the extreme spareness of his person—his lower limbs much resembling those of John Randolph; and, also, for the whiteness of his whiskers, in violent contrast to the blackness of his hair—the latter, in consequence, being very generally mistaken for a wig. His temperament was markedly nervous, and rendered him a good subject for mesmeric experiment. On two or three occasions I had put him to sleep with little difficulty, but was disappointed in other results which his peculiar constitution had naturally led me to anticipate. His will was at no period positively, or thoroughly, under my control, and in regard to *clairvoyance*, I could accomplish with him nothing to be relied upon. I always attributed my failure at these points to the disordered state of his health. For some months previous to my becoming acquainted with him, his physicians had declared him in a confirmed phthisis. It was his custom, indeed, to speak calmly of his approaching dissolution, as of a matter neither to be avoided nor regretted.

When the ideas to which I have alluded first occurred to me, it was of course very natural that I should think of M. Valdemar. I knew the steady philosophy of the man too well to apprehend any scruples from *him*; and he had no relatives in America who would be likely to interfere. I spoke to him frankly upon the subject; and, to my surprise, his interest seemed vividly excited. I say to my surprise; for, although he had always yielded his person freely to my experiments, he had never before given me any tokens of sympathy with what I did. His disease was of that character which would admit of exact calculation in respect to the epoch of its termination in death; and it was finally arranged between us that he would send for me about twenty-four hours before the period announced by his physicians as that of his decease.

It is now rather more than seven months since I received, from M. Valdemar himself, the subjoined note:

MY DEAR P——,
You may as well come *now*. D—— and F—— are agreed that I cannot hold out beyond to-morrow midnight; and I think they have hit the time very nearly.
VALDEMAR.

I received this note within half an hour after it was written, and in fifteen minutes more I was in the dying man's chamber. I had not seen him for ten days, and was appalled by the fearful alteration which the brief interval had wrought in him. His face wore a leaden hue; the eyes were utterly lustreless; and the emaciation was so extreme, that the skin had been broken through by the cheek-bones. His expectoration was excessive. The pulse was barely perceptible. He retained, nevertheless, in a very remarkable manner, both his mental power and a certain degree of physical strength. He spoke with distinctness—took some palliative medicines without aid—and, when I entered the room, was occupied in penciling memoranda in a pocket-book. He was propped up in the bed by pillows. Doctors D—— and F—— were in attendance.

After pressing Valdemar's hand, I took these gentlemen aside, and obtained from them a minute account of the patient's condition. The left lung had been for eighteen months in a semi-osseous or cartilaginous state, and was, of course, entirely useless for all purposes of vitality. The right, in its upper portion, was also partially, if not thoroughly, ossified, while the lower region was merely a mass of purulent tubercles, running one into another. Several extensive perforations existed; and, at one point, permanent adhesion to the ribs had taken place. These appearances in the right lobe were of comparatively recent date. The ossification had proceeded with very unusual rapidity; no sign of it had been discovered a month before, and the adhesion had only been observed during the three previous days. Independently of the phthisis, the patient was suspected of aneurism of the aorta; but on this point the osseous symptoms rendered an exact diagnosis impossible. It was the opinion of both physicians that M. Valdemar would die about midnight on the morrow (Sunday.) It was then seven o'clock on Saturday evening.

On quitting the invalid's bed-side to hold conversation with myself, Doctors D—— and F—— had bidden him a final farewell. It had not been their intention to return; but, at my request, they agreed to look in upon the patient about ten the next night.

When they had gone, I spoke freely with M. Valdemar on the subject of his approaching dissolution, as well as, more particularly, of the experiment proposed. He still professed himself quite willing and even anxious to have it made, and urged me to commence it at once. A male and a female nurse were in attendance; but I did not feel myself altogether at liberty to engage in a task of this character with no more reliable witnesses than these people, in case of sudden accident, might prove. I therefore postponed operations until about eight the next night, when the arrival of a medical student, with whom I had some acquaintance, (Mr. Theodore L——l,) relieved me from farther embarrassment. It had been my design, originally, to wait for the physicians; but I was induced to proceed, first, by the urgent entreaties of M. Valdemar, and secondly, by my conviction that I had not a moment to lose, as he was evidently sinking fast.

Mr. L——l was so kind as to accede to my desire that he would take notes of all that occurred; and it is from his memoranda that what I now have to relate is, for the most part, either condensed or copied *verbatim.*

It wanted about five minutes of eight when, taking the patient's hand, I begged him to state, as distinctly as he could, to Mr. L——l, whether he (M. Valdemar,) was entirely willing that I should make the experiment of mesmerizing him in his then condition.

He replied feebly, yet quite audibly, "Yes, I wish to be mesmerized"—adding immediately afterwards, "I fear you have deferred it too long."

While he spoke thus, I commenced the passes which I had already found most effectual in subduing him. He was evidently influenced with the first lateral stroke of my hand across his forehead; but although I exerted all my powers, no farther perceptible effect was induced until some minutes after ten o'clock, when Doctors D——— and F——— called, according to appointment. I explained to them, in a few words, what I designed, and as they opposed no objection, saying that the patient was already in the death agony, I proceeded without hesitation—exchanging, however, the lateral passes for downward ones, and directing my gaze entirely into the right eye of the sufferer.

By this time his pulse was imperceptible and his breathing was stertorious, and at intervals of half a minute.

This condition was nearly unaltered for a quarter of an hour. At the expiration of this period, however, a natural although a very deep sigh escaped the bosom of the dying man, and the stertorious breathing ceased—that is to say, its stertoriousness was no longer apparent; the intervals were undiminished. The patient's extremities were of an icy coldness.

At five minutes before eleven, I perceived unequivocal signs of the mesmeric influence. The glassy roll of the eye was changed for that expression of uneasy *inward* examination which is never seen except in cases of sleep-waking, and which it is quite impossible to mistake. With a few rapid lateral passes I made the lids quiver, as in incipient sleep, and with a few more I closed them altogether. I was not satisfied, however, with this, but continued the manipulations vigorously, and with the fullest exertion of the will, until I had completely stiffened the limbs of the slumberer, after placing them in a seemingly easy position. The legs were at full length; the arms were nearly so, and reposed on the bed at a moderate distance from the loins. The head was very slightly elevated.

When I had accomplished this, it was fully midnight, and I requested the gentlemen present to examine M. Valdemar's condition. After a few experiments, they admitted him to be in an unusually perfect state of mesmeric trance. The curiosity of both the physicians was greatly excited. Dr. D—— resolved at once to remain with the patient all night, while Dr. F—— took leave with a promise to return at daybreak. Mr. L——l and the nurses remained.

We left M. Valdemar entirely undisturbed until about three o'clock in the morning, when I approached him and found him in precisely the same condition as when Dr. F—— went away—that is to say, he lay in the same position; the pulse was imperceptible; the breathing was gentle (scarcely noticeable, unless through the application of a mirror to the lips;) the eyes were closed naturally; and the limbs were as rigid and as cold as marble. Still, the general appearance was certainly not that of death.

As I approached M. Valdemar I made a kind of half effort to influence his right arm into pursuit of my own, as I passed the latter gently to and fro above his person. In such experiments with this patient, I had never perfectly succeeded before, and assuredly I had little thought of succeeding now; but to my astonishment, his arm very readily, although feebly, followed every direction I assigned it with mine. I determined to hazard a few words of conversation.

"M. Valdemar," I said, "are you asleep?" He made no answer, but I perceived a tremor about the lips, and was thus induced to repeat the question, again and again. At its third repetition, his whole frame was agitated by a very slight shivering; the eye-lids unclosed themselves so far as to display a white line of a ball; the lips moved sluggishly, and from between them, in a barely audible whisper, issued the words:

"Yes;—asleep now. Do not wake me!—let me die so!"

I here felt the limbs and found them as rigid as ever. The right arm, as before, obeyed the direction of my hand. I questioned the sleep-waker again:

"Do you still feel pain in the breast, M. Valdemar?"

The answer now was immediate, but even less audible than before:

"No pain—I am dying."

I did not think it advisable to disturb him farther just then, and nothing more was said or done until the arrival of Dr. F——, who came a little before sunrise, and expressed unbounded astonishment at finding the patient still alive. After feeling the pulse and applying a mirror to the lips, he requested me to speak to the sleep-waker again. I did so, saying:

"M. Valdemar, do you still sleep?"

As before, some minutes elapsed ere a reply was made; and during the interval the dying man seemed to be collecting his energies to speak. At my fourth repetition of the question, he said very faintly, almost inaudibly:

"Yes; still asleep—dying."

It was now the opinion, or rather the wish, of the physicians, that M. Valdemar should be suffered to remain undisturbed in his present apparently tranquil condition, until death should supervene—and this, it was generally agreed, must now take place within a few minutes. I concluded, however, to speak to him once more, and merely repeated my previous question.

While I spoke, there came a marked change over the countenance of the sleep-waker. The eyes rolled themselves slowly open, the pupils disappearing upwardly; the skin generally assumed a cadaverous hue, resembling not so much parchment as white paper; and the circular hectic spots which, hitherto, had been strongly defined in the centre of each cheek, *went out* at once. I use this expression, because the suddenness of their departure put me in mind of nothing so much as the extinguishment of a candle by a puff of the breath. The upper lip, at the same time, writhed itself away from the teeth, which it had previously covered completely; while the lower jaw fell with an audible jerk, leaving the mouth widely extended, and disclosing in full view the swollen and blackened tongue. I presume that no member of the party then present had been unaccustomed to death-bed horrors; but so hideous beyond conception was the appearance of M. Valdemar at this moment, that there was a general shrinking back from the region of the bed.

I now feel that I have reached a point of this narrative at which every reader will be startled into positive disbelief. It is my business, however, simply to proceed.

There was no longer the faintest sign of vitality in M. Valdemar; and concluding him to be dead, we were consigning him to the charge of the nurses, when a strong vibratory motion was observable in the tongue. This continued for perhaps a minute. At the expiration of this period, there issued from the distended and motionless jaws a voice—such as it would be madness in me to attempt describing. There are, indeed, two or three epithets which might be considered as applicable to it in part; I might say, for example, that the sound was harsh, and broken and hollow; but the hideous whole is indescribable, for the simple reason that no similar sounds have ever jarred upon the ear of humanity. There were two particulars, nevertheless, which I thought then, and still think, might fairly be stated as characteristic of the intonation—as well adapted to convey some idea of its unearthly peculiarity. In the first place, the voice seemed to reach our ears—at least mine—from a vast distance, or from some deep cavern within the earth. In the second place, it impressed me (I fear, indeed, that it will be impossible to make myself comprehended) as gelatinous or glutinous matters impress the sense of touch.

I have spoken both of "sound" and of "voice." I mean to say that the sound was one of distinct—of even wonderfully, thrillingly distinct—syllibification. M. Valdemar *spoke*—obviously in reply to the question I had propounded to him a few minutes before. I had asked him, it will be remembered, if he still slept. He now said:

"Yes;—no;—I *have been* sleeping—and now—now—*I am dead.*"

No person present even affected to deny, or attempted to repress, the unutterable, shuddering horror which these few words, thus uttered, were so well calculated to convey. Mr. L——l (the student) swooned. The nurses immediately left the chamber, and could not be induced to return. My own impressions I would not pretend to render intelligible to the reader. For nearly an hour, we busied ourselves, silently—without the utterance of a word—in endeavors to revive Mr. L——l. When he came to himself, we addressed ourselves again to an investigation of M. Valdemar's condition.

It remained in all respects as I have last described it, with the exception that the mirror no longer afforded evidence of respiration. An attempt to draw blood from the arm failed. I should mention, too, that this limb was no farther subject to my will. I endeavored in vain to make it follow the direction of my hand. The only real indication, indeed, of the mesmeric influence, was now found in the vibratory movement of the tongue, whenever I addressed M. Valdemar a question. He seemed to be making an effort to reply, but had no longer sufficient volition. To queries put to him by any other person than myself he seemed utterly insensible—although I endeavored to place each member of the company in mesmeric *rapport* with him. I believe that I have now related all that is necessary to an understanding of the sleep-waker's state at this epoch. Other nurses were procured; and at ten o'clock I left the house in company with the two physicians and Mr. L——l.

In the afternoon we all called again to see the patient. His condition remained precisely the same. We had now some discussion as to the propriety and feasibility of awakening him; but we had little difficulty in agreeing that no good purpose would be served by so doing. It was evident that, so far, death (or what is usually termed death) had been arrested by the mesmeric process. It seemed clear to us all that to awaken M. Valdemar would be merely to insure his instant, or at least his speedy dissolution.

From this period until the close of last week—*an interval of nearly seven months*—we continued to make daily calls at M. Valdemar's house, accompanied, now and then, by medical and other friends. All this time the sleeper-waker remained *exactly* as I have last described him. The nurses' attentions were continual.

It was on Friday last that we finally resolved to make the experiment of awakening, or attempting to awaken him; and it is the (perhaps) unfortunate result of this latter experiment which has given rise to so much discussion in private circles—to so much of what I cannot help thinking unwarranted popular feeling.

For the purpose of relieving M. Valdemar from the mesmeric trance, I made use of the customary passes. These, for a time, were unsuccessful. The first indication of revival was afforded by a partial descent of the iris. It was observed, as especially remarkable, that this lowering of the pupil was accompanied by the profuse outflowing of a yellowish ichor (from beneath the lids) of a pungent and highly offensive odor.

It was now suggested that I should attempt to influence the patient's arm, as heretofore. I made the attempt and failed. Dr. F—— then intimated a desire to have me put a question. I did so, as follows:

"M. Valdemar, can you explain to us what are your feelings or wishes now?"

There was an instant return of the hectic circles on the cheeks; the tongue quivered, or rather rolled violently in the mouth (although the jaws and lips remained rigid as before;) and at length the same hideous voice which I have already described, broke forth:

"For God's sake!—quick!—quick!—put me to sleep—or, quick!—waken me!—quick!—*I say to you that I am dead!*"

I was thoroughly unnerved, and for an instant remained undecided what to do. At first I made an endeavor to re-compose the patient; but, failing in this through total abeyance of the will, I retraced my steps and as earnestly struggled to awaken him. In this attempt I soon saw that I should be successful—or at least I soon fancied that my success would be complete—and I am sure that all in the room were prepared to see the patient awaken.

For what really occurred, however, it is quite impossible that any human being could have been prepared.

As I rapidly made the mesmeric passes, amid ejaculations of "dead! dead!" absolutely *bursting* from the tongue and not from the lips of the sufferer, his whole frame at once—within the space of a single minute, or even less, shrunk—crumbled—absolutely *rotted* away beneath my hands. Upon the bed, before that whole company, there lay a nearly liquid mass of loathsome—of detestable putrescence.

❋

Jules Verne

(1828–1905)

"I REALLY THINK THAT my love for maps and the great explorers," remarked Jules Verne when interviewed by the *Strand* in 1895, "led to my composing the first of my long series of geographical stories." The parade of Verne titles include some of the most popular and influential novels in nineteenth-century science fiction: *Journey to the Center of the Earth, From the Earth to the Moon* and its sequel, *Around the Moon, Twenty Thousand Leagues under the Seas* and its sequel, *The Mysterious Island*—not to mention the irresistible (and perennially popular) farce *Around the World in Eighty Days.*

Voyages extraordinaires, the series of fifty-four novels was called. In a prologue to an 1866 publication, Verne's original French publisher, Pierre-Jules Hetzel, declaimed with typical ambition that the series' goal was "to outline all the geographical, geological, physical, and astronomical knowledge amassed by modern science and to recount, in an entertaining and picturesque format . . . the history of the universe." A culture benefiting financially and spiritually from real-life exploration welcomed fictional adventures surpassing terrestrial limitations. "Mr. Verne is the creator of a genre," proclaimed *Le Temps* in 1864, "and he will have a place of his own. What Walter Scott's novels are for the teaching of history . . . Mr. Verne's books are for geographical science."

The novels appeared in a succession of formats. Most were first serialized in Hetzel's *Le Magasin d'éducation et de récréation*. Then came an illustrated gift edition (dubbed *Cartonnages dorés et colorés*, for gilded and colored bindings), a cheap popular edition, and so on. The series made both author and publisher rich and famous.

Verne said that he chose Africa as the setting for much of his first novel, *Five Weeks in a Balloon*, "for the simple reason that less was, and is, known about that continent than any other." He meant "known in Europe and the United States," of course, which were his primary markets. Exhausting the surface of the earth, Verne took readers inside it, and then to the moon and underneath the sea. In his most fantastic outing, Verne even wrote a novel about a group of people dislodged from Earth when a comet brushes against the planet, who find themselves trying to survive on the comet itself.

Even for Jules Verne, however, not every imaginative work was applauded—especially when breaking new ground for him. In 1863, following immediately upon the popular reception of *Five Weeks in a Balloon*, Verne wrote a darkly dystopian novel, *Paris in the Twentieth Century*, that looked ahead to the technologically advanced but spiritually arid world of 1960. This era of what Verne called "picture-telegraphs" (remarkably like fax machines) and automobiles powered by internal combustion engines struck Hetzel as too fantastic, not to mention depressing. Verne set the novel aside and returned to the more realistic—or at least almost possible—adventures in exotic settings. Not until 1994 did his second novel see the light of day, with a first publication in France.

The notion that the earth might be hollow, or might contain other formations that could conceivably house prehistoric worlds or lost colonies of human beings, evolved into an odd perennial theme in science fiction. Verne's 1864 novel translated into English as *Journey to the Center of the Earth* is the most famous "hollow earth" story. It follows the adventures of a neurotic German scholar named Otto Lidenbrock, whose descent ever deeper into the planet reveals a hollow interior, with a vast subterranean ocean populated by plesiosaurs and other creatures that had become extinct on the surface of Earth. Clearly Arthur Conan Doyle derived many of the ideas for his 1912 novel *The Lost World* from Verne's adventure, which was published during Doyle's youth. Edgar Rice Burroughs, creator of Tarzan in the same year, credited Verne's novel with inspiring his later works such as *The Land That Time Forgot*.

Verne was born on Île Feydeau, a built-up man-made island surrounded by the Loire River, in the city of Nantes near the coast of France. It ceased to be an island when part of the Erdre, a tributary of the Loire, was filled in during the early twentieth century. Throughout his career he spent much of his time on a boat he owned. Not surprisingly, his best and most popular novel takes place at sea. In *Twenty Thousand Leagues under the Seas* ("Seas" was mistranslated as singular early on, an error since endlessly perpetuated), Verne accomplished what science fiction writers at their best do so well, and what storytellers have done since Homer: he woke up our attention to the real world by animating it with fantastic stories. The novel recounts dramatic undersea adventures narrated by the enthusiastic marine scientist Pierre Arronax, who is accompanied by his servant Conseil, as they are captured by the submarine *Nautilus* and held as prisoners by the mysterious Captain Nemo, who at first seems like a villain but is gradually revealed as a hero of classical stature. An unknown "sea monster" had been glimpsed in many locations around the world, and Arronax signed on to help hunt down and identify the creature. It turns out to be the *Nautilus*, Nemo's electrically powered submarine. Nemo cannot afford to release them with his secret, and Arronax regards this enforced voyage as a gift for a biologist such as himself.

"Ancient epic heroes like Aeneas are set in motion against their wishes," the scholar Benjamin Eldon Stevens has remarked,

> struggling to get home or, as in Aeneas' case, to reach a new place that must substitute for a home that has been lost. By contrast, modern heroes like Verne's leave home in order to explore unknown places *and then return*, finding that little if anything has

changed . . . Such modern travelers may have more in common with ancient explorers like the Greek historian Herodotus (fifth century B.C.E.), possessed of a certain rationalizing impulse, than with heroes like Aeneas, driven by powers beyond their comprehension and control.

Twenty Thousand Leagues under the Seas first appeared in Hetzel's *Magasin*, between March 1869 and June 1870. A handsome illustrated edition appeared in 1871. Two years later, the Reverend Lewis Page Mercier, working under his pseudonym Mercier Lewis, published the first major English translation. Lewis did not hesitate to cut out material he considered objectionable, and he is often considered the primary villain in the saga of Verne's diverse reputations in France and in anglophone countries. He also made numerous scientific errors which reviewers carelessly attributed to Verne. The U.S. scholar Frederick Paul Walter published a public domain translation in 1991 in which he corrected many of Verne's errors, and the following chapters are taken from this edition.

A Walk on the Bottom of the Sea

(from *Twenty Thousand Leagues under the Seas*)

Chapter XV

A Walk on the Bottom of the Sea

THIS CELL WAS, TO speak correctly, the arsenal and wardrobe of the *Nautilus*. A dozen diving apparatuses hung from the partition waiting our use.

Ned Land, on seeing them, showed evident repugnance to dress himself in one.

"But, my worthy Ned, the forests of the Island of Crespo are nothing but submarine forests."

"Good!" said the disappointed harpooner, who saw his dreams of fresh meat fade away. "And you, M. Aronnax, are you going to dress yourself in those clothes?"

"There is no alternative, Master Ned."

"As you please, sir," replied the harpooner, shrugging his shoulders; "but, as for me, unless I am forced, I will never get into one."

"No one will force you, Master Ned," said Captain Nemo.

"Is Conseil going to risk it?" asked Ned.

"I follow my master wherever he goes," replied Conseil.

At the Captain's call two of the ship's crew came to help us dress in these heavy and impervious clothes, made of india-rubber without seam, and constructed expressly to resist considerable pressure. One would have thought it a suit of armour, both supple and resisting. This suit formed trousers and waistcoat. The trousers were finished off with thick boots, weighted with heavy leaden soles. The texture of the waistcoat was held together by bands of copper, which crossed the chest, protecting it from the great pressure of the water, and leaving the lungs free to act; the sleeves ended in gloves, which in no way restrained the movement of the hands. There was a vast difference noticeable between these consummate apparatuses and the old cork breastplates, jackets, and other contrivances in vogue during the eighteenth century.

Captain Nemo and one of his companions (a sort of Hercules, who must have possessed great strength), Conseil and myself were soon enveloped in the dresses. There remained nothing more to be done but to enclose our heads in the metal box. But, before proceeding to this operation, I asked the Captain's permission to examine the guns.

One of the *Nautilus* men gave me a simple gun, the butt end of which, made of steel, hollow in the centre, was rather large. It served as a reservoir for compressed air, which a valve, worked by a spring, allowed to escape into a metal tube. A box of projectiles in a groove in the thickness of the butt end contained about twenty of these electric balls, which, by means of a spring, were forced into the barrel of the gun. As soon as one shot was fired, another was ready.

"Captain Nemo," said I, "this arm is perfect, and easily handled: I only ask to be allowed to try it. But how shall we gain the bottom of the sea?"

"At this moment, Professor, the *Nautilus* is stranded in five fathoms, and we have nothing to do but to start."

"But how shall we get off?"

"You shall see."

Captain Nemo thrust his head into the helmet, Conseil and I did the same, not without hearing an ironical "Good sport!" from the Canadian. The upper part of our dress terminated in a copper collar upon which was screwed the metal helmet. Three holes, protected by thick glass, allowed us to see in all directions, by simply turning our head in the interior of the head-dress. As soon as it was in position, the Rouquayrol apparatus on our backs began to act; and, for my part, I could breathe with ease.

With the Ruhmkorff lamp hanging from my belt, and the gun in my hand, I was ready to set out. But to speak the truth, imprisoned in these heavy garments, and glued to the deck by my leaden soles, it was impossible for me to take a step.

But this state of things was provided for. I felt myself being pushed into a little room contiguous to the wardrobe room. My companions followed, towed along in the same way. I heard a water-tight door, furnished with stopper plates, close upon us, and we were wrapped in profound darkness.

After some minutes, a loud hissing was heard. I felt the cold mount from my feet to my chest. Evidently from some part of the vessel they had, by means of a tap, given entrance to the water, which was invading us, and with which the room was soon filled. A second door cut in the side of the *Nautilus* then opened. We saw a faint light. In another instant our feet trod the bottom of the sea.

And now, how can I retrace the impression left upon me by that walk under the waters? Words are impotent to relate such wonders! Captain Nemo walked in front, his companion followed some steps behind. Conseil and I remained near each other, as if an exchange of words had been possible through our metallic cases. I no longer felt the weight of my clothing, or of my shoes, of my reservoir of air, or my thick helmet, in the midst of which my head rattled like an almond in its shell.

The light, which lit the soil thirty feet below the surface of the ocean, astonished me by its power. The solar rays shone through the watery mass easily, and dissipated all colour, and I clearly distinguished objects at a distance of a hundred and fifty yards. Beyond that the tints darkened into fine gradations of ultramarine, and faded into vague obscurity. Truly this water which surrounded me was but another air denser than the terrestrial atmosphere, but almost as transparent. Above me was the calm surface of the sea. We were walking on fine, even sand, not wrinkled, as on a flat shore, which retains the impression of the billows. This dazzling carpet, really a reflector, repelled the rays of the sun with wonderful intensity, which accounted for the vibration which penetrated every atom of liquid. Shall I be believed when I say that, at the depth of thirty feet, I could see as if I was in broad daylight?

For a quarter of an hour I trod on this sand, sown with the impalpable dust of shells. The hull of the *Nautilus*, resembling a long shoal, disappeared by degrees; but its lantern, when darkness should overtake us in the waters, would help to guide us on board by its distinct rays.

Soon forms of objects outlined in the distance were discernible. I recognised magnificent rocks, hung with a tapestry of zoophytes of the most beautiful kind, and I was at first struck by the peculiar effect of this medium.

It was then ten in the morning; the rays of the sun struck the surface of the waves at rather an oblique angle, and at the touch of their light, decomposed by refraction as through a prism, flowers, rocks, plants, shells, and polypi were shaded at the edges by the seven solar colours. It was marvellous, a feast for the eyes, this complication of coloured tints, a perfect kaleidoscope of green, yellow, orange, violet, indigo, and blue; in one word, the whole palette of an enthusiastic colourist! Why could I not communicate to Conseil the lively sensations which were mounting to my brain, and rival him in expressions of admiration? For aught I knew, Captain Nemo and his companion might be able to exchange thoughts by means of signs previously agreed upon. So, for want of better, I talked to myself; I declaimed in the copper box which covered my head, thereby expending more air in vain words than was perhaps wise.

Various kinds of isis, clusters of pure tuft-coral, prickly fungi, and anemones formed a brilliant garden of flowers, decked with their collarettes of blue tentacles, sea-stars studding the sandy bottom. It was a real grief to me to crush under my feet the brilliant specimens of molluscs which strewed the ground by thousands, of hammerheads, donaciae (veritable bounding shells), of staircases, and red helmet-shells, angel-wings, and many others produced by this inexhaustible ocean. But we were bound to walk, so we went on, whilst above our heads waved medusae whose umbrellas of opal or rose-pink, escalloped with a band of blue, sheltered us from the rays of the sun and fiery pelagiae, which, in the darkness, would have strewn our path with phosphorescent light.

All these wonders I saw in the space of a quarter of a mile, scarcely stopping, and following Captain Nemo, who beckoned me on by signs. Soon the nature of the soil changed; to the sandy plain succeeded an extent of slimy mud which the Americans call "ooze," composed of equal parts of silicious and calcareous shells. We then travelled over a plain of seaweed of wild and luxuriant vegetation. This sward was of close texture, and soft to the feet, and rivalled the softest carpet woven by the hand of man. But whilst verdure was spread at our feet, it did not abandon our heads. A light network of marine plants, of that inexhaustible family of seaweeds of which more than two thousand kinds are known, grew on the surface of the water.

I noticed that the green plants kept nearer the top of the sea, whilst the red were at a greater depth, leaving to the black or brown the care of forming gardens and parterres in the remote beds of the ocean.

We had quitted the *Nautilus* about an hour and a half. It was near noon; I knew by the perpendicularity of the sun's rays, which were no longer refracted. The magical colours disappeared by degrees, and the shades of emerald and sapphire were effaced. We walked with a regular step, which rang upon the ground with astonishing intensity; the slightest noise was transmitted with a quickness to which the ear is unaccustomed on the earth; indeed, water is a better conductor of sound than air, in the ratio of four to one. At this period the earth sloped downwards; the light took a uniform tint.

We were at a depth of a hundred and five yards and twenty inches, undergoing a pressure of six atmospheres.

At this depth I could still see the rays of the sun, though feebly; to their intense brilliancy had succeeded a reddish twilight, the lowest state between day and night; but we could still see well enough; it was not necessary to resort to the Ruhmkorff apparatus as yet. At this moment Captain Nemo stopped; he waited till I joined him, and then pointed to an obscure mass, looming in the shadow, at a short distance.

"It is the forest of the Island of Crespo," thought I; and I was not mistaken.

Chapter XVI

A Submarine Forest

We had at last arrived on the borders of this forest, doubtless one of the finest of Captain Nemo's immense domains. He looked upon it as his own, and considered he had the same right over it that the first men had in the first days of the world. And, indeed, who would have disputed with him the possession of this submarine property? What other hardier pioneer would come, hatchet in hand, to cut down the dark copses?

This forest was composed of large tree-plants; and the moment we penetrated under its vast arcades, I was struck by the singular position of their branches—a position I had not yet observed.

Not an herb which carpeted the ground, not a branch which clothed the trees, was either broken or bent, nor did they extend horizontally; all stretched up to the surface of the ocean. Not a filament, not a ribbon, however thin they might be, but kept as straight as a rod of iron. The fuci and llianas grew in rigid perpendicular lines, due to the density of the element which had produced them. Motionless yet, when bent to one side by the hand, they directly resumed their former position. Truly it was the region of perpendicularity!

I soon accustomed myself to this fantastic position, as well as to the comparative darkness which surrounded us. The soil of the forest seemed covered with sharp blocks, difficult to avoid. The submarine flora struck me as being very perfect, and richer even than it would have been in the arctic or tropical zones, where these productions are not so plentiful. But for some minutes I involuntarily confounded the genera, taking animals for plants; and who would not have been mistaken? The fauna and the flora are too closely allied in this submarine world.

These plants are self-propagated, and the principle of their existence is in the water, which upholds and nourishes them. The greater number, instead of leaves, shoot forth blades of capricious shapes, comprised within a scale of colours pink, carmine, green, olive, fawn, and brown.

"Curious anomaly, fantastic element!" said an ingenious naturalist, "in which the animal kingdom blossoms, and the vegetable does not!"

In about an hour Captain Nemo gave the signal to halt; I, for my part, was not sorry, and we stretched ourselves under an arbour of alariae, the long thin blades of which stood up like arrows.

This short rest seemed delicious to me; there was nothing wanting but the charm of conversation; but, impossible to speak, impossible to answer, I only put my great copper head to Conseil's. I saw the worthy fellow's eyes glistening with delight, and, to show his satisfaction, he shook himself in his breastplate of air, in the most comical way in the world.

After four hours of this walking, I was surprised not to find myself dreadfully hungry. How to account for this state of the stomach I could not tell. But instead I felt an insurmountable desire to sleep, which happens to all divers. And my eyes soon closed behind the thick glasses, and I fell into a heavy slumber, which the movement alone had prevented before. Captain Nemo and his robust companion, stretched in the clear crystal, set us the example.

How long I remained buried in this drowsiness I cannot judge, but, when I woke, the sun seemed sinking towards the horizon. Captain Nemo had already risen, and I was beginning to stretch my limbs, when an unexpected apparition brought me briskly to my feet.

A few steps off, a monstrous sea-spider, about thirty-eight inches high, was watching me with squinting eyes, ready to spring upon me. Though my diver's dress was thick enough to defend me from the bite of this animal, I could not help shuddering with horror. Conseil and the sailor of the *Nautilus* awoke at this moment. Captain Nemo pointed out the hideous crustacean, which a blow from the butt end of the gun knocked over, and I saw the horrible claws of the monster writhe in terrible convulsions. This incident reminded me that other animals more to be feared might haunt these obscure depths, against whose attacks my diving-dress would not protect me. I had never thought of it before, but I now resolved to be upon my guard. Indeed, I thought that this halt would mark the termination of our walk; but I was mistaken, for, instead of returning to the *Nautilus*, Captain Nemo continued his bold excursion. The ground was still on the incline, its declivity seemed to be getting greater, and to be leading us to greater depths. It must have been about three o'clock when we reached a narrow valley, between high perpendicular walls, situated about seventy-five fathoms deep. Thanks to the perfection of our apparatus, we were forty-five fathoms below the limit which nature seems to have imposed on man as to his submarine excursions.

I say seventy-five fathoms, though I had no instrument by which to judge the distance. But I knew that even in the clearest waters the solar rays could not penetrate further. And accordingly the darkness deepened. At ten paces not an object was visible. I was groping my way, when I suddenly saw a brilliant white light. Captain Nemo had just put his electric apparatus into use; his companion did the same, and Conseil and I followed their example. By turning a screw I established a communication between the wire and the spiral glass, and the sea, lit by our four lanterns, was illuminated for a circle of thirty-six yards.

As we walked I thought the light of our Ruhmkorff apparatus could not fail to draw some inhabitant from its dark couch. But if they did approach us, they at least kept at a respectful distance from the hunters. Several times I saw Captain Nemo stop, put his gun to his shoulder, and after some moments drop it and walk on. At last, after about four hours, this marvellous excursion came to an end. A wall of superb rocks, in an imposing mass, rose before us, a heap of gigantic blocks, an enormous, steep granite shore, forming dark grottos, but which presented no practicable slope; it was the prop of the Island of Crespo. It was the earth! Captain Nemo stopped suddenly. A gesture of his brought us all to a halt; and, however desirous I might be to scale the wall, I was obliged to stop. Here ended Captain Nemo's domains. And he would not go beyond them. Further on was a portion of the globe he might not trample upon.

The return began. Captain Nemo had returned to the head of his little band, directing their course without hesitation. I thought we were not following the same road to return to the *Nautilus*. The new road was very steep, and consequently very painful. We approached the surface of the sea rapidly. But this return to the upper strata was not so sudden as to cause relief from the pressure too rapidly, which might have produced serious disorder in our organisation, and brought on internal lesions, so fatal to divers. Very soon light reappeared and grew, and, the sun being low on the horizon, the refraction edged the different objects with a spectral ring. At ten yards and a half deep, we walked amidst a shoal of little fishes of all kinds, more numerous than the birds of the air, and also more agile; but no aquatic game worthy of a shot had as yet met our gaze, when at that moment I saw the Captain shoulder his gun quickly, and follow a moving object into the shrubs. He fired; I heard a slight hissing, and a creature fell stunned at some distance from us. It was a magnificent sea-otter, an enhydrus, the only exclusively marine quadruped. This otter was five feet long, and must have been very valuable. Its skin, chestnut-brown above and silvery underneath, would have made one of those beautiful furs so sought after in the Russian and Chinese markets: the fineness and the lustre of its coat would certainly fetch L80. I admired this curious mammal, with its rounded head ornamented with short ears, its round eyes, and white whiskers like those of a cat, with webbed feet and nails, and tufted tail. This precious animal, hunted and tracked by fishermen, has now become very rare, and taken refuge chiefly in the northern parts of the Pacific, or probably its race would soon become extinct.

Captain Nemo's companion took the beast, threw it over his shoulder, and we continued our journey. For one hour a plain of sand lay stretched before us. Sometimes it rose to within two yards and some inches of the surface of the water. I then saw our image clearly reflected, drawn inversely, and above us appeared an identical group reflecting our movements and our actions; in a word, like us in every point, except that they walked with their heads downward and their feet in the air.

Another effect I noticed, which was the passage of thick clouds which formed and vanished rapidly; but on reflection I understood that these seeming clouds were due to the varying thickness of the reeds at the bottom, and I could even see the fleecy foam which their broken tops multiplied on the water, and the shadows of large birds passing above our heads, whose rapid flight I could discern on the surface of the sea.

On this occasion I was witness to one of the finest gun shots which ever made the nerves of a hunter thrill. A large bird of great breadth of wing, clearly visible, approached, hovering over us. Captain Nemo's companion shouldered his gun and fired, when it was only a few yards above the waves. The creature fell stunned, and the force of its fall brought it within the reach of dexterous hunter's grasp. It was an albatross of the finest kind.

Our march had not been interrupted by this incident. For two hours we followed these sandy plains, then fields of algae very disagreeable to cross. Candidly, I could do no more when I saw a glimmer of light, which, for a half mile, broke the darkness of the waters. It was the lantern of the *Nautilus*. Before twenty minutes were over we should be on board, and I should be able to breathe with ease, for it seemed that my reservoir supplied air very deficient in oxygen. But I did not reckon on an accidental meeting which delayed our arrival for some time.

I had remained some steps behind, when I presently saw Captain Nemo coming hurriedly towards me. With his strong hand he bent me to the ground, his companion doing the same to Conseil. At first I knew not what to think of this sudden attack, but I was soon reassured by seeing the Captain lie down beside me, and remain immovable.

I was stretched on the ground, just under the shelter of a bush of algae, when, raising my head, I saw some enormous mass, casting phosphorescent gleams, pass blusteringly by.

My blood froze in my veins as I recognised two formidable sharks which threatened us. It was a couple of tintoreas, terrible creatures, with enormous tails and a dull glassy stare, the phosphorescent matter ejected from holes pierced around the muzzle. Monstrous brutes! which would crush a whole man in their iron jaws. I did not know whether Conseil stopped to classify them; for my part, I noticed their silver bellies, and their huge mouths bristling with teeth, from a very unscientific point of view, and more as a possible victim than as a naturalist.

Happily the voracious creatures do not see well. They passed without seeing us, brushing us with their brownish fins, and we escaped by a miracle from a danger certainly greater than meeting a tiger full-face in the forest. Half an hour after, guided by the electric light we reached the *Nautilus*. The outside door had been left open, and Captain Nemo closed it as soon as we had entered the first cell. He then pressed a knob. I heard the pumps working in the midst of the vessel, I felt the water sinking from around me, and in a few moments the cell was entirely empty. The inside door then opened, and we entered the vestry.

There our diving-dress was taken off, not without some trouble, and, fairly worn out from want of food and sleep, I returned to my room, in great wonder at this surprising excursion at the bottom of the sea.

✳

William Henry Rhodes

(1822–1876)

IN E. NESBIT'S STORY "The Five Senses," included in this anthology, a scientist develops a drug that enhances sensory perception to a dangerous level. In "The Automaton Ear," also found within these pages, Florence McLandburgh's narrator finds a way to enhance hearing until even sounds from the past can be heard again. Each author follows her concept along surprising narrative byways conjured by these technological developments. William Henry Rhodes, in contrast, eschews technology entirely in his initial premise; he imagines a boy born with a mutant eye that enables him to see past Earth and into space.

Rhodes was born in Windsor, North Carolina, in 1822. Six years later his mother died. When his father was appointed United States consul to the Republic of Texas, Rhodes left Princeton University and accompanied him. In 1844 he returned to the northeast and entered Harvard Law School. He continued throughout his life to pursue encyclopedic knowledge of U.S. history and the workings of the legal and social systems that were reshaping the nation. "He became a good lawyer," wrote one of his friends after his death, "but was an unwilling practitioner." He practiced law in Texas and then California, where he settled and remained, but his compass pointed toward literature. Often he wrote under the pen name Caxton. Like Richard Adams Locke, who anonymously authored the moon hoax (parts of which appear in this anthology as "Man-Bats on the Moon"), Rhodes wrote with a convincingly factual-sounding tone that led many readers to wonder if his outrageous tales were true.

In 1876 "The Telescopic Eye" appeared in the *San Francisco Evening Post* and was reprinted the same year in *Caxton's Book: A Collection of Essays, Poems, Tales, and Sketches*, published in San Francisco by A. L. Bancroft and Company. This posthumous gathering was assembled by friends of Rhodes. The preface, "In Memoriam," says of him, "His writings are illumined by powerful fancy, scientific knowledge, and a reasoning power which gave to his most weird imaginations the similitude of truth and the apparel of facts." *Caxton's Book* brought together Rhodes's stories from various venues and his poems, most of which he had written to read aloud at monthly gatherings of San Francisco's Bohemian Club, which had been founded a few years earlier. (It still exists.)

The collection demonstrates Rhodes's preoccupation with both vision and mad scientists. It opens with Rhodes's best-known story, "The Case of Summerfield," in which the kind of megalomaniacal villain later relegated to James Bond movies extorts money by threatening to burn the very oceans of Earth with potassium. The story "Phases in the Life of John Pollexfen" features a horrific mad scientist who invents a camera that requires human eyes for its lenses. The eyes of the boy in "The Telescopic Eye" are safe but troubled— blind to mundane Earth, yet, in a secular reimagining of the sacred visions of older literature, able to glimpse celestial life beyond the clouds.

The Telescopic Eye

A Leaf from a Reporter's Notebook

FOR THE PAST FIVE or six weeks, rumors of a strange abnormal development of the powers of vision of a youth named Johnny Palmer, whose parents reside at South San Francisco, have been whispered around in scientific circles in the city, and one or two short notices have appeared in the columns of some of our contemporaries relative to the prodigious *lusus naturæ*, as the scientists call it.

Owing to the action taken by the California College of Sciences, whose members comprise some of our most scientific citizens, the affair has assumed such importance as to call for a careful and exhaustive investigation.

Being detailed to investigate the flying stories, with regard to the powers of vision claimed for a lad named John or "Johnny" Palmer, as his parents call him, we first of all ventured to send in our card to Professor Gibbins, the President of the California College of Sciences. It is always best to call at the fountain-head for useful information, a habit which our two hundred thousand readers on this coast can never fail to see and appreciate. An estimable gentleman of the African persuasion, to whom we handed our "pasteboard," soon returned with the polite message, "Yes, sir; *in*. Please walk up." And so we followed our conductor through several passages almost as dark as the face of the *cicerone*, and in a few moments found ourselves in the presence of, perhaps, the busiest man in the city of San Francisco.

Without any flourish of trumpets, the Professor inquired our object in seeking him and the information we desired. "Ah," said he, "that is a long story. I have no time to go into particulars just now. I am computing the final sheet of Professor Davidson's report of the Transit of Venus, last year, at Yokohama and Loo-Choo. It must be ready before May, and it requires six months' work to do it correctly."

"But," I rejoined, "can't you tell me where the lad is to be found?"

"And if I did, they will not let you see him."

"Let me alone for that," said I, smiling; "a reporter, like love, finds his way where wolves would fear to tread."

"Really, my dear sir," quickly responded the Doctor, "I have no time to chat this morning. Our special committee submitted its report yesterday, which is on file in that book-case; and if you will promise not to publish it until after it has been read in open session of the College, you may take it to your sanctum, run it over, and clip from it enough to satisfy the public for the present."

Saying this, he rose from his seat, opened the case, took from a pigeon-hole a voluminous written document tied up with red tape, and handed it to me, adding, "Be careful!" Seating himself without another word, he turned his back on me, and I sallied forth into the street.

Reaching the office, I scrutinized the writing on the envelope, and found it as follows: "Report of Special Committee—Boy Palmer— Vision—Laws of Light—Filed February 10, 1876—Stittmore, Sec." Opening the document, I saw at once that it was a full, accurate, and, up to the present time, complete account of the phenomenal case I was after, and regretted the promise made not to publish the entire report until read in open session of the College. Therefore, I shall be compelled to give the substance of the report in my own words, only giving *verbatim* now and then a few scientific phrases which are not fully intelligible to me, or susceptible of circumlocution in common language.

The report is signed by Doctors Bryant, Gadbury and Golson, three of our ablest medical men, and approved by Professor Smyth, the oculist. So far, therefore, as authenticity and scientific accuracy are concerned, our readers may rely implicitly upon the absolute correctness of every fact stated and conclusion reached.

The first paragraph of the report gives the name of the child, "John Palmer, age, nine years, and place of residence, South San Francisco, Culp Hill, near Catholic Orphan Asylum;" and then plunges at once into *in medias res.*

It appears that the period through which the investigation ran was only fifteen days; but it seems to have been so thorough, by the use of the ophthalmoscope and other modern appliances and tests, that no regrets ought to be indulged as to the brevity of the time employed in experiments. Besides, we have superadded a short and minute account of our own, verifying some of the most curious facts reported, with several tests proposed by ourselves and not included in the statement of the scientific committee.

To begin, then, with the beginning of the inquiries by the committee. They were conducted into a small back room, darkened by old blankets hung up at the window, for the purpose of the total exclusion of daylight; an absurd remedy for blindness, recommended by a noted quack whose name adorns the extra fly-leaf of the San Francisco *Truth Teller.* The lad was reclining upon an old settee, ill-clad and almost idiotic in expression. As the committee soon ascertained, his mother only was at home, the father being absent at his customary occupation—that of switch-tender on the San Jose Rail-road. She notified her son of the presence of strangers and he rose and walked with a firm step toward where the gentlemen stood, at the entrance of the room. He shook them all by the hand and bade them good morning. In reply to questions rapidly put and answered by his mother, the following account of the infancy of the boy and the accidental discovery of his extraordinary powers of vision was given:

He was born in the house where the committee found him, nine years ago the 15th of last January. Nothing of an unusual character occurred until his second year, when it was announced by a neighbor that the boy was completely blind, his parents never having been suspicious of the fact before that time, although the mother declared that for some months anterior to the discovery she had noticed some acts of the child that seemed to indicate mental imbecility rather than blindness. From this time forward until a few months ago nothing happened to vary the boy's existence except a new remedy now and then prescribed by neighbors for the supposed malady. He was mostly confined to a darkened chamber, and was never trusted alone out of doors. He grew familiar, by touch and sound, with the forms of most objects about him, and could form very accurate guesses of the color and texture of them all. His conversational powers did not seem greatly impaired, and he readily acquired much useful knowledge from listening attentively to everything that was said in his presence. He was quite a musician, and touched the harmonicon, banjo and accordeon with skill and feeling. He was unusually sensitive to the presence of light, though incapable of seeing any object with any degree of distinctness; and hence the attempt to exclude light as the greatest enemy to the recovery of vision. It was very strange that up to the time of the examination of the committee, no scientific examination of the boy's eye had been made by a competent oculist, the parents contenting themselves with the chance opinions of visitors or the cheap nostrums of quacks. It is perhaps fortunate for science that this was the case, as a cure for the eye might have been an extinction of its abnormal power.

On the evening of the 12th of December last (1875), the position of the child's bed was temporarily changed to make room for a visitor. The bed was placed against the wall of the room, fronting directly east, with the window opening at the side of the bed next to the head. The boy was sent to bed about seven o'clock, and the parents and their visitor were seated in the front room, spending the evening in social intercourse. The moon rose full and cloudless about half-past seven o'clock, and shone full in the face of the sleeping boy.

Something aroused him from slumber, and when he opened his eyes the first object they encountered was the round disk of her orb. By some oversight the curtain had been removed from the window, and probably for the first time in his life he beheld the lustrous queen of night swimming in resplendent radiance, and bathing hill and bay in effulgent glory. Uttering a cry, equally of terror and delight, he sprang up in bed and sat there like a statue, with eyes aglare, mouth open, finger pointed, and astonishment depicted on every feature. His sudden, sharp scream brought his mother to his side, who tried for some moments in vain to distract his gaze from the object before him. Failing even to attract notice, she called in her husband and friend, and together they besought the boy to lie down and go to sleep, but to no avail. Believing him to be ill and in convulsions, they soon seized him, and were on the point of immersing him in a hot bath, when, with a sudden spring, he escaped from their grasp and ran out the front door. Again he fixed his unwinking eyes upon the moon, and remained speechless for several seconds. At length, having seemingly satisfied his present curiosity, he turned on his mother, who stood wringing her hands in the doorway and moaning piteously, and exclaimed, "I can see the moon yonder, and it is so beautiful that I am going there to-morrow morning, as soon as I get up."

"How big does it look?" said his mother.

"So big," he replied, "that I cannot see it all at one glance—as big as all out of doors."

"How far off from you does it seem to be?"

"About half a car's distance," he quickly rejoined.

It may be here remarked that the boy's idea of distance had been measured all his life by the distance from his home to the street-car station at the foot of the hill. This was about two hundred yards, so that the reply indicated that the moon appeared to be only one hundred yards from the spectator. The boy then proceeded of his own accord to give a very minute description of the appearance of objects which he beheld, corresponding, of course, to his poverty of words with which to clothe his ideas.

His account of things beheld by him was so curious, wonderful and apparently accurate, that the little group about him passed rapidly from a conviction of his insanity to a belief no less absurd— that he had become, in the cant lingo of the day, a seeing, or "clairvoyant" medium. Such was the final conclusion to which his parents had arrived at the time of the visit of the scientific committee. He had been classed with that credulous school known to this century as spiritualists, and had been visited solely by persons of that ilk heretofore.

The committee having fully examined the boy, and a number of independent witnesses, as to the facts, soon set about a scientific investigation of the true causes of the phenomenon. The first step, of course, was to examine the lad's eye with the modern ophthalmoscope, an invention of Professor Helmholtz, of Heidelberg, a few years ago, by means of which the depths of this organ can be explored, and the smallest variations from a healthy or normal condition instantaneously detected.

The mode of using the instrument is as follows: The room is made perfectly dark; a brilliant light is then placed near the head of the patient, and the rays are reflected by a series of small mirrors into his eye, as if they came from the eye of the observer; then, by looking through the central aperture of the instrument, the oculist can examine the illuminated interior of the eyeball, and perceive every detail of structure, healthy or morbid, as accurately and clearly as we can see any part of the exterior of the body. No discomfort arises to the organ examined, and all its hidden mysteries can be studied and understood as clearly as those of any other organ of the body.

This course was taken with John Palmer, and the true secret of his mysterious power of vision detected in an instant.

On applying the ophthalmoscope, the committee ascertained in a moment that the boy's eye was abnormally shaped. A natural, perfect eye is perfectly round. But the eye examined was exceedingly flat, very thin, with large iris, flat lens, immense petira, and wonderfully dilated pupil. The effect of the shape was at once apparent. It was utterly impossible to see any object with distinctness at any distance short of many thousands of miles. Had the eye been elongated inward, or shaped like an egg—to as great an extent, the boy would have been effectually blind, for no combination of lens power could have placed the image of the object beyond the coat of the retina. In other words, there are two common imperfections of the human organ of sight; one called *myopia*, or "near-sightedness;" the *presbyopia*, or "far-sightedness."

"The axis being too long," says the report, "in myopic eyes, parallel rays, such as proceed from distant objects, are brought to a focus at a point so far in front of the retina, that only confused images are formed upon it. Such a malformation, constituting an excess of refractive power, can only be neutralized by concave glasses, which give such a direction to rays entering the eye as will allow of their being brought to a focus at a proper point for distant perception."

"Presbyopia is the reverse of all this. The antero-posterior axis of such eyes being too short, owing to the flat plate-like shape of the ball, their refractive power is not sufficient to bring even parallel rays to a focus upon the retina, but is adapted for convergent rays only. Convex glasses, in a great measure, compensate for this quality by rendering parallel rays convergent; and such glasses, in ordinary cases, bring the rays to a focus at a convenient distance from the glass, corresponding to its degree of curvature." But in the case under examination, no glass or combination of glasses could be invented sufficiently concave to remedy the malformation. By a mathematical problem of easy solution, it was computed that the nearest distance from the unaided eye of the patient at which a distinct image could be formed upon the retina, was two hundred and forty thousand miles, a fraction short of the mean distance of the moon from the earth; and hence it became perfectly clear that the boy could see with minute distinctness whatever was transpiring on the surface of the moon.

Such being the undeniable truth as demonstrated by science, the declaration of the lad assumed a far higher value than the mere dicta of spiritualists, or the mad ravings of a monomaniac; and the committee at once set to work to glean all the astronomical knowledge they could by frequent and prolonged night interviews with the boy.

It was on the night of January 9, 1876, that the first satisfactory experiment was tried, testing beyond all cavil or doubt the powers of the subject's eye. It was full moon, and that luminary rose clear and dazzlingly bright. The committee were on hand at an early hour, and the boy was in fine condition and exuberant spirits. The interview was secret, and none but the members of the committee and the parents of the child were present. Of course the first proposition to be settled was that of the inhabitability of that sphere. This the boy had frequently declared was the case, and he had on several previous occasions described minutely the form, size and means of locomotion of the Lunarians. On this occasion he repeated in almost the same language, what he had before related to his parents and friends, but was more minute, owing to the greater transparency of the atmosphere and the experience in expression already acquired.

The Lunarians are not formed at all like ourselves. They are less in height, and altogether of a different appearance. When fully grown, they resemble somewhat a chariot wheel, with four spokes, converging at the center or axle. They have four eyes in the head, which is the axle, so to speak, and all the limbs branch out directly from the center, like some sea-forms known as "Radiates." They move by turning rapidly like a wheel, and travel as fast as a bird through the air. The children are undeveloped in form, and are perfectly round, like a pumpkin or orange. As they grow older, they seem to drop or absorb the rotundity of the whole body, and finally assume the appearance of a chariot wheel.

They are of different colors, or nationalities—bright red, orange and blue being the predominant hues. The reds are in a large majority. They do no work, but sleep every four or five hours. They have no houses, and need none. They have no clothing, and do not require it. There being no night on the side of the moon fronting the sun, and no day on the opposite side, all the inhabitants, apparently at a given signal of some kind, form into vast armies, and flock in myriads to the sleeping grounds on the shadow-side of the planet. They do not appear to go very far over the dark rim, for they reappear in immense platoons in a few hours, and soon spread themselves over the illuminated surface. They sleep and wake about six times in one ordinary day of twenty-four hours. Their occupations cannot be discerned; they must be totally different from anything upon the earth.

The surface of the moon is all hill and hollow. There are but few level spots, nor is there any water visible. The atmosphere is almost as refined and light as hydrogen gas. There is no fire visible, nor are there any volcanoes. Most of the time of the inhabitants seems to be spent in playing games of locomotion, spreading themselves into squares, circles, triangles, and other mathematical figures. They move always in vast crowds. No one or two are ever seen separated from the main bodies. The children also flock in herds, and seem to be all of one family. Individualism is unknown. They seem to spawn like herring or shad, or to be propagated like bees, from the queen, in myriads. Motion is their normal condition. The moment after a mathematical figure is formed, it is dissolved, and fresh combinations take place, like the atoms in a kaleidoscope. No other species of animal, bird, or being exist upon the illuminated face of the moon.

The shrubbery and vegetation of the moon is all metallic. Vegetable life nowhere exists; but the forms of some of the shrubs and trees are exceedingly beautiful. The highest trees do not exceed twenty-five feet, and they appear to have all acquired their full growth. The ground is strewn with flowers, but they are all formed of metals—gold, silver, copper, and tin predominating. But there is a new kind of metal seen everywhere on tree, shrub and flower, nowhere known on the earth. It is of a bright vermilion color, and is semi-transparent. The mountains are all of bare and burnt granite, and appear to have been melted with fire. The committee called the attention of the boy to the bright "sea of glass" lately observed near the northern rim of the moon, and inquired of what it is composed. He examined it carefully, and gave such a minute description of it that it became apparent at once to the committee that it was pure mercury or quicksilver. The reason why it has but very recently shown itself to astronomers is thus accounted for: it appears close up to the line of demarcation separating the light and shadow upon the moon's disk; and on closer inspection a distinct cataract of the fluid—in short, a metallic Niagara, was clearly seen falling from the night side to the day side of the luminary. It has already filled up a vast plain—one of the four that exist on the moon's surface—and appears to be still emptying itself with very great rapidity and volume. It covers an area of five by seven hundred miles in extent, and may possibly deluge one half the entire surface of the moon. It does not seem to occasion much apprehension to the inhabitants, as they were soon skating, so to speak, in platoons and battalions, over and across it. In fact, it presents the appearance of an immense park, to which the Lunarians flock, and disport themselves with great gusto upon its polished face. One of the most beautiful sights yet seen by the lad was the formation of a new figure, which he drew upon the sand with his finger.

The central heart was of crimson-colored natives; the one to the right of pale orange, and the left of bright blue. It was ten seconds in forming, and five seconds in dispersing. The number engaged in the evolution could not be less than half a million.

Thus has been solved one of the great astronomical questions of the century.

The next evening the committee assembled earlier, so as to get a view of the planet Venus before the moon rose. It was the first time that the lad's attention had been drawn to any of the planets, and he evinced the liveliest joy when he first beheld the cloudless disk of that resplendent world. It may here be stated that his power of vision, in looking at the fixed stars, was no greater or less than that of an ordinary eye. They appeared only as points of light, too far removed into the infinite beyond to afford any information concerning their properties. But the committee were doomed to a greater disappointment when they inquired of the boy what he beheld on the surface of Venus. He replied, "Nothing clearly; all is confused and watery; I see nothing with distinctness." The solution of the difficulty was easily apprehended, and at once surmised. The focus of the eye was fixed by nature at 240,000 miles, and the least distance of Venus from the earth being 24,293,000 miles, it was, of course, impossible to observe that planet's surface with distinctness. Still she appeared greatly enlarged, covering about one hundredth part of the heavens, and blazing with unimaginable splendor.

Experiments upon Jupiter and Mars were equally futile, and the committee half sorrowfully turned again to the inspection of the moon.

The report then proceeds at great length to give full descriptions of the most noted geographical peculiarities of the lunar surface, and corrects many errors fallen into by Herschel, Leverrier and Proctor. Professor Secchi informs us that the surface of the moon is much better known to astronomers than the surface of the earth is to geographers; for there are two zones on the globe within the Arctic and Antarctic circles, that we can never examine. But every nook and cranny of the illuminated face of the moon has been fully delineated, examined and named, so that no object greater than sixty feet square exists but has been seen and photographed by means of Lord Rosse's telescope and De la Ruis' camera and apparatus. As the entire report will be ordered published at the next weekly meeting of the College, we refrain from further extracts, but now proceed to narrate the results of our own interviews with the boy.

It was on the evening of the 17th of February, 1876, that we ventured with rather a misgiving heart to approach Culp Hill, and the humble residence of a child destined, before the year is out, to become the most celebrated of living beings. We armed ourselves with a pound of sugar candy for the boy, some *muslin-de-laine* as a present to the mother, and a box of cigars for the father. We also took with us a very large-sized opera-glass, furnished for the purpose by M. Muller. At first we encountered a positive refusal; then, on exhibiting the cigars, a qualified negative; and finally, when the muslin and candy were drawn on the enemy, we were somewhat coldly invited in and proffered a seat. The boy was pale and restless, and his eyes without bandage or glasses. We soon ingratiated ourself into the good opinion of the whole party, and henceforth encountered no difficulty in pursuing our investigations. The moon being nearly full, we first of all verified the tests by the committee. These were all perfectly satisfactory and reliable. Requesting, then, to stay until after midnight, for the purpose of inspecting Mars with the opera-glass, we spent the interval in obtaining the history of the child, which we have given above.

The planet Mars being at this time almost in dead opposition to the sun, and with the earth in conjunction, is of course as near to the earth as he ever approaches, the distance being thirty-five millions of miles. He rises toward midnight, and is in the constellation Virgo, where he may be seen to the greatest possible advantage, being in perigee. Mars is most like the earth of all the planetary bodies. He revolves on his axis in a little over twenty-four hours, and his surface is pleasantly variegated with land and water, pretty much like our own world—the land, however, being in slight excess. He is, therefore, the most interesting of all the heavenly bodies to the inhabitants of the earth.

Having all things in readiness, we directed the glass to the planet.

Alas, for all our calculations, the power was insufficient to clear away the obscurity resulting from imperfect vision and short focus.

Swallowing the bitter disappointment, we hastily made arrangements for another interview, with a telescope, and bade the family good night.

There is but one large telescope properly mounted in the city, and that is the property and pride of its accomplished owner, J. P. Manrow, Esq. We at once procured an interview with that gentleman, and it was agreed that on Saturday evening the boy should be conveyed to his residence, picturesquely situated on Russian Hill, commanding a magnificent view of the Golden Gate and the ocean beyond.

At the appointed hour the boy, his parents and myself presented ourselves at the door of that hospitable mansion. We were cordially welcomed, and conducted without further parley into the lofty observatory on the top of the house. In due time the magnificent tube was presented at the planet, but it was discovered that the power it was set for was too low. It was then gauged for 240,000 diameters, being the full strength of the telescope, and the eye of the boy observer placed at the eye-glass. One cry of joy, and unalloyed delight told the story! Mars, and its mountains and seas, its rivers, vales, and estuaries, its polar snow-caps and grassy plains—its inhabitants, palaces, ships, villages and cities, were all revealed, as distinctly, clearly and certainly, as the eye of Kit Carson, from the summits of the Sierra Nevada range, beheld the stupendous panorama of the Sacramento Valley, and the snow-clad summits of Mount Hood and Shasta Butte.

❋

Florence McLandburgh

(1850–1934)

FLORENCE MCLANDBURGH WAS BORN in Chillicothe, Ohio, and died at the age of eighty-four in Akron. In between she lived in Chicago and elsewhere. She published both light verse and more serious poetry under the name McLandburgh Wilson, in periodicals such as *Smart Set* and the *Atlantic Monthly*. Starting out as a poet with a critical eye on war and patriotism and hopes for a women's peace movement, she grew more conservative over the decades, not only applauding U.S. involvement in World War I but mocking activists who were opposed to it. When Macmillan published her collection *The Little Flag on Main Street* in 1917, the year that the United States joined the fighting in Europe, McLandburgh dedicated the volume "To Uncle Sam and His Allies."

Her light verse included a sometimes remembered definition of optimism ("The optimist sees the doughnut, / The pessimist sees the hole"), as well as this sort of jaunty observation, from her poem "Four Ages of the Drama," published in *Munsey's Magazine* in 1916:

> In melodrama, which to-day
>   True art derides,
> They always had in every play
>   Asides.

McLandburgh has curious honors to her credit, such as being quoted in Frank J. Wilstach's 1916 *Dictionary of Similes*, a dusty old amusement for the terminally bookish, for her line "Dark as the waiting tomb," quoted alongside Swinburne and Whittier and other writers better remembered in the twenty-first century.

Nowadays, when McLandburgh is remembered at all, fans of nineteenth-century science fiction applaud her story "The Automaton Ear." It first appeared in the May 1873 issue of *Scribner's Monthly* and was reprinted as the opening story in McLandburgh's 1876 collection *The Automaton Ear, and Other Sketches*, which brought together stories from *Appleton's Journal* and *Scribner's Monthly* and other periodicals, as well as including some tales never before published.

"The Automaton Ear" is one of the earliest examples of a subspecies of science fiction sometimes called "time-viewer" tales. Rather than bodily travel in time themselves, the protagonists of such stories invent technology that enables them to see into the past or future. The first technology-based story of this kind seems to have been the 1883 adventure "L'Historioscope," by Eugène Mouton, in which an electrical telescope can view past events. However, an 1872 tale, by the prolific and versatile French astronomer and writer Camille Flammarion, featured the same ability in a bodiless spirit that traveled through space faster than light itself and thus could see into the past. Many such tales followed, notably John Taine's "Before the Dawn" in 1934, in which characters can peer all the way back to the time of dinosaurs. In "A View from a Hill," by the great English ghost-story writer M. R. James, a character finds a pair of binoculars through which he can see the past. Rather than a technological invention, however, they were once bewitched, and the sights visible through them comprise a form of haunting.

The artistic opportunities in such plot devices can be demonstrated by a fine recent example—in Bob Shaw's poignant and now legendary 1966 story "Light of Other Days," and in related stories in his 1972 collection *Other Days, Other Eyes*. In these stories, the physical properties of what Shaw calls "slow glass" include a refractive index—the measurement of the rate at which a ray of light propagates through a medium, relative to its speed in a vacuum—so large that it reduces the light's progress until it can take months to pass through a pane of this material. Thus a pane of slow glass can be left out in a rain forest to absorb months of daily views, then installed in a window thousands of miles away, where the light's slowed progress results in the window appearing to look out upon the rain forest. The glass is constantly showing a scene that has already ceased to exist—such as a man's deceased wife and son playing in a yard.

In McLandburgh's story, which preceded Shaw's by almost a century, the narrator invents a "time-hearer," with results quite as dramatic and heartbreaking as in Shaw's story, which she brings about with echoes of Shelley and Poe.

The Automaton Ear

THE DAY WAS HARDLY different from many another day, though I will likely recall it even when the mist of years has shrouded the past in an undefined hueless cloud. The sunshine came in at my open window. Out of doors it flooded all the land in its warm summer light—the spires of the town and the bare college campus; farther, the tall bearded barley and rustling oats; farther still, the wild grass and the forest, where the river ran and the blue haze dipped from the sky.

The temptation was greater than I could stand, and taking my book I shut up the "study," as the students called my small apartment, leaving it for one bounded by no walls or ceiling.

The woods rang with the hum and chirp of insects and birds. I threw myself down beneath a tall, broad-spreading tree. Against its moss-covered trunk I could hear the loud tap of the woodpecker secreted high up among its leaves, and off at the end of a tender young twig a robin trilled, swinging himself to and fro through the checkered sunlight. I never grew weary listening to the changeful voice of the forest and the river, and was hardly conscious of reading until I came upon this paragraph:—

As a particle of the atmosphere is never lost, so sound is never lost. A strain of music or a simple tone will vibrate in the air

forever and ever, decreasing according to a fixed ratio. The diffu-
sion of the agitation extends in all directions, like the waves in
a pool, but the ear is unable to detect it beyond a certain point.
It is well known that some individuals can distinguish sounds
which to others under precisely similar circumstances are wholly
lost. Thus the fault is not in the sound itself, but in our organ of
hearing, and a tone once in existence is always in existence.

This was nothing new to me. I had read it before, though I had
never thought of it particularly; but while I listened to the robin, it
seemed singular to know that all the sounds ever uttered, ever born,
were floating in the air *now*—all music, every tone, every bird-song—
and we, alas! could not hear them.

Suddenly a strange idea shot through my brain—Why not?
Ay, *why not hear*? Men had constructed instruments which could
magnify to the eye and—was it possible?—Why not?

I looked up and down the river, but saw neither it, nor the sky,
nor the moss that I touched. Did the woodpecker still tap secreted
among the leaves, and the robin sing, and the hum of insects run
along the bank as before? I can not recollect, I can not recollect
anything, only Mother Flinse, the deaf and dumb old crone that
occasionally came to beg, and sell nuts to the students, was standing
in the gateway. I nodded to her as she passed, and walked up her
long, slim shadow that lay on the path. It was a strange idea that
had come so suddenly into my head and startled me. I hardly dared
to think of it, but I could think of nothing else. It could not be
possible, and yet—why not?

Over and over in the restless hours of the night, I asked myself,
I said aloud, Why not? Then I laughed at my folly, and wondered
what I was thinking of and tried to sleep—but if it *could* be done?

The idea clung to me. It forced itself up in class hours and made
confusion in the lessons. Some said the professor was ill those two
or three days before the vacation; perhaps I was. I scarcely slept; only
the one thought grew stronger—Men had done more wonderful

things; it certainly was possible, and I would accomplish this grand invention. I would construct the king of all instruments—I would construct an instrument which could catch these faint tones vibrating in the air and render them audible. Yes, and I would labor quietly until it was perfected, or the world might laugh.

The session closed, and the college was deserted, save by the few musty students whom, even in imagination, one could hardly separate or distinguish from the old books on the library shelves. I could wish for no better opportunity to begin my great work. The first thing would be to prepare for it by a careful study of acoustics, and I buried myself among volumes on the philosophy of sound.

I went down to London and purchased a common ear-trumpet. My own ear was exceedingly acute, and to my great delight I found that, with the aid of the trumpet just as it was, I could distinguish sounds at a much greater distance, and those nearer were magnified in power. I had only to improve upon this instrument; careful study, careful work, careful experiment, and my hopes would undoubtedly be realized.

Back to my old room in the college I went with a complete set of tools. So days and weeks I shut myself in, and every day and every week brought nothing but disappointment. The instrument seemed only to diminish sound rather than increase it, yet still I worked on and vowed I would not grow discouraged.

Hour after hour I sat, looking out of my narrow window. The fields of barley and waving oats had been reaped, the wheat too had ripened and gone, but I did not notice. I sprang up with a joyful exclamation—Strange never to have thought of it before! Perhaps I had not spent my time in vain, after all. How could I expect to test my instrument in this close room with only that little window? It should be removed from immediate noises, high up in the open air, where there would be no obstructions. I would never succeed here—but where should I go? It must be some place in which I would never be liable to interruption, for my first object was to be shielded and work in secret.

I scoured the neighborhood for an appropriate spot without success, when it occurred to me that I had heard some say the old gray church was shut up. This church was situated just beyond the suburbs of the town. It was built of rough stone, mottled and stained by unknown years. The high, square tower, covered by thick vines that clung and crept round its base, was the most venerable monument among all the slabs and tombs where it stood sentinel. Only graves deserted and uncared for by the living kept it company. People said the place was too damp for use, and talked of rebuilding, but it had never been done. Now if I could gain access to the tower, that was the very place for my purpose.

I found the door securely fastened, and walked round and round without discovering any way of entrance; but I made up my mind, if it were possible to get inside of that church I would do it, and without the help of keys. The high windows were not to be thought of; but in the rear of the building, lower down, where the fuel had probably been kept, there was a narrow opening which was boarded across. With very little difficulty I knocked out the planks and crept through. It was a cellar, and, as I had anticipated, the coal receptacle. After feeling about, I found a few rough steps which led to a door that was unlocked and communicated with the passage back of the vestry-room.

The tower I wished to explore was situated in the remote corner of the building. I passed on to the church. Its walls were discolored by green mould, and blackened where the water had dripped through. The sun, low down in the sky, lit the tall, arched windows on the west, and made yellow strips across the long aisles, over the faded pews with their stiff, straight backs, over the chancel rail, over the altar with its somber wood-work; but there was no warmth; only the cheerless glare seemed to penetrate the cold, dead atmosphere,—only the cheerless glare without sparkle, without life, came into that voiceless sanctuary where the organ slept. At the right of the vestibule, a staircase led to the tower; it ascended to a platform laid on a level with the four windows and a little above the point of the church roof. These four windows were situated one on each side of the tower, running high up, and the lower casement folding inward.

Here was my place. Above the tree-tops, in the free open air, with no obstacle to obstruct the wind, I could work unmolested by people or noise. The fresh breeze that fanned my face was cool and pleasant. An hour ago I had been tired, disappointed, and depressed; but now, buoyant with hope, I was ready to begin work again— work that I was determined to accomplish.

The sun had gone. I did not see the broken slabs and urns in the shadow down below; I did not see the sunken graves and the rank grass and the briers. I looked over them and saw the gorgeous fringes along the horizon, scarlet and gold and pearl; saw them quiver and brighten to flame, and the white wings of pigeons whirl and circle in the deepening glow.

I closed the windows, and when I had crawled out of the narrow hole, carefully reset the boards just as I had found them. In another day all the tools and books that I considered necessary were safely deposited in the tower. I only intended to make this my workshop, still, of course, occupying my old room in the college.

Here I matured plan after plan. I studied, read, worked, knowing, *feeling* that at last I must succeed; but failure followed failure, and I sank into despondency only to begin again with a kind of desperation. When I went down to London and wandered about, hunting up different metals and hard woods, I never encountered a concert-room or an opera-house. Was there not music in store for me, such as no mortal ear had ever heard? *All* the music, every strain that had sounded in the past ages? Ah, I could wait; I would work patiently and wait.

I was laboring now upon a theory that I had not tried heretofore. It was my last resource; if this failed, then—but it would not fail! I resolved not to make any test, not to put it near my ear until it was completed. I discarded all woods and used only the metals which best transmitted sound. Finally it was finished, even to the

ivory ear-piece. I held the instrument all ready—I held it and looked
eastward and westward and back again. Suddenly all control over
the muscles of my hand was gone, it felt like stone; then the strange
sensation passed away. I stood up and lifted the trumpet to my
ear—What! Silence? No, no—I was faint, my brain was confused,
whirling. I would not believe it; I would wait a moment until this
dizziness was gone, and then—then I would be able to hear. I was
deaf now. I still held the instrument; in my agitation the ivory tip
shook off and rolled down rattling on the floor. I gazed at it mechanically, as if it had been a pebble; I never thought of replacing it, and,
mechanically, I raised the trumpet a second time to my ear. A crash
of discordant sounds, a confused jarring noise broke upon me and
I drew back, trembling, dismayed.

Fool! O fool of fools never to have thought of this, which a child,
a dunce, would not have over-looked! My great invention was
nothing, was worse than nothing, was worse than a failure. I might
have known that my instrument would magnify present sounds in
the air to such a degree as to make them utterly drown all others,
and, clashing together, produce this noise like the heavy rumble of
thunder.

The college reopened, and I took up my old line of duties, or at
least attempted them, for the school had grown distasteful to me. I
was restless, moody, and discontented. I tried to forget my disappointment, but the effort was vain.

The spires of the town and the college campus glittered white,
the fields of barley and oats were fields of snow, the forest leaves
had withered and fallen, and the river slumbered, wrapped in a
sheeting of ice. Still I brooded over my failure, and when again the
wild grass turned green, I no longer cared. I was not the same man
that had looked out at the waving grain and the blue haze only a
year before. A gloomy despondency had settled upon me, and I grew
to hate the students, to hate the college, to hate society. In the first
shock of discovered failure I had given up all hope, and the Winter
passed I knew not how. I never wondered if the trouble could be

remedied. Now it suddenly occurred to me, perhaps it was no failure after all. The instrument might be made adjustable, so as to be sensible to faint or severe vibrations at pleasure of the operator, and thus separate the sounds. I remembered how but for the accidental removal of the ivory my instrument perhaps would not have reflected any sound. I would work again and persevere.

I would have resigned my professorship, only it might create suspicion. I knew not that already they viewed me with curious eyes and sober faces. When the session finally closed, they tried to persuade me to leave the college during vacation and travel on the continent. I would feel much fresher, they told me, in the Autumn. In the Autumn? Ay, perhaps I might, perhaps I might, and I would not go abroad.

Once more the reapers came unnoticed. My work progressed slowly. Day by day I toiled up in the old church tower, and night by night I dreamed. In my sleep it often seemed that the instrument was suddenly completed, but before I could raise it to my ear I would always waken with a nervous start, So the feverish time went by, and at last I held it ready for a second trial. Now the instrument was adjustable, and I had also improved it so far as to be able to set it very accurately for any particular period, thus rendering it sensible only to sounds of that time, all heavier and fainter vibrations being excluded.

I drew it out almost to its limits.

All the maddening doubts that had haunted me like grinning specters died. I felt no tremor, my hand was steady, my pulse-beat regular.

The soft breeze had fallen away. No leaf stirred in the quiet that seemed to await my triumph. Again the crimson splendor of sunset illumined the western sky and made a glory overhead—and the dusk was thickening down below among the mouldering slabs. But that mattered not.

I raised the trumpet to my ear.

Hark!—The hum of mighty hosts! It rose and fell, fainter and more faint; then the murmur of water was heard and lost again, as it swelled and gathered and burst in one grand volume of sound like a hallelujah from myriad lips. Out of the resounding echo, out of the dying cadence a single female voice arose. Clear, pure, rich, it soared above the tumult of the host that hushed itself, a living thing. Higher, sweeter, it seemed to break the fetters of mortality and tremble in sublime adoration before the Infinite. My breath stilled with awe. Was it a spirit-voice—one of the glittering host in the jasper city "that had no need of the sun, neither of the moon to shine in it?" And the water, was it the river flowing clear as crystal from the great white throne? But no! The tone now floated out soft, sad, human. There was no sorrowful strain in that nightless land where the leaves of the trees were for the healing of the nations. The beautiful voice was of the earth and sin-stricken. From the sobbing that mingled with the faint ripple of water it went up once more, ringing gladly, joyfully; it went up inspired with praise to the sky, and—hark! the Hebrew tongue:—

"The horse and his rider hath he thrown into the sea."

Then the noise of the multitude swelled again, and a crash of music broke forth from innumerable timbrels. I raised my head quickly—it was the song of Miriam after the passage of the Red Sea.

I knew not whether I lived.

I bent my ear eagerly to the instrument again and heard—the soft rustle, the breathing as of a sleeping forest. A plaintive note stole gently out, more solemn and quiet than the chant of the leaves. The mournful lay, forlorn, frightened, trembled on the air like the piteous wail of some wounded creature. Then it grew stronger. Clear, brilliant, it burst in a shower of silver sounds like a whole choir of birds in the glitter of the tropical sunlight. But the mournful wail crept back, and the lonely heart-broken strain was lost, while the leaves still whispered to one another in the midnight.

Like the light of a distant star came to me this song of some nightingale, thousands of years after the bird had mouldered to nothing.

At last my labor had been rewarded. As sound travels in waves, and these waves are continually advancing as they go round and round the world, therefore I would never hear the same sound over again at the same time, but it passed beyond and another came in its stead.

All night I listened with my ear pressed to the instrument. I heard the polished, well-studied compliments, the rustle of silks, and the quick music of the dance at some banquet. I could almost see the brilliant robes and glittering jewels of the waltzers, and the sheen of light, and the mirrors. But hush! a cry, a stifled moan. Was that at the—No, the music and the rustle of silk were gone.

"Mother, put your hand here,—I am tired, and my head feels hot and strange. Is it night, already, that it has grown so dark? I am resting now, for my book is almost done, and then, mother, we can go back to the dear old home where the sun shines so bright and the honeysuckles are heavy with perfume. And, mother, we will never be poor any more. I know you are weary, for your cheeks are pale and your fingers are thin; but they shall not touch a needle then, and you will grow better, mother, and we will forget these long, bitter years. I will not write in the evenings then, but sit with you and watch the twilight fade as we used to do and listen to the murmur of the frogs. I described the little stream, our little stream, mother, in my book.—Hark! I hear the splash of its waves now. Hold me by the hand tight, mother. I am tired, but we are almost there. See! the house glimmers white through the trees, and the red bird has built its nest again in the cedar. Put your arm around me, mother, mother—"

Then single, echoless, the mother's piercing cry went up—"O my God!"

Great Heaven! It would not always be music that I should hear. Into this ear, where all the world poured its tales, sorrow and suffering and death would come in turn with mirth and gladness.

I listened again. The long-drawn ahoy!—ahoy!—of the sailor rang out in slumbrous musical monotone, now free, now muffled—gone. The gleeful laugh of children at play, then the drunken boisterous shout of the midnight reveler—What was that? A chime of bells, strange, sublime, swimming in the air they made a cold, solemn harmony. But even over them dashed the storm-blast of passion that sweeps continually up and down the earth, and the harmony that bound them in peace broke up in a wild, angry clamor, that set loose shrill screams which were swallowed up in a savage page tumult of discord, like a mad carnival of yelling demons. Then, as if terrified by their own fiendish rage, they retreated shivering, remorseful, and hushed themselves in hoarse whispers about the gray belfry. It was the Carillonneur, Matthias Vander Gheyn, playing at Louvain on the first of July, 1745.

Yes, my invention had proved a grand success. I had worked and worked in order to give this instrument to the world; but now when it was finished, strange to say, all my ambition, all my desire for fame left me, and I was anxious only to guard it from discovery, to keep it secret, to keep it more jealously than a miser hoards his gold. An undefinable delight filled my soul that I alone out of all humanity possessed this treasure, this great Ear of the World, for which kings might have given up their thrones. Ah! they dreamed not of the wonders I could relate. It was a keen, intense pleasure to see the public for which I had toiled live on, deaf forever save to the few transient sounds of the moment, while I, their slave, reveled in another world above, beyond theirs. But they should never have this instrument; no, not for kingdoms would I give it up, not for life itself.

It exerted a strange fascination over me, and in my eager desire to preserve my secret a tormenting fear suddenly took possession of me that some one might track me to the tower and discover all. It seemed as if the people looked after me with curious faces as I passed. I went no longer on the main road that led to the church, but, when I left my room, took an opposite direction until out of sight, and then made a circuit across the fields. I lived in a continual fear of betraying myself, so that at night I closed my window and door lest I might talk aloud in my sleep. I could never again bear the irksome duties of my office, and when the college re-opened I gave up my situation and took lodgings in town. Still the dread of detection haunted me. Every day I varied my route to the church, and every day the people seemed to stare at me with a more curious gaze. Occasionally some of my old pupils came to visit me, but they appeared constrained in my presence and were soon gone. However, no one seemed to suspect my secret; perhaps all this was merely the work of my imagination, for I had grown watchful and reticent.

I hardly ate or slept. I lived perpetually in the past listening to the echoing song of the Alpine shepherd; the rich, uncultivated soprano of the Southern slave making strange wild melody. I heard grand organ fugues rolling, sweeping over multitudes that kneeled in awe, while a choir of voices broke into a gloria that seemed to sway the great cathedral. The thrilling artistic voices of the far past rang again, making my listening soul tremble in their magnificent harmony. It was music of which we could not dream.

Then suddenly I determined to try the opera once more; perhaps I was prejudiced: I had not been inside of a concert-room for more than a year.

I went down to London. It was just at the beginning of the season. I could hardly wait that evening until the curtain rose; the orchestra was harsh and discordant, the house hot and disagreeable, the gas painfully bright. My restlessness had acquired a feverish pitch before the prima donna made her appearance. Surely that voice was not the one before which the world bowed! Malibran's song stood out in my memory clearly defined and complete, like a magnificent cathedral of pure marble, with faultless arches and skillfully chiseled carvings, where the minarets rose from wreaths of lilies and vine-leaves cut in bas-relief, and the slender spire shot high, glittering yellow in the upper sunlight, its golden arrow, burning like flame, pointing towards the East. But this prima donna built only a flat, clumsy structure of wood ornamented by gaudily painted lattice.

I left the opera amid the deafening applause of the audience with a smile of scorn upon my face. Poor deluded creatures! they knew nothing of music, they knew not what they were doing.

I went to St. Paul's on the Sabbath. There was no worship in the operatic voluntary sung by hired voices; it did not stir my soul and their cold hymns did not warm with praise to the Divine Creator, or sway the vast pulseless congregation that came and went without one quickened breath.

All this time I felt a singular, inexpressible pleasure in the consciousness of my great secret, and I hurried back with eager haste. In London I had accidentally met two or three of my old acquaintances. I was not over glad to see them myself: as I have said, I had grown utterly indifferent to society; but I almost felt ashamed when they offered me every attention within their power, for I had not anticipated it, nor was it deserved on my part. Now, when I returned, every body in the street stopped to shake hands with me and inquire for my health. At first, although I was surprised at the interest they manifested, I took it merely as the common civility on meeting, but when the question was repeated so particularly by each one, I thought it appeared strange, and asked if they had ever heard to the contrary; no, oh no, they said, but still I was astonished at the unusual care with which they all made the same inquiry.

I went up to my room and walked directly to the glass. It was the first time I had consciously looked into a mirror for many weeks. Good Heavens! The mystery was explained now. *I could hardly recognise myself.* At first the shock was so great that I stood gazing, almost petrified. The demon of typhus fever could not have wrought a more terrific change in my face if he had held it in his clutches for months. My hair hung in long straggling locks around my neck. I was thin and fearfully haggard. My eyes sunken far back in my head, looked out from dark, deep hollows; my heavy black eyebrows were knit together by wrinkles that made seams over my forehead: my fleshless cheeks clung tight to the bone, and a bright red spot on either one was half covered by thick beard. I had thought so little about my personal appearance lately that I had utterly neglected my hair, and I wondered now that it had given me no annoyance. I smiled while I still looked at myself. This was the effect of the severe study and loss of sleep, and the excitement under which I had labored for months, yes, for more than a year. I had not been conscious of fatigue, but my work was done now and I would soon regain my usual weight. I submitted myself immediately to the hands of a barber, dressed with considerable care, and took another look in the glass. My face appeared pinched and small since it had been freed from beard. The caverns around my eyes seemed even larger, and the bright color in my cheeks contrasted strangely with the extremely sallow tint of my complexion. I turned away with an uncomfortable feeling, and started on a circuitous route to the church, for I never trusted my instrument in any other place.

It was a sober autumn day. Every thing looked dreary with that cold, gray, sunless sky stretched overhead. The half-naked trees shivered a little in their seared garments of ragged leaves. Occasionally a cat walked along the fence-top, or stood trembling on three legs. Sometimes a depressed bird tried to cheer its drooping spirits and uttered a few sharp, discontented chirps. Just in front of me two boys were playing ball on the road-side.

As I passed I accidentally caught this sentence:

"They say the professor ain't just right in his head."

For a moment I stood rooted to the ground; then wheeled round and cried out fiercely,

"What did you say?"

"Sir?"

"What was that you said just now?" I repeated still more fiercely.

The terrified boys looked at me an instant, then without answering turned and ran as fast as fright could carry them.

So the mystery now was really explained! It was not sick the people thought me, but crazy. I walked on with a queer feeling and began vaguely to wonder why I had been so savage to those boys. The fact which I had learned so suddenly certainly gave me a shock, but it was nothing to me. What did I care, even if the people did think me crazy? Ah! perhaps if I told my secret they would consider it a desperate case of insanity. But the child's words kept ringing in my ears until an idea flashed upon me even more terrifying than death itself. How did I know that I was *not* insane? How did I know that my great invention might be only a hallucination of my brain?

Instantly a whole army of thoughts crowded up like ghostly witnesses to affright me. I had studied myself to a shadow; my pallid face, with the red spots on the cheeks and the blue hollows around the eyes, came before my mental vision afresh. The fever in my veins told me I was unnaturally excited. I had not slept a sound, dreamless sleep for weeks. Perhaps in the long, long days and nights my brain, like my body, had been over-wrought; perhaps in my eager desire to succeed, in my desperate determination, the power of my will had disordered my mind, and it was all deception: the sounds, the music I had heard, merely the creation of my diseased fancy, and the instrument I had handled useless metal. The very idea was inexpressible torture to me. I could not bear that a single doubt of its reality should exist; but after once entering my head, how would I ever be able to free myself from distrust? I could not do it; I would be obliged to live always in uncertainty. It was maddening: now I felt as if I might have struck the child in my rage if I could have found him. Then suddenly it occurred to me, for the first time, that my invention could easily be tested by some other person. Almost instantly I rejected the thought, for it would compel me to betray my secret, and in my strange infatuation I would rather have destroyed the instrument. But the doubts of my sanity on this subject returned upon me with tenfold strength, and again I thought in despair of the only method left me by which they could ever be settled.

In the first shock, when the unlucky sentence fell upon my ear, I had turned after the boys, and then walked on mechanically towards the town. Now, when I looked up I found myself almost at the college gate. No one was to be seen, only Mother Flinse with her basket on her arm was just raising the latch. Half bewildered I turned hastily round and bent my steps in the direction of my lodgings, while I absently wondered whether that old woman had stood there ever since, since—when? I did not recollect, but her shadow was long and slim—no, there were no shadows this afternoon; it was sunless.

As I reached the stairs leading to my room, my trouble, which I had forgotten for the moment, broke upon me anew. I dragged myself up and sat down utterly overwhelmed. As I have said, I would sooner destroy the instrument than give it to a thankless world; but to endure the torturing doubt of its reality was impossible. Suddenly it occurred to me that Mother Flinse was mute. I might get her to test my invention without fear of betrayal, for she could neither speak nor write, and her signs on this subject, if she attempted to explain, would be altogether unintelligible to others. I sprang up in wild delight, then immediately fell back in my chair with a hoarse laugh—Mother Flinse was *deaf* as well as dumb. I had not remembered that. I sat quietly a moment trying to calm myself and think. Why need this make any difference? The instrument ought to, at least it was possible that it might, remedy loss of hearing. I too was deaf to these sounds in the air that it made audible. They would have to be magnified to a greater degree for her. I might set it for the present and use the full power of the instrument: there certainly would be no harm in trying, at any rate, and if it failed it would prove nothing, if it did not fail it would prove every thing. Then a new difficulty presented itself. How could I entice the old woman into the church?

I went back towards the college expecting to find her, but she was nowhere to be seen, and I smiled that only a few moments ago I had wondered if she did not always stand in the gateway. Once, I could not exactly recall the time, I had passed her hut. I remembered distinctly that there was a line full of old ragged clothes stretched across from the fence to a decayed tree, and a bright red flannel petticoat blew and flapped among the blackened branches. It was a miserable frame cabin, set back from the Spring road, about half a mile out of town. There I went in search of her.

The blasted tree stood out in bold relief against the drab sky. There appeared no living thing about the dirty, besmoked hovel except one lean rat, that squatted with quivering nose and stared a moment, then retreated under the loose plank before the door, leaving its smellers visible until I stepped upon the board. I knocked loudly without receiving any reply; then, smiling at the useless ceremony I had performed, pushed it open. The old woman, dressed in her red petticoat and a torn calico frock, with a faded shawl drawn over her head, was standing with her back towards me, picking over a pile of rags. She did not move. I hesitated an instant, then walked in. The moment I put my foot upon the floor she sprang quickly round. At first she appeared motionless, with her small, piercing gray eyes fixed upon me, holding a piece of orange-and-black spotted muslin; evidently she recognized me, for, suddenly dropping it, she began a series of wild gestures, grinning until all the wrinkles of her skinny face converged in the region of her mouth, where a few scattered teeth, long and sharp, gleamed strangely white. A rim of grizzled hair stood out round the edge of the turbaned shawl and set off the withered and watchful countenance of the speechless old crone. The yellow, shriveled skin hung loosely about her slim neck like leather, and her knotted hands were brown and dry as the claws of an eagle.

I went through the motion of sweeping and pointed over my shoulder, making her understand that I wished her to do some cleaning. She drew the seams of her face together into a new grimace by way of assent, and, putting the piece of orange-and-black spotted muslin around her shoulders in lieu of a cloak, preceded me out of the door. She started immediately in the direction of the college, and I was obliged to take hold of her before I could attract her attention; then, when I shook my head, she regarded me in surprise, and fell once more into a series of frantic gesticulations. With considerable trouble I made her comprehend that she was merely to follow me. The old woman was by no means dull, and her small, steel-gray eyes had a singular sharpness about them that is only found in the deaf-mute, where they perform the part of the ear and tongue. As soon as we came in sight of the church she was perfectly satisfied. I walked up to the main entrance, turned the knob and shook it, then suddenly felt in all my pockets, shook the door over, and felt through all my pockets again. This hypocritical pantomime had the desired effect. The old beldam slapped her hands together and poked her lean finger at the hole of the lock, apparently amused that I had forgotten the key. Then of her own accord she went round and tried the other doors, but without success. As we passed the narrow window in the rear I made a violent effort in knocking out the loose boards. The old woman seemed greatly delighted, and when I crawled through willingly followed. I gave her a brush, which fortunately one day I had discovered lying in the vestibule, and left her in the church to dust, while I went up in the tower to prepare and remove from sight all the tools which were scattered about. I put them in a recess and screened it from view by a map of the Holy Land. Then I took my instrument and carefully adjusted it, putting on its utmost power.

In about an hour I went down and motioned to Mother Flinse that I wanted her up stairs. She came directly after me without hesitation, and I felt greatly relieved, for I saw that I would likely have no trouble with the old woman. When we got into the tower she pointed down to the trees and then upward, meaning, I presume, that it was high. I nodded, and taking the instrument placed my ear to it for a moment. A loud blast of music, like a dozen bands playing in concert, almost stunned me. She watched me very attentively, but when I made signs for her to come and try she drew back. I held up the instrument and went through all manner of motions indicating that it would not hurt her, but she only shook her head. I persevered in my endeavor to coax her until she seemed to gain courage and walked up within a few feet of me, then suddenly stopped and stretched out her hands for the instrument. As she did not seem afraid, provided she had it herself, I saw that she took firm hold.

In my impatience to know the result of this experiment, I was obliged to repeat my signs again and again before I could prevail upon her to raise it to her ear. Then breathlessly I watched her face, a face I thought which looked as if it might belong to some mummy that had been withering for a thousand years. Suddenly it was convulsed as if by a galvanic shock, then the shriveled features seemed to dilate, and a great light flashed through them, transforming them almost into the radiance of youth; a strange light as of some seraph had taken possession of the wrinkled old frame and looked out at the gray eyes, making them shine with unnatural beauty. No wonder the dumb countenance reflected a brightness inexpressible, for the Spirit of Sound had just alighted with silvery wings upon a silence of seventy years.

A heavy weight fell unconsciously from my breast while I stood almost awed before this face, which was transfigured, as if it might have caught a glimmer of that mystical morn when, in a moment, in the twinkling of an eye, we shall all be changed.

My instrument had stood the test; it was proved forever. I could no longer cherish any doubts of its reality, and an indescribable peace came into my soul, like a sudden awakening from some frightful dream. I had not noticed the flight of time. A pale shadow hung already over the trees—yes, and under them on the slime-covered stones. Ay! and a heavier shadow than the coming night was even then gathering unseen its rayless folds. The drab sky had blanched and broken, and the sinking sun poured a fading light through its ragged fissures.

The old woman, as if wrapped in an enchantment, had hardly moved. I tried vainly to catch her attention; she did not even appear conscious of my presence. I walked up and shook her gently by the shoulder, and, pointing to the setting sun, held out my hand for the instrument. She looked at me a moment with the singular unearthly beauty shining through every feature; then suddenly clutching the trumpet tight between her skinny claws, sprang backward towards the stairs, uttering a sound that was neither human nor animal, that was not a wail or a scream, but it fell upon my ears like some palpable horror. Merciful Heaven! Was that thing yonder a woman? The shriveled, fleshless lips gaped apart, and a small pointed tongue lurked behind five glittering, fang-like teeth. The wild beast had suddenly been developed in the hag. Like a hungry tigress defending its prey, she stood hugging the trumpet to her, glaring at me with stretched neck and green eyes.

A savage fierceness roused within me when I found she would not give up the instrument, and I rushed at her with hands ready to snatch back the prize I valued more than my life—*or hers*; but, quicker than a hunted animal, she turned and fled with it down the stairs, making the tower ring with the hideous cries of her wordless voice. Swiftly—it seemed as if the danger of losing the trumpet gave me wings to fly in pursuit—I crossed the vestibule. She was not there. Every thing was silent, and I darted with fleet steps down the dusky aisle of the church, when suddenly the jarring idiotic sounds broke loose again, echoing up in the organ-pipes and rattling along the galleries. The fiend sprang from behind the altar, faced about an instant with flashing eyes and gleaming teeth, then fled through the vestry-room into the passage. The sight of her was fresh fuel to my rage, and it flamed into a frenzy that seemed to burn the human element out of my soul. When I gained the steps leading into the coal-room, she was already in the window, but I cleared the distance at a single bound and caught hold of her clothes as she leaped down. I crawled through, but she clutched the instrument tighter. I could not prize it out of her grasp; and in her ineffectual efforts to free herself from my hold she made loud, grating cries, that seemed to me to ring and reverberate all though the forest; but presently they grew smothered, gurgled, then ceased. Her clasp relaxed in a convulsive struggle, and the trumpet was in my possession. It was easily done, for her neck was small and lean, and my hands made a circle strong as a steel band.

The tremor died out of her frame and left it perfectly still. Through the silence I could hear the hiss of a snake in the nettleweeds, and the flapping wings of some night bird fanned my face as it rushed swiftly through the air in its low flight. The gray twilight had deepened to gloom and the graves seemed to have given up their tenants. The pale monuments stood out like shrouded specters. But all the dead in that church-yard were not under the ground, for on the wet grass at my feet there was something stark and stiff, more frightful than any phantom of imagination—something that the daylight would not rob of its ghastly features. It must be put out of sight, yes, it must be hid, to save my invention from discovery. The old hag might be missed, and if she was found here it would ruin me and expose my secret. I placed the trumpet on the window-ledge, and, carrying the grim burden in my arms, plunged into the damp tangle of weeds and grass.

In a lonesome corner far back from the church, in the dense shade of thorn-trees, among the wild brambles where poisonous vines grew, slippery with the mould of forgotten years, unsought, uncared for by any human hand, was a tomb. Its sides were half buried in the tall under-brush, and the long slab had been broken once, for a black fissure ran zigzag across the middle. In my muscles that night there was the strength of two men. I lifted off one-half of the stone and heard the lizards dart startled from their haunt, and felt the spiders crawl. When the stone was replaced it covered more than the lizards or the spiders in the dark space between the narrow walls.

As I have said, the instrument possessed a singular fascination over me. I had grown to love it, not alone as a piece of mechanism for the transmission of sound, but like a *living* thing, and I replaced it in the tower with the same pleasure one feels who has rescued a friend from death. My listening ear never grew weary, but now I drew quickly away. It was not music I heard, or the ripple of water, or the prattle of merry tongues, but the harsh grating cries that had echoed in the church, that had rattled and died out in the forest— that voice which was not a voice. I shivered while I readjusted the instrument; perhaps it was the night wind which chilled me, but the rasping sounds were louder than before. *I could not exclude them.* There was no element of superstition in my nature, and I tried it over again: still I heard them—sometimes sharp, sometimes only a faint rumbling. Had the soul of the deaf-mute come in retribution to haunt me and cry eternally in my instrument? Perhaps on the morrow it would not disturb me, but there was no difference. I could hear only it, though I drew out the trumpet for vibrations hundreds of years old. I had rid myself of the withered hag who would have stolen my treasure, but now I could not rid myself of her invisible ghost. She had conquered, even through death, and come from the spirit world to gain possession of the prize for which she had given up her life. The instrument was no longer of any value to me, though cherishing a vague hope I compelled myself to listen, even with chattering teeth; for it was a terrible thing to hear those hoarse, haunting cries of the dumb soul—of the soul I had strangled from its body, a soul which I would have killed itself if it were possible. But my hope was vain, and the trumpet had become not only worthless to me, but an absolute horror.

Suddenly I determined to destroy it. I turned it over ready to dash it in pieces, but it cost me a struggle to destroy this work of my life, and while I stood irresolute a small green-and-gold beetle crawled out of it and dropped like a stone to the floor. The insect was an electric flash to me, that dispelled the black gloom through which I had been battling. It had likely fallen into the instrument down in the church-yard, or when I laid it upon the window-sill, and the rasping of its wings, magnified, had produced the sounds which resembled the strange grating noise uttered by the deaf-mute.

Instantly I put the trumpet to my ear. Once more the music of the past surged in. Voices, leaves, water, all murmured to me their changeful melody; every zephyr wafting by was filled with broken but melodious whispers.

Relieved from doubts, relieved from fears and threatening dangers, I slept peacefully, dreamlessly as a child. With a feeling of rest to which I had long been unused, I walked out in the soft, clear morning. Every thing seemed to have put on new life, for the sky was not gray or sober, and the leaves, if they were brown, trimmed their edges in scarlet, and if many had fallen, the squirrels played among them on the ground. But suddenly the sky and the leaves and the squirrels might have been blotted from existence. I did not see them, but I saw—*I saw Mother Flinse come through the college gateway and walk slowly down the road!*

The large faded shawl pinned across her shoulders nearly covered the red flannel petticoat and the orange-and-black spotted muslin was wrapped into a turban on her head. Without breathing, almost without feeling, I watched the figure until at the corner it turned out of sight, and a long dark outline on the grass behind it ran into the fence. The shadow! Then it was not a ghost. Had the grave given up its dead? I would see.

At the churchyard the briers tore my face and clothes, but I plunged deeper where the shade thickened under the thorn-trees. There in the corner I stooped to lift the broken slab of a tomb, but all my strength would not avail to move it. As I leaned over, bruising my hands in a vain endeavor to raise it, my eyes fell for an instant on the stone, and with a start I turned quickly and ran to the church; then I stopped—the narrow fissure that cut zigzag across the slab on the tomb was filled with green moss, and this window was nailed up, and hung full of heavy cobwebs.

And my instrument?

Suddenly, while I stood there, some substance in my brain seemed to break up—it was the fetters of monomania which had bound me since that evening long ago, when, by the river in the oak-forest, I had heard the robin trill.

No murder stained my soul: and there, beside the black waves of insanity through which I had passed unharmed, I gave praise to the great Creator—praise silent, but intense as Miriam's song by the sea.

✤

Thomas Wentworth Higginson

(1823–1911)

THE APRIL 1862 ISSUE of the *Atlantic Monthly* included an essay by the U.S. writer and editor Thomas Wentworth Higginson, "Advice to a Young Contributor," in which he encouraged aspiring writers to study their craft, learn the rudiments of publishing, and persevere in their ambitions. From Amherst, Massachusetts, a reclusive thirty-one-year-old poet named Emily Dickinson immediately sent Higginson a few poems and a letter in which she asked, "Are you too deeply occupied to say if my Verse is alive?"

He was not. He assured her that her poetry lived and breathed, and in time he became her mentor and editor. His respect for her genius grew ever stronger. After Dickinson's death in 1886, Higginson coedited, with Mabel Loomis Todd, collections of her poetry; both tinkered shamelessly with Dickinson's shockingly original diction, punctuation, and lineation.

He wrote about myths (*Tales of the Enchanted Islands of the Atlantic*), his highly selective memories (*Cheerful Yesterdays*), and writers such as Longfellow and Whittier. Remaining ahead of his time among the male writers of this period, he even wrote various books and articles on behalf of feminism. "I love to do everything," he once wrote, "to study everything, to contemplate and to write."

Nowadays Higginson is remembered for his position in the career of Emily Dickinson and for his role in helping preserve the cultural and musical legacy of African American slaves, as in his 1867 essay "Negro Spirituals." An abolitionist to the point of participating in the group of sponsors known as the Secret Six, Higginson helped fund John Brown's raid on Harpers Ferry in 1859. In his 1870 account *Army Life in a Black Regiment*, he wrote sympathetically of his time as colonel of the First South Carolina Volunteers, a Union regiment comprising freedmen and escaped slaves from Florida and South Carolina.

And he is remembered for a pioneer science fiction story, "The Monarch of Dreams." When he wrote it in the summer of 1861, the prominent Higginson seldom found his writings rejected. But this wildly imaginative story, written only a few months after Emily Dickinson's death, could not find a home. Finally the author himself paid for printing it, to the dismay of his family, who found the story disturbing. After reading the story, Higginson's sister worried that he was about to have a nervous collapse. The story's protagonist, Francis Ayrault, tries to control his own dreams, to influence their direction, to return to their plots.

Higginson included it as the lead story in his 1887 collection of the same title, published in Boston by Lee and Shepard. It is a tempestuous fable about, in part, the danger of indulging the kind of sympathetic imagination that writers employ. Higginson was, after all, an activist first and a writer second; he had long understood that he would never stand amid the ranks of the Emily Dickinsons of the world. Perhaps he was reassuring himself that he had made the right choice.

The Monarch of Dreams

H E WHO FORSAKES THE railways and goes wandering through the hill-country of New England, must adopt one rule as invariable. When he comes to a fork in the road, and is assured that both ways lead to the desired point, he must simply ask which road is the best; and, on its being pointed out, must at once take the other. Nothing can be easier than the explanation of this method. The passers-by will always recommend the new road, which keeps to the valley and avoids the hills; but the old road, deserted by the general public, ascends the steeper grades, and has a monopoly of the wider views.

Turning to the old road, you soon feel that both houses and men are, in a manner, stranded. They see very little of the world, and are under no stimulus to keep themselves in repair. You are wholly beyond the dreary sway of French roofs; and the caricatures of good Queen Anne's day are far from you. If any farm-house on the hill-road was really built within the reign of that much-abused potentate, it is probably a solid, square mansion of brick, three stories high, blackened with time, and frowning rather gloomily from some hilltop,—as essentially a part of the past as an Irish round-tower or a Scotch border-fortress. . . .

It was in such a house that Francis Ayrault had finally taken up his abode, leaving behind him the old family homestead in a

Rhode Island seaside town. A series of domestic cares and watchings had almost broken him down: nothing debilitates a man of strong nature like the too prolonged and exclusive exercise of the habit of sympathy. At last, when the very spot where he was born had been chosen as a site for a new railway-station, there seemed nothing more to retain him. He needed utter rest and change; and there was no one left on earth whom he profoundly loved, except a little sunbeam of a sister, the child of his father's second marriage. This little five-year-old girl, of whom he was sole guardian, had been christened by the quaint name of Hart, after an ancestor, Hart Ayrault, whose moss-covered tombstone the child had often explored with her little fingers, to trace the vanishing letters of her own name.

The two had arrived one morning from the nearest railway station to take possession of the old brick farm-house. Ayrault had spent the day in unpacking and in consultations with Cyrus Gerry,—the farmer from whom he had bought the place, and who was still to conduct all outdoor operations. The child, for her part, had compelled her old nurse to follow her through every corner of the buildings. They were at last seated at an early supper, during which little Hart was too much absorbed in the novelty of wild red raspberries to notice, even in the most casual way, her brother's worn and exhausted look.

"Brother Frank," she incidentally remarked, as she began upon her second saucerful of berries, "I love you!"

"Thank you, darling," was his mechanical reply to the customary ebullition. She was silent for a time, absorbed in her pleasing pursuit, and then continued more specifically, "Brother Frank, you are the kindest person in the whole world! I am so glad we came here! May we stay here all winter? It must be lovely in the winter; and in the barn there is a little sled with only one runner gone. Brother Frank, I love you so much, I don't know what I shall do! I love you a thousand pounds, and fifteen, and eleven and a half, and more than tongue can tell besides! And there are three gray kittens,—only one of them is almost all white,—and Susan says I may bring them for you to see in the morning."

Half an hour later, the brilliant eyes were closed in slumber; the vigorous limbs lay in perfect repose; and the child slept that night in the little room inside her brother's, on the same bed that she had occupied ever since she had been left motherless. But her brother lay awake, absorbed in a project too fantastic to be talked about, yet which had really done more than anything else to bring him to that lonely house.

There has belonged to Rhode Islanders, ever since the days of Roger Williams, a certain taste for the ideal side of existence. It is the only State in the American Union where chief justices habitually write poetry, and prosperous manufacturers print essays on the Freedom of the Will. Perhaps, moreover, Francis Ayrault held something of these tendencies from a Huguenot ancestry, crossed with a strain of Quaker blood. At any rate it was there, and asserted itself at this crisis of his life. Being in a manner detached from almost all ties, he resolved to use his opportunity in a direction yet almost unexplored by man. His earthly joys being prostrate, he had resolved to make a mighty effort at self-concentration, and to render himself what no human being had ever yet been—the ruler of his own dreams.

Coming from a race of day-dreamers, Ayrault had inherited an unusual faculty of dreaming also by night; and, like all persons having an especial gift, he perhaps overestimated its importance. He easily convinced himself that no exertion of the intellect during wakeful hours can for an instant be compared with that we employ in dreams. The finest brain-structures of Shakespeare or Dante, he reasoned, are yet but such stuff as dreams are made of; and the stupidest rustic, the most untrained mind, will sometimes have, could they be but written out, visions that surpass those of these masters. . . .

But Ayrault had been vexed, like all others, by the utter incongruity of successive dreams. This sublime navigation still waited, like that of balloon voyages, for a rudder. Dreams, he reasoned, plainly try to connect themselves. We all have the frequent experience of half-recognizing new situations or even whole trains of ideas. We have seen this view before; reached this point; struck in some way the exquisite chord of memory. When half-aroused, or sometimes even long after clear consciousness, we seem to draw a half-drowned image of association from the deep waters of the mind; then another, then another, until dreaming seems inseparably entangled with waking. Again, over nightly dreams we have at least a certain amount of negative control, sufficient to bring them to an end. . . .

The thought had occurred to him, long since, at what point to apply his efforts for the control of his dreams. He had been quite fascinated, some time before, by a large photograph in a shop window, of the well-known fortress known as Mont Saint Michel, in Normandy. Its steepness, its airy height, its winding and returning stairways, its overhanging towers and machicolations, had struck him as appealing powerfully to that sense of the vertical, which is, for some reason or other, so peculiarly strong in dreams. We are rarely haunted by visions of plains; often of mountains. The sensation of uplifting or down-looking is one of our commonest nightly experiences. It seemed to Ayrault that by going to sleep with the vivid mental image in his brain of a sharp and superb altitude like that of Mont Saint Michel, he could avail himself of this magic, whatever it was, that lay in the vertical line. Casting himself off into the vast sphere of dreams, with the thread of his fancy attached to this fine image, he might risk what would next come to him; as a spider anchors his web and then floats away on it. In the silence of the first night at the farmhouse,—a stillness broken only by the answering cadence of two whippoorwills in the neighboring pine-wood,—Ayrault pondered long over the beautiful details of the photograph, and then went to sleep.

That night he was held, with the greatest vividness and mastery, in the grasp of a dream such as he had never before experienced.

He found himself on the side of a green hill, so precipitous that he could only keep his position by lying at full length, clinging to the short soft grass, and imbedding his feet in the turf. There were clouds about him: he could see but a short distance in any direction, nor was any sign of a human being within sight. He was absolutely alone upon the dizzy slope, where he hardly dared to look up or down, and where it took all his concentration of effort to keep a position at all. Yet there was a kind of friendliness in the warm earth; a comfort and fragrance in the crushed herbage. The vision seemed to continue indefinitely; but at last he waked and it was clear day. He rose with a bewildered feeling, and went to little Hart's room. The child lay asleep, her round face tangled in her brown curls, and one plump, tanned arm stretched over her eyes. She waked at his step, and broke out into her customary sweet asseveration, "Brother Frank, I love you!"

Dismissing the child, he pondered on his first experiment. It had succeeded, surely, in so far as he had given something like a direction to his nightly thought. He could not doubt that it was the picture of Mont Saint Michel which had transported him to the steep hillside. That day he spent in the most restless anxiety to see if the dream would come again. Writing down all that he could remember of the previous night's vision, he studied again the photograph that had so touched his fancy, and then he closed his eyes. Again he found himself—at some time between night and morning— on the same high elevation, with the clouds around him. But this time the vapors lifted, and he could see that the hill stretched for an immeasurable distance on each side, always at the same steep slope. Everywhere it was covered with human beings,—men, women, and children,—all trying to pursue various semblances of occupations; but all clinging to the short grass. Sometimes, he thought—but this was not positive—that he saw one of them lose his hold and glide downwards. For this he cared strangely little; but he waked feverish, excited, trembling. At last his effort had succeeded: he had, by an effort of will, formed a connection between two dreams. . . .

On the following night he grasped his dream once more. Again he found himself on the precipitous slope, this time looking off through clear air upon that line of detached mountain peaks, Wachusett, Monadnock, Moosilauke, which make the southern outposts of New England hills. In the valley lay pellucid lakes, set in summer beauty,—while he clung to his perilous hold. Presently there came a change; the mountain sank away softly beneath him, and the grassy slope remained a plain. The men and women, his former companions, had risen from their reclining postures and were variously busy; some of them even looked at him, but there was nothing said. Great spaces of time appeared to pass: suns rose and set. Sometimes one of the crowd would throw down his implements of labor, turn his face to the westward, walk swiftly away, and disappear. Yet some one else would take his place, so that the throng never perceptibly diminished. Ayrault began to feel rather unimportant in all this gathering, and the sensation was not agreeable.

On the succeeding night the hillside vanished, never to recur; but the vast plain remained, and the people. Over the wide landscape the sunbeams shed passing smiles of light, now here, now there. Where these shone for a moment, faces looked joyous, and Ayrault found, with surprise, that he could control the distribution of light and shade. This pleased him; it lifted him into conscious importance. There was, however, a singular want of all human relation in the tie between himself and all these people. He felt as if he had called them into being, which indeed he had; and could annihilate them at pleasure, which perhaps could not be so easily done. Meanwhile, there was a certain hardness in his state of mind toward them; indeed, why should a dreamer feel patience or charity or mercy toward those who exist but in his mind? Ayrault at any rate felt none; the sole thing which disturbed him was that they sometimes grew a little dim, as if they might vanish and leave him unaccompanied. When this happened, he drew with conscious volition a gleam of light over them, and thereby refreshed their life. They

enhanced his weight in the universe: he would no more have parted
with them than a Highland chief with his clansmen.

For several nights after this he did not dream. Little Hart became
ill and his mind was preoccupied. He had to send for physicians, to
give medicine, to be up with the child at night. . . . Then, with the
rapidity of childish convalescence, she grew well again; and he found
with joy that he could resume the thread of his dream-life.

Again he was on his boundless plain, with his circle of silent allies
around him. Suddenly they all vanished, and there rose before him,
as if built out of the atmosphere, a vast building, which he entered.
It included all structures in one,—legislative halls where men were
assembled by hundreds, waiting for him: libraries, where all the
books belonged to him, and whole alcoves were filled with his own
publications; galleries of art, where he had painted many of the
pictures, and selected the rest. Doors and corridors led to private
apartments; lines of obsequious servants stood for him to pass. There
seemed no other proprietor, no guests; all was for him; all flattered
his individual greatness. Suddenly it occurred to him that he was
painfully alone. Then he began to pass eagerly from hall to hall,
seeking an equal companion, but in vain. Wherever he went, there
was a trace of some one just vanished,—a book laid down, a curtain
still waving. Once he fairly came, he thought, upon the object of
his pursuit; all retreat was cut off, and he found himself face to face
with a mirror that reflected back to him only his own features. They
had never looked to him less attractive.

Ayrault's control of his visions became plainly more complete
with practice, at least as to their early stages. He could lie down to
sleep with almost a perfect certainty that he should begin where he
left off. Beyond this, alas! he was powerless. Night after night he
was in the same palace, but always differently occupied, and always
pursuing, with unabated energy, some new vocation. Sometimes the
books were at his command, and he grappled with whole alcoves;
sometimes he ruled a listening senate in the halls of legislation; but

the peculiarity was, that there were always menials and subordinates about him, never an equal. One night, in looking over these obsequious crowds, he made a startling discovery. They either had originally, or were acquiring, a strange resemblance to one another, and to some person whom he had somewhere seen. All the next day, in his waking hours, this thought haunted him. The next night it flashed upon him that the person whom they all so closely resembled, with a likeness that now amounted to absolute identity, was himself.

From the moment of this discovery, these figures multiplied; they assumed a mocking, taunting, defiant aspect. The thought was almost more than he could bear, that there was around him a whole world of innumerable and uncontrollable beings, every one of whom was Francis Ayrault. As if this were not sufficient, they all began visibly to duplicate themselves before his eyes. The confusion was terrific. Figures divided themselves into twins, laughing at each other, jeering, running races, measuring heights, actually playing leap-frog with one another. Worst of all, each one of these had as much apparent claim to his personality as he himself possessed. He could no more retain his individual hold upon his consciousness than the infusorial animalcule in a drop of water can know to which of its subdivided parts the original individuality attaches. It became insufferable, and by a mighty effort he waked.

The next day, after breakfast, old Susan sought an interview with Ayrault, and taxed him roundly with neglect of little Hart's condition. Since her former illness she never had been quite the same; she was growing pale and thin. As her brother no longer played with her, she only moped about with her kitten, and talked to herself. It touched Ayrault's heart. He took pains to be with the child that day, carried her for a long drive, and went to see her Guinea hen's eggs. That night he kept her up later than usual, instead of hurrying her off as had become his wont; he really found himself shrinking from the dream-world he had with such effort created. The most timid and shy person can hardly hesitate more about venturing among a crowd of strangers than Francis Ayrault recoiled, that evening, from the thought of this mob of intrusive persons, every one of whom reflected his own image. Gladly would he have undone the past, and swept them all away forever. But the shrinking was all on one side: the moment he sank to sleep, they all crowded upon him, laughing, frolicking, claiming detestable intimacy. No one among strangers ever longed for a friendly face, as he, among these intolerable duplicates, longed for the sight of a stranger. It was worse yet when the images grew smaller and smaller, until they had shrunk to a pin's length. He found himself trying with all his strength of will to keep them at their ampler size, with only the effect that they presently became no larger than the heads of pins. Yet his own individuality was still so distributed among them that it could not be distinguished from them; but he found himself merged in this crowd of little creatures an eighth of an inch long. . . .

Having long since fallen out of the way of action, or at best grown satisfied to imagine enterprises and leave others to execute them, he now, more than ever, drifted on from day to day. There had been a strike at the neighboring manufacturing village, and there was to be a public meeting, at which he was besought, as a person not identified with either party, to be present, and throw his influence for peace. It touched him, and he meant to attend. He even thought of a few things, which, if said, might do good; then forgot the day of the meeting, and rode ten miles in another direction. Again, when at the little post-office one day, he was asked by the postmaster to translate several letters in the French language, addressed to that official, and coming from an unknown village in Canada. They proved to contain anxious inquiries as to the whereabouts of a handsome young French girl, whom Ayrault had occasionally met driving about in what seemed doubtful company. His sympathy was thoroughly aroused by the anxiety of the poor parents, from whom the letters came. He answered them himself, promising to interfere in behalf of the girl; delayed, day by day, to fulfil the promise; and,

when he at last looked for her, she was not to be found. Yet, while
his power of efficient action waned, his dream-power increased.
His little people were busier about him than ever, though he
controlled them less and less. He was Gulliver bound and fettered
by Lilliputians.

But a more stirring appeal was on its way to him. The storm of the
Civil War began to roll among the hills; regiments were recruited,
camps were formed. The excitement reached the benumbed energies
of Ayrault. Never, indeed, had he felt such a thrill. The old Huguenot
pulse beat strongly within him. For days, and even nights, these
thoughts possessed his mind, and his dreams utterly vanished. Then
there was a lull in the excitement; recruiting stopped, and his nightly
habit of confusing visions set in again with dreary monotony. Then
there was a fresh call for troops. An old friend of Ayrault's came to
a neighboring village, and held a noonday meeting in one of the
churches to recruit a company. Ayrault listened with absorbed
interest to the rousing appeal, and, when recruits were called for,
was the first to rise. It turned out that the matter could not be at once
consummated, as the proper papers were not there. Other young
men from the neighborhood followed Ayrault's example, and it was
arranged that they should all go to the city for regular enlistment
the next day. All that afternoon was spent in preparations, and in
talking with other eager volunteers, who seemed to look to Ayrault
as their head. It was understood, they told him, that he would probably be an officer in the company. He felt himself a changed being;
he was as if floating in air, and ready to swim off to some new planet.
What had he now to do with that pale dreamer who had nourished
his absurd imaginings until he had barely escaped being controlled
by them? When they crossed his mind it was only to make him
thank God for his escape. He flung wide the windows of his chamber.
He hated the very sight of the scene where his proud vision had
been fulfilled, and he had been Monarch of Dreams. No matter: he
was now free, and the spell was broken. Life, action, duty, honor, a
redeemed nation, lay before him; all entanglements were cut away.

That evening there went through the little village a summons that opened the door of every house. A young man galloped out from the city, waking the echoes of the hills with his somewhat untutored bugle-notes, as he dashed along. Riding from house to house of those who had pledged themselves, he told the news. There had been a great defeat; reinforcements had been summoned instantly; and the half-organized regiment, undrilled, unarmed, not even uniformed, was ordered to proceed that night to the front, and replace in the forts round Washington other levies that were a shade less raw. Every man desiring to enlist must come instantly; yet, as before daybreak the regiment would pass by special train on the railway that led through the village, those in that vicinity might join it at the station, and have still a few hours at home. They were hurried hours for Ayrault, and toward midnight he threw himself on his bed for a moment's repose, having left strict orders for his awakening. He gave not one thought to his world of visions; had he done so, it would have only been to rejoice that he had eluded them forever.

Let a man at any moment attempt his best, and his life will still be at least half made up of the accumulated results of past action. Never had Ayrault seemed so absolutely safe from the gathered crowd of his own delusions: never had they come upon him with a power so terrific. Again he was in those stately halls which his imagination had so laboriously built up; again the mob of unreal beings came around him, each more himself than he was. Ayrault was beset, encircled, overwhelmed; he was in a manner lost in the crowd of himself. . . .

In the midst of this tumultuous dreaming, came confused sounds from without. There was the rolling of railway wheels, the scream of locomotive engines, the beating of drums, the cheers of men, the report and glare of fireworks. Mingled with all, there came the repeated sound of knocking at his own door, which he had locked, from mere force of habit, ere he lay down. The sounds seemed only to rouse into new tumult the figures of his dream. These suddenly began to increase steadily in size, even as they had before diminished; and the waxing was more fearful than the waning. From being Gulliver among the Lilliputians, Ayrault was Gulliver in Brobdingnag. Each image of himself, before diminutive, became colossal: they blocked his path; he actually could not find himself, could not tell which was he that should arouse himself in their vast and endless self-multiplication. He became vaguely conscious, amidst the bewilderment, that the shouts in the village were subsiding, the illuminations growing dark; and the train with its young soldiers was again in motion, throbbing and resounding among the hills, and bearing the lost opportunity of his life away—away—away.

Edward Page Mitchell

(1852–1927)

IN 1874, NEW YORK'S daily paper the *Sun* published the first of many stories by Edward Page Mitchell. Over the next decade and a half, writing anonymously as was common at the time, Mitchell pioneered many of the lasting tropes of science fiction still in use today. He was first to write about faster-than-light travel, in his early story "The Tachypomp." In 1881, fourteen years before the first appearance of H. G. Wells's novel *The Invisible Man*, the *Sun* published Mitchell's own pioneer take on invisibility, "The Crystal Man." Mitchell also loved and wrote ghost stories, and even in this genre he could not stop innovating. In his story "An Uncommon Sort of Spectre," a ghost comes not from the past but from the future to haunt a character.

Mitchell was so full of revolutionary ideas that you will find two stories to represent him within the pages of this anthology. Set in faraway 1937, "The Senator's Daughter" casually envisions an America in which the Chinese have won a war with the United States and characters communicate by personal radio, travel from New York to Washington, D.C., via fast pneumatic tubes, dine on pills of condensed nutrition, choose to cryogenically store themselves in suspended animation, and argue the virtues of the Mongol-Vegetarian political party. Like Wells and other science fiction writers, Mitchell often wove a story around a single large idea. In

"The Senator's Daughter," in contrast, he conjures a future society and performs the crucial task for making characters in such tales convincingly human: they take their world for granted, living immersed in it the way that we do in ours, the way that 1870s New Yorkers did in theirs. Ideas shoot out from this story like fireworks. It was published in the July 27, 1879, issue of the *Sun*.

In the same year, Mitchell beat Wells to the punch on time travel too, with "The Clock That Went Backward" on September 18, 1881—fourteen years before readers encountered *The Time Machine*. However, a backward-moving clock does not subvert time the way that Wells's narrator's machine does; Mitchell basically replaces magic with technology to establish his initial premise. But then he uses his time clock to poignantly explore the first known iteration of what science fiction critics now call a temporal paradox—the sort of logical contradiction that could result from even minor tinkering with the past. The "grandfather paradox" is an example: if you travel to the past and kill your own grandfather, then your parents never existed and neither did you, and thus you could not travel to the past.

Published anonymously in newspapers, Mitchell's stories were largely forgotten. He wasn't even identified as the author of most of them until decades after his death in 1927. In 1973, however, science fiction fan, historian, and critic Sam Moskowitz published a new collection of Mitchell's stories, which led a quiet revival of interest in this pioneering science fiction writer. Mitchell's is still not a household name, even in diehard science fiction fan circles, but his star is on the rise again.

The Senator's Daughter

I

THE SMALL GOLD BOX

O N THE EVENING OF the fourth of March, year of grace nineteen hundred and thirty-seven, Mr. Daniel Webster Wanlee devoted several hours to the consummation of a rather elaborate toilet. That accomplished, he placed himself before a mirror and critically surveyed the results of his patient art.

The effect appeared to give him satisfaction. In the glass he beheld a comely young man of thirty, something under the medium stature, faultlessly attired in evening dress. The face was a perfect oval, the complexion delicate, the features refined. The high cheekbones and a slight elevation of the outer corners of the eyes, the short upper lip, from which drooped a slender but aristocratic mustache, the tapered fingers of the hand, and the remarkably small feet, confined tonight in dancing pumps of polished red morocco, were all unmistakable heirlooms of a pure Mongolian ancestry. The long, stiff, black hair, brushed straight back from the forehead, fell in profusion over the neck and shoulders. Several rich decorations shone on the breast of the black broadcloth coat. The knickerbocker breeches were tied at the knees with scarlet ribbons. The stockings were of a flowered silk. Mr. Wanlee's face sparked with intelligent good sense; his figure poised itself before the glass with easy grace.

A soft, distinct utterance, filling the room yet appearing to proceed from no particular quarter, now attracted Mr. Wanlee's attention. He at once recognized the voice of his friend, Mr. Walsingham Brown.

"How are we off for time, old fellow?"

"It's getting late," replied Mr. Wanlee, without turning his face from the mirror. "You had better come over directly."

In a very few minutes the curtains at the entrance to Mr. Wanlee's apartments were unceremoniously pulled open, and Mr. Walsingham Brown strode in. The two friends cordially shook hands.

"How is the honorable member from the Los Angeles district?" inquired the newcomer gaily. "And what is there new in Washington society? Prepared to conquer tonight, I see. What's all this? Red ribbons and flowered silk hose! Ah, Wanlee. I thought you had outgrown these frivolities!"

The faintest possible blush appeared on Mr. Daniel Webster Wanlee's cheeks. "It is cool tonight?" he asked, changing the subject.

"Infernally cold," replied his friend. "I wonder you have no snow here. It is snowing hard in New York. There were at least three inches on the ground just now when I took the Pneumatic."

"Pull an easy chair up to the thermo-electrode," said the Mongolian. "You must get the New York climate thawed out of your joints if you expect to waltz creditably. The Washington women are critical in that respect."

Mr. Walsingham Brown pushed a comfortable chair toward a sphere of shining platinum that stood on a crystal pedestal in the center of the room. He pressed a silver button at the base, and the metal globe began to glow incandescently. A genial warmth diffused itself through the apartment. "That feels good," said Mr. Walsingham Brown, extending both hands to catch the heat from the thermo-electrode.

"By the way," he continued, "you haven't accounted to me yet for the scarlet bows. What would your constituents say if they saw you thus—you, the impassioned young orator of the Pacific slope; the thoughtful student of progressive statesmanship; the mainstay and hope of the Extreme Left; the thorn in the side of conservative Vegetarianism; the bete noire of the whole Indo-European gang— you, in knee ribbons and florid extensions, like a club man at a fashionable Harlem hop, or a—"

Mr. Brown interrupted himself with a hearty but goodnatured laugh.

Mr. Wanlee seemed ill at ease. He did not reply to his friend's raillery. He cast a stealthy glance at his knees in the mirror, and then went to one side of the room, where an endless strip of printed paper, about three feet wide, was slowly issuing from between noiseless rollers and falling in neat folds into a willow basket placed on the floor to receive it. Mr. Wanlee bent his head over the broad strip of paper and began to read attentively.

"You take the *Contemporaneous News*, I suppose," said the other.

"No, I prefer the *Interminable Intelligencer*," replied Mr. Wanlee. "The *Contemporaneous* is too much of my own way of thinking. Why should a sensible man ever read the organ of his own party? How much wiser it is to keep posted on what your political opponents think and say."

"Do you find anything about the event of the evening?"

"The ball has opened," said Mr. Wanlee, "and the floor of the Capitol is already crowded. Let me see," he continued, beginning to read aloud: "'The wealth, the beauty, the chivalry, and the brains of the nation combine to lend unprecedented luster to the Inauguration Ball, and the brilliant success of the new Administration is assured beyond all question.'"

"That is encouraging logic," Mr. Brown remarked.

"'President Trimbelly has just entered the rotunda, escorting his beautiful and stately wife, and accompanied by ex-President Riley, Mrs. Riley, and Miss Norah Riley. The illustrious group is of course the cynosure of all eyes. The utmost cordiality prevails among statesmen of all shades of opinion. For once, bitter political animosities seem to have been laid aside with the ordinary habiliments of everyday wear. Conspicuous among the guests are some of the most distinguished radicals of the opposition. Even General Quong, the defeated Mongol-Vegetarian candidate, is now proceeding across the rotunda, leaning on the arm of the Chinese ambassador, with the evident intention of paying his compliments to his successful rival. Not the slightest trace of resentment or hostility is visible upon his strongly marked Asiatic features.'

"The hero of the Battle of Cheyenne can afford to be magnanimous," remarked Mr. Wanlee, looking up from the paper.

"True," said Mr. Walsingham Brown, warmly. "The noble old hoodlum fighter has settled forever the question of the equality of your race. The presidency could have added nothing to his fame."

Mr. Wanlee went on reading: "'The toilets of the ladies are charming. Notable among those which attract the reportorial eye are the peacock feather train of the Princess Hushyida; the mauve—'"

"Cut that," suggested Mr. Brown. "We shall see for ourselves presently. And give me a dinner, like a good fellow. It occurs to me that I have eaten nothing for fifteen days."

The Honorable Mr. Wanlee drew from his waistcoat pocket a small gold box, oval in form. He pressed a spring and the lid flew open. Then he handed the box to his friend. It contained a number of little gray pastilles, hardly larger than peas. Mr. Brown took one between his thumb and forefinger and put it into his mouth. "Thus do I satisfy mine hunger," he said, "or, to borrow the language of the opposition orators, thus do I lend myself to the vile and degrading practice, subversive of society as at present constituted, and outraging the very laws of nature."

Mr. Wanlee was paying no attention. With eager gaze he was again scanning the columns of the *Interminable Intelligencer*. As if involuntarily, he read aloud: "'—Secretary Quimby and Mrs. Quimby, Count Schneeke, the Austrian ambassador, Mrs. Hoyette and the Misses Hoyette of New York, Senator Newton of Massachusetts, whose arrival with his lovely daughter is causing no small sensation—'"

He paused, stammering, for he became aware that his friend was regarding him earnestly. Coloring to the roots of his hair, he affected indifference and began to read again: "'Senator Newton of Massachusetts, whose arrival with his lovely—'"

"I think, my dear boy," said Mr. Walsingham Brown, with a smile, "that it is high time for us to proceed to the Capitol."

II

THE BALL AT THE CAPITOL

Through a brilliant throng of happy men and charming women, Mr. Wanlee and his friend made their way into the rotunda of the Capitol. Accustomed as they both were to the spectacular efforts which society arranged for its own delectation, the young men were startled by the enchantment of the scene before them. The dingy historical panorama that girds the rotunda was hidden behind a wall of flowers. The heights of the dome were not visible, for beneath that was a temporary interior dome of red roses and white lilies, which poured down from the concavity a continual and almost oppressive shower of fragrance. From the center of the floor ascended to the height of forty or fifty feet a single jet of water, rendered intensely luminous by the newly discovered hydrolectric process, and flooding the room with a light ten times brighter than daylight, yet soft and grateful as the light of the moon. The air pulsated with music, for every flower in the dome overhead gave utterance to the notes which Ratibolial, in the conservatoire at Paris, was sending across the Atlantic from the vibrant tip of his baton.

The friends had hardly reached the center of the rotunda, where the hydrolectric fountain threw aloft its jet of blazing water, and where two opposite streams of promenaders from the north and the south wings of the Capitol met and mingled in an eddy of polite humanity, before Mr. Walsingham Brown was seized and led off captive by some of his Washington acquaintances.

Wanlee pushed on, scarcely noticing his friend's defection. He directed his steps wherever the crowd seemed thickest, casting ahead and on either side of him quick glances of inquiry, now and then exchanging bows with people whom he recognized, but pausing only once to enter into conversation. That was when he was accosted by General Quong, the leader of the Mongol-Vegetarian party and the defeated candidate for President in the campaign of 1936. The veteran spoke familiarly to the young congressman and detained him only a moment. "You are looking for somebody, Wanlee," said General Quong, kindly. "I see it in your eyes. I grant you leave of absence."

Mr. Wanlee proceeded down the long corridor that leads to the Senate chamber, and continued there his eager search. Disappointed, he turned back, retraced his steps to the rotunda, and went to the other extremity of the Capitol. The Hall of Representatives was reserved for the dancers. From the great clock above the Speaker's desk issued the music of a waltz, to the rhythm of which several hundred couples were whirling over the polished floor.

Wanlee stood at the door, watching the couples as they moved before him in making the circuit of the hall. Presently his eyes began to sparkle. They were resting upon the beautiful face and supple figure of a girl in white satin, who waltzed in perfect form with a young man, apparently an Italian. Wanlee advanced a step or two, and at the same instant the lady became aware of his presence. She said a word to her partner, who immediately relinquished her waist.

"I have been expecting you this age," said the girl, holding out her hand to Wanlee. "I am delighted that you have come."

"Thank you, Miss Newton," said Wanlee.

"You may retire, Francesco," she continued, turning to the young man who had just been her partner. "I shall not need you again."

The young man addressed as Francesco bowed respectfully and departed without a word.

"Let us not lose this lovely waltz," said Miss Newton, putting her hand upon Wanlee's shoulder. "It will be my first this evening."

"Then you have not danced?" asked Wanlee, as they glided off together.

"No, Daniel," said Miss Newton, "I haven't danced with any gentlemen."

The Mongolian thanked her with a smile.

"I have made good use of Francesco, however," she went on. "What a blessing a competent protectional partner is! Only think, our grandmothers, and even our mothers, were obliged to sit dismally around the walls waiting the pleasure of their high and mighty—"

She paused suddenly, for a shade of annoyance had fallen upon her partner's face. "Forgive me," she whispered, her head almost upon his shoulder. "Forgive me if I have wounded you. You know, love, that I would not—"

"I know it," he interrupted. "You are too good and too noble to let that weigh a feather's weight in your estimation of the Man. You never pause to think that my mother and my grandmother were not accustomed to meet your mother and your grandmother in society—for the very excellent reason," he continued, with a little bitterness in his tone, "that my mother had her hands full in my father's laundry in San Francisco, while my grandmother's social ideas hardly extended beyond the cabin of our ancestral san-pan on the Yangtze Kiang. *You* do not care for that. But there are others—"

They waltzed on for some time in silence, he, thoughtful and moody, and she, sympathetically concerned.

"And the senator; where is he tonight?" asked Wanlee at last.

"Papa!" said the girl, with a frightened little glance over her shoulder. "Oh! Papa merely made his appearance here to bring me and because it was expected of him. He has gone home to work on his tiresome speech against the vegetables."

"Do you think," asked Wanlee, after a few minutes, whispering the words very slowly and very low, "that the senator has any suspicion?"

It was her turn now to manifest embarrassment. "I am very sure," she replied, "that Papa has not the least idea in the world of it all. And that is what worries me. I constantly feel that we are walking together on a volcano. I know that we are right, and that heaven means it to be just as it is; yet, I cannot help trembling in my happiness. You know as well as I do the antiquated and absurd notions that still prevail in Massachusetts, and that Papa is a conservative among the conservatives. He respects your ability, that I discovered long ago. Whenever you speak in the House, he reads your remarks with great attention. I think," she continued with a forced laugh, "that your arguments bother him a good deal."

"This must have an end, Clara," said the Chinaman, as the music ceased and the waltzers stopped. "I cannot allow you to remain a day longer in an equivocal position. My honor and your own peace of mind require that there shall be an explanation to your father. Have you the courage to stake all our happiness on one bold move?"

"I have courage," frankly replied the girl, "to go with you before my father and tell him all. And furthermore," she continued, slightly pressing his arm and looking into his face with a charming blush, "I have courage even beyond that."

"You beloved little Puritan!" was his reply.

As they passed out of the Hall of Representatives, they encountered Mr. Walsingham Brown with Miss Hoyette of New York. The New York lady spoke cordially to Miss Newton, but recognized Wanlee with a rather distant bow. Wanlee's eyes sought and met those of his friend. "I may need your counsel before morning," he said in a low voice.

"All right, my dear fellow," said Mr. Brown. "Depend on me." And the two couples separated.

The Mongolian and his Massachusetts sweetheart drifted with the tide into the supper room. Both were preoccupied with their own thoughts. Almost mechanically, Wanlee led his companion to a corner of the supper room and established her in a seat behind a screen of palmettos, sheltered from the observation of the throne.

"It is nice of you to bring me here," said the girl, "for I am hungry after our waltz."

Intimate as their souls had become, this was the first time that she had ever asked him for food. It was an innocent and natural request, yet Wanlee shuddered when he heard it, and bit his under lip to control his agitation. He looked from behind the palmettos at the tables heaped with delicate viands and surrounded by men, eagerly pressing forward to obtain refreshment for the ladies in their care. Wanlee shuddered again at the spectacle. After a momentary hesitation he returned to Miss Newton, seated himself beside her, and taking her hand in his, began to speak deliberately and earnestly.

"Clara," he said, "I am going to ask you for a final proof of your affection. Do not start and look alarmed, but hear me patiently. If, after hearing me, you still bid me bring you a *pâté*, or the wing of a fowl, or a salad, or even a plate of fruit, I will do so, though it wrench the heart in my bosom. But first listen to what I have to say."

"Certainly I will listen to all you have to say," she replied.

"You know enough of the political theories that divide parties," he went on, nervously examining the rings on her slender fingers, "to be aware that what I conscientiously believe to be true is very different from what you have been educated to believe."

"I know," said Miss Newton, "that you are a Vegetarian and do not approve the use of meat. I know that you have spoken eloquently in the House on the right of every living being to protection in its life, and that that is the theory of your party. Papa says that it is demagogy—that the opposition parade an absurd and sophistical theory in order to win votes and get themselves into office. Still, I know that a great many excellent people, friends of ours in Massachusetts, are coming to believe with you, and, of course, loving you as I do, I have the firmest faith in the honesty of your convictions.

You are not a demagogue, Daniel. You are above pandering to the radicalism of the rabble. Neither my father nor all the world could make me think the contrary."

Mr. Daniel Webster Wanlee squeezed her hand and went on:

"Living as you do in the most ultra-conservative of circles, dear Clara, you have had no opportunity to understand the tremendous significance and force of the movement that is now sweeping over the land, and of which I am a very humble representative. It is something more than a political agitation; it is an upheaval and reorganization of society on the basis of science and abstract right. It is fit and proper that I, belonging to a race that has only been emancipated and enfranchised by the march of time, should stand in the advance guard—in the forlorn hope, it may be—of the new revolution."

His flaming eyes were now looking directly into hers. Although a little troubled by his earnestness, she could not hide her proud satisfaction in his manly bearing.

"We believe that every animal is born free and equal," he said. "That the humblest polyp or the most insignificant mollusk has an equal right with you or me to life and the enjoyment of happiness. Why, are we not all brothers? Are we not all children of a common evolution? What are we human animals but the more favored members of the great family? Is Senator Newton of Massachusetts further removed in intelligence from the Australian bushman, than the Australian bushman or the Flathead Indian is removed from the ox which Senator Newton orders slain to yield food for his family? Have we a right to take the paltriest life that evolution has given? Is not the butchery of an ox or of a chicken murder—nay, fratricide—in the view of absolute justice? Is it not cannibalism of the most repulsive and cowardly sort to prey upon the flesh of our defenseless brother animals, and to sacrifice their lives and rights to an unnatural appetite that has no foundation save in the habit of long ages of barbarian selfishness?"

"I have never thought of these things," said Miss Clara, slowly.

"Would you elevate them to the suffrage—I mean the ox and the chicken and the baboon?"

"There speaks the daughter of the senator from Massachusetts," cried Wanlee. "No, we would not give them the suffrage—at least, not at present. The right to live and enjoy life is a natural, an inalienable right. The right to vote depends upon conditions of society and of individual intelligence. The ox, the chicken, the baboon are not yet prepared for the ballot. But they are voters in embryo; they are struggling up through the same process that our own ancestors underwent, and it is a crime, an unnatural, horrible thing, to cut off their career, their future, for the sake of a meal!"

"Those are noble sentiments, I must admit," said Miss Newton, with considerable enthusiasm.

"They are the sentiments of the Mongol-Vegetarian party," said Wanlee. "They will carry the country in 1940, and elect the next President of the United States."

"I admire your earnestness," said Miss Newton after a pause, "and I will not grieve you by asking you to bring me even so much as a chicken wing. I do not think I could eat it now, with your words still in my ears. A little fruit is all that I want."

"Once more," said Wanlee, taking the tall girl's hand again, "I must request you to consider. The principles, my dearest, that I have already enunciated are the principles of the great mass of our party. They are held even by the respectable, easygoing, not oversensitive voters such as constitute the bulk of every political organization. But there are a few of us who stand on ground still more advanced. We do not expect to bring the laggards up to our line for years, perhaps in our lifetime. We simply carry the accepted theory to its logical conclusions and calmly await ultimate results."

"And what is your ground, pray?" she inquired. "I cannot see how anything could be more dreadfully radical—that is, more bewildering and generally upsetting at first sight—than the ground which you just took."

"If what I have said is true, and I believe it to be true, then how

can we escape including the Vegetable Kingdom in our proclama-
tion of emancipation from man's tyranny? The tree, the plant, even
the fungus, have they not individual life, and have they not also the
right to live?"

"But how—"

"And indeed," continued the Chinaman, not noticing the interruption, "who can say where vegetable life ends and animal life
begins? Science has tried in vain to draw the boundary line. I hold
that to uproot a potato is to destroy an existence certainly, although
perhaps remotely akin to ours. To pluck a grape is to maim the
living vine; and to drink the juice of that grape is to outrage consan-
guinity. In this broad, elevated view of the matter it becomes a duty
to refrain from vegetable food. Nothing less than the vital principal
itself becomes the test and tie of universal brotherhood. 'All living
things are born free and equal, and have a right to existence and
the enjoyment of existence.' Is not that a beautiful thought?"

"It is a beautiful thought," said the maiden. "But—I know you
will think me dreadfully cold, and practical, and unsympathetic—
but how are *we* to live? Have *we* no right, too, to existence? Must
we starve to death in order to establish the theoretical right of vegetables not to be eaten?"

"My dear love," said Wanlee, "that would be a serious and
perplexing question, had not the latest discovery of science already
solved it for us."

He took from his waistcoat pocket the small gold box, scarcely
larger than a watch, and opened the cover. In the palm of her white
hand he placed one of the little pastilles.

"Eat it," said he. "It will satisfy your hunger."

She put the morsel into her mouth. "I would do as you bade me,"
she said, "even if it were poison."

"It is not poison," he rejoined. "It is nourishment in the only
rational form."

"But it is tasteless; almost without substance."

"Yet it will support life for from eighteen to twenty-five days.

This little gold box holds food enough to afford all subsistence to the entire Seventy-sixth Congress for a month."

She took the box and curiously examined its contents.

"And how long would it support my life—for more than a year, perhaps?"

"Yes, for more than ten—more than twenty years."

"I will not bore you with chemical and physiological facts," continued Wanlee, "but you must know that the food which we take, in whatever form, resolves itself into what are called proximate principles—starch, sugar, oleine, flurin, albumen, and so on. These are selected and assimilated by the organs of the body, and go to build up the necessary tissues. But all these proximate principles, in their turn, are simply combinations of the ultimate chemical elements, chiefly carbon, nitrogen, hydrogen, and oxygen. It is upon these elements that we depend for sustenance. By the old plan we obtained them indirectly. They passed from the earth and the air into the grass; from the grass into the muscular tissues of the ox; and from the beef into our own persons, loaded down and encumbered by a mass of useless, irrelevant matter. The German chemists have discovered how to supply the needed elements in compact, undiluted form—here they are in this little box. Now shall mankind go direct to the fountainhead of nature for his aliment; now shall the old roundabout, cumbrous, inhuman method be at an end; now shall the evils of gluttony and the attendant vices cease; now shall the brutal murdering of fellow animals and brother vegetables forever stop—now shall all this be, since the new, holy cause has been consecrated by the lips I love!"

He bent and kissed those lips. Then he suddenly looked up and saw Mr. Walsingham Brown standing at his elbow.

"You are observed—compromised, I fear," said Mr. Brown, hurriedly. "That Italian dancer in your employ, Miss Newton, has been following you like a hound. I have been paying him the same gracious attention. He has just left the Capitol post haste. I fear there may be a scene."

The brave girl, with clear eyes, gave her Mongolian lover a look worth to him a year of life. "There shall be no scene," she said; "we will go at once to my father, Daniel, and bear ourselves the tale which Francesco would carry."

The three left the Capitol without delay. At the head of Pennsylvania Avenue they entered a great building, lighted up as brilliantly as the Capitol itself. An elevator took them down toward the bowels of the earth. At the fourth landing they passed from the elevator into a small carriage, luxuriously upholstered. Mr. Walsingham Brown touched an ivory knob at the end of the conveyance. A man in uniform presented himself at the door.

"To Boston," said Mr. Walsingham Brown.

III

THE FROZEN BRIDE

The senator from Massachusetts sat in the library of his mansion on North Street at two o'clock in the morning. An expression of astonishment and rage distorted his pale, cold features. The pen had dropped from his fingers, blotting the last sentences written upon the manuscript of his great speech—for Senator Newton still adhered to the ancient fashion of recording thought. The blotted sentences were these:

The logic of events compels us to acknowledge the political equality of those Asiatic invaders—shall I say conquerors?—of our Indo-European institutions. But the logic of events is often repugnant to common sense, and its conclusions abhorrent to patriotism and right. The sword has opened for them the way to the ballot box; but, Mr. President, and I say it deliberately, no power under heaven can unlock for these aliens the sacred approaches to our homes and hearts!

Beside the senator stood Francesco, the professional dancer. His face wore a smile of malicious triumph.

"With the Chinaman? Miss Newton—my daughter?" gasped the senator. "I do not believe you. It is a lie."

"Then come to the Capitol, Your Excellency, and see it with your own eyes," said the Italian.

The door was quickly opened and Clara Newton entered the room, followed by the Honorable Mr. Wanlee and his friend.

"There is no need of making that excursion, Papa," said the girl. "You can see it with your own eyes here and now. Francesco, leave the house!"

The senator bowed with forced politeness to Mr. Walsingham Brown. Of the presence of Wanlee he took not the slightest notice.

Senator Newton attempted to laugh. "This is a pleasantry, Clara," he said; "a practical jest, designed by yourself and Mr. Brown for my midnight diversion. It is a trifle unseasonable."

"It is no jest," replied his daughter, bravely. She then went up to Wanlee and took his hand in hers. "Papa," she said, "this is a gentleman of whom you already know something. He is our equal in station, in intellect, and in moral worth. He is in every way worthy of my friendship and your esteem. Will you listen to what he has to say to you? Will you, Papa?"

The senator laughed a short, hard laugh, and turned to Mr. Walsingham Brown. "I have no communication to make to the member of the lower branch," said he. "Why should he have any communication to make to me?"

Miss Newton put her arm around the waist of the young Chinaman and led him squarely in front of her father. "Because," she said, in a voice as firm and clear as the note of a silver bell "—because I love him."

In recalling with Wanlee the circumstances of this interview, Mr. Walsingham Brown said long afterward, "She glowed for a moment like the platinum of your thermo-electrode."

"If the member from California," said Senator Newton, without changing the tone of his voice, and still continuing to address himself to Mr. Brown, "has worked upon the sentimentality of this foolish child, that is her misfortune, and mine. It cannot be helped now. But if the member from California presumes to hope to profit in the least by his sinister operations, or to enjoy further opportunities for pursuing them, the member from California deceives himself."

So saying he turned around in his chair and began to write on his great speech.

"I come," said Wanlee slowly, now speaking for the first time, "as an honorable man to ask of Senator Newton the hand of his daughter in honorable marriage. Her own consent has already been given."

"I have nothing further to say," said the Senator, once more turning his cold face toward Mr. Brown. Then he paused an instant, and added with a sting, "I am told that the member from California is a prophet and apostle of Vegetable Rights. Let him seek a cactus in marriage. He should wed on his own level."

Wanlee, coloring at the wanton insult, was about to leave the room. A quick sign from Miss Newton arrested him.

"But I have something further to say," she cried with spirit. "Listen, Father; it is this. If Mr. Wanlee goes out of the house without a word from you—a word such as is due him from you as a gentleman and as my father—I go with him to be his wife before the sun rises!"

"Go if you will, girl," the senator coldly replied. "But first consult with Mr. Walsingham Brown, who is a lawyer and a gentleman, as to the tenor and effect of the Suspended Animation Act."

Miss Newton looked inquiringly from one face to another. The words had no meaning to her. Her lover turned suddenly pale and clutched at the back of a chair for support. Mr. Brown's cheeks were also white. He stepped quickly forward, holding out his hands as if to avert some dreadful calamity.

"Surely you would not—" he began. "But no! That is an absolute low, an inhuman, outrageous enactment that has long been as dead as the partisan fury that prompted it. For a quarter of a century it has been a dead letter on the statute books."

"I was not aware," said the senator, from between firmly set teeth, "that the act had ever been repealed."

He took from the shelf a volume of statutes and opened the book. "I will read the text," he said. "It will form an appropriate part of the ritual of this marriage." He read as follows:

"'Section 7.391. No male person of Caucasian descent, of or under the age of 25 years, shall marry, or promise or contract himself in marriage with any female person of Mongolian descent without the full written consent of his male parent or guardian, as provided by law; and no female person, either maid or widow, under the age of 30 years, of Caucasian parentage, shall give, promise, or contract herself in marriage with any male person of Mongolian descent without the full written and registered consent of her male and female parents or guardians, as provided by law. And any marriage obligations so contracted shall be null and void, and the Caucasian so contracting shall be guilty of a misdemeanor and liable to punishment at the discretion of his or her male parent or guardian as provided by law.

"'Section 7.392. Such parents or guardians may, at their discretion and upon application to the authorities of the United States District Court for the district within which the offense is committed, deliver the offending person of Caucasian descent to the designated officers, and require that his or her consciousness, bodily activities, and vital functions be suspended by the frigorific process known as the Werkomer process, for a period equal to that which must elapse before the offending person will arrive at the age of 25 years, if a male, or 30 years, if a female; or for a shorter period at the discretion of the parent or guardian; said shorter period to be fixed in advance.'"

"What does it mean?" demanded Miss Newton, bewildered by the verbiage of the act, and alarmed by her lover's exclamation of despair.

Mr. Walsingham Brown shook his head, sadly. "It means," said he, "that the cruel sin of the fathers is to be visited upon the children."

"It means, Clara," said Wanlee with a great effort, "that we must part."

"Understand me, Mr. Brown," said the senator, rising and motioning impatiently with the hand that held the pen, as if to dismiss both the subject and the intruding party. "I do not employ the Suspended Animation Act as a bugaboo to frighten a silly girl out of her lamentable infatuation. As surely as the law stands, so surely will I put it to use."

Miss Newton gave her father a long, steady look which neither Wanlee nor Mr. Brown could interpret and then slowly led the way to the parlor. She closed the door and locked it. The clock on the mantel said four.

A complete change had come over the girl's manner. The spirit of defiance, of passionate appeal, of outspoken love, had gone. She was calm now, as cold and self-possessed as the senator himself. "Frozen!" she kept saying under her breath. "He has frozen me already with his frigid heart."

She quickly asked Mr. Walsingham Brown to explain clearly the force and bearings of the statute which her father had read from the book. When he had done so, she inquired, "Is there not also a law providing for voluntary suspension of animation?"

"The Twenty-seventh Amendment to the Constitution," replied the lawyer, "recognizes the right of any individual, not satisfied with the condition of his life, to suspend that life for a time, long or short, according to his pleasure. But it is rarely, as you know, that any one avails himself of the right—practically never, except as the only means to procure divorce from uncongenial marriage relations."

"Still," she persisted, "the right exists and the way is open?" He bowed. She went to Wanlee and said:

"My darling, it must be so. I must leave you for a time, but as your wife. We will arrange a wedding"—and she smiled sadly—"within this hour. Mr. Brown will go with us to the clergyman. Then we will proceed at once to the Refuge, and you yourself shall lead me to the cloister that is to keep me safe till times are better for us. No, do not be startled, my love! The resolution is taken; you cannot alter it. And it will not be so very long, dear. Once, by accident, in arranging my father's papers, I came across his Life Probabilities, drawn up by the Vital Bureau at Washington. He has less than ten years to live. I never thought to calculate in cold blood on the chances of my father's life, but it must be. In ten years, Daniel, you may come to the Refuge again and claim your bride. You will find me as you left me."

With tears streaming down his pale cheeks, the Mongolian strove to dissuade the Caucasian from her purpose. Hardly less affected, Mr. Walsingham Brown joined his entreaties and arguments.

"Have you ever seen," he asked, "a woman who has undergone what you propose to undergo? She went into the Refuge, perhaps, as you will go, fresh, rosy, beautiful, full of life and energy. She comes out a prematurely aged, withered, sallow, flaccid body, a living corpse—a skeleton, a ghost of her former self. In spite of all they say, there can be no absolute suspension of animation. Absolute suspension would be death. Even in the case of the most perfect freezing there is still some activity of the vital functions, and they gnaw and prey upon the existence of the unconscious subject. Will you risk," he suddenly demanded, using the last and most perfect argument that can be addressed to a woman "—will you risk the effect your loss of beauty may have upon Wanlee's love after ten years' separation?"

Clara Newton was smiling now. "For my poor beauty," she replied, "I care very little. Yet perhaps even that may be preserved."

She took from the bosom of her dress the little gold box which the Chinaman had given her in the supper room of the Capitol, and hastily swallowed its entire contents.

Wanlee now spoke with determination: "Since you have resolved to sacrifice ten years of your life my duty is with you. I shall share with you the sacrifice and share also the joy of awakening."

She gravely shook her head. "It is no sacrifice for me," she said. "But you must remain in life. You have a great and noble work to perform. Till the oppressed of the lower orders of being are emancipated from man's injustice and cruelty, you cannot abandon their cause. I think your duty is plain."

"You are right," he said, bowing his head to his breast.

In the gray dawn of the early morning the officials at the Frigorific Refuge in Cambridgeport were astonished by the arrival of a bridal party. The bridegroom's haggard countenance contrasted strangely with the elegance of his full evening toilet, and the bright scarlet bows at his knees seemed a mockery of grief. The bride, in white satin, wore a placid smile on her lovely face. The friend accompanying the two was grave and silent.

Without delay the necessary papers of admission were drawn up and signed and the proper registration was made upon the books of the establishment. For an instant husband and wife rested in each other's arms. Then she, still cheerful, followed the attendants toward the inner door, while he, pressing both hands upon his tearless eyes, turned away sobbing.

A moment later the intense cold of the congealing chamber caught the bride and wrapped her close in its icy embrace.

The Clock That Went Backward

I

A ROW OF LOMBARDY poplars stood in front of my great-aunt Gertrude's house, on the bank of the Sheepscot River. In personal appearance my aunt was surprisingly like one of those trees. She had the look of hopeless anemia that distinguishes them from fuller blooded sorts. She was tall, severe in outline, and extremely thin. Her habiliments clung to her. I am sure that had the gods found occasion to impose upon her the fate of Daphne she would have taken her place easily and naturally in the dismal row, as melancholy a poplar as the rest.

Some of my earliest recollections are of this venerable relative. Alive and dead she bore an important part in the events I am about to recount: events which I believe to be without parallel in the experience of mankind.

During our periodical visits of duty to Aunt Gertrude in Maine, my cousin Harry and myself were accustomed to speculate much on her age. Was she sixty, or was she six score? We had no precise information; she might have been either. The old lady was surrounded by old-fashioned things. She seemed to live altogether in the past. In her short half-hours of communicativeness, over her second cup of tea, or on the piazza where the poplars sent slim shadows directly toward the east, she used to tell us stories of her alleged ancestors. I say alleged, because we never fully believed that she had ancestors.

A genealogy is a stupid thing. Here is Aunt Gertrude's, reduced to its simplest forms:

Her great-great-grandmother (1599–1642) was a woman of Holland who married a Puritan refugee, and sailed from Leyden to Plymouth in the ship Ann in the year of our Lord 1632. This Pilgrim mother had a daughter, Aunt Gertrude's great-grandmother (1640–1718). She came to the Eastern District of Massachusetts in the early part of the last century, and was carried off by the Indians in the Penobscot wars. Her daughter (1680–1776) lived to see these colonies free and independent, and contributed to the population of the coming republic not less than nineteen stalwart sons and comely daughters. One of the latter (1735–1802) married a Wiscasset skipper engaged in the West India trade, with whom she sailed. She was twice wrecked at sea—once on what is now Seguin Island and once on San Salvador. It was on San Salvador that Aunt Gertrude was born.

We got to be very tired of hearing this family history. Perhaps it was the constant repetition and the merciless persistency with which the above dates were driven into our young ears that made us skeptics. As I have said, we took little stock in Aunt Gertrude's ancestors. They seemed highly improbable. In our private opinion the great-grandmothers and grandmothers and so forth were pure myths, and Aunt Gertrude herself was the principal in all the adventures attributed to them, having lasted from century to century while generations of contemporaries went the way of all flesh.

On the first landing of the square stairway of the mansion loomed a tall Dutch clock. The case was more than eight feet high, of a dark red wood, not mahogany, and it was curiously inlaid with silver. No common piece of furniture was this. About a hundred years ago there flourished in the town of Brunswick a horologist named Cary, an industrious and accomplished workman. Few well-to-do houses on that part of the coast lacked a Cary timepiece. But Aunt Gertrude's clock had marked the hours and minutes of two full centuries before the Brunswick artisan was born. It was running when William the Taciturn pierced the dikes to relieve Leyden. The name of the maker, Jan Lipperdam, and the date, 1572, were still legible in broad black letters and figures reaching quite across the dial. Cary's master-pieces were plebeian and recent beside this ancient aristocrat. The jolly Dutch moon, made to exhibit the phases over a landscape of windmills and polders, was cunningly painted. A skilled hand had carved the grim ornament at the top, a death's head transfixed by a two-edged sword. Like all timepieces of the sixteenth century, it had no pendulum. A simple Van Wyck escapement governed the descent of the weights to the bottom of the tall case.

But these weights never moved. Year after year, when Harry and I returned to Maine, we found the hands of the old clock pointing to the quarter past three, as they had pointed when we first saw them. The fat moon hung perpetually in the third quarter, as motionless as the death's head above. There was a mystery about the silenced movement and the paralyzed hands. Aunt Gertrude told us that the works had never performed their functions since a bolt of lightning entered the clock; and she showed us a black hole in the side of the case near the top, with a yawning rift that extended down-ward for several feet. This explanation failed to satisfy us. It did not account for the sharpness of her refusal when we proposed to bring over the watchmaker from the village, or for her singular agita-tion once when she found Harry on a stepladder, with a borrowed key in his hand, about to test for himself the clock's suspended vitality.

One August night, after we had grown out of boyhood, I was awakened by a noise in the hallway. I shook my cousin. "Some-body's in the house," I whispered.

We crept out of our room and on to the stairs. A dim light came from below. We held breath and noiselessly descended to the second landing. Harry clutched my arm. He pointed down over the banisters, at the same time drawing me back into the shadow.

We saw a strange thing.

Aunt Gertrude stood on a chair in front of the old clock, as spectral in her white nightgown and white nightcap as one of the poplars when covered with snow. It chanced that the floor creaked slightly under our feet. She turned with a sudden movement, peering intently into the darkness, and holding a candle high toward us, so that the light was full upon her pale face. She looked many years older than when I bade her good night. For a few minutes she was motionless, except in the trembling arm that held aloft the candle. Then, evidently reassured, she placed the light upon a shelf and turned again to the clock.

We now saw the old lady take a key from behind the face and proceed to wind up the weights. We could hear her breath, quick and short. She rested a band on either side of the case and held her face close to the dial, as if subjecting it to anxious scrutiny. In this attitude she remained for a long time. We heard her utter a sigh of relief, and she half turned toward us for a moment. I shall never forget the expression of wild joy that transfigured her features then.

The hands of the clock were moving; they were moving backward.

Aunt Gertrude put both arms around the clock and pressed her withered cheek against it. She kissed it repeatedly. She caressed it in a hundred ways, as if it had been a living and beloved thing. She fondled it and talked to it, using words which we could hear but could not understand. The hands continued to move backward.

Then she started back with a sudden cry. The clock had stopped. We saw her tall body swaying for an instant on the chair. She stretched out her arms in a convulsive gesture of terror and despair, wrenched the minute hand to its old place at a quarter past three, and fell heavily to the floor.

II

Aunt Gertrude's will left me her bank and gas stocks, real estate, rail-road bonds, and city sevens, and gave Harry the clock. We thought at the time that this was a very unequal division, the more surprising because my cousin had always seemed to be the favorite. Half in seriousness we made a thorough examination of the ancient timepiece, sounding its wooden case for secret drawers, and even probing the not complicated works with a knitting needle to ascertain if our whimsical relative had bestowed there some codicil or other document changing the aspect of affairs. We discovered nothing.

There was testamentary provision for our education at the University of Leyden. We left the military school in which we had learned a little of the theory of war, and a good deal of the art of standing with our noses over our heels, and took ship without delay. The clock went with us. Before many months it was established in a corner of a room in the Breede Straat.

The fabric of Jan Lipperdam's ingenuity, thus restored to its native air, continued to tell the hour of quarter past three with its old fidelity. The author of the clock had been under the sod for nearly three hundred years. The combined skill of his successors in the craft at Leyden could make it go neither forward nor backward.

We readily picked up enough Dutch to make ourselves under-stood by the townspeople, the professors, and such of our eight hundred and odd fellow students as came into intercourse. This language, which looks so hard at first, is only a sort of polarized English. Puzzle over it a little while and it jumps into your comprehension like one of those simple cryptograms made by running together all the words of a sentence and then dividing in the wrong places.

The language acquired and the newness of our surroundings worn off, we settled into tolerably regular pursuits. Harry devoted himself with some assiduity to the study of sociology, with especial reference to the round-faced and not unkind maidens of Leyden. I went in for the higher metaphysics.

Outside of our respective studies, we had a common ground of unfailing interest. To our astonishment, we found that not one in twenty of the faculty or students knew or cared a sliver about the glorious history of the town, or even about the circumstances under which the university itself was founded by the Prince of Orange. In marked contrast with the general indifference was the enthusiasm of Professor Van Stopp, my chosen guide through the cloudiness of speculative philosophy.

This distinguished Hegelian was a tobacco-dried little old man, with a skullcap over features that reminded me strangely of Aunt Gertrude's. Had he been her own brother the facial resemblance could not have been closer. I told him so once, when we were together in the Stadthuis looking at the portrait of the hero of the siege, the Burgomaster Van der Werf. The professor laughed. "I will show you what is even a more extraordinary coincidence," said he; and, leading the way across the hall to the great picture of the siege, by Warmers, he pointed out the figure of a burgher participating in the defense. It was true. Van Stopp might have been the burgher's son; the burgher might have been Aunt Gertrude's father.

The professor seemed to be fond of us. We often went to his rooms in an old house in the Rapenburg Straat, one of the few houses remaining that antedate 1574. He would walk with us through the beautiful suburbs of the city, over straight roads lined with poplars that carried us back to the bank of the Sheepscot in our minds. He took us to the top of the ruined Roman tower in the center of the town, and from the same battlements from which anxious eyes three centuries ago had watched the slow approach of Admiral Boisot's fleet over the submerged polders, he pointed out the great dike of the Landscheiding, which was cut that the oceans might bring Boisot's Zealanders to raise the leaguer and feed the starving. He showed us the headquarters of the Spaniard Valdez at Leyderdorp, and told us how heaven sent a violent northwest wind on the night of the first of October, piling up the water deep where it had been shallow and sweeping the fleet on between Zoeterwoude and Zwieten up to the very walls of the fort at Lammen, the last stronghold of the besiegers and the last obstacle in the way of succor to the famishing inhabitants. Then he showed us where, on the very night before the retreat of the besieging army, a huge breach was made in the wall of Leyden, near the Cow Gate, by the Walloons from Lammen.

"Why!" cried Harry, catching fire from the eloquence of the professor's narrative, "that was the decisive moment of the siege."

The professor said nothing. He stood with his arms folded, looking intently into my cousin's eyes.

"For," continued Harry, "had that point not been watched, or had defense failed and the breach been carried by the night assault from Lammen, the town would have been burned and the people massacred under the eyes of Admiral Boisot and the fleet of relief. Who defended the breach?"

Van Stopp replied very slowly, as if weighing every word:

"History records the explosion of the mine under the city wall on the last night of the siege; it does not tell the story of the defense or give the defender's name. Yet no man that ever lived had a more tremendous charge than fate entrusted to this unknown hero. Was it chance that sent him to meet that unexpected danger? Consider some of the consequences had he failed. The fall of Leyden would have destroyed the last hope of the Prince of Orange and of the free states. The tyranny of Philip would have been reestablished. The birth of religious liberty and of self-government by the people would have been postponed, who knows for how many centuries? Who knows that there would or could have been a republic of the United States of America had there been no United Netherlands? Our University, which has given to the world Grotius, Scaliger, Arminius, and Descartes, was founded upon this hero's successful defense of the breach. We owe to him our presence here today. Nay, you owe to him your very existence. Your ancestors were of

Leyden; between their lives and the butchers outside the walls he stood that night."

The little professor towered before us, a giant of enthusiasm and patriotism. Harry's eyes glistened and his cheeks reddened.

"Go home, boys," said Van Stopp, "and thank God that while the burghers of Leyden were straining their gaze toward Zoeter-woude and the fleet, there was one pair of vigilant eyes and one stout heart at the town wall just beyond the Cow Gate!"

III

The rain was splashing against the windows one evening in the autumn of our third year at Leyden, when Professor Van Stopp honored us with a visit in the Breede Straat. Never had I seen the old gentleman in such spirits. He talked incessantly. The gossip of the town, the news of Europe, science, poetry, philosophy, were in turn touched upon and treated with the same high and good humor. I sought to draw him out on Hegel, with whose chapter on the complexity and interdependency of things I was just then struggling.

"You do not grasp the return of the Itself into Itself through its Otherself?" he said smiling. "Well, you will, sometime."

Harry was silent and preoccupied. His taciturnity gradually affected even the professor. The conversation flagged, and we sat a long while without a word. Now and then there was a flash of light-ning succeeded by distant thunder.

"Your clock does not go," suddenly remarked the professor. "Does it ever go?"

"Never since we can remember," I replied. "That is, only once, and then it went backward. It was when Aunt Gertrude—"

Here I caught a warning glance from Harry. I laughed and stam-mered, "The clock is old and useless. It cannot be made to go."

"Only backward?" said the professor, calmly, and not appearing to notice my embarrassment. "Well, and why should not a clock go backward? Why should not Time itself turn and retrace its course?"

He seemed to be waiting for an answer. I had none to give.

"I thought you Hegelian enough," he continued, "to admit that every condition includes its own contradiction. Time is a condition, not an essential. Viewed from the Absolute, the sequence by which future follows present and present follows past is purely arbitrary. Yesterday, today, tomorrow; there is no reason in the nature of things why the order should not be tomorrow, today, yesterday."

A sharper peal of thunder interrupted the professor's speculations.

"The day is made by the planet's revolution on its axis from west to east. I fancy you can conceive conditions under which it might turn from east to west, unwinding, as it were, the revolutions of past ages. Is it so much more difficult to imagine Time unwinding itself; Time on the ebb, instead of on the flow; the past unfolding as the future recedes; the centuries countermarching; the course of events proceeding toward the Beginning and not, as now, toward the End?"

"But," I interposed, "we know that as far as we are concerned the—"

"We know!" exclaimed Van Stopp, with growing scorn. "Your intelligence has no wings. You follow in the trail of Compte and his slimy brood of creepers and crawlers. You speak with amazing assurance of your position in the universe. You seem to think that your wretched little individuality has a firm foothold in the Absolute. Yet you go to bed tonight and dream into existence men, women, children, beasts of the past or of the future. How do you know that at this moment you yourself, with all your conceit of nineteenth-century thought, are anything more than a creature of a dream of the future, dreamed, let us say, by some philosopher of the sixteenth century? How do you know that you are anything more than a creature of a dream of the past, dreamed by some

Hegelian of the twenty-sixth century? How do you know, boy, that you will not vanish into the sixteenth century or 2060 the moment the dreamer awakes?"

There was no replying to this, for it was sound metaphysics. Harry yawned. I got up and went to the window. Professor Van Stopp approached the clock.

"Ah, my children," said he, "there is no fixed progress of human events. Past, present, and future are woven together in one inextricable mesh. Who shall say that this old clock is not right to go backward?"

A crash of thunder shook the house. The storm was over our heads.

When the blinding glare had passed away, Professor Van Stopp was standing upon a chair before the tall timepiece. His face looked more than ever like Aunt Gertrude's. He stood as she had stood in that last quarter of an hour when we saw her wind the clock.

The same thought struck Harry and myself.

"Hold!" we cried, as he began to wind the works. "It may be death if you—"

The professor's sallow features shone with the strange enthusiasm that had transformed Aunt Gertrude's.

"True," he said, "it may be death; but it may be the awakening. Past, present, future; all woven together! The shuttle goes to and fro, forward and back—"

He had wound the clock. The hands were whirling around the dial from right to left with inconceivable rapidity. In this whirl we ourselves seemed to be borne along. Eternities seemed to contract into minutes while lifetimes were thrown off at every tick. Van Stopp, both arms outstretched, was reeling in his chair. The house shook again under a tremendous peal of thunder. At the same instant a ball of fire, leaving a wake of sulphurous vapor and filling the room with dazzling light, passed over our heads and smote the clock. Van Stopp was prostrated. The hands ceased to revolve.

IV

The roar of the thunder sounded like heavy cannonading. The lightning's blaze appeared as the steady light of a conflagration. With our hands over our eyes, Harry and I rushed out into the night.

Under a red sky people were hurrying toward the Stadthuis. Flames in the direction of the Roman tower told us that the heart of the town was afire. The faces of those we saw were haggard and emaciated. From every side we caught disjointed phrases of complaint or despair. "Horseflesh at ten schillings the pound," said one, "and bread at sixteen schillings." "Bread indeed!" an old woman retorted: "It's eight weeks gone since I have seen a crumb." "My little grandchild, the lame one, went last night." "Do you know what Gekke Betje, the washerwoman, did? She was starving. Her babe died, and she and her man—"

A louder cannon burst cut short this revelation. We made our way on toward the citadel of the town, passing a few soldiers here and there and many burghers with grim faces under their broad-brimmed felt hats.

"There is bread plenty yonder where the gunpowder is, and full pardon, too. Valdez shot another amnesty over the walls this morning."

An excited crowd immediately surrounded the speaker. "But the fleet!" they cried.

"The fleet is grounded fast on the Greenway polder. Boisot may turn his one eye seaward for a wind till famine and pestilence have carried off every mother's son of ye, and his ark will not be a rope's length nearer. Death by plague, death by starvation, death by fire and musketry—that is what the burgomaster offers us in return for glory for himself and kingdom for Orange."

"He asks us," said a sturdy citizen, "to hold out only twenty-four hours longer, and to pray meanwhile for an ocean wind."

"Ah, yes!" sneered the first speaker. "Pray on. There is bread enough locked in Pieter Adriaanszoon van der Werf's cellar. I warrant you that is what gives him so wonderful a stomach for resisting the Most Catholic King."

A young girl, with braided yellow hair, pressed through the crowd and confronted the malcontent. "Good people," said the maiden, "do not listen to him. He is a traitor with a Spanish heart. I am Pieter's daughter. We have no bread. We ate malt cakes and rapeseed like the rest of you till that was gone. Then we stripped the green leaves from the lime trees and willows in our garden and ate them. We have eaten even the thistles and weeds that grew between the stones by the canal. The coward lies."

Nevertheless, the insinuation had its effect. The throng, now become a mob, surged off in the direction of the burgomaster's house. One ruffian raised his hand to strike the girl out of the way. In a wink the cur was under the feet of his fellows, and Harry, panting and glowing, stood at the maiden's side, shouting defiance in good English at the backs of the rapidly retreating crowd.

With the utmost frankness she put both her arms around Harry's neck and kissed him.

"Thank you," she said. "You are a hearty lad. My name is Gertruyd van der Wert."

Harry was fumbling in his vocabulary for the proper Dutch phrases, but the girl would not stay for compliments. "They mean mischief to my father"; and she hurried us through several exceedingly narrow streets into a three-cornered market place dominated by a church with two spires. "There he is," she exclaimed, "on the steps of St. Pancras."

There was a tumult in the market place. The conflagration raging beyond the church and the voices of the Spanish and Walloon cannon outside of the walls were less angry than the roar of this multitude of desperate men clamoring for the bread that a single word from their leader's lips would bring them. "Surrender to the King!" they cried, "or we will send your dead body to Lammen as Leyden's token of submission."

One tall man, taller by half a head than any of the burghers confronting him, and so dark of complexion that we wondered how he could be the father of Gertruyd, heard the threat in silence. When the burgomaster spoke, the mob listened in spite of themselves.

"What is it you ask, my friends? That we break our vow and surrender Leyden to the Spaniards? That is to devote ourselves to a fate far more horrible than starvation. I have to keep the oath! Kill me, if you will have it so. I can die only once, whether by your hands, by the enemy's, or by the hand of God. Let us starve, if we must, welcoming starvation because it comes before dishonor. Your menaces do not move me; my life is at your disposal. Here, take my sword, thrust it into my breast, and divide my flesh among you to appease your hunger. So long as I remain alive expect no surrender."

There was silence again while the mob wavered. Then there were mutterings around us. Above these rang out the clear voice of the girl whose hand Harry still held—unnecessarily, it seemed to me.

"Do you not feel the sea wind? It has come at last. To the tower! And the first man there will see by moonlight the full white sails of the prince's ships."

For several hours I scoured the streets of the town, seeking in vain my cousin and his companion; the sudden movement of the crowd toward the Roman tower had separated us. On every side I saw evidences of the terrible chastisement that had brought this stout-hearted people to the verge of despair. A man with hungry eyes chased a lean rat along the bank of the canal. A young mother, with two dead babes in her arms, sat in a doorway to which they bore the bodies of her husband and father, just killed at the walls. In the middle of a deserted street I passed unburied corpses in a pile twice as high as my head. The pestilence had been there—kinder than the Spaniard, because it held out no treacherous promises while it dealt its blows.

Toward morning the wind increased to a gale. There was no sleep in Leyden, no more talk of surrender, no longer any thought or care about defense. These words were on the lips of everybody I met: "Daylight will bring the fleet!"

Did daylight bring the fleet? History says so, but I was not a witness. I know only that before dawn the gale culminated in a violent thunderstorm, and that at the same time a muffled explosion, heavier than the thunder, shook the town. I was in the crowd that watched from the Roman Mound for the first signs of the approaching relief. The concussion shook hope out of every face. "Their mine has reached the wall!" But where? I pressed forward until I found the burgomaster, who was standing among the rest. "Quick!" I whispered. "It is beyond the Cow Gate, and this side of the Tower of Burgundy." He gave me a searching glance, and then strode away, without making any attempt to quiet the general panic. I followed close at his heels.

It was a tight run of nearly half a mile to the rampart in question. When we reached the Cow Gate this is what we saw:

A great gap, where the wall had been, opening to the swampy fields beyond: in the moat, outside and below, a confusion of upturned faces, belonging to men who struggled like demons to achieve the breach, and who now gained a few feet and now were forced back; on the shattered rampart a handful of soldiers and burghers forming a living wall where masonry had failed; perhaps a double handful of women and girls, serving stones to the defenders and boiling water in buckets, besides pitch and oil and unslaked lime, and some of them quoiting tarred and burning hoops over the necks of the Spaniards in the moat; my cousin Harry leading and directing the men; the burgomaster's daughter Gertruyd encouraging and inspiring the women.

But what attracted my attention more than anything else was the frantic activity of a little figure in black, who, with a huge ladle, was showering molten lead on the heads of the assailing party. As he turned to the bonfire and kettle which supplied him with ammunition, his features came into the full light. I gave a cry of surprise: the ladler of molten lead was Professor Van Stopp.

The burgomaster Van der Werf turned at my sudden exclamation. "Who is that?" I said. "The man at the kettle?"

"That," replied Van der Werf, "is the brother of my wife, the clockmaker Jan Lipperdam."

The affair at the breach was over almost before we had had time to grasp the situation. The Spaniards, who had overthrown the wall of brick and stone, found the living wall impregnable. They could not even maintain their position in the moat; they were driven off into the darkness. Now I felt a sharp pain in my left arm. Some stray missile must have hit me while we watched the fight.

"Who has done this thing?" demanded the burgomaster. "Who is it that has kept watch on today while the rest of us were straining fools' eyes toward tomorrow?"

Gertruyd van der Werf came forward proudly, leading my cousin. "My father," said the girl, "he has saved my life."

"That is much to me," said the burgomaster, "but it is not all. He has saved Leyden and he has saved Holland."

I was becoming dizzy. The faces around me seemed unreal. Why were we here with these people? Why did the thunder and lightning forever continue? Why did the clockmaker, Jan Lipperdam, turn always toward me the face of Professor Van Stopp? "Harry!" I said, "come back to our rooms."

But though he grasped my hand warmly his other hand still held that of the girl, and he did not move. Then nausea overcame me. My head swam, and the breach and its defenders faded from sight.

V

Three days later I sat with one arm bandaged in my accustomed seat in Van Stopp's lecture room. The place beside me was vacant.

"We hear much," said the Hegelian professor, reading from a notebook in his usual dry, hurried tone, "of the influence of the sixteenth century upon the nineteenth. No philosopher, as far as I am aware, has studied the influence of the nineteenth century upon the sixteenth. If cause produces effect, does effect never induce cause? Does the law of heredity, unlike all other laws of this universe of mind and matter, operate in one direction only? Does the descendant owe everything to the ancestor, and the ancestor nothing to the descendant? Does destiny, which may seize upon our existence, and for its own purposes bear us far into the future, never carry us back into the past?"

I went back to my rooms in the Breede Straat, where my only companion was the silent clock.

✳

Thomas Hardy

(1840–1928)

THOMAS HARDY'S 1882 NOVEL, *Two on a Tower*, is not science fiction. However, a brief excerpt from it appears in this anthology because it addresses the kind of science-induced anxiety that pervades science fiction of the nineteenth century—and which continues today. A lively and interesting, if admittedly minor, novel of Hardy's, it demonstrates the limitations and virtues of realistic fiction in addressing the emotional and intellectual vertigo inspired by revelations of the ever larger and older cosmos—"a peep into a maelstrom of fire," as Hardy remarks.

The novel opens with a description of a solitary tower on the estate of the wealthy Lady Constantine, telling how she encounters therein an aspiring amateur astronomer, a young man named Swithin St. Cleeve. Hardy uses telescopic views of the heavens to inspire philosophical discussions about the impact of scientific discovery on thoughtful nonspecialists. These characters are more alive and convincing than many genre characters, but Jules Verne would have taken them into space for an unclouded gaze at the stars. No, he would have left Lady Constantine behind completely, but he would have made the stars themselves (not to mention his characters' vehicle) as important in the tale as St. Cleeve's yearning for them.

In her biography of Hardy, Claire Tomalin notes that he wrote

Two on a Tower for serialization, scribbling too quickly and cram-
ming the book with "far too much plot." It is rife with Hardy's usual
Shakespearean dependence upon coincidence and "hap," and also
infected with Hardy's conviction that women are intellectually inferior to men. St. Cleeve doesn't generously share his knowledge
with Lady Constantine; he condescendingly assumes that she won't
be able to understand his passion for science, and in doing so he
seems to reflect Hardy's own views.

The following passage, however, beautifully demonstrates how
some nineteenth-century intellectuals responded to the dizzying
way that the cosmos seemed to be growing larger and older by
the day. Hardy poignantly has his characters realize their cosmic
insignificance even as they are drawn to each other through the
primordial chemistry of romantic and sexual attraction. "This
slightly-built romance," writes Hardy in his preface to the 1895
edition, "was the outcome of a wish to set the emotional history of
two infinitesimal lives against the stupendous background of the
stellar universe, and to impart to readers the sentiment that of these
contrasting magnitudes the smaller might be the greater to them
as men."

The following excerpt comprises a section from chapter one and
a section from chapter two.

Monsters of Magnitude

(from *Two on a Tower*)

THE COLUMN NOW SHOWED itself as a much more important erection than it had appeared from the road, or the park, or the windows of Welland House, her residence hard by, whence she had surveyed it hundreds of times without ever feeling a sufficient interest in its details to investigate them. The column had been erected in the last century, as a substantial memorial of her husband's great-grandfather, a respectable officer who had fallen in the American war, and the reason of her lack of interest was partly owing to her relations with this husband, of which more anon. It was little beyond the sheer desire for something to do—the chronic desire of her curiously lonely life—that had brought her here now. She was in a mood to welcome anything that would in some measure disperse an almost killing ennui. She would have welcomed even a misfortune. She had heard that from the summit of the pillar four counties could be seen. Whatever pleasurable effect was to be derived from looking into four counties she resolved to enjoy to-day.

The fir-shrouded hill-top was (according to some antiquaries) an old Roman camp,—if it were not (as others insisted) an old British castle, or (as the rest swore) an old Saxon field of Witenagemote,—with remains of an outer and an inner vallum, a winding path leading up between their overlapping ends by an easy ascent. The spikelets from the trees formed a soft carpet over the route, and occasionally a brake of brambles barred the interspaces of the trunks. Soon she stood immediately at the foot of the column.

It had been built in the Tuscan order of classic architecture, and was really a tower, being hollow with steps inside. The gloom and solitude which prevailed round the base were remarkable. The sob of the environing trees was here expressively manifest; and moved by the light breeze their thin straight stems rocked in seconds, like inverted pendulums; while some boughs and twigs rubbed the pillar's sides, or occasionally clicked in catching each other. Below the level of their summits the masonry was lichen-stained and mildewed, for the sun never pierced that moaning cloud of blue-black vegetation. Pads of moss grew in the joints of the stone-work, and here and there shade-loving insects had engraved on the mortar patterns of no human style or meaning; but curious and suggestive. Above the trees the case was different: the pillar rose into the sky a bright and cheerful thing, unimpeded, clean, and flushed with the sunlight.

The spot was seldom visited by a pedestrian, except perhaps in the shooting season. The rarity of human intrusion was evidenced by the mazes of rabbit-runs, the feathers of shy birds, the exuviae of reptiles; as also by the well-worn paths of squirrels down the sides of trunks, and thence horizontally away. The fact of the plantation being an island in the midst of an arable plain sufficiently accounted for this lack of visitors. Few unaccustomed to such places can be aware of the insulating effect of ploughed ground, when no necessity compels people to traverse it. This rotund hill of trees and brambles, standing in the centre of a ploughed field of some ninety or a hundred acres, was probably visited less frequently than a rock would have been visited in a lake of equal extent.

She walked round the column to the other side, where she found the door through which the interior was reached. The paint, if it had ever had any, was all washed from the wood, and down the decaying surface of the boards liquid rust from the nails and hinges had run in red stains. Over the door was a stone tablet, bearing, apparently, letters or words; but the inscription, whatever it was, had been smoothed over with a plaster of lichen.

Here stood this aspiring piece of masonry, erected as the most conspicuous and ineffaceable reminder of a man that could be thought of; and yet the whole aspect of the memorial betokened forgetfulness. Probably not a dozen people within the district knew the name of the person commemorated, while perhaps not a soul remembered whether the column were hollow or solid, whether with or without a tablet explaining its date and purpose. She herself had lived within a mile of it for the last five years, and had never come near it till now.

She hesitated to ascend alone, but finding that the door was not fastened she pushed it open with her foot, and entered. A scrap of writing-paper lay within, and arrested her attention by its freshness. Some human being, then, knew the spot, despite her surmises. But as the paper had nothing on it no clue was afforded; yet feeling herself the proprietor of the column and of all around it her self-assertiveness was sufficient to lead her on. The staircase was lighted by slits in the wall, and there was no difficulty in reaching the top, the steps being quite unworn. The trap-door leading on to the roof was open, and on looking through it an interesting spectacle met her eye.

A youth was sitting on a stool in the centre of the lead flat which formed the summit of the column, his eye being applied to the end of a large telescope that stood before him on a tripod. This sort of presence was unexpected, and the lady started back into the shade of the opening. The only effect produced upon him by her footfall was an impatient wave of the hand, which he did without removing his eye from the instrument, as if to forbid her to interrupt him.

Pausing where she stood the lady examined the aspect of the individual who thus made himself so completely at home on a building which she deemed her unquestioned property. He was a youth who might properly have been characterized by a word the judicious chronicler would not readily use in such a connexion, preferring to

reserve it for raising images of the opposite sex. Whether because
no deep felicity is likely to arise from the condition, or from any
other reason, to say in these days that a youth is beautiful is not to
award him that amount of credit which the expression would have
carried with it if he had lived in the times of the Classical Dictionary.
So much, indeed, is the reverse the case that the assertion creates
an awkwardness in saying anything more about him. The beautiful
youth usually verges so perilously on the incipient coxcomb, who
is about to become the Lothario or Juan among the neighbouring
maidens, that, for the due understanding of our present young man,
his sublime innocence of any thought concerning his own material
aspect, or that of others, is most fervently asserted, and must be as
fervently believed.

Such as he was, there the lad sat. The sun shone full in his face,
and on his head he wore a black velvet skull-cap, leaving to view
below it a curly margin of very light shining hair, which accorded
well with the flush upon his cheek.

He had such a complexion as that with which Raffaelle enriches
the countenance of the youthful son of Zacharias,—a complexion
which, though clear, is far enough removed from virgin delicacy,
and suggests plenty of sun and wind as its accompaniment. His
features were sufficiently straight in the contours to correct the
beholder's first impression that the head was the head of a girl. Beside
him stood a little oak table, and in front was the telescope.

His visitor had ample time to make these observations; and she
may have done so all the more keenly through being herself of a
totally opposite type. Her hair was black as midnight, her eyes had no
less deep a shade, and her complexion showed the richness demanded
as a support to these decided features. As she continued to look at
the pretty fellow before her, apparently so far abstracted into some
speculative world as scarcely to know a real one, a warmer wave of
her warm temperament glowed visibly through her, and a qualified observer might from this have hazarded a guess that there was
Romance blood in her veins.

But even the interest attaching to the youth could not arrest her attention for ever, and as he made no further signs of moving his eye from the instrument she broke the silence with—

"What do you see?—something happening somewhere?"

"Yes, quite a catastrophe!" he automatically murmured, without moving round.

"What?"

"A cyclone in the sun."

The lady paused, as if to consider the weight of that event in the scale of terrene life.

"Will it make any difference to us here?" she asked.

The young man by this time seemed to be awakened to the consciousness that somebody unusual was talking to him; he turned, and started.

"I beg your pardon," he said. "I thought it was my relative come to look after me! She often comes about this time."

He continued to look at her and forget the sun, just such a reciprocity of influence as might have been expected between a dark lady and a flaxen-haired youth making itself apparent in the faces of each.

"Don't let me interrupt your observations," said she.

"Ah, no," said he, again applying his eye; whereupon his face lost the animation which her presence had lent it, and became immutable as that of a bust, though superadding to the serenity of repose the sensitiveness of life. The expression that settled on him was one of awe. Not unaptly might it have been said that he was worshipping the sun. Among the various intensities of that worship which have prevailed since the first intelligent being saw the luminary decline westward, as the young man now beheld it doing, his was not the weakest. He was engaged in what may be called a very chastened or schooled form of that first and most natural of adorations.

"But would you like to see it?" he recommended. "It is an event that is witnessed only about once in two or three years, though it may occur often enough."

She assented, and looked through the shaded eyepiece, and saw a whirling mass, in the centre of which the blazing globe seemed to be laid bare to its core. It was a peep into a maelstrom of fire, taking place where nobody had ever been or ever would be.

"It is the strangest thing I ever beheld," she said. Then he looked again; till wondering who her companion could be she asked, "Are you often here?"

"Every night when it is not cloudy, and often in the day."

"Ah, night, of course. The heavens must be beautiful from this point."

"They are rather more than that.". . . .

. . ."I aim at nothing less than the dignity and office of Astronomer Royal, if I live. Perhaps I shall not live."

"I don't see why you should suppose that," said she. "How long are you going to make this your observatory?"

"About a year longer—till I have obtained a practical familiarity with the heavens. Ah, if I only had a good equatorial!"

"What is that?"

"A proper instrument for my pursuit. But time is short, and science is infinite,—how infinite only those who study astronomy fully realize,—and perhaps I shall be worn out before I make my mark."

She seemed to be greatly struck by the odd mixture in him of scientific earnestness and melancholy mistrust of all things human. Perhaps it was owing to the nature of his studies.

"You are often on this tower alone at night?" she said.

"Yes; at this time of the year particularly, and while there is no moon. I observe from seven or eight till about two in the morning, with a view to my great work on variable stars. But with such a telescope as this—well, I must put up with it!"

"Can you see Saturn's ring and Jupiter's moons?"

He said drily that he could manage to do that, not without some contempt for the state of her knowledge.

"I have never seen any planet or star through a telescope."

"If you will come the first clear night, Lady Constantine, I will show you any number. I mean, at your express wish; not otherwise."

"I should like to come, and possibly may at some time. These stars that vary so much—sometimes evening stars, sometimes morning stars, sometimes in the east, and sometimes in the west— have always interested me."

"Ah—now there is a reason for your not coming. Your ignorance of the realities of astronomy is so satisfactory that I will not disturb it except at your serious request."

"But I wish to be enlightened."

"Let me caution you against it."

"Is enlightenment on the subject, then, so terrible?"

"Yes, indeed."

★   ★   ★   ★   ★

The stars were so bright as distinctly to show her the place, and now she could see a faint light at the top of the column, which rose like a shadowy finger pointing to the upper constellations. There was no wind, in a human sense; but a steady stertorous breathing from the fir-trees showed that, now as always, there was movement in apparent stagnation. Nothing but an absolute vacuum could paralyze their utterance.

The door of the tower was shut. It was something more than the freakishness which is engendered by a sickening monotony that had led Lady Constantine thus far, and hence she made no ado about admitting herself. Three years ago, when her every action was a thing of propriety, she had known of no possible purpose which could have led her abroad in a manner such as this.

She ascended the tower noiselessly. On raising her head above the hatchway she beheld Swithin bending over a scroll of paper which lay on the little table beside him. The small lantern that

illuminated it showed also that he was warmly wrapped up in
a coat and thick cap, behind him standing the telescope on its
frame.

What was he doing? She looked over his shoulder upon the paper,
and saw figures and signs. When he had jotted down something he
went to the telescope again.

"What are you doing to-night?" she said in a low voice.

Swithin started, and turned. The faint lamp-light was sufficient
to reveal her face to him.

"Tedious work, Lady Constantine," he answered, without
betraying much surprise. "Doing my best to watch phenomenal
stars, as I may call them."

"You said you would show me the heavens if I could come on a
starlight night. I have come."

Swithin, as a preliminary, swept round the telescope to Jupiter,
and exhibited to her the glory of that orb. Then he directed the
instrument to the less bright shape of Saturn.

"Here," he said, warming up to the subject, "we see a world
which is to my mind by far the most wonderful in the solar system.
Think of streams of satellites or meteors racing round and round
the planet like a fly-wheel, so close together as to seem solid matter!"
He entered further and further into the subject, his ideas gathering
momentum as he went on, like his pet heavenly bodies.

When he paused for breath she said, in tones very different from
his own, "I ought now to tell you that, though I am interested in
the stars, they were not what I came to see you about. . . . I first
thought of disclosing the matter to Mr. Torkingham; but I altered
my mind, and decided on you."

She spoke in so low a voice that he might not have heard her.
At all events, abstracted by his grand theme, he did not heed her. He
continued,—

"Well, we will get outside the solar system altogether,—leave the
whole group of sun, primary and secondary planets quite behind us
in our flight, as a bird might leave its bush and sweep into the whole

forest. Now what do you see, Lady Constantine?" He levelled the achromatic at Sirius.

She said that she saw a bright star, though it only seemed a point of light now as before.

"That's because it is so distant that no magnifying will bring its size up to zero. Though called a fixed star, it is, like all fixed stars, moving with inconceivable velocity; but no magnifying will show that velocity as anything but rest."

And thus they talked on about Sirius, and then about other stars

> . . . in the scrowl
> Of all those beasts, and fish, and fowl,
> With which, like Indian plantations,
> The learned stock the constellations,

till he asked her how many stars she thought were visible to them at that moment.

She looked around over the magnificent stretch of sky that their high position unfolded. "Oh, thousands, hundreds of thousands," she said absently.

"No. There are only about three thousand. Now, how many do you think are brought within sight by the help of a powerful telescope?"

"I won't guess."

"Twenty millions. So that, whatever the stars were made for, they were not made to please our eyes. It is just the same in everything; nothing is made for man."

"Is it that notion which makes you so sad for your age?" she asked, with almost maternal solicitude. "I think astronomy is a bad study for you. It makes you feel human insignificance too plainly."

"Perhaps it does. However," he added more cheerfully, "though I feel the study to be one almost tragic in its quality, I hope to be the new Copernicus. What he was to the solar system I aim to be to the systems beyond."

Then, by means of the instrument at hand, they travelled together from the earth to Uranus and the mysterious outskirts of the solar system; from the solar system to a star in the Swan, the nearest fixed star in the northern sky; from the star in the Swan to remoter stars; thence to the remotest visible; till the ghastly chasm which they had bridged by a fragile line of sight was realized by Lady Constantine.

"We are now traversing distances beside which the immense line stretching from the earth to the sun is but an invisible point," said the youth. "When, just now, we had reached a planet whose remoteness is a hundred times the remoteness of the sun from the earth, we were only a two thousandth part of the journey to the spot at which we have optically arrived now."

"Oh, pray don't; it overpowers me!" she replied, not without seriousness. "It makes me feel that it is not worth while to live; it quite annihilates me."

"If it annihilates your ladyship to roam over these yawning spaces just once, think how it must annihilate me to be, as it were, in constant suspension amid them night after night."

"Yes. . . . It was not really this subject that I came to see you upon, Mr. St. Cleeve," she began a second time. "It was a personal matter."

"I am listening, Lady Constantine."

"I will tell it you. Yet no,—not this moment. Let us finish this grand subject first; it dwarfs mine."

It would have been difficult to judge from her accents whether she were afraid to broach her own matter, or really interested in his. Or a certain youthful pride that he evidenced at being the elucidator of such a large theme, and at having drawn her there to hear and observe it, may have inclined her to indulge him for kindness' sake.

Thereupon he took exception to her use of the word "grand" as descriptive of the actual universe:

"The imaginary picture of the sky as the concavity of a dome whose base extends from horizon to horizon of our earth is grand, simply grand, and I wish I had never got beyond looking at it in that way. But the actual sky is a horror."

"A new view of our old friends, the stars," she said, smiling up at them.

"But such an obviously true one!" said the young man. "You would hardly think, at first, that horrid monsters lie up there waiting to be discovered by any moderately penetrating mind—monsters to which those of the oceans bear no sort of comparison."

"What monsters may they be?"

"Impersonal monsters, namely, Immensities. Until a person has thought out the stars and their inter-spaces, he has hardly learnt that there are things much more terrible than monsters of shape, namely, monsters of magnitude without known shape. Such monsters are the voids and waste places of the sky. Look, for instance, at those pieces of darkness in the Milky Way," he went on, pointing with his finger to where the galaxy stretched across over their heads with the luminousness of a frosted web. "You see that dark opening in it near the Swan? There is a still more remarkable one south of the equator, called the Coal Sack, as a sort of nickname that has a farcical force from its very inadequacy. In these our sight plunges quite beyond any twinkler we have yet visited. Those are deep wells for the human mind to let itself down into, leave alone the human body! and think of the side caverns and secondary abysses to right and left as you pass on!"

Lady Constantine was heedful and silent.

He tried to give her yet another idea of the size of the universe; never was there a more ardent endeavour to bring down the immeasurable to human comprehension! By figures of speech and apt comparisons he took her mind into leading-strings, compelling her to follow him into wildernesses of which she had never in her life even realized the existence.

"There is a size at which dignity begins," he exclaimed; "further on there is a size at which grandeur begins; further on there is a size at which solemnity begins; further on, a size at which awfulness begins; further on, a size at which ghastliness begins. That size faintly approaches the size of the stellar universe. So am I not right in saying that those minds who exert their imaginative powers to bury themselves in the depths of that universe merely strain their faculties to gain a new horror?"

Standing, as she stood, in the presence of the stellar universe, under the very eyes of the constellations, Lady Constantine apprehended something of the earnest youth's argument.

"And to add a new weirdness to what the sky possesses in its size and formlessness, there is involved the quality of decay. For all the wonder of these everlasting stars, eternal spheres, and what not, they are not everlasting, they are not eternal; they burn out like candles. You see that dying one in the body of the Greater Bear? Two centuries ago it was as bright as the others. The senses may become terrified by plunging among them as they are, but there is a pitifulness even in their glory. Imagine them all extinguished, and your mind feeling its way through a heaven of total darkness, occasionally striking against the black, invisible cinders of those stars. . . . If you are cheerful, and wish to remain so, leave the study of astronomy alone. Of all the sciences, it alone deserves the character of the terrible."

"I am not altogether cheerful."

"Then if, on the other hand, you are restless and anxious about the future, study astronomy at once. Your troubles will be reduced amazingly. But your study will reduce them in a singular way, by reducing the importance of everything. So that the science is still terrible, even as a panacea. It is quite impossible to think at all adequately of the sky—of what the sky substantially is, without feeling it as a juxtaposed nightmare. It is better—far better—for men to forget the universe than to bear it clearly in mind!. . . But you say the universe was not really what you came to see me about. What was it, may I ask, Lady Constantine?"

She mused, and sighed, and turned to him with something pathetic in her.

"The immensity of the subject you have engaged me on has completely crushed my subject out of me! Yours is celestial; mine lamentably human! And the less must give way to the greater."

※

Robert Louis Stevenson

(1850–1894)

AN EDINBURGH NATIVE, ROBERT Louis Stevenson was raised fiercely religious, but by his college years he was rejecting dogma. He enrolled in Edinburgh University in 1867, at the age of sixteen, studied engineering, then switched to law. He was called to the bar in 1876, the year after he published his first story, but he never worked in law. He wanted to write, and write he did, with luscious texture and contagious verve. Such decisions disappointed his father, who had repeatedly complained about young Robert's choices in education, companions, and beliefs or lack thereof—not to mention his broad-brimmed bohemian hats.

In 1880 Stevenson published *Edinburgh: Picturesque Notes*. In that small volume, in his letters, and in other writings, Stevenson recorded vivid glimpses of the crowded, lamplit streets of his native city. He immortalized a cripple leaning on a crutch in a gutter, wailing a sad Scottish song in a cracked voice as he held up his last three boxes of lucifer matches for sale. He wrote of the hush on Sunday mornings, when a man's footfall could be heard a few streets away, and the trees in walled gardens seemed to stand on tiptoe and listen to the silence, in stark contrast to a sickly little girl chanting obscene and blasphemous oaths while skipping rope.

This magical ability to conjure a scene, to sketch a character with a few quick brush strokes, served Stevenson well through a variety

of writings. One-legged Long John Silver in *Treasure Island* is a terri-
fyingly believable villain, in part because he often comes across as
sympathetic to the narrator, the convincingly brave but naive Jim
Hawkins. The personality of Modestine, the title character in his
1879 memoir *Travels with a Donkey in the Cévennes*, becomes as
memorable as the social dynamics of the South Sea island setting
of his 1892 novella *The Beach of Falesá*. His letters, diaries, notes—
all tremble with captured life. The same vivid sense of adventure
animates the rousing historical saga *Kidnapped*, mesmerizing ghost
stories such as "Olalla" and "Thrawn Janet," and his three-volume
account of journeying from Scotland to California (*The Amateur
Emigrant*, *Across the Plains*, and *The Silverado Squatters*). He even wrote
the perennially sunny compendium, *A Child's Garden of Verses*.

In October 1885, tormented by tubercular hemorrhaging aggra-
vated by medicinal cocaine, Stevenson's occasional slumber was
often interrupted by nightmares. One restless night he was calling
out in his sleep when his wife, Fanny, woke him.

"I was dreaming a fine bogey tale," he protested.

But it was too late; the dream was gone. The next morning he
began to write a story conjured by the dream. For three days he did
almost nothing but write, after which he read the thirty-thousand-
word novella to Fanny and her son, his stepson Lloyd Osbourne—
only to find his wife's response much cooler than he expected. It
should be more of an allegory, she argued, not just sensationalism.
Stevenson was furious, but apparently he also knew that Fanny was
an astute critic. He stomped back upstairs.

Osbourne recalled that soon Stevenson returned to say, "You're
right. I've missed the allegory, which is, after all, the whole point
of it."

To the dismay of wife and stepson, he tossed the rustling stack
of paper into the fireplace. Then he rewrote the book, making it
longer and richer. Accounts differ as to how much time Stevenson
invested in rewrite and polishing, but he was quick. Less than two
months later, Longmans, Green in London published it during the

first week of January 1886 as *Strange Case of Doctor Jekyll and Mister Hyde*. It was his greatest success so far. As the following selection demonstrates, Stevenson paid considerable attention to the ever-changing science around him. He wove many contemporary issues into his 1886 novella, beginning with well-known case studies of dual personality, but they gained resonance when he mixed in evolutionary fears and the recent notion of the violent criminal as an atavistic reversion to our brute past. The same year, Sigmund Freud set up a private practice in Vienna, and Frederic W. H. Myers, the founder of the Society for Psychical Research, described the "pitch to which the dissociation of memories, faculties, sensibilities may be carried, without resulting in mere insane chaos, mere demented oblivion." He called this condition "multiplex personality." Stevenson was way ahead of him.

A Horror of the Spirit

(from *Strange Case of Doctor Jekyll and Mister Hyde*)

DR. LANYON'S NARRATIVE

O N THE NINTH OF January, now four days ago, I received by the evening delivery a registered envelope, addressed in the hand of my colleague and old school-companion, Henry Jekyll. I was a good deal surprised by this; for we were by no means in the habit of correspondence; I had seen the man, dined with him, indeed, the night before; and I could imagine nothing in our intercourse that should justify formality of registration. The contents increased my wonder; for this is how the letter ran:

10th December, 18—

DEAR LANYON, You are one of my oldest friends; and although we may have differed at times on scientific questions, I cannot remember, at least on my side, any break in our affection. There was never a day when, if you had said to me, "Jekyll, my life, my honour, my reason, depend upon you," I would not have sacrificed my left hand to help you. Lanyon, my life, my honour my reason, are all at your mercy; if you fail me to-night I am lost. You might suppose, after this preface, that I am going to ask you for something dishonourable to grant. Judge for yourself.

I want you to postpone all other engagements for to-night—
ay, even if you were summoned to the bedside of an emperor; to
take a cab, unless your carriage should be actually at the door;
and with this letter in your hand for consultation, to drive straight
to my house. Poole, my butler, has his orders; you will find him
waiting your arrival with a locksmith. The door of my cabinet is
then to be forced: and you are to go in alone; to open the glazed
press (letter E) on the left hand, breaking the lock if it be shut;
and to draw out, with all its contents as they stand, the fourth
drawer from the top or (which is the same thing) the third from
the bottom. In my extreme distress of mind, I have a morbid fear
of misdirecting you; but even if I am in error, you may know
the right drawer by its contents: some powders, a phial and a
paper book. This drawer I beg of you to carry back with you to
Cavendish Square exactly as it stands.

That is the first part of the service: now for the second. You
should be back, if you set out at once on the receipt of this, long
before midnight; but I will leave you that amount of margin, not
only in the fear of one of those obstacles that can neither be
prevented nor foreseen, but because an hour when your servants
are in bed is to be preferred for what will then remain to do. At
midnight, then, I have to ask you to be alone in your consulting-
room, to admit with your own hand into the house a man who
will present himself in my name, and to place in his hands the
drawer that you will have brought with you from my cabinet.
Then you will have played your part and earned my gratitude
completely. Five minutes afterwards, if you insist upon an explanation, you will have understood that these arrangements are
of capital importance; and that by the neglect of one of them,
fantastic as they must appear, you might have charged your
conscience with my death or the shipwreck of my reason.

Confident as I am that you will not trifle with this appeal,
my heart sinks and my hand trembles at the bare thought of such
a possibility. Think of me at this hour, in a strange place, labouring

under a blackness of distress that no fancy can exaggerate, and yet well aware that, if you will but punctually serve me, my troubles will roll away like a story that is told.

Serve me, my dear Lanyon, and save
Your friend,
H. J.

P. S. I had already sealed this up when a fresh terror struck upon my soul. It is possible that the post office may fail me, and this letter not come into your hands until to-morrow morning. In that case, dear Lanyon, do my errand when it shall be most convenient for you in the course of the day; and once more expect my messenger at midnight. It may then already be too late; and if that night passes without event, you will know that you have seen the last of Henry Jekyll.

Upon the reading of this letter, I made sure my colleague was insane; but till that was proved beyond the possibility of doubt, I felt bound to do as he requested. The less I understood of this farrago, the less I was in a position to judge of its importance; and an appeal so worded could not be set aside without a grave responsibility. I rose accordingly from table, got into a hansom, and drove straight to Jekyll's house. The butler was awaiting my arrival; he had received by the same post as mine a registered letter of instruction, and had sent at once for a locksmith and a carpenter. The tradesmen came while we were yet speaking; and we moved in a body to old Dr. Denman's surgical theatre, from which (as you are doubtless aware) Jekyll's private cabinet is most conveniently entered. The door was very strong, the lock excellent; the carpenter avowed he would have great trouble and have to do much damage, if force were to be used; and the locksmith was near despair. But this last was a handy fellow, and after two hours' work, the door stood open. The press marked E was unlocked; and I took out the drawer, had it filled up with straw and tied in a sheet, and returned with it to Cavendish Square.

Here I proceeded to examine its contents. The powders were neatly enough made up, but not with the nicety of the dispensing chemist; so that it was plain they were of Jekyll's private manufacture; and when I opened one of the wrappers I found what seemed to me a simple crystalline salt of a white colour. The phial, to which I next turned my attention, might have been about half-full of a blood-red liquor, which was highly pungent to the sense of smell and seemed to me to contain phosphorus and some volatile ether. At the other ingredients I could make no guess.

The book was an ordinary version-book and contained little but a series of dates. These covered a period of many years, but I observed that the entries ceased nearly a year ago and quite abruptly. Here and there a brief remark was appended to a date, usually no more than a single word: "double" occurring perhaps six times in a total of several hundred entries; and once very early in the list and followed by several marks of exclamation, "total failure!!!" All this, though it whetted my curiosity, told me little that was definite. Here were a phial of some tincture, a paper of some salt, and the record of a series of experiments that had led (like too many of Jekyll's investigations) to no end of practical usefulness. How could the presence of these articles in my house affect either the honour, the sanity, or the life of my flighty colleague? If his messenger could go to one place, why could he not go to another? And even granting some impediment, why was this gentleman to be received by me in secret? The more I reflected the more convinced I grew that I was dealing with a case of cerebral disease: and though I dismissed my servants to bed, I loaded an old revolver, that I might be found in some posture of self-defence.

Twelve o'clock had scarce rung out over London, ere the knocker sounded very gently on the door. I went myself at the summons, and found a small man crouching against the pillars of the portico.

"Are you come from Dr. Jekyll?" I asked.

He told me "yes" by a constrained gesture; and when I had bidden him enter, he did not obey me without a searching backward glance into the darkness of the square. There was a policeman not far off, advancing with his bull's eye open; and at the sight, I thought my visitor started and made greater haste.

These particulars struck me, I confess, disagreeably; and as I followed him into the bright light of the consulting-room, I kept my hand ready on my weapon. Here, at last, I had a chance of clearly seeing him. I had never set eyes on him before, so much was certain. He was small, as I have said; I was struck besides with the shocking expression of his face, with his remarkable combination of great muscular activity and great apparent debility of constitution, and— last but not least—with the odd, subjective disturbance caused by his neighbourhood. This bore some resemblance to incipient rigour, and was accompanied by a marked sinking of the pulse. At the time, I set it down to some idiosyncratic, personal distaste, and merely wondered at the acuteness of the symptoms; but I have since had reason to believe the cause to lie much deeper in the nature of man, and to turn on some nobler hinge than the principle of hatred.

This person (who had thus, from the first moment of his entrance, struck in me what I can only describe as a disgustful curiosity) was dressed in a fashion that would have made an ordinary person laughable; his clothes, that is to say, although they were of rich and sober fabric, were enormously too large for him in every measurement— the trousers hanging on his legs and rolled up to keep them from the ground, the waist of the coat below his haunches, and the collar sprawling wide upon his shoulders. Strange to relate, this ludicrous accoutrement was far from moving me to laughter. Rather, as there was something abnormal and misbegotten in the very essence of the creature that now faced me—something seizing, surprising, and revolting—this fresh disparity seemed but to fit in with and to reinforce it; so that to my interest in the man's nature and character, there was added a curiosity as to his origin, his life, his fortune and status in the world.

These observations, though they have taken so great a space to be set down in, were yet the work of a few seconds. My visitor was, indeed, on fire with sombre excitement.

"Have you got it?" he cried. "Have you got it?" And so lively was his impatience that he even laid his hand upon my arm and sought to shake me.

I put him back, conscious at his touch of a certain icy pang along my blood. "Come, sir," said I. "You forget that I have not yet the pleasure of your acquaintance. Be seated, if you please." And I showed him an example, and sat down myself in my customary seat and with as fair an imitation of my ordinary manner to a patient, as the lateness of the hour, the nature of my pre-occupations, and the horror I had of my visitor, would suffer me to muster.

"I beg your pardon, Dr. Lanyon," he replied civilly enough. "What you say is very well founded; and my impatience has shown its heels to my politeness. I come here at the instance of your colleague, Dr. Henry Jekyll, on a piece of business of some moment; and I understood. . . ." He paused and put his hand to his throat, and I could see, in spite of his collected manner, that he was wrestling against the approaches of the hysteria—"I understood, a drawer . . ."

But here I took pity on my visitor's suspense, and some perhaps on my own growing curiosity.

"There it is, sir," said I, pointing to the drawer, where it lay on the floor behind a table and still covered with the sheet.

He sprang to it, and then paused, and laid his hand upon his heart: I could hear his teeth grate with the convulsive action of his jaws; and his face was so ghastly to see that I grew alarmed both for his life and reason.

"Compose yourself," said I.

He turned a dreadful smile to me, and as if with the decision of despair, plucked away the sheet. At sight of the contents, he uttered one loud sob of such immense relief that I sat petrified. And the next moment, in a voice that was already fairly well under control, "Have you a graduated glass?" he asked.

I rose from my place with something of an effort and gave him what he asked.

He thanked me with a smiling nod, measured out a few minims of the red tincture and added one of the powders. The mixture, which was at first of a reddish hue, began, in proportion as the crystals melted, to brighten in colour, to effervesce audibly, and to throw off small fumes of vapour. Suddenly and at the same moment, the ebullition ceased and the compound changed to a dark purple, which faded again more slowly to a watery green. My visitor, who had watched these metamorphoses with a keen eye, smiled, set down the glass upon the table, and then turned and looked upon me with an air of scrutiny.

"And now," said he, "to settle what remains. Will you be wise? will you be guided? will you suffer me to take this glass in my hand and to go forth from your house without further parley? or has the greed of curiosity too much command of you? Think before you answer, for it shall be done as you decide. As you decide, you shall be left as you were before, and neither richer nor wiser, unless the sense of service rendered to a man in mortal distress may be counted as a kind of riches of the soul. Or, if you shall so prefer to choose, a new province of knowledge and new avenues to fame and power shall be laid open to you, here, in this room, upon the instant; and your sight shall be blasted by a prodigy to stagger the unbelief of Satan."

"Sir," said I, affecting a coolness that I was far from truly possessing, "you speak enigmas, and you will perhaps not wonder that I hear you with no very strong impression of belief. But I have gone too far in the way of inexplicable services to pause before I see the end."

"It is well," replied my visitor. "Lanyon, you remember your vows: what follows is under the seal of our profession. And now, you who have so long been bound to the most narrow and material views, you who have denied the virtue of transcendental medicine, you who have derided your superiors—behold!"

He put the glass to his lips and drank at one gulp. A cry followed; he reeled, staggered, clutched at the table and held on, staring with injected eyes, gasping with open mouth; and as I looked there came, I thought, a change—he seemed to swell—his face became suddenly black and the features seemed to melt and alter—and the next moment, I had sprung to my feet and leaped back against the wall, my arm raised to shield me from that prodigy, my mind submerged in terror.

"O God!" I screamed, and "O God!" again and again; for there before my eyes—pale and shaken, and half-fainting, and groping before him with his hands, like a man restored from death—there stood Henry Jekyll!

What he told me in the next hour, I cannot bring my mind to set on paper. I saw what I saw, I heard what I heard, and my soul sickened at it; and yet now when that sight has faded from my eyes, I ask myself if I believe it, and I cannot answer. My life is shaken to its roots; sleep has left me; the deadliest terror sits by me at all hours of the day and night; I feel that my days are numbered, and that I must die; and yet I shall die incredulous. As for the moral turpitude that man unveiled to me, even with tears of penitence, I cannot, even in memory, dwell on it without a start of horror. I will say but one thing, Utterson, and that (if you can bring your mind to credit it) will be more than enough. The creature who crept into my house that night was, on Jekyll's own confession, known by the name of Hyde and hunted for in every corner of the land as the murderer of Carew.

HASTIE LANYON

HENRY JEKYLL'S FULL STATEMENT
OF THE CASE

I was born in the year 18—to a large fortune, endowed besides with excellent parts, inclined by nature to industry, fond of the respect of the wise and good among my fellow-men, and thus, as might have been supposed, with every guarantee of an honourable and distinguished future. And indeed the worst of my faults was a certain impatient gaiety of disposition, such as has made the happiness of many, but such as I found it hard to reconcile with my imperious desire to carry my head high, and wear a more than commonly grave countenance before the public. Hence it came about that I concealed my pleasures; and that when I reached years of reflection, and began to look round me and take stock of my progress and position in the world, I stood already committed to a profound duplicity of life. Many a man would have even blazoned such irreg- ularities as I was guilty of; but from the high views that I had set before me, I regarded and hid them with an almost morbid sense of shame. It was thus rather the exacting nature of my aspirations than any particular degradation in my faults, that made me what I was and, with even a deeper trench than in the majority of men, severed in me those provinces of good and ill which divide and compound man's dual nature. In this case, I was driven to reflect deeply and inveterately on that hard law of life, which lies at the root of reli- gion and is one of the most plentiful springs of distress. Though so profound a double-dealer, I was in no sense a hypocrite; both sides of me were in dead earnest; I was no more myself when I laid aside restraint and plunged in shame, than when I laboured, in the eye of day, at the furtherance of knowledge or the relief of sorrow and suffering. And it chanced that the direction of my scientific studies, which led wholly toward the mystic and the transcendental, re-acted and shed a strong light on this consciousness of the perennial war among my members. With every day, and from both sides of my intelligence, the moral and the intellectual, I thus drew steadily

nearer to that truth, by whose partial discovery I have been doomed
to such a dreadful shipwreck: that man is not truly one, but truly
two. I say two, because the state of my own knowledge does not
pass beyond that point. Others will follow, others will outstrip me
on the same lines; and I hazard the guess that man will be ultimately
known for a mere polity of multifarious, incongruous, and independent denizens. I, for my part, from the nature of my life, advanced
infallibly in one direction and in one direction only. It was on the
moral side, and in my own person, that I learned to recognise the
thorough and primitive duality of man; I saw that, of the two natures
that contended in the field of my consciousness, even if I could
rightly be said to be either, it was only because I was radically both;
and from an early date, even before the course of my scientific
discoveries had begun to suggest the most naked possibility of such
a miracle, I had learned to dwell with pleasure, as a beloved day-
dream, on the thought of the separation of these elements. If each,
I told myself, could but be housed in separate identities, life would
be relieved of all that was unbearable; the unjust delivered from the
aspirations might go his way, and remorse of his more upright twin;
and the just could walk steadfastly and securely on his upward path,
doing the good things in which he found his pleasure, and no longer
exposed to disgrace and penitence by the hands of this extraneous
evil. It was the curse of mankind that these incongruous fagots were
thus bound together that in the agonised womb of consciousness,
these polar twins should be continuously struggling. How, then,
were they dissociated?

I was so far in my reflections when, as I have said, a side-light
began to shine upon the subject from the laboratory table. I began
to perceive more deeply than it has ever yet been stated, the trembling immateriality, the mist-like transience of this seemingly so
solid body in which we walk attired. Certain agents I found to have
the power to shake and to pluck back that fleshly vestment, even as
a wind might toss the curtains of a pavilion. For two good reasons,
I will not enter deeply into this scientific branch of my confession.

First, because I have been made to learn that the doom and burthen of our life is bound for ever on man's shoulders, and when the attempt is made to cast it off, it but returns upon us with more unfamiliar and more awful pressure. Second, because, as my narrative will make, alas! too evident, my discoveries were incomplete. Enough, then, that I not only recognised my natural body for the mere aura and effulgence of certain of the powers that made up my spirit, but managed to compound a drug by which these powers should be dethroned from their supremacy, and a second form and countenance substituted, none the less natural to me because they were the expression, and bore the stamp, of lower elements in my soul.

I hesitated long before I put this theory to the test of practice. I knew well that I risked death; for any drug that so potently controlled and shook the very fortress of identity, might by the least scruple of an overdose or at the least inopportunity in the moment of exhibition, utterly blot out that immaterial tabernacle which I looked to it to change. But the temptation of a discovery so singular and profound, at last overcame the suggestions of alarm. I had long since prepared my tincture; I purchased at once, from a firm of wholesale chemists, a large quantity of a particular salt which I knew, from my experiments, to be the last ingredient required; and late one accursed night, I compounded the elements, watched them boil and smoke together in the glass, and when the ebullition had subsided, with a strong glow of courage, drank off the potion.

The most racking pangs succeeded: a grinding in the bones, deadly nausea, and a horror of the spirit that cannot be exceeded at the hour of birth or death. Then these agonies began swiftly to subside, and I came to myself as if out of a great sickness. There was something strange in my sensations, something indescribably new and, from its very novelty, incredibly sweet. I felt younger, lighter, happier in body; within I was conscious of a heady recklessness, a current of disordered sensual images running like a mill-race in my fancy, a solution of the bonds of obligation, an unknown but not an innocent freedom of the soul. I knew myself, at the first breath of this new life, to be more wicked, tenfold more wicked, sold a slave to my original evil; and the thought, in that moment, braced and delighted me like wine. I stretched out my hands, exulting in the freshness of these sensations; and in the act, I was suddenly aware that I had lost in stature.

There was no mirror, at that date, in my room; that which stands beside me as I write, was brought there later on and for the very purpose of these transformations. The night, however, was far gone into the morning—the morning, black as it was, was nearly ripe for the conception of the day—the inmates of my house were locked in the most rigorous hours of slumber; and I determined, flushed as I was with hope and triumph, to venture in my new shape as far as to my bedroom. I crossed the yard, wherein the constellations looked down upon me, I could have thought, with wonder, the first creature of that sort that their unsleeping vigilance had yet disclosed to them; I stole through the corridors, a stranger in my own house; and coming to my room, I saw for the first time the appearance of Edward Hyde.

I must here speak by theory alone, saying not that which I know, but that which I suppose to be most probable. The evil side of my nature, to which I had now transferred the stamping efficacy, was less robust and less developed than the good which I had just deposed. Again, in the course of my life, which had been, after all, nine-tenths a life of effort, virtue, and control, it had been much less exercised and much less exhausted. And hence, as I think, it came about that Edward Hyde was so much smaller, slighter, and younger than Henry Jekyll. Even as good shone upon the countenance of the one, evil was written broadly and plainly on the face of the other. Evil besides (which I must still believe to be the lethal side of man) had left on that body an imprint of deformity and decay. And yet when I looked upon that ugly idol in the glass, I was conscious of no repugnance, rather of a leap of welcome. This, too, was myself. It seemed natural and human. In my eyes it bore a livelier image of the spirit, it seemed more express and single, than the

imperfect and divided countenance I had been hitherto accustomed to call mine. And in so far I was doubtless right. I have
observed that when I wore the semblance of Edward Hyde, none
could come near to me at first without a visible misgiving of the
flesh. This, as I take it, was because all human beings, as we meet
them, are commingled out of good and evil: and Edward Hyde,
alone in the ranks of mankind, was pure evil.

I lingered but a moment at the mirror: the second and conclu-
sive experiment had yet to be attempted; it yet remained to be seen
if I had lost my identity beyond redemption and must flee before
daylight from a house that was no longer mine; and hurrying back
to my cabinet, I once more prepared and drank the cup, once more
suffered the pangs of dissolution, and came to myself once more with
the character, the stature, and the face of Henry Jekyll.

That night I had come to the fatal cross-roads. Had I approached
my discovery in a more noble spirit, had I risked the experiment
while under the empire of generous or pious aspirations, all must
have been otherwise, and from these agonies of death and birth, I
had come forth an angel instead of a fiend. The drug had no discrim-
inating action; it was neither diabolical nor divine; it but shook the
doors of the prison-house of my disposition; and like the captives
of Philippi, that which stood within ran forth. At that time my
virtue slumbered; my evil, kept awake by ambition, was alert and
swift to seize the occasion; and the thing that was projected was
Edward Hyde. Hence, although I had now two characters as well
as two appearances, one was wholly evil, and the other was still the
old Henry Jekyll, that incongruous compound of whose reformation
and improvement I had already learned to despair. The movement
was thus wholly toward the worse.

Even at that time, I had not yet conquered my aversion to the
dryness of a life of study. I would still be merrily disposed at times;
and as my pleasures were (to say the least) undignified, and I was
not only well known and highly considered, but growing toward
the elderly man, this incoherency of my life was daily growing more

unwelcome. It was on this side that my new power tempted me until I fell in slavery. I had but to drink the cup, to doff at once the body of the noted professor, and to assume, like a thick cloak, that of Edward Hyde. I smiled at the notion; it seemed to me at the time to be humorous; and I made my preparations with the most studious care. I took and furnished that house in Soho, to which Hyde was tracked by the police; and engaged as housekeeper a creature whom I well knew to be silent and unscrupulous. On the other side, I announced to my servants that a Mr. Hyde (whom I described) was to have full liberty and power about my house in the square; and to parry mishaps, I even called and made myself a familiar object, in my second character. I next drew up that will to which you so much objected; so that if anything befell me in the person of Dr. Jekyll, I could enter on that of Edward Hyde without pecuniary loss. And thus fortified, as I supposed, on every side, I began to profit by the strange immunities of my position.

Men have before hired bravos to transact their crimes, while their own person and reputation sat under shelter. I was the first that ever did so for his pleasures. I was the first that could thus plod in the public eye with a load of genial respectability, and in a moment, like a schoolboy, strip off these lendings and spring headlong into the sea of liberty. But for me, in my impenetrable mantle, the safety was complete. Think of it—I did not even exist! Let me but escape into my laboratory door, give me but a second or two to mix and swallow the draught that I had always standing ready; and whatever he had done, Edward Hyde would pass away like the stain of breath upon a mirror; and there in his stead, quietly at home, trimming the midnight lamp in his study, a man who could afford to laugh at suspicion, would be Henry Jekyll.

The pleasures which I made haste to seek in my disguise were, as I have said, undignified; I would scarce use a harder term. But in the hands of Edward Hyde, they soon began to turn toward the monstrous. When I would come back from these excursions, I was often plunged into a kind of wonder at my vicarious depravity. This familiar that I called out of my own soul, and sent forth alone to do his good pleasure, was a being inherently malign and villainous; his every act and thought centred on self; drinking pleasure with bestial avidity from any degree of torture to another; relentless like a man of stone. Henry Jekyll stood at times aghast before the acts of Edward Hyde; but the situation was apart from ordinary laws, and insidiously relaxed the grasp of conscience. It was Hyde, after all, and Hyde alone, that was guilty. Jekyll was no worse; he woke again to his good qualities seemingly unimpaired; he would even make haste, where it was possible, to undo the evil done by Hyde. And thus his conscience slumbered.

Into the details of the infamy at which I thus connived (for even now I can scarce grant that I committed it) I have no design of entering; I mean but to point out the warnings and the successive steps with which my chastisement approached. I met with one accident which, as it brought on no consequence, I shall no more than mention. An act of cruelty to a child aroused against me the anger of a passer-by, whom I recognised the other day in the person of your kinsman; the doctor and the child's family joined him; there were moments when I feared for my life; and at last, in order to pacify their too just resentment, Edward Hyde had to bring them to the door, and pay them in a cheque drawn in the name of Henry Jekyll. But this danger was easily eliminated from the future, by opening an account at another bank in the name of Edward Hyde himself; and when, by sloping my own hand backward, I had supplied my double with a signature, I thought I sat beyond the reach of fate.

Some two months before the murder of Sir Danvers, I had been out for one of my adventures, had returned at a late hour, and woke the next day in bed with somewhat odd sensations. It was in vain I looked about me; in vain I saw the decent furniture and tall proportions of my room in the square; in vain that I recognised the pattern of the bed-curtains and the design of the mahogany frame; something still kept insisting that I was not where I was, that I had not wakened where I seemed to be, but in the little room in Soho where I was accustomed to sleep in the body of Edward Hyde. I smiled to myself, and, in my psychological way began lazily to inquire into the elements of this illusion, occasionally, even as I did so, dropping back into a comfortable morning doze. I was still so engaged when, in one of my more wakeful moments, my eyes fell upon my hand. Now the hand of Henry Jekyll (as you have often remarked) was professional in shape and size: it was large, firm, white, and comely. But the hand which I now saw, clearly enough, in the yellow light of a mid-London morning, lying half shut on the bed-clothes, was lean, corded, knuckly, of a dusky pallor and thickly shaded with a swart growth of hair. It was the hand of Edward Hyde.

I must have stared upon it for near half a minute, sunk as I was in the mere stupidity of wonder, before terror woke up in my breast as sudden and startling as the crash of cymbals; and bounding from my bed, I rushed to the mirror. At the sight that met my eyes, my blood was changed into something exquisitely thin and icy. Yes, I had gone to bed Henry Jekyll, I had awakened Edward Hyde. How was this to be explained? I asked myself, and then, with another bound of terror—how was it to be remedied? It was well on in the morning; the servants were up; all my drugs were in the cabinet— a long journey down two pairs of stairs, through the back passage, across the open court and through the anatomical theatre, from where I was then standing horror-struck. It might indeed be possible to cover my face; but of what use was that, when I was unable to conceal the alteration in my stature? And then with an overpowering sweetness of relief, it came back upon my mind that the servants were already used to the coming and going of my second self. I had soon dressed, as well as I was able, in clothes of my own size: had soon passed through the house, where Bradshaw stared and drew back at seeing Mr. Hyde at such an hour and in such a strange array; and ten minutes later, Dr. Jekyll had returned to his own shape and was sitting down, with a darkened brow, to make a feint of breakfasting.

Small indeed was my appetite. This inexplicable incident, this reversal of my previous experience, seemed, like the Babylonian finger on the wall, to be spelling out the letters of my judgment; and I began to reflect more seriously than ever before on the issues and possibilities of my double existence. That part of me which I had the power of projecting, had lately been much exercised and nourished; it had seemed to me of late as though the body of Edward Hyde had grown in stature, as though (when I wore that form) I were conscious of a more generous tide of blood; and I began to spy a danger that, if this were much prolonged, the balance of my nature might be permanently overthrown, the power of voluntary change be forfeited, and the character of Edward Hyde become irrevocably mine. The power of the drug had not been always equally displayed. Once, very early in my career, it had totally failed me; since then I had been obliged on more than one occasion to double, and once, with infinite risk of death, to treble the amount; and these rare uncertainties had cast hitherto the sole shadow on my contentment. Now, however, and in the light of that morning's accident, I was led to remark that whereas, in the beginning, the difficulty had been to throw off the body of Jekyll, it had of late gradually but decidedly transferred itself to the other side. All things therefore seemed to point to this: that I was slowly losing hold of my original and better self, and becoming slowly incorporated with my second and worse.

Between these two, I now felt I had to choose. My two natures had memory in common, but all other faculties were most unequally shared between them. Jekyll (who was composite) now with the most sensitive apprehensions, now with a greedy gusto, projected and shared in the pleasures and adventures of Hyde; but Hyde was indifferent to Jekyll, or but remembered him as the mountain bandit remembers the cavern in which he conceals himself from pursuit. Jekyll had more than a father's interest; Hyde had more than a son's indifference. To cast in my lot with Jekyll, was to die to those appetites which I had long secretly indulged and had of late begun to pamper. To cast it in with Hyde, was to die to a thousand interests and aspirations, and to become, at a blow and for ever, despised and friendless. The bargain might appear unequal; but there was still another consideration in the scales; for while Jekyll would suffer smartingly in the fires of abstinence, Hyde would be not even conscious of all that he had lost. Strange as my circumstances were, the terms of this debate are as old and commonplace as man; much the same inducements and alarms cast the die for any tempted and trembling sinner; and it fell out with me, as it falls with so vast a majority of my fellows, that I chose the better part and was found wanting in the strength to keep to it.

Yes, I preferred the elderly and discontented doctor, surrounded by friends and cherishing honest hopes; and bade a resolute farewell to the liberty, the comparative youth, the light step, leaping impulses and secret pleasures, that I had enjoyed in the disguise of Hyde. I made this choice perhaps with some unconscious reservation, for I neither gave up the house in Soho, nor destroyed the clothes of Edward Hyde, which still lay ready in my cabinet. For two months, however, I was true to my determination; for two months I led a life of such severity as I had never before attained to, and enjoyed the compensations of an approving conscience. But time began at last to obliterate the freshness of my alarm; the praises of conscience began to grow into a thing of course; I began to be tortured with throes and longings, as of Hyde struggling after freedom; and at last, in an hour of moral weakness, I once again compounded and swallowed the transforming draught.

I do not suppose that, when a drunkard reasons with himself upon his vice, he is once out of five hundred times affected by the dangers that he runs through his brutish, physical insensibility; neither had I, long as I had considered my position, made enough allowance for the complete moral insensibility and insensate readiness to evil, which were the leading characters of Edward Hyde. Yet it was by these that I was punished. My devil had been long caged, he came out roaring. I was conscious, even when I took the draught, of a more unbridled, a more furious propensity to ill. It must have been this, I suppose, that stirred in my soul that tempest of impatience with which I listened to the civilities of my unhappy victim; I declare, at least, before God, no man morally sane could have been guilty of that crime upon so pitiful a provocation; and that I struck in no more reasonable spirit than that in which a sick child may break a plaything. But I had voluntarily stripped myself of all those balancing instincts by which even the worst of us continues to walk with some degree of steadiness among temptations; and in my case, to be tempted, however slightly, was to fall.

Instantly the spirit of hell awoke in me and raged. With a transport of glee, I mauled the unresisting body, tasting delight from every blow; and it was not till weariness had begun to succeed, that I was suddenly, in the top fit of my delirium, struck through the heart by a cold thrill of terror. A mist dispersed; I saw my life to be forfeit; and fled from the scene of these excesses, at once glorying and trembling, my lust of evil gratified and stimulated, my love of life screwed to the topmost peg. I ran to the house in Soho, and (to make assurance doubly sure) destroyed my papers; thence I set out through the lamplit streets, in the same divided ecstasy of mind, gloating on my crime, light-headedly devising others in the future, and yet still hastening and still hearkening in my wake for the steps of the avenger. Hyde had a song upon his lips as he compounded the draught, and as he drank it, pledged the dead man. The pangs of transformation had not done tearing him, before Henry Jekyll, with streaming tears of gratitude and remorse, had fallen upon his knees and lifted his clasped hands to God. The veil of self-indulgence was rent from head to foot, I saw my life as a whole: I followed it up from the days of childhood, when I had walked with my father's hand, and through the self-denying toils of my professional life, to arrive again and again, with the same sense of unreality, at the damned horrors of the evening. I could have screamed aloud; I sought with tears and prayers to smother down the crowd of hideous images and sounds with which my memory swarmed against me; and still, between the petitions, the ugly face of my iniquity stared into my soul. As the acuteness of this remorse began to die away, it was succeeded by a sense of joy. The problem of my conduct was solved. Hyde was thenceforth impossible; whether I would or not, I was now confined to the better part of my existence; and oh, how I rejoiced to think it! with what willing humility, I embraced anew the restrictions of natural life! with what sincere renunciation, I locked the door by which I had so often gone and come, and ground the key under my heel!

The next day, came the news that the murder had been over-looked, that the guilt of Hyde was patent to the world, and that the victim was a man high in public estimation. It was not only a crime, it had been a tragic folly. I think I was glad to know it; I think I was glad to have my better impulses thus buttressed and guarded by the terrors of the scaffold. Jekyll was now my city of refuge; let but Hyde peep out an instant, and the hands of all men would be raised to take and slay him.

I resolved in my future conduct to redeem the past; and I can say with honesty that my resolve was fruitful of some good. You know yourself how earnestly in the last months of last year, I laboured to relieve suffering; you know that much was done for others, and that the days passed quietly, almost happily for myself. Nor can I truly say that I wearied of this beneficent and innocent life; I think instead that I daily enjoyed it more completely; but I was still cursed with my duality of purpose; and as the first edge of my penitence wore off, the lower side of me, so long indulged, so recently chained down, began to growl for licence. Not that I dreamed of resuscitating Hyde; the bare idea of that would startle me to frenzy: no, it was in my own person, that I was once more tempted to trifle with my conscience; and it was as an ordinary secret sinner, that I at last fell before the assaults of temptation.

There comes an end to all things; the most capacious measure is filled at last; and this brief condescension to evil finally destroyed the balance of my soul. And yet I was not alarmed; the fall seemed natural, like a return to the old days before I had made discovery. It was a fine, clear, January day, wet under foot where the frost had melted, but cloudless overhead; and the Regent's Park was full of winter chirrupings and sweet with spring odours. I sat in the sun on a bench; the animal within me licking the chops of memory; the spiritual side a little drowsed, promising subsequent penitence, but not yet moved to begin. After all, I reflected, I was like my neighbours; and then I smiled, comparing myself with other men, comparing my active goodwill with the lazy cruelty of their neglect. And at the very moment of that vain-glorious thought, a qualm came over me, a horrid nausea and the most deadly shuddering. These passed away, and left me faint; and then as in its turn the faint-ness subsided, I began to be aware of a change in the temper of my thoughts, a greater boldness, a contempt of danger, a solution of the bonds of obligation. I looked down; my clothes hung formlessly on my shrunken limbs; the hand that lay on my knee was corded and hairy. I was once more Edward Hyde. A moment before I had been safe of all men's respect, wealthy, beloved—the cloth laying for me in the dining-room at home; and now I was the common quarry of mankind, hunted, houseless, a known murderer, thrall to the gallows.

My reason wavered, but it did not fail me utterly. I have more than once observed that, in my second character, my faculties seemed sharpened to a point and my spirits more tensely elastic; thus it came about that, where Jekyll perhaps might have succumbed, Hyde rose to the importance of the moment. My drugs were in one of the presses of my cabinet; how was I to reach them? That was the problem that (crushing my temples in my hands) I set myself to solve. The laboratory door I had closed. If I sought to enter by the house, my own servants would consign me to the gallows. I saw I must employ another hand, and thought of Lanyon. How was he to be reached? how persuaded? Supposing that I escaped capture in the streets, how was I to make my way into his presence? and how should I, an unknown and displeasing visitor, prevail on the famous

physician to rifle the study of his colleague, Dr. Jekyll? Then I
remembered that of my original character, one part remained to me:
I could write my own hand; and once I had conceived that kindling
spark, the way that I must follow became lighted up from end to
end.

Thereupon, I arranged my clothes as best I could, and summoning
a passing hansom, drove to an hotel in Portland Street, the name of
which I chanced to remember. At my appearance (which was indeed
comical enough, however tragic a fate these garments covered) the
driver could not conceal his mirth. I gnashed my teeth upon him
with a gust of devilish fury; and the smile withered from his face—
happily for him—yet more happily for myself, for in another instant
I had certainly dragged him from his perch. At the inn, as I entered,
I looked about me with so black a countenance as made the attendants tremble; not a look did they exchange in my presence; but
obsequiously took my orders, led me to a private room, and brought
me wherewithal to write. Hyde in danger of his life was a creature
new to me; shaken with inordinate anger, strung to the pitch of
murder, lusting to inflict pain. Yet the creature was astute; mastered
his fury with a great effort of the will; composed his two important letters, one to Lanyon and one to Poole; and that he might
receive actual evidence of their being posted, sent them out with
directions that they should be registered.

Thenceforward, he sat all day over the fire in the private room,
gnawing his nails; there he dined, sitting alone with his fears, the
waiter visibly quailing before his eye; and thence, when the night
was fully come, he set forth in the corner of a closed cab, and was
driven to and fro about the streets of the city. He, I say—I cannot
say, I. That child of Hell had nothing human; nothing lived in him
but fear and hatred. And when at last, thinking the driver had begun
to grow suspicious, he discharged the cab and ventured on foot,
attired in his misfitting clothes, an object marked out for observation, into the midst of the nocturnal passengers, these two base
passions raged within him like a tempest. He walked fast, hunted

by his fears, chattering to himself, skulking through the less-
frequented thoroughfares, counting the minutes that still divided
him from midnight. Once a woman spoke to him, offering, I think,
a box of lights. He smote her in the face, and she fled.

When I came to myself at Lanyon's, the horror of my old friend
perhaps affected me somewhat: I do not know; it was at least but a
drop in the sea to the abhorrence with which I looked back upon
these hours. A change had come over me. It was no longer the fear
of the gallows, it was the horror of being Hyde that racked me. I
received Lanyon's condemnation partly in a dream; it was partly in
a dream that I came home to my own house and got into bed. I
slept after the prostration of the day, with a stringent and profound
slumber which not even the nightmares that wrung me could avail
to break. I awoke in the morning shaken, weakened, but refreshed.
I still hated and feared the thought of the brute that slept within
me, and I had not of course forgotten the appalling dangers of the
day before; but I was once more at home, in my own house and
close to my drugs; and gratitude for my escape shone so strong in
my soul that it almost rivalled the brightness of hope.

I was stepping leisurely across the court after breakfast, drinking
the chill of the air with pleasure, when I was seized again with those
indescribable sensations that heralded the change; and I had but the
time to gain the shelter of my cabinet, before I was once again raging
and freezing with the passions of Hyde. It took on this occasion a
double dose to recall me to myself; and alas! Six hours after, as I sat
looking sadly in the fire, the pangs returned, and the drug had to
be re-administered. In short, from that day forth it seemed only by
a great effort as of gymnastics, and only under the immediate stimulation of the drug, that I was able to wear the countenance of Jekyll.
At all hours of the day and night, I would be taken with the premonitory shudder; above all, if I slept, or even dozed for a moment in
my chair, it was always as Hyde that I awakened. Under the strain
of this continually-impending doom and by the sleeplessness to
which I now condemned myself, ay, even beyond what I had thought

possible to man, I became, in my own person, a creature eaten up
and emptied by fever, languidly weak both in body and mind, and
solely occupied by one thought: the horror of my other self. But
when I slept, or when the virtue of the medicine wore off, I would
leap almost without transition (for the pangs of transformation grew
daily less marked) into the possession of a fancy brimming with
images of terror, a soul boiling with causeless hatreds, and a body
that seemed not strong enough to contain the raging energies of life.
The powers of Hyde seemed to have grown with the sickliness of
Jekyll. And certainly the hate that now divided them was equal on
each side. With Jekyll, it was a thing of vital instinct. He had now
seen the full deformity of that creature that shared with him some
of the phenomena of consciousness, and was co-heir with him to
death: and beyond these links of community, which in themselves
made the most poignant part of his distress, he thought of Hyde,
for all his energy of life, as of something not only hellish but inorganic. This was the shocking thing; that the slime of the pit seemed
to utter cries and voices; that the amorphous dust gesticulated and
sinned; that what was dead, and had no shape, should usurp the
offices of life. And this again, that that insurgent horror was knit
to him closer than a wife, closer than an eye; lay caged in his flesh,
where he heard it mutter and felt it struggle to be born; and at every
hour of weakness, and in the confidence of slumber, prevailed
against him and deposed him out of life. The hatred of Hyde for
Jekyll, was of a different order. His terror of the gallows drove him
continually to commit temporary suicide, and return to his subor-
dinate station of a part instead of a person; but he loathed the necessity, he loathed the despondency into which Jekyll was now fallen,
and he resented the dislike with which he was himself regarded.
Hence the ape-like tricks that he would play me, scrawling in my
own hand blasphemies on the pages of my books, burning the letters
and destroying the portrait of my father; and indeed, had it not been
for his fear of death, he would long ago have ruined himself in order
to involve me in the ruin. But his love of life is wonderful; I go

further: I, who sicken and freeze at the mere thought of him, when I recall the abjection and passion of this attachment, and when I know how he fears my power to cut him off by suicide, I find it in my heart to pity him.

It is useless, and the time awfully fails me, to prolong this description; no one has ever suffered such torments, let that suffice; and yet even to these, habit brought—no, not alleviation—but a certain callousness of soul, a certain acquiescence of despair; and my punishment might have gone on for years, but for the last calamity which has now fallen, and which has finally severed me from my own face and nature. My provision of the salt, which had never been renewed since the date of the first experiment, began to run low. I sent out for a fresh supply, and mixed the draught; the ebullition followed, and the first change of colour, not the second; I drank it and it was without efficiency. You will learn from Poole how I have had London ransacked; it was in vain; and I am now persuaded that my first supply was impure, and that it was that unknown impurity which lent efficacy to the draught.

About a week has passed, and I am now finishing this statement under the influence of the last of the old powders. This, then, is the last time, short of a miracle, that Henry Jekyll can think his own thoughts or see his own face (now how sadly altered!) in the glass. Nor must I delay too long to bring my writing to an end; for if my narrative has hitherto escaped destruction, it has been by a combination of great prudence and great good luck. Should the throes of change take me in the act of writing it, Hyde will tear it in pieces; but if some time shall have elapsed after I have laid it by, his wonderful selfishness and Circumscription to the moment will probably save it once again from the action of his ape-like spite. And indeed the doom that is closing on us both, has already changed and crushed him. Half an hour from now, when I shall again and for ever re-indue that hated personality, I know how I shall sit shuddering and weeping in my chair, or continue, with the most strained and fear-struck ecstasy of listening, to pace up and down this room (my last earthly refuge) and give ear to every sound of menace. Will Hyde die upon the scaffold? or will he find courage to release himself at the last moment? God knows; I am careless; this is my true hour of death, and what is to follow concerns another than myself. Here then, as I lay down the pen and proceed to seal up my confession, I bring the life of that unhappy Henry Jekyll to an end.

Alice W. Fuller

(dates unknown)

ALTHOUGH HERMAN MELVILLE ENVISIONED an automaton in his 1855 story "The Bell-Tower," Alice W. Fuller seems to have been the first writer to explore the possibilities of a convincingly human-looking robot. Her particular category, the android robot as romantic interest, has flourished ever since the 1895 publication of her story "A Wife Manufactured to Order." When Fritz Lang's brilliant silent film *Metropolis* premiered in 1927, the actress Brigitte Helm was so memorable in her dual role as Maria and the robot Maschinen-mensch that she appeared on many of the movie posters. In 1959 the TV program *The Twilight Zone* broadcast an episode about a man sentenced to fifty years of solitary confinement on an alien planet—until a compassionate former colleague brought the prisoner company in the form of a female robot. The actress Julie Newmar, probably best remembered as the first Catwoman on the campy 1960s *Batman* television series, had earlier starred as Rhoda the Robot in a 1964–65 series entitled *My Living Doll*. The idea is still flourishing in science fiction books and movies, with the disturbing 2015 movie *Ex Machina* a prime example.

"Alice W. Fuller" may have been a pseudonym. The author seems to have left behind no other work under this name, and her personal life is a blank. "A Wife Manufactured to Order" first appeared in the July 1895 issue of the diverse progressive monthly the *Arena*, which had been founded in Boston six years earlier and would survive only until 1909. Publishing writers such as Upton Sinclair and Hamlin Garland, the periodical supported human rights issues such as birth control, the right to unionize, and unchecked trusts' danger to democracy, and opposed child labor and other forms of exploitation of the powerless. It must have seemed a likely venue to be sympathetic to the tone of Fuller's pointed satire.

A Wife Manufactured to Order

A s I was going down G Street in the city of W—— a strange sign attracted my attention. I stopped, looked, fairly rubbed my eyes to see if they were rightly focused; yes, there it was plainly lettered in gilt: "Wives made to order! Satisfaction guaranteed or money refunded."

Well! well! does some lunatic live here, I wonder? By Jove! I will investigate. I had inherited (I suppose from my mother) a bit of curiosity, and the truth of the matter was this: now nearing the age of forty, I thought it might be advisable to settle down in a home of my own; but alas! to settle down to a life of strife and turmoil, that would not be pleasant; and that I should have to do, I knew very well, if I should marry any of my numerous lady acquaintances—especially Florence Ward, the one I most admired. She unfortunately had strong-minded ways, and inclinations to be investigating woman's rights, politics, theosophy, and all that sort of thing. Bah! I could never endure it. I should be miserable, and the outcome would be a separation; I knew it. To be dictated to, perhaps found fault with—no, no, it would never do; better be a bachelor and at least live in peace. But—what does this sign mean? I'll find out for myself.

A ring of the bell brought a little white-haired, wiry sort of a man to the door. "Walk in, walk in, sir," he said.

I asked for an explanation of the strange sign over the door.

"Just step right in here and be seated, sir. My master is engaged at present, sir, with a great politician who had to separate from his wife; was so fractious, sir, got so many strange notions in her head; in fact, she wanted to hold the reins herself. You may have seen it— the papers have been full of it. Why, law bless you, sir, the poor man couldn't say his soul was his own, and he is here now making arrangements with master to make him a quieter sort of wife, some one to do the honors of the home without feelin' neglected if he happens to be a little courteous to some of his young lady friends. You see, master makes 'em to order, makes 'em to think just as you do, just as you want 'em to; then you've got a happy home, something to live for. Beautiful—golly! I've seen some of the beautifulest women turned out, 'most make your mouth water to look at." And so the old man rattled on until I was quite bewildered.

I interrupted him by asking if I could see his master.

"Oh, certainly, sir; you just make yourself comfortable and I will let you know when he is through."

I sat for some time like one in a dream, wondering if this could be so, and with many wonderful modern inventions in mind I began to think it possible. And then there was a vision of a happy home, a wife beautiful as a dream, gentle and loving, without a thought for anyone but me; one who would never reproach me if I didn't happen to get home just at what she thought was the proper time; one who would not ask me to go to church when she knew it was against my wishes; one who would never find fault with me if I wished to go to a base-ball game on Sunday, or bother me to take her to the theatre or opera. A man, you know, can't give much time to such things without interfering greatly with his comfort. Oh! could all this be realized? But just then my reverie was broken by the old man, who was saying: "Just step this way. Master, let me introduce you to Mr. Charles Fitzsimmons."

Short, thick-set, florid complexion, pale blue eyes with a sinister twinkle, was the description of Mr. Sharper, whom I confronted.

Reaching out his hand, which was cold and clammy and reminded me very much of a piece of cold boiled pork, he said:

"Now, young man, what can I do for you? Want a life-companion, a pleasant one? Man of means, no doubt, and can enjoy yourself; a little fun now and then with the boys and no harm at all—none in the least. When a man comes home tired, doesn't like to be dictated to; want some one always to meet you with a smile, some one that doesn't expect you to be fondlin' and pettin' 'em all the time. I understand it—I know just how it is. Law bless my soul, I'e made more'n one man happy, and I've only been in the business a short time, too. Now, sir, I can get you up any style you want—*wax*, but can't be detected."

"Do you mean to say you manufacture a woman out of wax, who will talk?"

"That's just what I do; you give me the subjects you most enjoy talking upon, and tell me what kind of a looking wife you want, and leave the rest to me, and you will never regret it. I will furnish as many 'phones' as you wish; most men don't care for such a variety for a wife—too much talk, you know;" and he chuckled and laughed like a big baby.

"What are your prices, may I ask?"

"Well, it's owing a good deal to how they are got up—from five hundred to a thousand dollars."

"Well," I said, "I think that rather high."

"Dear man alive, a pleasant companion for life for a few hundred dollars! Most men don't grumble at all for the sake of having their own way and a pleasant home, and you see she ain't always asking for money." (Sure enough, I hadn't thought of that.)

"Very well, I will decide upon the matter and let you know."

"All right, young man; you'll come back. They all do, them as knows about it."

I went to my room at the hotel and thought it all out, thought of the pleasant evenings I could have with some one whose thoughts were like my own, some one who would not vex me by differing in opinion. I wondered what Florence would say. I really believed she cared for me, but she knew how I disliked so many of the topics she persisted in talking upon. What mattered it to me what Emerson said, or Edward Bellamy wrote, or Henry George, or Pentecost? what did I care about Hume or Huxley or Stuart Mill? any of those sciences, Christian Science or Divine Science or mind cure?—bah! it was all nonsense. The topics of the day were enough, and if I attended closely to my business I needed recreation, not such things as she would prescribe. Still Florence was interesting to talk to, and I rather liked her at times when she talked every-day talk; but I could not marry her, and it was her own fault. She knew my senti-ments, and if she would persist in going on as she did I couldn't help it.

Yes, I decided I would have a home of my own, and a wife made to order at once. Before leaving the city I made all necessary arrange-ments, hurried home, rented a house, and went to see old Susan Tyler, whom I engaged as housekeeper; she was deaf and had an impediment in her speech, but she was a fine housekeeper. All my preparations made, the ideal home! Oh! how my heart beat as I looked around!—what happiness to do as I liked, a beautiful, uncomplaining wife ready to grant every wish and meet me with a smile! What would the boys say when, out a little late at night, I should be so perfectly at ease? I could just see jealousy on their faces, and I laughed outright for joy. To-morrow I was going for my bride. Side-looks and innuendos were thrust at me from all quarters, but I was too happy to demur or explain. When I reached the city I could scarcely wait for the appointed time.

Alighting from the carriage the door was opened, and I was ushered into the presence of the most beautiful creature I had ever beheld. The hands extended towards mine, the lips opened, and a low, sweet voice said, "Dear Charles, how glad I am you have come!" I stood spellbound, and only a chuckle from Mr. Sharper brought me to my senses.

"Kiss your affianced, why don't you?" he said, and chuckled again.

I felt as though I wanted to knock him down for speaking so in that beautiful creature's presence. And then a little soft rippling laugh, and she moved towards me. Oh, could I get that beast to leave the room! Why did he stand there chuckling in that manner?

"Sir," I said, "you will oblige me by leaving the room for a few moments."

With that he chuckled still louder and muttered, "Bless me, I really believe he thinks her alive." Then to me: "To be sure, to be sure, but you only have a short time before going to the minister's, and I must show you how to adjust her. When you get home"— and he chuckled again—"you can be just as sentimental as you please, but just now we will attend to business. Here are a box of tubes made to talk as you wished them. They are adjusted so. Place the one you wish in your sleeve. You can carelessly touch her right here if there is any one around. Here is a spring in each hand and the tips of her fingers. I will give you a book of instructions, and you will soon learn to arrange her with very little effort, just to suit your- self, and I am sure you will be very happy. Now, sir, the time is up; you can go to the minister's."

As I put her wraps around her and drew her arm through mine she murmured so sweetly, "Thank you, dear." How glad I was to get out of the presence of that vile man who was constantly pulling or pushing her; I could scarcely keep my hands off from him, and my serene Margurette—for I decided to call her that—would only smile and say, "Thank you!" "Oh, how lovely!" "Ah, indeed!" I was almost vexed with her to think she did not resent it. I wanted her all to myself where I could have the smiles, and thought I should be thankful when we were in our own home.

During our journey I could not help noticing the admiring glances from my fellow travellers, but my beautiful wife did not return any of their looks. In fact, I overheard a couple of young dudes say, "Just wait till that old codger's back is turned, and we shall see whether she will have no smiles for any but him." I had half a notion to adjust her to give them some cutting reply and then go into the smoker awhile, for I was sure they would try to get into conversation with her; but pshaw! I hadn't ordered any tubes of that kind. I believed I'd send and get one in case of an emergency. No, I wouldn't have such in the house; I wanted an amiable wife, and when we were once at home it would not be necessary. I wouldn't *have* to go with her anywhere unless I wanted to. Only think of that!—never feel that my wife would ask me to go with her and I have to refuse, then ten to one have her cry and make a fuss about it. I knew how it was, for I had seen too much of that sort of thing in the homes of my friends.

Business ran smoothly; everything was perfect harmony; my home was heaven on earth. I smoked when I wished to, I went to my base-ball games, I stayed out as long as I pleased, played cards when I wished, drank champagne or whatever I fancied, in fact had as good a time as I did before marriage. My male friends congratu-lated me upon my good fortune, and I was considered the luckiest man anywhere around. No one knew how I had made the good luck for myself.

There are some things in life I could never understand. One of them is that, when everything seems so prosperous, calamity is so often in the wake. And that was the case with me. After so many prosperous years a financial crash came. I tried to ward it off; I was up early and late. Margurette never complained, but was always sweet and smiling, with the same endearing words. Sometimes as the years went by I felt as though I would not object to her differing with me a little, for variety's sake; still it was best. When I would say, "Margurette, do you really think so?" and I would speak so cross to her often—I don't know but that I did so more than was necessary; still a man must have some place where he can be himself, and if he can't have that privilege at home, what's the use of having a home?—but she was never out of patience, and my wife would only say, "Yes, darling," so low and sweet. I remember once I said, when I was worried more than usual, "I am damned tired of this sort of thing," and she laughed so sweetly and called me her "own precious boy."

But the crash came, and there was no use trying to stay it any longer. I came home sick and tired. It was nine o'clock at night, with a cold, drizzling rain falling. Susan had gone to bed sick, and forgotten to light a fire in the grate. I went into the library, where Margurette always waited for me. No lights; I stumbled over a chair. I accidentally touched Margurette. She put up her lips to kiss me and laughingly said, "Precious darling, tired to-night?" Great God! I came very near striking her.

"Margurette, don't call me darling, talk to me; talk to me about something—anything sensible. Don't you know I am a ruined man? Everything I have got has been swept away from me."

"There, precious, I love you;" and she laughed again.

"Did you not hear what I said?" I screamed.

But she only laughed the more and said, "Oh, how lovely!"

I rushed from the house. I could not endure it longer; I was like one mad. My first thought was, Where can I go, to whom can I go for sympathy? I cannot stand this strain much longer, and to show weakness to men, I could never do that. I will go to Florence, I said. I will see what she says. Strange I should think of her just then!

I asked the servant who admitted me for Miss Florence.

"She is indisposed and cannot see anyone to-night."

"But," I said, writing on a card hastily, "take this to her."

Only a few moments elapsed and she came in, holding out her hand in an assuring and friendly way. "I am surprised to see you to-night, Mr. Fitzsimmons."

"O Florence!" I cried, "I am in trouble. I believe I shall lose my mind if I cannot have someone to go to; and you, dear Florence, you will know my needs; you can counsel, you can understand me."

"Sir!" Florence said, "are you mad, that you come here to insult me?"

"But I love you. I know it. I love the traits that I once thought I despised."

"Stop where you are! I did not receive you to hear such language. You forget yourself and me; you forget that you are a married man—shame upon you for humiliating me so!"

"Florence, Florence, I am not married; it is all a lie, a deception."

"Have you lost your reason, Mr. Fitzsimmons? Sit down, pray, and let me call my father. You are ill."

"Stop," I cried, "I do not need your father. I need you. Listen to me. I imagined I could never be happy with a wife who differed in opinion from me. In fact, I had almost decided to remain single all the rest of my days, until I came across a man who manufactured wives to order. Wait, Florence, until I have finished—do not look at me so. I am indeed sane. My wife was manufactured to my own ideas, a perfect human being as I supposed."

"Mr. Fitzsimmons, let me call my father." And Florence started towards the door. She was so pale that she frightened me, but I clutched her frantically.

"Listen," I said; "will you go with me? I will prove that all I have told you is true."

My earnestness seemed to reassure her. She stopped as if carefully thinking, then asked me to repeat what I had already told her. Finally she said yes, she would go.

We were soon in the presence of my beautiful Margurette, whom I literally hated—I could not endure her face. "Now, Florence, see," I cried; and I had my wife talk the namby-pamby lingo I once thought so sweet. "Oh! how I hate her!" and I glared at her like a madman. "Florence, save me. I am a ruined man. Everything has been swept away—the last to-day. I am a pauper, an egotist, a bigot, a selfish—"

"Stop!" cried Florence. "You wrong yourself; you are a man in your prime. What if your money has gone, you have your health and your faculties, I guess" (and there was a merry twinkle in her eyes); "the whole world is before you, and best of all, no one to interfere with you or argue on disagreeable topics."

"O Florence! I am punished enough for my selfishness. O God!" and I threw myself on the couch, "were I not a pauper, too, there might be some hope for happiness yet."

"You are not a pauper," said Florence; "you are the master of your fate, and if you are not happy it is your own fault."

"Florence, I can never be happy without you. I know now it is too late."

"Too late—never say that. But could you be happy with me, 'a woman wedded to an idea,' 'strongminded'? Why, Charles, I am liable to investigate all sorts of scientific subjects and reforms. And then supposing I should talk about it sometimes; if it was not for that I might think of the matter. As far as money is concerned, that would have little to do with my actions. Still, Charles, upon the whole I should be afraid to marry the 'divorced' husband of so amiable a wife as your present one is. I, with my faults and imperfections!—the contrast would be too great."

"Florence, Florence," I said, "say no more. All I ask is, can you overlook my folly and take me for better, for worse? I have learned my lesson. I see now it is only a petty and narrow type of man who would wish to live only with his own personal echo. I want a woman, one who retains her individuality, a thinking woman. Will you be mine?"

"I will consider the matter favorably," said Florence; "but we shall have to wait a year, for opinion's sake, as I suppose there are not many who know how you had your late wife manufactured to order."

And we both laughed.

❋

Ambrose Bierce

(1842–1914?)

"*INFIDEL*: IN NEW YORK, one who does not believe in the Christian religion; in Constantinople, one who does."

This sly comment appeared first in Ambrose Bierce's newspaper column and in 1906 in his satirical collection *The Cynic's Word Book*, which was later redubbed with the title we know today: *The Devil's Dictionary*. It is a form of skepticism and pessimism as cure for social and linguistic codswallop. "Bitter Bierce," they called him, for his gloomy view of humanity. In one portrait, he leans against a mantle beside a skull whose stare can't match his own thoughtful frown.

Born in Ohio, Ambrose Gwinnett Bierce spent his adolescence in Indiana and his early adulthood managing a mine in the Dakotas. He served with distinction in the Civil War, fought at both Kennesaw Mountain and Shiloh, rescued a wounded comrade under fire, and suffered a severe head wound that kept him out of combat for only a few months before he returned. He edited various newspapers and magazines. He wrote for William Randolph Hearst's *San Francisco Examiner*, then continued the association from Washington, D.C.

In October 1913, at the age of seventy-one, Bierce decided to visit Mexico to learn more about its revolution and to interview the outlaw and revolutionary leader Pancho Villa. Along the way he visited the sites of his war experience. Traveling via Chattanooga and New Orleans, he crossed over the Rio Bravo into Ciudad Juárez in late November. The day after Christmas 1913, Bierce wrote to his secretary from Chihuahua, stating his plan to travel to where Pancho Villa was supposedly plotting to attack troops. Bierce was never heard from again. His disappearance without a trace has piqued the imagination of other writers ever since. Bierce appears in numerous fantasy and science fiction stories, as well as in a series of detective novels. Even Mexican novelist Carlos Fuentes couldn't resist the mystique; Bierce is a central character in his 1985 novel, *The Old Gringo*. One of Gregory Peck's last roles was playing Bierce in the 1989 film version.

Bierce wrote poetry and essays. Not surprisingly, the man who described a novel as "a short story padded" is best remembered for his elegant, economical stories. Probably his best known are "Chickamauga" and "An Occurrence at Owl Creek Bridge," either of which if published now would be called postmodern. A year after "Owl Creek" came another enduring story, a creepy oedipal vampire tale called "The Death of Halpin Frayser." Bierce reprinted all three in a collection with the perfect title of *Can Such Things Be?*, published on the first day of 1893. This volume has been hugely influential and is now a legendary milestone in the evolution of the weird tale.

The following brief accounts were first published under the title "Whither?" in the *San Francisco Examiner* in October 1888, signed "A. G. B.," but Bierce later retitled them with the more provocative "Mysterious Disappearances." The title sounds like a headline, and the overall tone mimics that of sensationalist news stories, so it is worth noting that the quoted expert Dr. Hern is fictional, like all the other details. Even now, however, you may run across them cited as true, at least in the rootless, self-sustaining literature of the occult. Because this anthology reprints Bierce's revised versions that appeared in book form before anywhere else, in its chronological roster the little group of anecdotes is dated 1893 rather than 1888. This is one of the first known stories about the possibility of moving from one dimension to another—in these cases, apparently unintentionally. Whether Bierce's own disappearance was voluntary, and whether it was into another dimension, is still not known.

Mysterious Disappearances

THE DIFFICULTY OF CROSSING A FIELD

One morning in July, 1854, a planter named Williamson, living six miles from Selma, Alabama, was sitting with his wife and a child on the veranda of his dwelling. Immediately in front of the house was a lawn, perhaps fifty yards in extent between the house and public road, or, as it was called, the "pike." Beyond this road lay a close-cropped pasture of some ten acres, level and without a tree, rock, or any natural or artificial object on its surface. At the time there was not even a domestic animal in the field. In another field, beyond the pasture, a dozen slaves were at work under an overseer.

Throwing away the stump of a cigar, the planter rose, saying: "I forgot to tell Andrew about those horses." Andrew was the overseer.

Williamson strolled leisurely down the gravel walk, plucking a flower as he went, passed across the road and into the pasture, pausing a moment as he closed the gate leading into it, to greet a passing neighbor, Armour Wren, who lived on an adjoining plantation. Mr. Wren was in an open carriage with his son James, a lad of thirteen. When he had driven some two hundred yards from the point of meeting, Mr. Wren said to his son: "I forgot to tell Mr. Williamson about those horses."

Mr. Wren had sold to Mr. Williamson some horses, which were to have been sent for that day, but for some reason not now remembered it would be inconvenient to deliver them until the morrow. The coachman was directed to drive back, and as the vehicle turned Williamson was seen by all three, walking leisurely across the pasture. At that moment one of the coach horses stumbled and came near falling. It had no more than fairly recovered itself when James Wren cried: "Why, father, what has become of Mr. Williamson?"

It is not the purpose of this narrative to answer that question.

Mr. Wren's strange account of the matter, given under oath in the course of legal proceedings relating to the Williamson estate, here follows:

My son's exclamation caused me to look toward the spot where I had seen the deceased [sic] an instant before, but he was not there, nor was he anywhere visible. I cannot say that at the moment I was greatly startled, or realized the gravity of the occurrence, though I thought it singular. My son, however, was greatly astonished and kept repeating his question in different forms until we arrived at the gate. My black boy Sam was similarly affected, even in a greater degree, but I reckon more by my son's manner than by anything he had himself observed. [This sentence in the testimony was stricken out.] As we got out of the carriage at the gate of the field, and while Sam was hanging [sic] the team to the fence, Mrs. Williamson, with her child in her arms and followed by several servants, came running down the walk in great excitement, crying: "He is gone, he is gone! O God! what an awful thing!" and many other such exclamations, which I do not distinctly recollect. I got from them the impression that they related to something more than the mere disappearance of her husband, even if that had occurred before her eyes. Her manner was wild, but not more so, I think, than was natural under the circumstances. I have no reason to think she had at that time lost her mind. I have never since seen nor heard of Mr. Williamson.

This testimony, as might have been expected, was corroborated in almost every particular by the only other eye-witness (if that is a proper term)—the lad James. Mrs. Williamson had lost her reason and the servants were, of course, not competent to testify. The boy James Wren had declared at first that he saw the disappearance, but there is nothing of this in his testimony given in court. None of the field hands working in the field to which Williamson was going had seen him at all, and the most rigorous search of the entire plantation and adjoining country failed to supply a clew. The most monstrous and grotesque fictions, originating with the blacks, were current in that part of the State for many years, and probably are to this day; but what has been here related is all that is certainly known of the matter. The courts decided that Williamson was dead, and his estate was distributed according to law.

AN UNFINISHED RACE

James Burne Worson was a shoemaker who lived in Leamington, Warwickshire, England. He had a little shop in one of the by-ways leading off the road to Warwick. In his humble sphere he was esteemed an honest man, although like many of his class in English towns he was somewhat addicted to drink. When in liquor he would make foolish wagers. On one of these too frequent occasions he was boasting of his prowess as a pedestrian and athlete, and the outcome was a match against nature. For a stake of one sovereign he undertook to run all the way to Coventry and back, a distance of something more than forty miles. This was on the 3rd day of September in 1873. He set out at once, the man with whom he had made the bet—whose name is not remembered—accompanied by Barham

Wise, a linen draper, and Hamerson Burns, a photographer, I think, following in a light cart or wagon.

For several miles Worson went on very well, at an easy gait, without apparent fatigue, for he had really great powers of endurance and was not sufficiently intoxicated to enfeeble them. The three men in the wagon kept a short distance in the rear, giving him occasional friendly "chaff" or encouragement, as the spirit moved them. Suddenly—in the very middle of the roadway, not a dozen yards from them, and with their eyes full upon him—the man seemed to stumble, pitched headlong forward, uttered a terrible cry and vanished! He did not fall to the earth—he vanished before touching it. No trace of him was ever discovered.

After remaining at and about the spot for some time, with aimless irresolution, the three men returned to Leamington, told their astonishing story and were afterward taken into custody. But they were of good standing, had always been considered truthful, were sober at the time of the occurrence, and nothing ever transpired to discredit their sworn account of their extraordinary adventure, concerning the truth of which, nevertheless, public opinion was divided, throughout the United Kingdom. If they had something to conceal, their choice of means is certainly one of the most amazing ever made by sane human beings.

CHARLES ASHMORE'S TRAIL

The family of Christian Ashmore consisted of his wife, his mother, two grown daughters, and a son of sixteen years. They lived in Troy, New York, were well-to-do, respectable persons, and had many friends, some of whom, reading these lines, will doubtless learn for the first time the extraordinary fate of the young man. From Troy the Ashmores moved in 1871 or 1872 to Richmond, Indiana, and a year or two later to the vicinity of Quincy, Illinois, where

Mr. Ashmore bought a farm and lived on it. At some little distance from the farmhouse was a spring with a constant flow of clear, cold water, whence the family derived its supply for domestic use at all seasons.

On the evening of the 9th of November in 1878, at about nine o'clock, young Charles Ashmore left the family circle about the hearth, took a tin bucket and started toward the spring. As he did not return, the family became uneasy, and going to the door by which he had left the house, his father called without receiving an answer. He then lighted a lantern and with the eldest daughter, Martha, who insisted on accompanying him, went in search. A light snow had fallen, obliterating the path, but making the young man's trail conspicuous; each footprint was plainly defined. After going a little more than half-way—perhaps seventy-five yards—the father, who was in advance, halted, and elevating his lantern stood peering intently into the darkness ahead.

"What is the matter, father?" the girl asked.

This was the matter: the trail of the young man had abruptly ended, and all beyond was smooth, unbroken snow. The last footprints were as conspicuous as any in the line; the very nail-marks were distinctly visible. Mr. Ashmore looked upward, shading his eyes with his hat held between them and the lantern. The stars were shining; there was not a cloud in the sky; he was denied the explanation which had suggested itself, doubtful as it would have been—a new snowfall with a limit so plainly defined. Taking a wide circuit round the ultimate tracks, so as to leave them undisturbed for further examination, the man proceeded to the spring, the girl following, weak and terrified. Neither had spoken a word of what both had observed. The spring was covered with ice, hours old.

Returning to the house they noted the appearance of the snow on both sides of the trail its entire length. No tracks led away from it.

The morning light showed nothing more. Smooth, spotless, unbroken, the shallow snow lay everywhere.

Four days later the grief-stricken mother herself went to the spring for water. She came back and related that in passing the spot where the footprints had ended she had heard the voice of her son and had been eagerly calling to him, wandering about the place, as she had fancied the voice to be now in one direction, now in another, until she was exhausted with fatigue and emotion. Questioned as to what the voice had said, she was unable to tell, yet averred that the words were perfectly distinct. In a moment the entire family was at the place, but nothing was heard, and the voice was believed to be an hallucination caused by the mother's great anxiety and her disordered nerves. But for months afterward, at irregular intervals of a few days, the voice was heard by the several members of the family, and by others. All declared it unmistakably the voice of Charles Ashmore; all agreed that it seemed to come from a great distance, faintly, yet with entire distinctness of articulation; yet none could determine its direction, nor repeat its words. The intervals of silence grew longer and longer, the voice fainter and farther, and by midsummer it was heard no more.

If anybody knows the fate of Charles Ashmore it is probably his mother. She is dead.

SCIENCE TO THE FRONT

In connection with this subject of "mysterious disappearance"—of which every memory is stored with abundant example—it is pertinent to note the belief of Dr. Hern, of Leipsic; not by way of explanation, unless the reader may choose to take it so, but because of its intrinsic interest as a singular speculation. This distinguished scientist has expounded his views in a book entitled "Verschwinden und Seine Theorie," which has attracted some attention, "particularly," says one writer, "among the followers of Hegel, and mathematicians who hold to the actual existence of a so-called non-Euclidean space—that is to say, of space which has more dimensions than length, breadth, and thickness—space in which it would be possible to tie a knot in an endless cord and to turn a rubber ball inside out without 'a solution of its continuity,'" or in other words, "without breaking or cracking it."

Dr. Hern believes that in the visible world there are void places— vacua, and something more—holes, as it were, through which animate and inanimate objects may fall into the invisible world and be seen and heard no more. The theory is something like this: Space is pervaded by luminiferous ether, which is a material thing—as much a substance as air or water, though almost infinitely more attenuated. All force, all forms of energy must be propagated in this; every process must take place in it which takes place at all. But let us suppose that cavities exist in this otherwise universal medium, as caverns exist in the earth, or cells in a Swiss cheese. In such a cavity there would be absolutely nothing. It would be such a vacuum as cannot be artificially produced; for if we pump the air from a receiver there remains the luminiferous ether. Through one of these cavities light could not pass, for there would be nothing to bear it. Sound could not come from it; nothing could be felt in it. It would not have a single one of the conditions necessary to the action of any of our senses. In such a void, in short, nothing whatever could occur. Now, in the words of the writer before quoted—the learned doctor himself nowhere puts it so concisely: "A man inclosed in such a closet could neither see nor be seen; neither hear nor be heard; neither feel nor be felt; neither live nor die, for both life and death are processes which can take place only where there is force, and in empty space no force could exist." Are these the awful conditions (some will ask) under which the friends of the lost are to think of them as existing, and doomed forever to exist?

Baldly and imperfectly as here stated, Dr. Hern's theory, in so far as it professes to be an adequate explanation of "mysterious disappearances," is open to many obvious objections; to fewer as he states it himself in the "spacious volubility" of his book. But even as expounded by its author it does not explain, and in truth is incompatible with some incidents of, the occurrences related in these memoranda: for example, the sound of Charles Ashmore's voice. It is not my duty to imbue facts and theories with affinity.

A. B.

H. G. Wells

(1866–1946)

IN 1885, THOMAS HUXLEY began his fifth and last year as professor of biology and dean of the Normal School of Science, which evolved into the Royal College of Science and is now part of Imperial College London. One of his students was a skinny, unkempt, but attentive nineteen-year-old named Herbert George Wells. He had previously slogged through unimpressive-sounding apprenticeships as draper, teacher, and chemist's assistant, before winning a scholarship that enabled him to study under his idol—the great Mr. Huxley, "Darwin's bulldog." Later Wells praised Huxley's morphology course for teaching "coherence and consistency," and most of all for instilling in his students a sense of research as not only the key to unlocking the secrets of the cosmos but also an exciting and ever-changing adventure. Slowly Wells earned a bachelor's degree in zoology.

Huxley died in 1895, the year that Wells published his first "scientific romance," *The Time Machine.* An uneven work, half satire and half melodrama, it often stops for speeches inspired by the author's Fabian socialism; throughout, it seems marked by Huxley's pessimistic view of the future of humanity. In Wells's version of evolution, adaptation to decadent civilization splits human beings into the effete Eloi and the Morlocks, a cross between Victorian ideas of the lumpenproletariat and prevailing notions about our simian ancestors. Wells explored a similar idea in his later dystopian novel *When the Sleeper Wakes.*

Apparently never resting his pen, Wells would go on to write dozens of novels and nonfiction books, leaving his mark on everyone from Arthur C. Clarke to Woody Allen. Although he wrote relatively realistic novels such as *The History of Mr. Polly,* Wells is remembered mostly for his pioneer science fiction. The straightforward titles of his books still conjure images that influenced not only a fledgling genre but much of twentieth-century literature and film: *The War of the Worlds, The Invisible Man, The Food of the Gods.* His shorter stories—such as "The Country of the Blind," "The Empire of the Ants," and "The Man Who Could Work Miracles"—have had almost as wide an influence.

From the first, Wells was analyzing the world around him and thinking ahead to how it might change in the future. In 1920, with the first edition of his monumental (if sometimes simplistic) *Outline of History*—which Wells began with prehistory—he began looking backward as well. In his books Wells not only responded to scientific advances but, like Jules Verne before him and many writers since, also predicted them. Leo Szilard, the Hungarian American physicist behind much of the Manhattan Project, claimed that his own work on the nuclear chain reaction was inspired by Wells's envisioning of accelerated radioactive decay in his 1914 novel *The World Set Free.*

Few cautionary fables about Frankensteinian tinkering are more powerful than the grisly account of a mad vivisectionist in the 1896 novel *The Island of Dr. Moreau.* Vivisection was a ferociously divisive topic in late Victorian England, having occupied the attention of everyone from Charles Darwin to Lewis Carroll. Racial degeneration, the influence of our animal nature on our supposedly nobler side, evolutionary legacies and potential, the dangers of dispassionate scientific tinkering—these and many other issues crowd the story, which is one of Wells's most suspenseful novels and surely his most horrific.

The general narrative is so well-known through movie versions that perhaps the reader will forgive the following spoilers. The novel follows the discoveries of shipwrecked Edward Prendick, an upper-class Englishman whose horror expresses the likely response of most of Wells's readers. Prendick himself becomes a captive of the greatest mad scientist in literature, as he witnesses the many creatures who suffer daily in Moreau's quest, both godlike and demonic, to reshape nature in his own form. In the fifteenth chapter—which follows in its entirety—Moreau finally describes his motivations and methods to Prendick. A student of Victorian natural history can't read H. G. Wells's pages without wondering what Thomas Huxley might have thought of them had he lived only one more year.

Monsters Manufactured

(from *The Island of Doctor Moreau*)

"AND NOW, PRENDICK, I will explain," said Doctor Moreau, so soon as we had eaten and drunk. "I must confess that you are the most dictatorial guest I ever entertained. I warn you that this is the last I shall do to oblige you. The next thing you threaten to commit suicide about, I shan't do,—even at some personal inconvenience."

He sat in my deck chair, a cigar half consumed in his white, dexterous-looking fingers. The light of the swinging lamp fell on his white hair; he stared through the little window out at the star-light. I sat as far away from him as possible, the table between us and the revolvers to hand. Montgomery was not present. I did not care to be with the two of them in such a little room.

"You admit that the vivisected human being, as you called it, is, after all, only the puma?" said Moreau. He had made me visit that horror in the inner room, to assure myself of its inhumanity.

"It is the puma," I said, "still alive, but so cut and mutilated as I pray I may never see living flesh again. Of all vile—"

"Never mind that," said Moreau; "at least, spare me those youthful horrors. Montgomery used to be just the same. You admit that it is the puma. Now be quiet, while I reel off my physiological lecture to you."

And forthwith, beginning in the tone of a man supremely bored, but presently warming a little, he explained his work to me. He was very simple and convincing. Now and then there was a touch of sarcasm in his voice. Presently I found myself hot with shame at our mutual positions.

The creatures I had seen were not men, had never been men. They were animals, humanised animals,—triumphs of vivisection.

"You forget all that a skilled vivisector can do with living things," said Moreau. "For my own part, I'm puzzled why the things I have done here have not been done before. Small efforts, of course, have been made,—amputation, tongue-cutting, excisions. Of course you know a squint may be induced or cured by surgery? Then in the case of excisions you have all kinds of secondary changes, pigmentary disturbances, modifications of the passions, alterations in the secretion of fatty tissue. I have no doubt you have heard of these things?"

"Of course," said I. "But these foul creatures of yours—"

"All in good time," said he, waving his hand at me; "I am only beginning. Those are trivial cases of alteration. Surgery can do better things than that. There is building up as well as breaking down and changing. You have heard, perhaps, of a common surgical operation resorted to in cases where the nose has been destroyed: a flap of skin is cut from the forehead, turned down on the nose, and heals in the new position. This is a kind of grafting in a new position of part of an animal upon itself. Grafting of freshly obtained material from another animal is also possible,—the case of teeth, for example. The grafting of skin and bone is done to facilitate healing: the surgeon places in the middle of the wound pieces of skin snipped from another animal, or fragments of bone from a victim freshly killed. Hunter's cock-spur—possibly you have heard of that— flourished on the bull's neck; and the rhinoceros rats of the Algerian zouaves are also to be thought of,—monsters manufactured by transferring a slip from the tail of an ordinary rat to its snout, and allowing it to heal in that position."

"Monsters manufactured!" said I. "Then you mean to tell me—"

"Yes. These creatures you have seen are animals carven and

wrought into new shapes. To that, to the study of the plasticity of living forms, my life has been devoted. I have studied for years, gaining in knowledge as I go. I see you look horrified, and yet I am telling you nothing new. It all lay in the surface of practical anatomy years ago, but no one had the temerity to touch it. It is not simply the outward form of an animal which I can change. The physiology, the chemical rhythm of the creature, may also be made to undergo an enduring modification,—of which vaccination and other methods of inoculation with living or dead matter are examples that will, no doubt, be familiar to you. A similar operation is the transfusion of blood,—with which subject, indeed, I began. These are all familiar cases. Less so, and probably far more extensive, were the operations of those mediaeval practitioners who made dwarfs and beggar-cripples, show-monsters,—some vestiges of whose art still remain in the preliminary manipulation of the young mountebank or contortionist. Victor Hugo gives an account of them in 'L'Homme qui Rit.'—But perhaps my meaning grows plain now. You begin to see that it is a possible thing to transplant tissue from one part of an animal to another, or from one animal to another; to alter its chemical reactions and methods of growth; to modify the articulations of its limbs; and, indeed, to change it in its most intimate structure.

"And yet this extraordinary branch of knowledge has never been sought as an end, and systematically, by modern investigators until I took it up! Some of such things have been hit upon in the last resort of surgery; most of the kindred evidence that will recur to your mind has been demonstrated as it were by accident,—by tyrants, by criminals, by the breeders of horses and dogs, by all kinds of untrained clumsy-handed men working for their own immediate ends. I was the first man to take up this question armed with antiseptic surgery, and with a really scientific knowledge of the laws of growth. Yet one would imagine it must have been practised in secret before. Such creatures as the Siamese Twins—And in the vaults of the Inquisition. No doubt their chief aim was artistic torture, but some at least of the inquisitors must have had a touch of scientific curiosity."

"But," said I, "these things—these animals talk!"

He said that was so, and proceeded to point out that the possibility of vivisection does not stop at a mere physical metamorphosis. A pig may be educated. The mental structure is even less determinate than the bodily. In our growing science of hypnotism we find the promise of a possibility of superseding old inherent instincts by new suggestions, grafting upon or replacing the inherited fixed ideas. Very much indeed of what we call moral education, he said, is such an artificial modification and perversion of instinct; pugnacity is trained into courageous self-sacrifice, and suppressed sexuality into religious emotion. And the great difference between man and monkey is in the larynx, he continued,—in the incapacity to frame delicately different sound-symbols by which thought could be sustained. In this I failed to agree with him, but with a certain incivility he declined to notice my objection. He repeated that the thing was so, and continued his account of his work.

I asked him why he had taken the human form as a model. There seemed to me then, and there still seems to me now, a strange wickedness for that choice.

He confessed that he had chosen that form by chance. "I might just as well have worked to form sheep into llamas and llamas into sheep. I suppose there is something in the human form that appeals to the artistic turn more powerfully than any animal shape can. But I've not confined myself to man-making. Once or twice—" He was silent, for a minute perhaps. "These years! How they have slipped by! And here I have wasted a day saving your life, and am now wasting an hour explaining myself!"

"But," said I, "I still do not understand. Where is your justification for inflicting all this pain? The only thing that could excuse vivisection to me would be some application—"

"Precisely," said he. "But, you see, I am differently constituted. We are on different platforms. You are a materialist."

"I am not a materialist," I began hotly.

"In my view—in my view. For it is just this question of pain that parts us. So long as visible or audible pain turns you sick; so long as your own pains drive you; so long as pain underlies your propositions about sin,—so long, I tell you, you are an animal, thinking a little less obscurely what an animal feels. This pain—"

I gave an impatient shrug at such sophistry.

"Oh, but it is such a little thing! A mind truly opened to what science has to teach must see that it is a little thing. It may be that save in this little planet, this speck of cosmic dust, invisible long before the nearest star could be attained—it may be, I say, that nowhere else does this thing called pain occur. But the laws we feel our way towards—Why, even on this earth, even among living things, what pain is there?"

As he spoke he drew a little penknife from his pocket, opened the smaller blade, and moved his chair so that I could see his thigh. Then, choosing the place deliberately, he drove the blade into his leg and withdrew it.

"No doubt," he said, "you have seen that before. It does not hurt a pin-prick. But what does it show? The capacity for pain is not needed in the muscle, and it is not placed there,—is but little needed in the skin, and only here and there over the thigh is a spot capable of feeling pain. Pain is simply our intrinsic medical adviser to warn us and stimulate us. Not all living flesh is painful; nor is all nerve, not even all sensory nerve. There's no tint of pain, real pain, in the sensations of the optic nerve. If you wound the optic nerve, you merely see flashes of light,—just as disease of the auditory nerve merely means a humming in our ears. Plants do not feel pain, nor the lower animals; it's possible that such animals as the starfish and crayfish do not feel pain at all. Then with men, the more intelligent they become, the more intelligently they will see after their own welfare, and the less they will need the goad to keep them out of danger. I never yet heard of a useless thing that was not ground out of existence by evolution sooner or later. Did you? And pain gets needless.

"Then I am a religious man, Prendick, as every sane man must be. It may be, I fancy, that I have seen more of the ways of this world's Maker than you,—for I have sought his laws, in my way, all my life, while you, I understand, have been collecting butter-flies. And I tell you, pleasure and pain have nothing to do with heaven or hell. Pleasure and pain—bah! What is your theologian's ecstasy but Mahomet's houri in the dark? This store which men and women set on pleasure and pain, Prendick, is the mark of the beast upon them,—the mark of the beast from which they came! Pain, pain and pleasure, they are for us only so long as we wriggle in the dust.

"You see, I went on with this research just the way it led me. That is the only way I ever heard of true research going. I asked a question, devised some method of obtaining an answer, and got a fresh question. Was this possible or that possible? You cannot imagine what this means to an investigator, what an intellectual passion grows upon him! You cannot imagine the strange, colour-less delight of these intellectual desires! The thing before you is no longer an animal, a fellow-creature, but a problem! Sympathetic pain,—all I know of it I remember as a thing I used to suffer from years ago. I wanted—it was the one thing I wanted—to find out the extreme limit of plasticity in a living shape."

"But," said I, "the thing is an abomination—"

"To this day I have never troubled about the ethics of the matter," he continued. "The study of Nature makes a man at last as remorse-less as Nature. I have gone on, not heeding anything but the ques-tion I was pursuing; and the material has—dripped into the huts yonder. It is really eleven years since we came here, I and Mont-gomery and six Kanakas. I remember the green stillness of the island and the empty ocean about us, as though it was yesterday. The place seemed waiting for me.

"The stores were landed and the house was built. The Kanakas founded some huts near the ravine. I went to work here upon what I had brought with me. There were some disagreeable things happened at first. I began with a sheep, and killed it after a day and a half by a slip of the scalpel. I took another sheep, and made a thing of pain and fear and left it bound up to heal. It looked quite human to me when I had finished it; but when I went to it I was discontented with it. It remembered me, and was terrified beyond imagination; and it had no more than the wits of a sheep. The more I looked at it the clumsier it seemed, until at last I put the monster out of its misery. These animals without courage, these fear-haunted, pain-driven things, without a spark of pugnacious energy to face torment,—they are no good for man-making.

"Then I took a gorilla I had; and upon that, working with infinite care and mastering difficulty after difficulty, I made my first man. All the week, night and day, I moulded him. With him it was chiefly the brain that needed moulding; much had to be added, much changed. I thought him a fair specimen of the negroid type when I had finished him, and he lay bandaged, bound, and motionless before me. It was only when his life was assured that I left him and came into this room again, and found Montgomery much as you are. He had heard some of the cries as the thing grew human,— cries like those that disturbed you so. I didn't take him completely into my confidence at first. And the Kanakas too, had realised something of it. They were scared out of their wits by the sight of me. I got Montgomery over to me—in a way; but I and he had the hardest job to prevent the Kanakas deserting. Finally they did; and so we lost the yacht. I spent many days educating the brute,—altogether I had him for three or four months. I taught him the rudiments of English; gave him ideas of counting; even made the thing read the alphabet. But at that he was slow, though I've met with idiots slower. He began with a clean sheet, mentally; had no memories left in his mind of what he had been. When his scars were quite healed, and he was no longer anything but painful and stiff, and able to converse a little, I took him yonder and introduced him to the Kanakas as an interesting stowaway.

"They were horribly afraid of him at first, somehow,—which offended me rather, for I was conceited about him; but his ways seemed so mild, and he was so abject, that after a time they received him and took his education in hand. He was quick to learn, very imitative and adaptive, and built himself a hovel rather better, it seemed to me, than their own shanties. There was one among the boys a bit of a missionary, and he taught the thing to read, or at least to pick out letters, and gave him some rudimentary ideas of morality; but it seems the beast's habits were not all that is desirable.

"I rested from work for some days after this, and was in a mind to write an account of the whole affair to wake up English physiology. Then I came upon the creature squatting up in a tree and gibbering at two of the Kanakas who had been teasing him. I threatened him, told him the inhumanity of such a proceeding, aroused his sense of shame, and came home resolved to do better before I took my work back to England. I have been doing better. But somehow the things drift back again: the stubborn beast-flesh grows day by day back again. But I mean to do better things still. I mean to conquer that. This puma—

"But that's the story. All the Kanaka boys are dead now; one fell overboard of the launch, and one died of a wounded heel that he poisoned in some way with plant-juice. Three went away in the yacht, and I suppose and hope were drowned. The other one—was killed. Well, I have replaced them. Montgomery went on much as you are disposed to do at first, and then—"

"What became of the other one?" said I, sharply,—"the other Kanaka who was killed?"

"The fact is, after I had made a number of human creatures I made a Thing." He hesitated.

"Yes," said I.

"It was killed."

"I don't understand," said I; "do you mean to say—"

"It killed the Kanakas—yes. It killed several other things that it caught. We chased it for a couple of days. It only got loose by accident—I never meant it to get away. It wasn't finished. It was purely an experiment. It was a limbless thing, with a horrible face, that writhed along the ground in a serpentine fashion. It was immensely strong, and in infuriating pain. It lurked in the woods for some days, until we hunted it; and then it wriggled into the northern part of the island, and we divided the party to close in upon it. Montgomery insisted upon coming with me. The man had a rifle; and when his body was found, one of the barrels was curved into the shape of an S and very nearly bitten through. Montgomery shot the thing. After that I stuck to the ideal of humanity—except for little things."

He became silent. I sat in silence watching his face.

"So for twenty years altogether—counting nine years in England—I have been going on; and there is still something in everything I do that defeats me, makes me dissatisfied, challenges me to further effort. Sometimes I rise above my level, sometimes I fall below it; but always I fall short of the things I dream. The human shape I can get now, almost with ease, so that it is lithe and graceful, or thick and strong; but often there is trouble with the hands and the claws,—painful things, that I dare not shape too freely. But it is in the subtle grafting and reshaping one must needs do to the brain that my trouble lies. The intelligence is often oddly low, with unaccountable blank ends, unexpected gaps. And least satisfactory of all is something that I cannot touch, somewhere—I cannot determine where—in the seat of the emotions. Cravings, instincts, desires that harm humanity, a strange hidden reservoir to burst forth suddenly and inundate the whole being of the creature with anger, hate, or fear. These creatures of mine seemed strange and uncanny to you so soon as you began to observe them; but to me, just after I make them, they seem to be indisputably human beings. It's afterwards, as I observe them, that the persuasion fades. First one animal trait, then another, creeps to the surface and stares out at me. But I will conquer yet! Each time I dip a living creature into the bath of burning pain, I say, 'This time I will burn out all the animal; this time I will make a rational creature of my own!' After all, what is ten years? Men have been a hundred thousand in the making." He thought darkly. "But I am drawing near the fastness. This puma of mine—" After a silence, "And they revert. As soon as my hand is taken from them the beast begins to creep back, begins to assert itself again." Another long silence.

"Then you take the things you make into those dens?" said I.

"They go. I turn them out when I begin to feel the beast in them, and presently they wander there. They all dread this house and me. There is a kind of travesty of humanity over there. Montgomery knows about it, for he interferes in their affairs. He has trained one or two of them to our service. He's ashamed of it, but I believe he half likes some of those beasts. It's his business, not mine. They only sicken me with a sense of failure. I take no interest in them. I fancy they follow in the lines the Kanaka missionary marked out, and have a kind of mockery of a rational life, poor beasts! There's something they call the Law. Sing hymns about 'all thine.' They build themselves their dens, gather fruit, and pull herbs—marry even. But I can see through it all, see into their very souls, and see there nothing but the souls of beasts, beasts that perish, anger and the lusts to live and gratify themselves.—Yet they're odd; complex, like everything else alive. There is a kind of upward striving in them, part vanity, part waste sexual emotion, part waste curiosity. It only mocks me. I have some hope of this puma. I have worked hard at her head and brain—

"And now," said he, standing up after a long gap of silence, during which we had each pursued our own thoughts, "what do you think? Are you in fear of me still?"

I looked at him, and saw but a white-faced, white-haired man, with calm eyes. Save for his serenity, the touch almost of beauty that resulted from his set tranquillity and his magnificent build, he might have passed muster among a hundred other comfortable old gentlemen. Then I shivered. By way of answer to his second question, I handed him a revolver with either hand.

"Keep them," he said, and snatched at a yawn. He stood up, stared at me for a moment, and smiled. "You have had two eventful days," said he. "I should advise some sleep. I'm glad it's all clear. Goodnight." He thought me over for a moment, then went out by the inner door.

I immediately turned the key in the outer one. I sat down again; sat for a time in a kind of stagnant mood, so weary, emotionally, mentally, and physically, that I could not think beyond the point at which he had left me. The black window stared at me like an eye. At last with an effort I put out the light and got into the hammock. Very soon I was asleep.

Wardon Allan Curtis

(1867–1940)

WARDON ALLAN CURTIS WAS born in the New Mexico Territory, to a father in the U.S. military, and graduated from the University of Wisconsin in 1889. For many years he was a journalist, writing for newspapers such as the *Chicago Daily News*, *Boston Herald*, and *Manchester Union*. A rambler, he settled in New Hampshire and died there.

He wrote numerous stories that fall into the science fiction category, including his novel *The Valley of Gwangi*, which was adapted into the 1969 movie of the same title, along with elements from many other monster movies, including dinosaurs animated by special-effects pioneer Ray Harryhausen. Curtis also wrote an Arabian Nights fantasy entitled "The Seal of Solomon the Great." Some of Curtis's strange and often gruesome tales were gathered, along with a sample of his detective and mainstream stories, into his 1903 collection *The Strange Adventures of Mr. Middleton*.

Curtis is forgotten now, except among cobwebbed anthologists who admire his outrageously free imagination in stories such as "The Monster of Lake LaMetrie," a pioneer in the now flourishing living-fossil scenario popular from Arthur Conan Doyle's *The Lost World* to Michael Crichton's modern take on it in *Jurassic Park*. It first appeared in the September 1899 issue of *Pearson's Magazine*. Nowadays it might be considered a founding text of the subgenre called "weird Western," an outlaw genus that comprises everything from the 1960s television program *The Wild Wild West* to the DC Comics series *Jonah Hex*, but which is particularly associated with contemporary writers such as Joe R. Lansdale, who merges Western themes with horror and fantasy.

The Monster of Lake LaMetrie

Being the narration of James McLennegan, M.D., Ph.D.

LAKE LAMETRIE, WYOMING.
APRIL 1ST, 1899.

Prof. Wilhelm G. Breyfogle,
University of Taychobera.
Dear Friend,—Inclosed you will find some portions of the diary it
has been my life-long custom to keep, arranged in such a manner
as to narrate connectedly the history of some remarkable occurrences that have taken place here during the last three years. Years
and years ago, I heard vague accounts of a strange lake high up in
an almost inaccessible part of the mountains of Wyoming. Various
incredible tales were related of it, such as that it was inhabited by
creatures which elsewhere on the globe are found only as fossils of
a long vanished time.

The lake and its surroundings are of volcanic origin, and not the
least strange thing about the lake is that it is subject to periodic
disturbances, which take the form of a mighty boiling in the centre,
as if a tremendous artesian well were rushing up there from the
bowels of the earth. The lake rises for a time, almost filling the basin
of black rocks in which it rests, and then recedes, leaving on the

shores mollusks and trunks of strange trees and bits of strange ferns which no longer grow—on the earth, at least—and are to be seen elsewhere only in coal measures and beds of stone. And he who casts hook and line into the dusky waters, may haul forth, ganoid fishes completely covered with bony plates.

All of this is described in the account written by Father LaMe-trie years ago, and he there advances the theory that the earth is hollow, and that its interior is inhabited by the forms of plant and animal life which disappeared from its surface ages ago, and that the lake connects with this interior region. Symmes' theory of polar orifices is well known to you. It is amply corroborated. I know that it is true now. Through the great holes at the poles, the sun sends light and heat into the interior.

Three years ago this month, I found my way through the mountains here to Lake LaMetrie accompanied by a single companion, our friend, young Edward Framingham. He was led to go with me not so much by scientific fervor, as by a faint hope that his health might be improved by a sojourn in the mountains, for he suffered from an acute form of dyspepsia that at times drove him frantic.

Beneath an overhanging scarp of the wall of rock surrounding the lake, we found a rudely-built stone-house left by the old cliff dwellers. Though somewhat draughty, it would keep out the infre-quent rains of the region, and serve well enough as a shelter for the short time which we intended to stay.

The extracts from my diary follow:

APRIL 29TH, 1896.
I have been occupied during the past few days in gathering spec-imens of the various plants which are cast upon the shore by the waves of this remarkable lake. Framingham does nothing but fish, and claims that he has discovered the place where the lake communicates with the interior of the earth, if, indeed, it does, and there seems to be little doubt of that. While fishing at a point

near the centre of the lake, he let down three pickerel lines tied together, in all nearly three hundred feet, without finding bottom. Coming ashore, he collected every bit of line, string, strap, and rope in our possession, and made a line five hundred feet long, and still he was unable to find the bottom.

MAY 2ND, EVENING.

The past three days have been profitably spent in securing specimens, and mounting and pickling them for preservation. Framingham has had a bad attack of dyspepsia this morning and is not very well. Change of climate had a brief effect for the better upon his malady, but seems to have exhausted its force much sooner than one would have expected, and he lies on his couch of dry water-weeds, moaning piteously. I shall take him back to civilisation as soon as he is able to be moved.

It is very annoying to have to leave when I have scarcely begun to probe the mysteries of the place. I wish Framingham had not come with me. The lake is roaring wildly without, which is strange, as it has been perfectly calm hitherto, and still more strange because I can neither feel nor hear the rushing of the wind, though perhaps that is because it is blowing from the south, and we are protected from it by the cliff. But in that case there ought to be no waves on this shore. The roaring seems to grow louder momentarily. Framingham——

MAY 3RD, MORNING.

Such a night of terror we have been through. Last evening, as I sat writing in my diary, I heard a sudden hiss, and, looking down, saw wriggling across the earthen floor what I at first took to be a serpent of some kind, and then discovered was a stream of water which, coming in contact with the fire, had caused the startling hiss. In a moment, other streams had darted in, and before I had collected my senses enough to move, the water was two inches deep everywhere and steadily rising.

Now I knew the cause of the roaring, and, rousing Framingham, I half dragged him, half carried him to the door, and digging our feet into the chinks of the wall of the house, we climbed up to its top. There was nothing else to do, for above us and behind us was the unscalable cliff, and on each side the ground sloped away rapidly, and it would have been impossible to reach the high ground at the entrance to the basin.

After a time we lighted matches, for with all this commotion there was little air stirring, and we could see the water, now halfway up the side of the house, rushing to the west with the force and velocity of the current of a mighty river, and every little while it hurled tree-trunks against the house-walls with a terrific shock that threatened to batter them down. After an hour or so, the roaring began to decrease, and finally there was an absolute silence. The water, which reached to within a foot of where we sat, was at rest, neither rising nor falling.

Presently a faint whispering began and became a stertorous breathing, and then a rushing like that of the wind and a roaring rapidly increasing in volume, and the lake was in motion again, but this time the water and its swirling freight of tree-trunks flowed by the house toward the east, and was constantly falling, and out in the centre of the lake the beams of the moon were darkly reflected by the sides of a huge whirlpool, streaking the surface of polished blackness down, down, down the vortex into the beginning of whose terrible depths we looked from our high perch.

This morning the lake is back at its usual level. Our mules are drowned, our boat destroyed, our food damaged, my specimens and some of my instruments injured, and Framingham is very ill. We shall have to depart soon, although I dislike exceedingly to do so, as the disturbance of last night, which is clearly like the one described by Father LaMetrie, has undoubtedly brought up from the bowels of the earth some strange and interesting things. Indeed, out in the middle of the lake where the whirlpool subsided, I can see a large quantity of floating things; logs and branches, most of them probably, but who knows what else?

Through my glass I can see a tree-trunk, or rather stump, of enormous dimensions. From its width I judge that the whole tree must have been as large as some of the Californian big trees. The main part of it appears to be about ten feet wide and thirty feet long. Projecting from it and lying prone on the water is a limb, or root, some fifteen feet long, and perhaps two or three feet thick. Before we leave, which will be as soon as Framingham is able to go, I shall make a raft and visit the mass of driftwood, unless the wind providentially sends it ashore.

MAY 4TH, EVENING.

A day of most remarkable and wonderful occurrences. When I arose this morning and looked through my glass, I saw that the mass of driftwood still lay in the middle of the lake, motionless on the glassy surface, but the great black stump had disappeared. I was sure it was not hidden by the rest of the driftwood, for yesterday it lay some distance from the other logs, and there had been no disturbance of wind or water to change its position. I therefore concluded that it was some heavy wood that needed to become but slightly waterlogged to cause it to sink.

Framingham having fallen asleep at about ten, I sallied forth to look along the shores for specimens, carrying with me a botanical can, and a South American machete, which I have possessed since a visit to Brazil three years ago, where I learned the usefulness of this sabre-like thing. The shore was strewn with bits of strange plants and shells, and I was stooping to pick one up, when suddenly I felt my clothes plucked, and heard a snap behind me, and turning about I saw—but I won't describe it until I tell what I did, for I did not fairly see the terrible creature until I had swung

my machete round and sliced off the top of its head, and then
tumbled down into the shallow water where I lay almost fainting.

Here was the black log I had seen in the middle of the lake, a
monstrous elasmosaurus, and high above me on the heap of rocks
lay the thing's head with its long jaws crowded with sabre-like
teeth, and its enormous eyes as big as saucers. I wondered that it
did not move, for I expected a series of convulsions, but no sound
of a commotion was heard from the creature's body, which lay
out of my sight on the other side of the rocks. I decided that my
sudden cut had acted like a stunning blow and produced a sort
of coma, and fearing lest the beast should recover the use of its
muscles before death fully took place, and in its agony roll away
into the deep water where I could not secure it, I hastily removed
the brain entirely, performing the operation neatly, though with
some trepidation, and restoring to the head the detached segment
cut off by my machete, I proceeded to examine my prize.

In length of body, it is exactly twenty-eight feet. In the widest
part it is eight feet through laterally, and is some six feet through
from back to belly. Four great flippers, rudimentary arms and
feet, and an immensely long, sinuous, swan-like neck, complete
the creature's body. Its head is very small for the size of the body
and is very round and a pair of long jaws project in front much
like a duck's bill. Its skin is a leathery integument of a lustrous
black, and its eyes are enormous hazel optics with a soft, melancholy stare in their liquid depths. It is an elasmosaurus, one of
the largest of antediluvian animals. Whether of the same species
as those whose bones have been discovered, I cannot say.

My examination finished, I hastened after Framingham, for I
was certain that this waif from a long past age would arouse
almost any invalid. I found him somewhat recovered from his
attack of the morning, and he eagerly accompanied me to the
elasmosaurus. In examining the animal afresh, I was astonished
to find that its heart was still beating and that all the functions of
the body except thought were being performed one hour after

the thing had received its death blow, but I knew that the hearts of sharks have been known to beat hours after being removed from the body, and that decapitated frogs live, and have all the powers of motion, for weeks after their heads have been cut off.

I removed the top of the head to look into it and here another surprise awaited me, for the edges of the wound were granulating and preparing to heal. The colour of the interior of the skull was perfectly healthy and natural, there was no undue flow of blood, and there was every evidence that the animal intended to get well and live without a brain. Looking at the interior of the skull, I was struck by its resemblance to a human skull; in fact, it is, as nearly as I can judge, the size and shape of the brain-pan of an ordinary man who wears a seven and an eighth hat. Examining the brain itself, I found it to be the size of an ordinary human brain, and singularly like it in general contour, though it is very inferior in fibre and has few convolutions.

MAY 5TH, MORNING.
Framingham is exceedingly ill and talks of dying, declaring that if a natural death does not put an end to his sufferings, he will commit suicide. I do not know what to do. All my attempts to encourage him are of no avail, and the few medicines I have no longer fit his case at all.

MAY 5TH, EVENING.
I have just buried Framingham's body in the sand of the lake shore. I performed no ceremonies over the grave, for perhaps the real Framingham is not dead, though such speculation seems utterly wild. To-morrow I shall erect a cairn upon the mound, unless indeed there are signs that my experiment is successful, though it is foolish to hope that it will be.

At ten this morning, Framingham's qualms left him, and he set forth with me to see the elasmosaurus. The creature lay in the place where we left it yesterday, its position unaltered, still breathing, all the bodily functions performing themselves. The wound in its head had healed a great deal during the night, and I daresay will be completely healed within a week or so, such is the rapidity with which these reptilian organisms repair damages to themselves. Collecting three or four bushels of mussels, I shelled them and poured them down the elasmosaurus's throat. With a convulsive gasp, they passed down and the great mouth slowly closed.

"How long do you expect to keep the reptile alive?" asked Framingham.

"Until I have gotten word to a number of scientific friends, and they have come here to examine it. I shall take you to the nearest settlement and write letters from there. Returning, I shall feed the elasmosaurus regularly until my friends come, and we decide what final disposition to make of it. We shall probably stuff it."

"But you will have trouble in killing it, unless you hack it to pieces, and that won't do. Oh, if I only had the vitality of that animal. There is a monster whose vitality is so splendid that the removal of its brain does not disturb it. I should feel very happy if someone would remove my body. If I only had some of that beast's useless strength."

"In your case, the possession of a too active brain has injured the body," said I. "Too much brain exercise and too little bodily exercise are the causes of your trouble. It would be a pleasant thing if you had the robust health of the elasmosaurus, but what a wonderful thing it would be if that mighty engine had your intelligence."

I turned away to examine the reptile's wounds, for I had brought my surgical instruments with me, and intended to dress them. I was interrupted by a burst of groans from Framingham and turning, beheld him rolling on the sand in an agony. I hastened to him, but before I could reach him, he seized my case of instruments, and taking the largest and sharpest knife, cut his throat from ear to ear.

"Framingham, Framingham," I shouted and, to my astonishment, he looked at me intelligently. I recalled the case of the
French doctor who, for some minutes after being guillotined,
answered his friends by winking.

"If you hear me, wink," I cried. The right eye closed and
opened with a snap. Ah, here the body was dead and the brain
lived. I glanced at the elasmosaurus. Its mouth, half closed over
its gleaming teeth, seemed to smile an invitation. The intelligence of the man and the strength of the brain. The living body
and the living brain. The curious resemblance of the reptile's
brain-pan to that of a man flashed across my mind.

"Are you still alive, Framingham?"

The right eye winked. I seized my machete, for there was no
time for delicate instruments. I might destroy all by haste and
roughness, I was sure to destroy all by delay. I opened the skull
and disclosed the brain. I had not injured it, and breaking the
wound of the elasmosaurus's head, placed the brain within. I
dressed the wound and, hurrying to the house, brought all my
store of stimulants and administered them.

For years the medical fraternity has been predicting that brain-
grafting will some time be successfully accomplished. Why has
it never been successfully accomplished? Because it has not been
tried. Obviously, a brain from a dead body cannot be used and
what living man would submit to the horrible process of having
his head opened, and portions of his brain taken for the use of
others?

The brains of men are frequently examined when injured and
parts of the brain removed, but parts of the brains of other men
have never been substituted for the parts removed. No uninjured
man has ever been found who would give any portion of his brain
for the use of another. Until criminals under sentence of death
are handed over to science for experimentation, we shall not
know what can be done in the way of brain-grafting. But public
opinion would never allow it.

Conditions are favourable for a fair and thorough trial of my experiment. The weather is cool and even, and the wound in the head of the elasmosaurus has every chance for healing. The animal possesses a vitality superior to any of our later day animals, and if any organism can successfully become the host of a foreign brain, nourishing and cherishing it, the elasmosaurus with its abundant vital forces can do it. It may be that a new era in the history of the world will begin here.

MAY 6TH, NOON.
I think I will allow my experiment a little more time.

MAY 7TH, NOON.
It cannot be imagination. I am sure that as I looked into the elasmosaurus's eyes this morning there was expression in them. Dim, it is true, a sort of mistiness that floats over them like the reflection of passing clouds.

MAY 8TH, NOON.
I am more sure than yesterday that there is expression in the eyes, a look of troubled fear, such as is seen in the eyes of those who dream nightmares with unclosed lids.

MAY 11TH, EVENING.
I have been ill, and have not seen the elasmosaurus for three days, but I shall be better able to judge the progress of the experiment by remaining away a period of some duration.

MAY 12TH, NOON.
I am overcome with awe as I realise the success that has so far crowned my experiment. As I approached the elasmosaurus this morning, I noticed a faint disturbance in the water near its flippers. I cautiously investigated, expecting to discover some fishes nibbling at the helpless monster, and saw that the commotion was

not due to fishes, but to the flippers themselves, which were feebly moving.

"Framingham, Framingham," I bawled at the top of my voice. The vast bulk stirred a little, a very little, but enough to notice. Is the brain, or Framingham, it would perhaps be better to say, asleep, or has he failed to establish connection with the body? Undoubtedly he has not yet established connection with the body, and this of itself would be equivalent to sleep, to unconsciousness. As a man born with none of the senses would be unconscious of himself, so Framingham, just beginning to establish connections with his new body, is only dimly conscious of himself and sleeps. I fed him, or it—which is the proper designation will be decided in a few days—with the usual allowance.

MAY 17TH, EVENING.

I have been ill for the past three days, and have not been out of doors until this morning. The elasmosaurus was still motionless when I arrived at the cove this morning. Dead, I thought; but I soon detected signs of breathing, and I began to prepare some mussels for it, and was intent upon my task, when I heard a slight, gasping sound, and looked up. A feeling of terror seized me. It was as if in response to some doubting incantations there had appeared the half-desired, yet wholly-feared and unexpected apparition of a fiend. I shrieked, I screamed, and the amphitheatre of rocks echoed and re-echoed my cries, and all the time the head of the elasmosaurus raised aloft to the full height of its neck, swayed about unsteadily, and its mouth silently struggled and twisted, as if in an attempt to form words, while its eyes looked at me now with wild fear and now with piteous intreaty.

"Framingham," I said.

The monster's mouth closed instantly, and it looked at me attentively, pathetically so, as a dog might look.

"Do you understand me?"

The mouth began struggling again, and little gasps and moans issued forth.

"If you understand me, lay your head on the rock."

Down came the head. He understood me. My experiment was a success. I sat for a moment in silence, meditating upon the wonderful affair, striving to realise that I was awake and sane, and then began in a calm manner to relate to my friend what had taken place since his attempted suicide.

"You are at present something in the condition of a partial paralytic, I should judge," said I, as I concluded my account. "Your mind has not yet learned to command your new body. I see you can move your head and neck, though with difficulty. Move your body if you can. Ah, you cannot, as I thought. But it will all come in time. Whether you will ever be able to talk or not, I cannot say, but I think so, however. And now if you cannot, we will arrange some means of communication. Anyhow, you are rid of your human body and possessed of the powerful vital apparatus you so much envied its former owner. When you gain control of yourself, I wish you to find the communication between this lake and the under-world, and conduct some explorations. Just think of the additions to geological knowledge you can make. I will write an account of your discovery, and the names of Framingham and McLennegan will be among those of the greatest geologists."

I waved my hands in my enthusiasm, and the great eyes of my friend glowed with a kindred fire.

JUNE 2ND, NIGHT.

The process by which Framingham has passed from his first powerlessness to his present ability to speak, and command the use of his corporeal frame, has been so gradual that there has been nothing to note down from day to day. He seems to have all the command over his vast bulk that its former owner had, and in addition speaks and sings. He is singing now. The north wind has risen with the fall of night, and out there in the darkness I hear the mighty organ pipe-tones of his tremendous, magnificent voice, chanting the solemn notes of the Gregorian, the full throated Latin words mingling with the roaring of the wind in a wild and weird harmony.

To-day he attempted to find the connection between the lake and the interior of the earth, but the great well that sinks down in the centre of the lake is choked with rocks and he has discovered nothing. He is tormented by the fear that I will leave him, and that he will perish of loneliness. But I shall not leave him. I feel too much pity for the loneliness he would endure, and besides, I wish to be on the spot should another of those mysterious convulsions open the connection between the lake and the lower world.

He is beset with the idea that should other men discover him, he may be captured and exhibited in a circus or museum, and declares that he will fight for his liberty even to the extent of taking the lives of those attempting to capture him. As a wild animal, he is the property of whomsoever captures him, though perhaps I can set up a title to him on the ground of having tamed him.

JULY 6TH.

One of Framingham's fears has been realised. I was at the pass leading into the basin, watching the clouds grow heavy and pendulous net appear over a knoll in the pass, followed by its bearer, a small man, unmistakably a scientist, but I did not note him well, for as he looked down into the valley, suddenly there burst forth with all the power and volume of a steam calliope, the tremendous voice of Framingham, singing a Greek song of Anacreon to the tune of "Where did you get that hat?" and the singer appeared in a little cove, the black column of his great neck raised aloft, his jagged jaws wide open.

That poor little scientist. He stood transfixed, his butterfly net dropped from his hand, and as Framingham ceased his singing, curvetted and leaped from the water and came down with a splash that set the whole cove swashing, and laughed a guffaw that echoed among the cliffs like the laughing of a dozen demons, he turned and sped through the pass at all speed.

I skip all entries for nearly a year. They are unimportant.

JUNE 30TH, 1897.

A change is certainly coming over my friend. I began to see it some time ago, but refused to believe it and set it down to imagination. A catastrophe threatens, the absorption of the human intellect by the brute body. There are precedents for believing it possible. The human body has more influence over the mind than the mind has over the body. The invalid, delicate Framingham with refined mind, is no more. In his stead is a roistering monster, whose boisterous and commonplace conversation betrays a constantly growing coarseness of mind.

No longer is he interested in my scientific investigations, but pronounces them all bosh. No longer is his conversation such as an educated man can enjoy, but slangy and diffuse iterations concerning the trivial happenings of our uneventful life. Where will it end? In the absorption of the human mind by the brute body? In the final triumph of matter over mind and the degradation of the most mundane force and the extinction of the celestial spark? Then, indeed, will Edward Framingham be dead, and over the grave of his human body can I fittingly erect a headstone, and then will my vigil in this valley be over.

FORT D. A. RUSSELL, WYOMING.
APRIL 15TH, 1899.

Prof. William G. Breyfogle.

DEAR SIR,—the inclosed intact manuscript and the fragments which accompany it, came into my possession in the manner I am about to relate and I inclose them to you, for whom they were intended by their late author. Two weeks ago, I was dispatched into the mountains after some Indians who had left their reservation, having under my command a company of infantry and two squads of cavalrymen with mountain howitzers. On the seventh day of our pursuit, which led us into a wild and unknown part of the mountains, we were startled at hearing from somewhere in front us a succession of bellowings of a very unusual nature, mingled with the cries of a human being apparently in the last extremity, and rushing over a rise before us, we looked down upon a lake and saw a colossal, indescribable thing engaged in rending the body of a man.

Observing us, it stretched its jaws and laughed, and in saying this, I wish to be taken literally. Part of my command cried out that it was the devil, and turned and ran. But I rallied them, and thoroughly enraged at what we had witnessed, we marched down to the shore, and I ordered the howitzers to be trained upon the murderous creature. While we were doing this, the thing kept up a constant blabbing that bore a distinct resemblance to human speech, sounding very much like the jabbering of an imbecile, or a drunk trying to talk. I gave the command to fire and to fire again, and the beast tore out into the lake in its death-agony, and sank.

With the remains of Dr. McLennegan, I found the foregoing manuscript intact, and the torn fragments of the diary from which it was compiled, together with other papers on scientific subjects, all of which I forward. I think some attempt should be made to secure the body of the elasmosaurus. It would be a priceless addition to any museum.

Arthur W. Fairchild.
Captain U.S.A.

❋

Grant Allen

(1848–1899)

NOWADAYS DISASTERS ARE A staple of both science fiction novels and Hollywood blockbusters, but they have a long heritage of folklore and literature behind them. Steeped from birth in the psychedelic revenge fantasies of the Book of Revelation, Western writers seem to have found it easy to replace religious with secular apocalypses, and like many other genres this one came of age during the nineteenth century. Mary Shelley wanders through nineteenth-century science fiction as often as she does through this anthology, and not surprisingly she wrote a novel on this theme—*The Last Man*, about a plague-ravaged society in the late twenty-first century. It was published in 1826 to mostly shocked reviews, but critics have since applauded its vision and daring. Six decades later, the English nature writer Richard Jefferies published *After London*, in which with Hitchcockian offhandedness he never explains the species of catastrophe that has destroyed the civilization whose return to nature he lovingly envisions. H. G. Wells playfully destroys half of England in *The War of the Worlds*, and in *The Time Machine* he envisions a far future time of apocalyptic decline.

Grant Allen's story "The Thames Valley Catastrophe" is a lesser work than these, but an example of the author's vivid imagination and breakneck narrative pacing, as well as his precise literate style. It fit not only into the disaster theme popular during the century, but even into its specialized habitat, the valley of the Thames River. Like many writers of his era, Allen disliked the noise and oppression of London—he fled to Sussex—and in this story he got his revenge.

Charles Grant Blairfindie Allen was born in Ontario, to a Scottish French mother from a prominent Canadian family and a father who had emigrated from Ireland. Homeschooled and then taught by a Yale tutor, he attended French and English universities and then majored in classics at Oxford. He taught Latin in various English schools and then moved to Jamaica to teach moral and mental philosophy. Such wide-ranging exposure to the world may have contributed to his lifelong freethinking approach to social conventions.

Soon Allen moved to England and pursued writing so passionately that his severe writer's cramp became a cautionary fable among colleagues, as he cranked out fifty or so volumes in a relatively short life. Beginning his career with the self-published volume *Physiological Aesthetics*, he eventually grew into a prolific and versatile professional. His nonfiction books ranged from *The Evolution of the Idea of God* to *The Colour-Sense* and included a brief biography of his friend Charles Darwin for Andrew Lang's series of "English Worthies." He was well versed in botany and wrote monographs on it; he was known for his encyclopedic ability to recognize countless plants at a glance.

Allen's diverse resume includes popular novels such as *The Typewriter Girl* and *A Bride from the Desert*. Perhaps his most famous work during his lifetime was the 1895 succès de scandale *The Woman Who Did*, a sympathetic novel about a well-educated young woman who chooses to have a child outside of wedlock. Marriage, religion, the rest of society—Allen remained a compassionate freethinker and skeptic about everything.

He is remembered now for his crime fiction. His legacy includes two memorable female amateur detectives, one featured in the 1899 episodic novel *Miss Cayley's Adventures* and the other the following year in *Hilda Wade: A Woman with Tenacity of Purpose*. (Allen died before he finished this novel, which his friend Arthur Conan Doyle then completed.) Both are indomitable adventurers, Miss Cayley for the thrill of adventure itself, Miss Wade to avenge the murder of her father. And Allen created one of the immortal rogues of the genre—the ingenious Colonel Clay, one of the earliest series characters who is a criminal yet appears in the role of hero rather than villain.

"The Thames Valley Catastrophe" first appeared in the December 1897 issue of the *Strand Magazine*. It was not Grant Allen's only foray into science fiction. In *The British Barbarians*, for example, he brought a twenty-fifth-century anthropologist back to Grant's own era to ruefully anatomize the author's fellow Brits.

The Thames Valley Catastrophe

IT CAN SCARCELY BE necessary for me to mention, I suppose, at this time of day, that I was one of the earliest and fullest observers of the sad series of events which finally brought about the transference of the seat of Government of these islands from London to Manchester. Nor need I allude here to the conspicuous position which my narrative naturally occupies in the Blue-book on the Thames Valley Catastrophe (vol. ii., part vii), ordered by Parliament in its preliminary Session under the new regime at Birmingham. But I think it also incumbent upon me, for the benefit of posterity, to supplement that necessarily dry and formal statement by a more circumstantial account of my personal adventures during the terrible period.

I am aware, of course, that my poor little story can possess little interest for our contemporaries, wearied out as they are with details of the disaster, and surfeited with tedious scientific discussions as to its origin and nature. But in after years, I venture to believe, when the crowning calamity of the nineteenth century has grown picturesque and, so to speak, ivy-clad, by reason of its remoteness (like the Great Plague or the Great Fire of London with ourselves), the world may possibly desire to hear how this unparalleled convulsion affected the feelings and fortunes of a single family in the middle rank of life, and in a part of London neither squalid nor fashionable.

It is such personal touches of human nature that give reality to history, which without them must become, as a great writer has finely said, nothing more than an old almanac. I shall not apologize, therefore, for being frankly egoistic and domestic in my reminiscences of that appalling day: for I know that those who desire to seek scientific information on the subject will look for it, not in vain, in the eight bulky volumes of the recent Blue-book. I shall concern myself here with the great event merely as it appeared to myself, a Government servant of the second grade, and in its relations to my own wife, my home, and my children.

On the morning of the 21st of August, in the memorable year of the calamity, I happened to be at Cookham, a pleasant and pretty village which then occupied the western bank of the Thames just below the spot where the Look-out Tower of the Earthquake and Eruption Department now dominates the whole wide plain of the Glassy Rock Desert. In place of the black lake of basalt which young people see nowadays winding its solid bays in and out among the grassy downs, most men still living can well remember a gracious and smiling valley, threaded in the midst by a beautiful river.

I had cycled down from London the evening before (thus forestalling my holiday), and had spent the night at a tolerable inn in the village. By a curious coincidence, the only other visitor at the little hotel that night was a fellow-cyclist, an American, George W. Ward by name, who had come over with his "wheel," as he called it, for six weeks in England, in order to investigate the geology of our southern counties for himself, and to compare it with that of the far western cretaceous system. I venture to describe this as a curious coincidence, because, as it happened, the mere accident of my meeting him gave me my first inkling of the very existence of that singular phenomenon of which we were all so soon to receive a startling example. I had never so much as heard before of fissure-eruptions; and if I had not heard of them from Ward that evening, I might not have recognised at sight the actuality when it first appeared, and therefore I might have been involved in the general disaster. In which case, of course, this unpretentious narrative would never have been written.

As we sat in the little parlour of the White Hart, however, over our evening pipe, it chanced that the American, who was a pleasant, conversable fellow, began talking to me of his reasons for visiting England. I was at that time a clerk in the General Post Office (of which I am now secretary), and was then no student of science; but his enthusiastic talk about his own country and its vastness amused and interested me. He had been employed for some years on the Geological Survey in the Western States, and he was deeply impressed by the solemnity and the colossal scale of everything American. "Mountains!" he said, when I spoke of Scotland; "why, for mountains, your Alps aren't in it! and as for volcanoes, your Vesuviuses and Etnas just spit fire a bit at infrequent intervals; while ours do things on a scale worthy of a great country, I can tell you. Europe is a circumstance: America is a continent."

"But surely," I objected, "that was a pretty fair eruption that destroyed Pompeii!"

The American rose and surveyed me slowly. I can see him to this day, with his close-shaven face and his contemptuous smile at my European ignorance. "Well," he said, after a long and impressive pause, "the lava-flood that destroyed a few acres about the Bay of Naples was what we call a trickle: it came from a crater; and the crater it came from was nothing more than a small round vent-hole; the lava flowed down from it in a moderate stream over a limited area. But what do you say to the earth opening in a huge crack, forty or fifty miles long—say, as far as from here right away to London, or farther—and lava pouring out from the orifice, not in a little rivulet as at Etna or Vesuvius, but in a sea or inundation, which spread at once over a tract as big as England? That's something like volcanic action, isn't it? And that's the sort of thing we have out in Colorado."

"You are joking," I replied, "or bragging. You are trying to astonish me with the familiar spread eagle."

He smiled a quiet smile. "Not a bit of it," he answered. "What I tell you is at least as true as Gospel. The earth yawns in Montana. There are fissure-eruptions, as we call them, in the Western States, out of which the lava has welled like wine out of a broken skin— welled up in vast roaring floods, molten torrents of basalt, many miles across, and spread like water over whole plains and valleys."

"Not within historical times!" I exclaimed.

"I'm not so sure about that," he answered, musing. "I grant you, not within times which are historical right there—for Colorado is a very new country: but I incline to think some of the most recent fissure eruptions took place not later than when the Tudors reigned in England. The lava oozed out, red-hot—gushed out— was squeezed out—and spread instantly everywhere; it's so comparatively recent that the surface of the rock is still bare in many parts, unweathered sufficiently to support vegetation. I fancy the stream must have been ejected at a single burst, in a huge white-hot dome, and then flowed down on every side, filling up the valleys to a certain level, in and out among the hills, exactly as water might do. And some of these eruptions, I tell you, by measured survey, would have covered more ground than from Dover to Liverpool, and from York to Cornwall."

"Let us be thankful," I said, carelessly, "that such things don't happen in our own times."

He eyed me curiously. "Haven't happened, you mean," he answered. "We have no security that they mayn't happen again to-morrow. These fissure-eruptions, though not historically described for us, are common events in geological history— commoner and on a larger scale in America than elsewhere. Still, they have occurred in all lands and at various epochs; there is no reason at all why one shouldn't occur in England at present."

I laughed, and shook my head. I had the Englishman's firm conviction—so rudely shattered by the subsequent events, but then so universal—that nothing very unusual ever happened in England.

Next morning I rose early, bathed in Odney Weir (a picturesque pool close by), breakfasted with the American, and then wrote a hasty line to my wife, informing her that I should probably sleep that night at Oxford; for I was off on a few days' holiday, and I liked Ethel to know where a letter or telegram would reach me each day, as we were both a little anxious about the baby's teething. Even while I pen these words now, the grim humour of the situation comes back to me vividly. Thousands of fathers and mothers were anxious that morning about similar trifles, whose pettiness was brought home to them with an appalling shock in the all-embracing horror of that day's calamity.

About ten o'clock I inflated my tyres and got under way. I meant to ride towards Oxford by a leisurely and circuitous route, along the windings of the river, past Marlow and Henley; so I began by crossing Cookham Bridge, a wooden or iron structure, I scarcely remember which. It spanned the Thames close by the village: the curious will find its exact position marked in the maps of the period.

In the middle of the bridge, I paused and surveyed that charming prospect, which I was the last of living men perhaps to see as it then existed. Close by stood a weir; beside it, the stream divided into three separate branches, exquisitely backed up by the gentle green slopes of Hedsor and Cliveden. I could never pass that typical English view without a glance of admiration; this morning, I pulled up my bicycle for a moment, and cast my eye down stream with more than my usual enjoyment of the smooth blue water and the tall white poplars whose leaves showed their gleaming silver in the breeze beside it. I might have gazed at it too long—and one minute more would have sufficed for my destruction—had not a cry from the tow-path a little farther up attracted my attention.

It was a wild, despairing cry, like that of a man being overpowered and murdered.

I am confident this was my first intimation of danger. Two minutes before, it is true, I had heard a faint sound like distant

rumbling of thunder; but nothing else. I am one of those who stren-
uously maintain that the catastrophe was not heralded by shocks of
earthquake.

I turned my eye up stream. For half a second I was utterly bewildered. Strange to say, I did not perceive at first the great flood of
fire that was advancing towards me. I saw only the man who had
shouted—a miserable, cowering, terror-stricken wretch, one of the
abject creatures who used to earn a dubious livelihood in those days
(when the river was a boulevard of pleasure) by towing boats up
stream. But now, he was rushing wildly forward, with panic in his
face; I could see he looked as if close pursued by some wild beast
behind him. "A mad dog!" I said to myself at the outset; "or else a
bull in the meadow!"

I glanced back to see what his pursuer might be; and then, in
one second, the whole horror and terror of the catastrophe burst
upon me. Its whole horror and terror, I say, but not yet its magnitude. I was aware at first just of a moving red wall, like dull, red-hot
molten metal. Trying to recall at so safe a distance in time and space
the feelings of the moment and the way in which they surged and
succeeded one another, I think I can recollect that my earliest idea
was no more than this: "He must run, or the moving wall will over-
take him!" Next instant, a hot wave seemed to strike my face. It
was just like the blast of heat that strikes one in a glasshouse when
you stand in front of the boiling and seething glass in the furnace.
At about the same point in time, I was aware, I believe, that the
dull red wall was really a wall of fire. But it was cooled by contact
with the air and the water. Even as I looked, however, a second wave
from behind seemed to rush on and break: it overlaid and outran
the first one. This second wave was white, not red—at white heat,
I realized. Then, with a burst of recognition, I knew what it all
meant. What Ward had spoken of last night—a fissure eruption!

I looked back. Ward was coming towards me on the bridge,
mounted on his Columbia. Too speechless to utter one word, I
pointed up stream with my hand. He nodded and shouted back, in

a singularly calm voice: "Yes; just what I told you. A fissure-eruption!"

They were the last words I heard him speak. Not that he appreciated the danger less than I did, though his manner was cool; but he was wearing no clips to his trousers, and at that critical moment he caught his leg in his pedals. The accident disconcerted him; he dismounted hurriedly, and then, panic-stricken as I judged, abandoned his machine. He tried to run. The error was fatal. He tripped and fell. What became of him afterward I will mention later.

But for the moment I saw only the poor wretch on the tow-path. He was not a hundred yards off, just beyond the little bridge which led over the opening to a private boat-house. But as he rushed forwards and shrieked, the wall of fire overtook him. I do not think it quite caught him. It is hard at such moments to judge what really happens; but I believe I saw him shrivel like a moth in a flame a few seconds before the advancing wall of fire swept over the boat-house. I have seen an insect shrivel just so when flung into the midst of white-hot coals. He seemed to go off in gas, leaving a shower or powdery ash to represent his bones behind him. But of this I do not pretend to be positive; I will allow that my own agitation was far too profound to permit of my observing anything with accuracy.

How high was the wall at that time? This has been much debated. I should guess, thirty feet (though it rose afterwards to more than two hundred), and it advanced rather faster than a man could run down the centre of the valley. (Later on, its pace accelerated greatly with subsequent outbursts.) In frantic haste, I saw or felt that only one chance of safety lay before me: I must strike up hill by the field path to Hedsor.

I rode for very life, with grim death behind me. Once well across the bridge, and turning up the hill, I saw Ward on the parapet, with his arms flung up, trying wildly to save himself by leaping into the river. Next instant he shrivelled I think, as the beggar had shrivelled; and it is to this complete combustion before the lava flood reached them that I attribute the circumstance (so much commented upon in the scientific excavations among the ruins) that no cast of dead bodies, like those at Pompeii, have anywhere been found in the Thames Valley Desert. My own belief is that every human body was reduced to a gaseous condition by the terrific heat several seconds before the molten basalt reached it.

Even at the distance which I had now attained from the central mass, indeed, the heat was intolerable. Yet, strange to say, I saw few or no people flying as yet from the inundation. The fact is, the eruption came upon us so suddenly, so utterly without warning or premonitory symptoms (for I deny the earthquake shocks), that whole towns must have been destroyed before the inhabitants were aware that anything out of the common was happening. It is a sort of alleviation to the general horror to remember that a large propor-tion of the victims must have died without even knowing it; one second, they were laughing, talking, bargaining; the next, they were asphyxiated or reduced to ashes as you have seen a small fly disap-pear in an incandescent gas flame.

This, however, is what I learned afterward. At that moment, I was only aware of a frantic pace uphill, over a rough, stony road, and with my pedals working as I had never before worked them; while behind me, I saw purgatory let loose, striving hard to over-take me. I just knew that a sea of fire was filling the valley from end to end, and that its heat scorched my face as I urged on my bicycle in abject terror.

All this time, I will admit, my panic was purely personal. I was too much engaged in the engrossing sense of my own pressing danger to be vividly alive to the public catastrophe. I did not even think of Ethel and the children. But when I reached the hill by Hedsor Church—a neat, small building, whose shell still stands, though scorched and charred, by the edge of the desert—I was able to pause for half a minute to recover breath, and to look back upon the scene of the first disaster.

It was a terrible and yet I felt even then a beautiful sight—beautiful with the awful and unearthly beauty of a great forest fire, or a mighty conflagration in some crowded city. The whole river valley, up which I looked, was one sea of fire. Barriers of red-hot lava formed themselves for a moment now and again where the outer edge or vanguard of the inundation had cooled a little on the surface by exposure: and over these temporary dams, fresh cataracts of white-hot material poured themselves afresh into the valley beyond it. After a while, as the deeper portion of basalt was pushed out all was white alike. So glorious it looked in the morning sunshine that one could hardly realize the appalling reality of that sea of molten gold; one might almost have imagined a splendid triumph of the scene painter's art, did one not know that it was actually a river of fire, overwhelming, consuming, and destroying every object before it in its devastating progress.

I tried vaguely to discover the source of the disaster. Looking straight up stream, past Bourne End and Marlow, I descried with bleared and dazzled eyes a whiter mass than any, glowing fiercely in the daylight like an electric light, and filling up the narrow gorge of the river towards Hurley and Henley. I recollected at once that this portion of the valley was not usually visible from Hedsor Hill, and almost without thinking of it I instinctively guessed the reason why it had become so now: it was the centre of disturbance—the earth's crust just there had bulged upward slightly, till it cracked and gaped to emit the basalt.

Looking harder, I could make out (though it was like looking at the sun) that the glowing white dome-shaped mass, as of an electric light, was the molten lava as it gurgled from the mouth of the vast fissure. I say vast, because so it seemed to me, though, as everybody now knows, the actual gap where the earth opened measures no more than eight miles across, from a point near what was once Shiplake Ferry to the site of the old lime-kilns at Marlow. Yet when one saw the eruption actually taking place, the colossal scale of it was what most appalled one. A sea of fire, eight to twelve miles broad, in the familiar Thames Valley, impressed and terrified one a thousand times more than a sea of fire ten times as vast in the nameless wilds of Western America.

I could see dimly, too, that the flood spread in every direction from its central point, both up and down the river. To right and left, indeed, it was soon checked and hemmed in by the hills about Wargrave and Medmenham; but downward, it had filled the entire valley as far as Cookham and beyond; while upward, it spread in one vast glowing sheet towards Reading and the flats by the confluence of the Kennet. I did not then know, of course, that this gigantic natural dam or barrier was later on to fill up the whole low-lying level, and so block the course of the two rivers as to form those twin expanses of inland water, Lake Newbury and Lake Oxford. Tourists who now look down on still summer evenings where the ruins of Magdalen and of Merton may be dimly descried through the pale green depths, their broken masonry picturesquely overgrown with tangled water-weeds, can form but little idea of the terrible scene which that peaceful bank presented while the incandescent lava was pouring forth in a scorching white flood towards the doomed district. Merchants who crowd the busy quays of those mushroom cities which have sprung up with greater rapidity than Chicago or Johannesburg on the indented shore where the new lakes abut upon the Berkshire Chalk Downs have half forgotten the horror of the intermediate time when the waters of the two rivers rose slowly, slowly, day after day, to choke their valleys and overwhelm some of the most glorious architecture in Britain. But though I did not know and could not then foresee the remoter effects of the great fire-flood in that direction, I saw enough to make my heart stand still within me. It was with difficulty that I grasped my bicycle, my hands trembled so fiercely. I realized that I was a spectator of the greatest calamity which had befallen a civilized land within the ken of history.

I looked southward along the valley in the direction of Maiden-head. As yet it did not occur to me that the catastrophe was anything more than a local flood, though even as such it would have been one of unexampled vastness. My imagination could hardly conceive that London itself was threatened. In those days one could not grasp the idea of the destruction of London. I only thought just at first, "It will go on towards Maidenhead!" Even as I thought it, I saw a fresh and fiercer gush of fire well out from the central gash, and flow still faster than ever down the centre of the valley, over the hardening layer already cooling on its edge by contact with the air and soil. This new outburst fell in a mad cataract over the end or van of the last, and instantly spread like water across the level expanse between the Cliveden hills and the opposite range at Pinkneys. I realized with a throb that it was advancing towards Windsor. Then a wild fear thrilled through me. If Windsor, why not Staines and Chertsey and Hounslow? If Hounslow, why not London?

In a second I remembered Ethel and the children. Hitherto, the immediate danger of my own position alone had struck me. The fire was so near; the heat of it rose up in my face and daunted me. But now I felt I must make a wild dash to warn—not London—no, frankly, I forgot those millions; but Ethel and my little ones. In that thought, for the first moment, the real vastness of the catastrophe came home to me. The Thames Valley was doomed! I must ride for dear life if I wished to save my wife and children!

I mounted again, but found my shaking feet could hardly work the pedals. My legs were one jelly. With a frantic effort, I struck off inland in the direction of Burnham. I did not think my way out definitely; I hardly knew the topography of the district well enough to form any clear conception of what route I must take in order to keep to the hills and avoid the flood of fire that was deluging the lowlands. But by pure instinct, I believe, I set my face Londonwards along the ridge of the chalk downs. In three minutes I had lost sight of the burning flood, and was deep among green lanes and under shadowy beeches. The very contrast frightened me. I wondered if I was going mad. It was all so quiet. One could not believe that scarce five miles off from that devastating sheet of fire, birds were singing in the sky and men toiling in the fields as if nothing had happened.

Near Lambourne Wood I met a brother cyclist, just about to descend the hill. A curve in the road hid the valley from him. I shouted aloud:

"For Heaven's sake, don't go down! There is danger, danger!"

He smiled and looked back at me. "I can take any hill in England," he answered.

"It's not the hill," I burst out. "There has been an eruption—a fissure-eruption at Marlow—great floods of fire—and all the valley is filled with burning lava!"

He stared at me derisively. Then his expression changed of a sudden. I suppose he saw I was white-faced and horror-stricken. He drew away as if alarmed. "Go back to Colney Hatch!" he cried, pedalling faster and rode hastily down the hill, as if afraid of me. I have no doubt he must have ridden into the very midst of the flood, and been scorched by its advance, before he could check his machine on so sudden a slope.

Between Lambourne Wood and Burnham I did not see the fire-flood. I rode on at full speed among green fields and meadows. Here and there I passed a labouring man on the road. More than one looked up at me and commented on the oppressive heat, but none of them seemed to be aware of the fate that was overtaking their own homes close by, in the valley. I told one or two, but they laughed and gazed after me as if I were a madman. I grew sick of warning them. They took no heed of my words, but went on upon their way as if nothing out of the common were happening to England.

On the edge of the down, near Burnham, I caught sight of the valley again. Here, people were just awaking to what was taking place near them. Half the population was gathered on the slope, looking down with wonder on the flood of fire, which had now just turned the corner of the hills by Taplow. Silent terror was the prevailing type of expression. But when I told them I had seen the lava bursting forth from the earth in a white dome above Marlow, they laughed me to scorn; and when I assured them I was pushing forward in hot haste to London, they answered, "London! It won't never get as far as London!" That was the only place on the hills, as is now well known, where the flood was observed long enough beforehand to telegraph and warn the inhabitants of the great city; but nobody thought of doing it; and I must say, even if they had done so, there is not the slightest probability that the warning would have attracted the least attention in our ancient Metropolis. Men on the Stock Exchange would have made jests about the slump, and proceeded to buy and sell as usual.

I measured with my eye the level plain between Burnham and Slough, calculating roughly with myself whether I should have time to descend upon the well-known road from Maidenhead to London by Colnbrook and Hounslow. (I advise those who are unacquainted with the topography of this district before the eruption to follow out my route on a good map of the period.) But I recognised in a moment that this course would be impossible. At the rate that the flood had taken to progress from Cookham Bridge to Taplow, I felt sure it would be upon me before I reached Upton, or Ditton Park at the outside. It is true the speed of the advance might slacken somewhat as the lava cooled; and strange to say, so rapidly do realities come to be accepted in one's mind, that I caught myself thinking this thought in the most natural manner, as if I had all my life long been accustomed to the ways of fissure-eruptions. But on the other hand, the lava might well out faster and hotter than before, as I had already seen it do more than once; and I had no certainty even that it would not rise to the level of the hills on which I was standing. You who read this narrative nowadays take it for granted, of course, that the extent and height of the inundation was bound to be exactly what you know it to have been; we at the time could not guess how high it might rise and how large an area of the country it might

overwhelm and devastate. Was it to stop at the Chilterns, or to go
north to Birmingham, York, and Scotland?

Still, in my trembling anxiety to warn my wife and children, I
debated with myself whether I should venture down into the valley,
and hurry along the main road with a wild burst for London. I
thought of Ethel, alone in our little home at Bayswater, and almost
made up my mind to risk it. At that moment, I became aware that
the road to London was already crowded with carriages, carts, and
cycles, all dashing at a mad pace unanimously towards London.
Suddenly a fresh wave turned the corner by Taplow and Maiden-
head Bridge, and began to gain upon them visibly. It was an awful
sight. I cannot pretend to describe it. The poor creatures on the
road, men and animals alike, rushed wildly, despairingly on; the fire
took them from behind, and, one by one, before the actual sea
reached them, I saw them shrivel and melt away in the fierce white
heat of the advancing inundation. I could not look at it any longer.
I certainly could not descend and court instant death. I felt that my
one chance was to strike across the downs, by Stoke Poges and
Uxbridge, and then try the line of northern heights to London.

Oh, how fiercely I pedalled! At Farnham Royal (where again
nobody seemed to be aware what had happened) a rural policeman
tried to stop me for frantic riding. I tripped him up, and rode on.
Experience had taught me it was no use telling those who had not
seen it of the disaster. A little beyond, at the entrance to a fine park,
a gatekeeper attempted to shut a gate in my face, exclaiming that
the road was private. I saw it was the only practicable way without
descending to the valley, and I made up my mind this was no time
for trifling. I am a man of peace, but I lifted my fist and planted it
between his eyes. Then, before he could recover from his astonishment, I had mounted again and ridden on across the park, while he
ran after me in vain, screaming to the men in the pleasure-grounds
to stop me. But I would not be stopped; and I emerged on the road
once more at Stoke Poges.

Near Galley Hill, after a long and furious ride, I reached the descent to Uxbridge. Was it possible to descend? I glanced across, once more by pure instinct, for I had never visited the spot before, towards where I felt the Thames must run. A great white cloud hung over it. I saw what that cloud must mean: it was the steam of the river, where the lava sucked it up and made it seethe and boil suddenly. I had not noticed this white fleece of steam at Cookham, though I did not guess why till afterwards. In the narrow valley where the Thames ran between hills, the lava flowed over it all at once, bottling the steam beneath; and it is this imprisoned steam that gave rise in time to the subsequent series of appalling earthquakes, to supply forecasts of which is now the chief duty of the Seismologer Royal; whereas, in the open plain, the basalt advanced more gradually and in a thinner stream, and therefore turned the whole mass of water into white cloud as soon as it reached each bend of the river.

At the time, however, I had no leisure to think out all this. I only knew by such indirect signs that the flood was still advancing, and, therefore, that it would be impossible for me to proceed towards London by the direct route via Uxbridge and Hanwell. If I meant to reach town (as we called it familiarly), I must descend to the valley at once, pass through Uxbridge streets as fast as I could, make a dash across the plain, by what I afterwards knew to be Hillingdon (I saw it then as a nameless village), and aim at a house-crowned hill which I only learned later was Harrow, but which I felt sure would enable me to descend upon London by Hampstead or Highgate.

I am no strategist; but in a second, in that extremity, I picked out these points, feeling dimly sure they would lead me home to Ethel and the children.

The town of Uxbridge (whose place you can still find marked on many maps) lay in the valley of a small river, a confluent of the Thames. Up this valley it was certain that the lava-stream must flow; and, indeed, at the present day, the basin around is completely filled by one of the solidest and most forbidding masses of black basalt in the country. Still, I made up my mind to descend and cut across the low-lying ground towards Harrow. If I failed, I felt, after all, I was but one unit more in what I now began to realize as a prodigious national calamity.

I was just coasting down the hill, with Uxbridge lying snug and unconscious in the glen below me, when a slight and unimportant accident occurred which almost rendered impossible my further progress. It was past the middle of August; the hedges were being cut; and this particular lane, bordered by a high thorn fence, was strewn with the mangled branches of the may-bushes. At any other time, I should have remembered the danger and avoided them; that day, hurrying down hill for dear life and for Ethel, I forgot to notice them. The consequence was, I was pulled up suddenly by finding my front wheel deflated; this untimely misfortune almost unmanned me. I dismounted and examined the tyre; it had received a bad puncture. I tried inflating again, in hopes the hole might be small enough to make that precaution sufficient. But it was quite useless. I found I must submit to stop and doctor up the puncture. Fortunately, I had the necessary apparatus in my wallet.

I think it was the weirdest episode of all that weird ride—this sense of stopping impatiently, while the fiery flood still surged on towards London, in order to go through all the fiddling and troublesome little details of mending a pneumatic tyre. The moment and the operation seemed so sadly out of harmony. A countryman passed by on a cart, obviously suspecting nothing; that was another point which added horror to the occasion—that so near the catastrophe, so very few people were even aware what was taking place beside them. Indeed, as is well known, I was one of the very few who saw the eruption during its course, and yet managed to escape from it. Elsewhere, those who tried to run before it, either to escape themselves or to warn others of the danger, were overtaken by the lava before they could reach a place of safety. I attribute this mainly to the fact that most of them continued along the high roads in the valley, or fled instinctively for shelter towards their homes, instead of making at once for the heights and the uplands.

The countryman stopped and looked at me.

"The more haste the less speed!" he said, with proverbial wisdom.

I glanced up at him, and hesitated. Should I warn him of his doom, or was it useless? "Keep up on the hills," I said, at last. "An unspeakable calamity is happening in the valley. Flames of fire are flowing down it, as from a great burning mountain. You will be cut off by the eruption."

He stared at me blankly, and burst into a meaningless laugh. "Why, you're one of them Salvation Army fellows," he exclaimed, after a short pause. "You're trying to preach to me. I'm going to Uxbridge." And he continued down the hill towards certain destruction.

It was hours, I feel sure, before I had patched up that puncture, though I did it by the watch in four and a half minutes. As soon as I had blown out my tyre again I mounted once more, and rode at a breakneck pace to Uxbridge. I passed down the straggling main street of the suburban town, crying aloud as I went, "Run, run, to the downs! A flood of lava is rushing up the valley! To the hills, for your lives! All the Thames bank is blazing!" Nobody took the slightest heed; they stood still in the street for a minute with open mouths: then they returned to their customary occupations. A quarter of an hour later, there was no such place in the world as Uxbridge.

I followed the main road through the village which I have since identified as Hillingdon; then I diverged to the left, partly by roads and partly by field paths of whose exact course I am still uncertain, towards the hill at Harrow. When I reached the town, I did not strive to rouse the people, partly because my past experience had taught me the futility of the attempt, and partly because I rightly judged that they were safe from the inundation; for as it never quite covered the dome of St. Paul's, part of which still protrudes from the sea of basalt, it did not reach the level of the northern heights of London. I rode on through Harrow without one word to any body. I did not desire to be stopped or harassed as an escaped lunatic.

From Harrow I made my way tortuously along the rising ground, by the light of nature, through Wembley Park, to Willesden. At Willesden, for the first time, I found to a certainty that London was threatened. Great crowds of people in the profoundest excitement stood watching a dense cloud of smoke and steam that spread rapidly over the direction of Shepherd's Bush and Hammersmith. They were speculating as to its meaning, but laughed incredulously when I told them what it portended. A few minutes later, the smoke spread ominously towards Kensington and Paddington. That settled my fate. It was clearly impossible to descend into London; and indeed, the heat now began to be unendurable. It drove us all back, almost physically. I thought I must abandon all hope. I should never even know what had become of Ethel and the children.

My first impulse was to lie down and await the fire-flood. Yet the sense of the greatness of the catastrophe seemed somehow to blunt one's own private grief. I was beside myself with fear for my darlings; but I realized that I was but one among hundreds of thousands of fathers in the same position. What was happening at that moment in the great city of five million souls we did not know, we shall never know; but we may conjecture that the end was mercifully too swift to entail much needless suffering. All at once, a gleam of hope struck me. It was my father's birthday. Was it not just possible that Ethel might have taken the children up to Hampstead to wish their grandpa many happy returns of the day? With a wild determination not to give up all for lost, I turned my front wheel in the direction of Hampstead Hill, still skirting the high ground as far as possible. My heart was on fire within me. A restless anxiety urged me to ride my hardest. As all along the route, I was still just a minute or two in front of the catastrophe. People were beginning to be aware that something was taking place; more than once as I passed they asked me eagerly where the fire was. It was impossible for me to believe by this time that they knew nothing of an event in whose midst I seemed to have been living for months; how could I realize that all the things which had happened since I started from Cookham

Bridge so long ago were really compressed into the space of a single morning?—nay, more, of an hour and a half only?

As I approached Windmill Hill, a terrible sinking seized me. I seemed to totter on the brink of a precipice. Could Ethel be safe? Should I ever again see little Bertie and the baby? I pedalled on as if automatically; for all life had gone out of me. I felt my hip-joint moving dry in its socket. I held my breath; my heart stood still. It was a ghastly moment.

At my father's door I drew up, and opened the garden gate. I hardly dared to go in. Though each second was precious, I paused and hesitated.

At last I turned the handle. I heard somebody within. My heart came up in my mouth. It was little Bertie's voice: "Do it again, Granpa; do it again; it amooses Bertie!"

I rushed into the room. "Bertie, Bertie!" I cried. "Is Mammy here?"

He flung himself upon me. "Mammy, Mammy, Daddy has comed home." I burst into tears. "And Baby?" I asked, trembling.

"Baby and Ethel are here, George," my father answered, staring at me. "Why, my boy, what's the matter?"

I flung myself into a chair and broke down. In that moment of relief, I felt that London was lost, but I had saved my wife and children.

I did not wait for explanations. A crawling four-wheeler was loitering by. I hailed it and hurried them in. My father wished to discuss the matter, but I cut him short. I gave the driver three pounds—all the gold I had with me. "Drive on!" I shouted, "drive on! Towards Hatfield—anywhere!"

He drove as he was bid. We spent that night, while Hampstead flared like a beacon, at an isolated farm-house on the high ground in Hertfordshire. For, of course, though the flood did not reach so high, it set fire to everything inflammable in its neighbourhood.

Next day, all the world knew the magnitude of the disaster. It can only be summed up in five emphatic words: There was no more London.

I have one other observation alone to make. I noticed at the time how, in my personal relief, I forgot for the moment that London was perishing. I even forgot that my house and property had perished. Exactly the opposite, it seemed to me, happened with most of those survivors who lost wives and children in the eruption. They moved about as in a dream, without a tear, without a complaint, helping others to provide for the needs of the homeless and houseless. The universality of the catastrophe made each man feel as though it were selfishness to attach too great an importance at such a crisis to his own personal losses. Nay, more; the burst of feverish activity and nervous excitement, I might even say enjoyment, which followed the horror, was traceable, I think, to this self-same cause. Even grave citizens felt they must do their best to dispel the universal gloom; and they plunged accordingly into a round of dissipations which other nations thought both unseemly and un-English. It was one way of expressing the common emotion. We had all lost heart and we flocked to the theatres to pluck up our courage. That, I believe, must be our national answer to M. Zola's strictures on our untimely levity. "This people," says the great French author, "which took its pleasures sadly while it was rich and prosperous, begins to dance and sing above the ashes of its capital—it makes merry by the open graves of its wives and children. What an enigma! What a puzzle! What chance of an Œdipus!"

Rudyard Kipling

(1865–1936)

"KIPLING TOWARD THE END," wrote Guy Davenport, "managed to write stories with complex layers of meaning, as rich as Shakespeare's." This claim might be extravagant, but Kipling's reputation has evolved curiously through the decades since the Nobel laureate's death. It reached its nadir during World War II, when George Orwell denounced Kipling as a prophet of relentless expansionism, a man who thought of the British Empire as "a sort of forcible evangelizing," when in fact, Orwell maintained, it was and had always been "primarily a money-making concern." Eton alumnus Orwell dismissed Kipling as "vulgar," mocked his attention to vernacular speech as a condescending failed comedy, and contrarily declared soldier poems such as the 1892 collection *Barrack-Room Ballads* "his best and most representative work." But then Orwell even complained that Kipling exaggerated the horrors of the wars he had seen, which he felt surely could not compare with the wars of Orwell's own benighted era.

Kipling's reputation rebounded from Orwell's attack. Nowadays literary critics lavish praise on many of his works, especially the 1901 novel *Kim*. It demonstrates not only Kipling's verve and style as a writer, but also his photographic observation of a setting and his broad compassion for a variety of human beings. In a 2006 *Guardian* interview, Salman Rushdie admitted that he has "many of the difficulties with Kipling that a lot of people from India have, but every true Indian reader knows that no non-Indian writer understood India as well as Kipling . . . If you want to look at the India of Kipling's time, there is no writer who will give it to you better."

In 1836 Joseph Rudyard Kipling was born to English parents in Mumbai (then still called Bombay by westerners), and after several unhappy years in England he returned in his late teens to the land of his birth. There he began working hard as a journalist and literary balladeer and by the age of twenty had published his first collection of poems, *Departmental Ditties*. Kipling's books are wildly varied, from the boarding school antics of M'Turk and the titular antihero against the brutal masters in *Stalky & Co.* to the playful history-minded fancy of *Puck of Pook's Hill*. Nowadays he is best known for *The Jungle Book*, *The Second Jungle Book*, and *Just So Stories*, his inspired volumes of talking-animal stories written mostly during the last few years of the nineteenth century, and for his grand stories of the supernatural. "His tales of the fantastic are chilling, or illuminating or remarkable or sad," remarked Neil Gaiman, "because his people breathe and dream."

So do his settings. In an insightful critique of Kipling, the poet and critic Randall Jarrell remarked, "Knowing what the peoples, animals, plants, weathers of the world look like, sound like, smell like, was Kipling's métier, and so was knowing the words that could make someone else know. You can argue about the judgment he makes of something, but the thing is there." As Jarrell points out, the man who began as a journeyman journalist, author of *Plain Tales from the Hills*, continued to mature as a bold and elegant writer for a half century.

Kipling wrote many fine and original stories about the supernatural, ranging from the ancient gods of "The Mark of the Beast" to the modern gods of "Wireless." Many, including his best-known ghost story, "The Phantom 'Rickshaw," are set in India. "Wireless," in contrast, takes place on the stormy southern coast of England. The story was published in the August 1902 issue of *Scribner's*

Magazine, and two years later Kipling included it in his collection *Traffics and Discoveries*.

Always curious about the workings of inspiration, Kipling would later write to his friend and colleague H. Rider Haggard, author of *King Solomon's Mines*, "We are only telephone wires."

Wireless

KASPAR'S SONG IN VARDA
(*From the Swedish of Stagnelius.*)

Eyes aloft, over dangerous places,
  The children follow where Psyche flies,
And, in the sweat of their upturned faces,
  Slash with a net at the empty skies.
So it goes they fall amid brambles,
  And sting their toes on the nettle-tops,
Till after a thousand scratches and scrambles
  They wipe their brows, and the hunting stops.
Then to quiet them comes their father
  And stills the riot of pain and grief,
Saying, "Little ones, go and gather
  Out of my garden a cabbage leaf.
"You will find on it whorls and clots of
  Dull grey eggs that, properly fed,
Turn, by way of the worm, to lots of
  Radiant Psyches raised from the dead."
★ ★ ★ ★ ★

"Heaven is beautiful, Earth is ugly,"
  The three-dimensioned preacher saith,

298

So we must not look where the snail and the slug lie
For Psyche's birth . . . And that is our death!

"It's a funny thing, this Marconi business, isn't it?" said Mr. Shaynor, coughing heavily. "Nothing seems to make any difference, by what they tell me—storms, hills, or anything; but if that's true we shall know before morning."

"Of course it's true," I answered, stepping behind the counter. "Where's old Mr. Cashell?"

"He's had to go to bed on account of his influenza. He said you'd very likely drop in."

"Where's his nephew?"

"Inside, getting the things ready. He told me that the last time they experimented they put the pole on the roof of one of the big hotels here, and the batteries electrified all the water-supply, and"— he giggled—"the ladies got shocks when they took their baths."

"I never heard of that."

"The hotel wouldn't exactly advertise it, would it? Just now, by what Mr. Cashell tells me, they're trying to signal from here to Poole, and they're using stronger batteries than ever. But, you see, he being the guvnor's nephew and all that (and it will be in the papers too), it doesn't matter how they electrify things in this house. Are you going to watch?"

"Very much. I've never seen this game. Aren't you going to bed?"

"We don't close till ten on Saturdays. There's a good deal of influenza in town, too, and there'll be a dozen prescriptions coming in before morning. I generally sleep in the chair here. It's warmer than jumping out of bed every time. Bitter cold, isn't it?"

"Freezing hard. I'm sorry your cough's worse."

"Thank you. I don't mind cold so much. It's this wind that fair cuts me to pieces." He coughed again hard and hackingly, as an old lady came in for ammoniated quinine. "We've just run out of it in bottles, madam," said Mr. Shaynor, returning to the professional tone, "but if you will wait two minutes, I'll make it up for you, madam."

I had used the shop for some time, and my acquaintance with
the proprietor had ripened into friendship. It was Mr. Cashell who
revealed to me the purpose and power of Apothecaries' Hall that
time a fellow-chemist had made an error in a prescription of mine,
had lied to cover his sloth, and when error and lie were brought
home to him had written vain letters.

"A disgrace to our profession," said the thin, mild-eyed man,
hotly, after studying the evidence. "You couldn't do a better service
to the profession than report him to Apothecaries' Hall."

I did so, not knowing what djinns I should evoke; and the result
was such an apology as one might make who had spent a night on
the rack. I conceived great respect for Apothecaries' Hall, and esteem
for Mr. Cashell, a zealous craftsman who magnified his calling.
Until Mr. Shaynor came down from the North his assistants had
by no means agreed with Mr. Cashell. "They forget," said he, "that,
first and foremost, the compounder is a medicine-man. On him
depends the physician's reputation. He holds it literally in the hollow
of his hand, Sir."

Mr. Shaynor's manners had not, perhaps, the polish of the grocery
and Italian warehouse next door, but he knew and loved his dispensary work in every detail. For relaxation he seemed to go no farther
afield than the romance of drugs—their discovery, preparation,
packing, and export—but it led him to the ends of the earth, and
on this subject, and the Pharmaceutical Formulary, and Nicholas
Culpepper, most confident of physicians, we met.

Little by little I grew to know something of his beginnings and
his hopes—of his mother, who had been a school-teacher in one
of the northern counties, and of his red-headed father, a small
job-master at Kirby Moors, who died when he was a child; of the
examinations he had passed and of their exceeding and increasing
difficulty; of his dreams of a shop in London; of his hate for the
price-cutting Co-operative stores; and, most interesting, of his
mental attitude towards customers.

"There's a way you get into," he told me, "of serving them

carefully, and I hope, politely, without stopping your own thinking. I've been reading Christie's *New Commercial Plants* all this autumn, and that needs keeping your mind on it, I can tell you. So long as it isn't a prescription, of course, I can carry as much as half a page of Christie in my head, and at the same time I could sell out all that window twice over, and not a penny wrong at the end. As to prescriptions, I think I could make up the general run of 'em in my sleep, almost."

For reasons of my own, I was deeply interested in Marconi experiments at their outset in England; and it was of a piece with Mr. Cashell's unvarying thoughtfulness that, when his nephew the electrician appropriated the house for a long-range installation, he should, as I have said, invite me to see the result.

The old lady went away with her medicine, and Mr. Shaynor and I stamped on the tiled floor behind the counter to keep ourselves warm. The shop, by the light of the many electrics, looked like a Paris-diamond mine, for Mr. Cashell believed in all the ritual of his craft. Three superb glass jars—red, green, and blue—of the sort that led Rosamund to parting with her shoes—blazed in the broad plate-glass windows, and there was a confused smell of orris, Kodak films, vulcanite, tooth-powder, sachets, and almond-cream in the air. Mr. Shaynor fed the dispensary stove, and we sucked cayenne-pepper jujubes and menthol lozenges. The brutal east wind had cleared the streets, and the few passers-by were muffled to their puckered eyes. In the Italian warehouse next door some gay feathered birds and game, hung upon hooks, sagged to the wind across the left edge of our window-frame.

"They ought to take these poultry in—all knocked about like that," said Mr. Shaynor. "Doesn't it make you feel fair perishing? See that old hare! The wind's nearly blowing the fur off him."

I saw the belly-fur of the dead beast blown apart in ridges and streaks as the wind caught it, showing bluish skin underneath. "Bitter cold," said Mr. Shaynor, shuddering. "Fancy going out on a night like this! Oh, here's young Mr. Cashell."

The door of the inner office behind the dispensary opened, and an energetic, spade-bearded man stepped forth, rubbing his hands.

"I want a bit of tin-foil, Shaynor," he said. "Good-evening. My uncle told me you might be coming." This to me, as I began the first of a hundred questions.

"I've everything in order," he replied. "We're only waiting until Poole calls us up. Excuse me a minute. You can come in whenever you like—but I'd better be with the instruments. Give me that tin-foil. Thanks."

While we were talking, a girl—evidently no customer—had come into the shop, and the face and bearing of Mr. Shaynor changed. She leaned confidently across the counter.

"But I can't," I heard him whisper uneasily—the flush on his cheek was dull red, and his eyes shone like a drugged moth's. "I can't. I tell you I'm alone in the place."

"No, you aren't. Who's *that*? Let him look after it for half an hour. A brisk walk will do you good. Ah, come now, John."

"But he isn't——"

"I don't care. I want you to; we'll only go round by St. Agnes. If you don't——"

He crossed to where I stood in the shadow of the dispensary counter, and began some sort of broken apology about a lady-friend.

"Yes," she interrupted. "You take the shop for half an hour—to oblige *me*, won't you?"

She had a singularly rich and promising voice that well matched her outline.

"All right," I said. "I'll do it—but you'd better wrap yourself up, Mr. Shaynor."

"Oh, a brisk walk ought to help me. We're only going round by the church."

I heard him cough grievously as they went out together.

I refilled the stove, and, after reckless expenditure of Mr. Cashell's coal, drove some warmth into the shop. I explored many of the glass-knobbed drawers that lined the walls, tasted some disconcerting drugs, and, by the aid of a few cardamoms, ground ginger, chloric-ether, and dilute alcohol, manufactured a new and wildish drink, of which I bore a glassful to young Mr. Cashell, busy in the back office. He laughed shortly when I told him that Mr. Shaynor had stepped out—but a frail coil of wire held all his attention, and he had no word for me bewildered among the batteries and rods. The noise of the sea on the beach began to make itself heard as the traffic in the street ceased. Then briefly, but very lucidly, he gave me the names and uses of the mechanism that crowded the tables and the floor.

"When do you expect to get the message from Poole?" I demanded, sipping my liquor out of a graduated glass.

"About midnight, if everything is in order. We've got our installation-pole fixed to the roof of the house. I shouldn't advise you to turn on a tap or anything tonight. We've connected up with the plumbing, and all the water will be electrified." He repeated to me the history of the agitated ladies at the hotel at the time of the first installation.

"But what *is* it?" I asked. "Electricity is out of my beat altogether."

"Ah, if you knew *that* you'd know something nobody knows. It's just It—what we call Electricity, but the magic—the manifestations—the Hertzian waves—are all revealed by *this*. The coherer, we call it."

He picked up a glass tube not much thicker than a thermometer, in which, almost touching, were two tiny silver plugs, and between them an infinitesimal pinch of metallic dust. "That's all," he said, proudly, as though himself responsible for the wonder. "That is the thing that will reveal to us the Powers—whatever the Powers may be—at work—through space—a long distance away."

Just then Mr. Shaynor returned alone and stood coughing his heart out on the mat.

"Serves you right for being such a fool," said young Mr. Cashell, as annoyed as myself at the interruption. "Never mind—we've all the night before us to see wonders."

Shaynor clutched the counter, his handkerchief to his lips. When he brought it away I saw two bright red stains.

"I—I've got a bit of a rasped throat from smoking cigarettes," he panted. "I think I'll try a cubeb."

"Better take some of this. I've been compounding while you've been away."

I handed him the brew.

"'Twon't make me drunk, will it? I'm almost a teetotaller. My word! That's grateful and comforting."

He sat down the empty glass to cough afresh.

"Brr! But it was cold out there! I shouldn't care to be lying in my grave a night like this. Don't *you* ever have a sore throat from smoking?" He pocketed the handkerchief after a furtive peep.

"Oh, yes, sometimes," I replied, wondering, while I spoke, into what agonies of terror I should fall if ever I saw those bright-red danger-signals under my nose. Young Mr. Cashell among the batteries coughed slightly to show that he was quite ready to continue his scientific explanations, but I was thinking still of the girl with the rich voice and the significantly cut mouth, at whose command I had taken charge of the shop. It flashed across me that she distantly resembled the seductive shape on a gold-framed toilet-water advertisement whose charms were unholily heightened by the glare from the red bottle in the window. Turning to make sure, I saw Mr. Shaynor's eyes bent in the same direction, and by instinct recognised that the flamboyant thing was to him a shrine. "What do you take for your—cough?" I asked.

"Well, I'm the wrong side of the counter to believe much in patent medicines. But there are asthma cigarettes and there are pastilles. To tell you the truth, if you don't object to the smell, which is very like incense, I believe, though I'm not a Roman Catholic, Blaudett's Cathedral Pastilles relieve me as much as anything."

"Let's try." I had never raided a chemist's shop before, so I was thorough. We unearthed the pastilles—brown, gummy cones of benzoin—and set them alight under the toilet-water advertisement, where they fumed in thin blue spirals.

"Of course," said Mr. Shaynor, to my question, "what one uses in the shop for one's self comes out of one's pocket. Why, stock-taking in our business is nearly the same as with jewellers—and I can't say more than that. But one gets them"—he pointed to the pastille-box—"at trade prices." Evidently the censing of the gay, seven-tinted wench with the teeth was an established ritual which cost something.

"And when do we shut up shop?"

"We stay like this all night. The gov—old Mr. Cashell—doesn't believe in locks and shutters as compared with electric light. Besides it brings trade. I'll just sit here in the chair by the stove and write a letter, if you don't mind. Electricity isn't my prescription."

The energetic young Mr. Cashell snorted within, and Shaynor settled himself up in his chair over which he had thrown a staring red, black, and yellow Austrian jute blanket, rather like a table-cover. I cast about, amid patent medicine pamphlets, for something to read, but finding little, returned to the manufacture of the new drink. The Italian warehouse took down its game and went to bed. Across the street blank shutters flung back the gaslight in cold smears; the dried pavement seemed to rough up in goose-flesh under the scouring of the savage wind, and we could hear, long ere he passed, the policeman flapping his arms to keep himself warm. Within, the flavours of cardamoms and chloric-ether disputed those of the pastilles and a score of drugs and perfume and soap scents. Our electric lights, set low down in the windows before the tunbellied Rosamund jars, flung inward three monstrous daubs of red, blue, and green, that broke into kaleidoscopic lights on the facetted knobs of the drug-drawers, the cut-glass scent flagons, and the bulbs of the sparklet bottles. They flushed the white-tiled floor in gorgeous patches; splashed along the nickel-silver counter-rails, and turned the polished mahogany counter-panels to the likeness of intricate grained marbles—slabs of porphyry and malachite. Mr. Shaynor unlocked a drawer, and ere he began to write, took out a meagre bundle of letters. From my place by the stove, I could see the scalloped edges of the paper with a flaring monogram in the corner and could even smell the reek of chypre. At each page he turned toward the toilet-water lady of the advertisement and devoured her with over-luminous eyes. He had drawn the Austrian blanket over his shoulders, and among those warring lights he looked more than ever the incarnation of a drugged moth—a tiger-moth as I thought.

He put his letter into an envelope, stamped it with stiff mechanical movements, and dropped it in the drawer. Then I became aware of the silence of a great city asleep—the silence that underlaid the even voice of the breakers along the sea-front—a thick, tingling quiet of warm life stilled down for its appointed time, and unconsciously I moved about the glittering shop as one moves in a sickroom. Young Mr. Cashell was adjusting some wire that crackled from time to time with the tense, knuckle-stretching sound of the electric spark. Upstairs, where a door shut and opened swiftly, I could hear his uncle coughing abed.

"Here," I said, when the drink was properly warmed, "take some of this, Mr. Shaynor."

He jerked in his chair with a start and a wrench, and held out his hand for the glass. The mixture, of a rich port-wine colour, frothed at the top.

"It looks," he said, suddenly, "it looks—those bubbles—like a string of pearls winking at you—rather like the pearls round that young lady's neck." He turned again to the advertisement where the female in the dove-coloured corset had seen fit to put on all her pearls before she cleaned her teeth.

"Not bad, is it?" I said.

"Eh?"

He rolled his eyes heavily full on me, and, as I stared, I beheld all meaning and consciousness die out of the swiftly dilating pupils. His figure lost its stark rigidity, softened into the chair, and, chin on chest, hands dropped before him, he rested open-eyed, absolutely still.

"I'm afraid I've rather cooked Shaynor's goose," I said, bearing the fresh drink to young Mr. Cashell. "Perhaps it was the chloric-ether."

"Oh, he's all right." The spade-bearded man glanced at him pity-ingly. "Consumptives go off in those sort of doses very often. It's exhaustion . . . I don't wonder. I dare say the liquor will do him good. It's grand stuff," he finished his share appreciatively. "Well, as I was saying—before he interrupted—about this little coherer. The pinch of dust, you see, is nickel-filings. The Hertzian waves, you see, come out of space from the station that despatches 'em, and all these little particles are attracted together—cohere, we call it—for just so long as the current passes through them. Now, it's impor-tant to remember that the current is an induced current. There are a good many kinds of induction——"

"Yes, but what *is* induction?"

"That's rather hard to explain untechnically. But the long and the short of it is that when a current of electricity passes through a wire there's a lot of magnetism present round that wire; and if you put another wire parallel to, and within what we call its magnetic field—why then, the second wire will also become charged with electricity."

"On its own account?"

"On its own account."

"Then let's see if I've got it correctly. Miles off, at Poole, or wher-ever it is——"

"It will be anywhere in ten years."

"You've got a charged wire——"

"Charged with Hertzian waves which vibrate, say, two hundred and thirty million times a second." Mr. Cashell snaked his forefinger rapidly through the air.

"All right—a charged wire at Poole, giving out these waves into space. Then this wire of yours sticking out into space—on the roof of the house—in some mysterious way gets charged with those waves from Poole——"

"Or anywhere—it only happens to be Poole tonight."

"And those waves set the coherer at work, just like an ordinary telegraph-office ticker?"

"No! That's where so many people make the mistake. The Hertzian waves wouldn't be strong enough to work a great heavy Morse instrument like ours. They can only just make that dust cohere, and while it coheres (a little while for a dot and a longer while for a dash) the current from this battery—the home battery"— he laid his hand on the thing—"can get through to the Morse printing-machine to record the dot or dash. Let me make it clearer. Do you know anything about steam?"

"Very little. But go on."

"Well, the coherer is like a steam-valve. Any child can open a valve and start a steamer's engines, because a turn of the hand lets in the main steam, doesn't it? Now, this home battery here ready to print is the main steam. The coherer is the valve, always ready to be turned on. The Hertzian wave is the child's hand that turns it."

"I see. That's marvellous."

"Marvellous, isn't it? And, remember, we're only at the beginning. There's nothing we sha'n't be able to do in ten years. I want to live—my God, how I want to live, and see it develop!" He looked through the door at Shaynor breathing lightly in his chair.

"Poor beast! And he wants to keep company with Fanny Brand."

"Fanny *who*?" I said, for the name struck an obscurely familiar chord in my brain—something connected with a stained handkerchief, and the word "arterial."

"Fanny Brand—the girl you kept shop for." He laughed, "That's all I know about her, and for the life of me I can't see what Shaynor sees in her, or she in him."

"*Can't* you see what he sees in her?" I insisted.

"Oh, yes, if *that's* what you mean. She's a great, big, fat lump of a girl, and so on. I suppose that's why he's so crazy after her. She isn't his sort. Well, it doesn't matter. My uncle says he's bound to die before the year's out. Your drink's given him a good sleep, at any rate." Young Mr. Cashell could not catch Mr. Shaynor's face, which was half turned to the advertisement.

I stoked the stove anew, for the room was growing cold, and lighted another pastille. Mr. Shaynor in his chair, never moving, looked through and over me with eyes as wide and lustreless as those of a dead hare.

"Poole's late," said young Mr. Cashell, when I stepped back. "I'll just send them a call."

He pressed a key in the semi-darkness, and with a rending crackle there leaped between two brass knobs a spark, streams of sparks, and sparks again.

"Grand, isn't it? *That's* the Power—our unknown Power— kicking and fighting to be let loose," said young Mr. Cashell. "There she goes—kick—kick—kick into space. I never get over the strange- ness of it when I work a sending-machine—waves going into space, you know. T.R. is our call. Poole ought to answer with L.L.L."

We waited two, three, five minutes. In that silence, of which the boom of the tide was an orderly part, I caught the clear "*kiss—kiss— kiss*" of the halliards on the roof, as they were blown against the installation-pole.

"Poole is not ready. I'll stay here and call you when he is."

I returned to the shop, and set down my glass on a marble slab with a careless clink. As I did so, Shaynor rose to his feet, his eyes fixed once more on the advertisement, where the young woman bathed in the light from the red jar simpered pinkly over her pearls. His lips moved without cessation. I stepped nearer to listen. "And threw—and threw—and threw," he repeated, his face all sharp with some inexplicable agony.

I moved forward astonished. But it was then he found words— delivered roundly and clearly. These:—

And threw warm gules on Madeleine's young breast.

The trouble passed off his countenance, and he returned lightly to his place, rubbing his hands.

It had never occurred to me, though we had many times discussed reading and prize-competitions as a diversion, that Mr. Shaynor ever read Keats, or could quote him at all appositely. There was, after all, a certain stained-glass effect of light on the high bosom of the highly-polished picture which might, by stretch of fancy, suggest, as a vile chromo recalls some incomparable canvas, the line he had spoken. Night, my drink, and solitude were evidently turning Mr. Shaynor into a poet. He sat down again and wrote swiftly on his villainous note-paper, his lips quivering.

I shut the door into the inner office and moved up behind him. He made no sign that he saw or heard. I looked over his shoulder, and read, amid half-formed words, sentences, and wild scratches:—

> —Very cold it was. Very cold
> The hare—the hare—the hare—
> The birds——

He raised his head sharply, and frowned toward the blank shutters of the poulterer's shop where they jutted out against our window. Then one clear line came:—

> The hare, in spite of fur, was very cold.

The head, moving machine-like, turned right to the advertisement where the Blaudett's Cathedral pastille reeked abominably. He grunted, and went on:—

> Incense in a censer—
> Before her darling picture framed in gold—
> Maiden's picture—angel's portrait—

"Hsh!" said Mr. Cashell guardedly from the inner office, as though in the presence of spirits. "There's something coming through from somewhere; but it isn't Poole." I heard the crackle of sparks as he depressed the keys of the transmitter. In my own brain, too, something crackled, or it might have been the hair on my head. Then I heard my own voice, in a harsh whisper: "Mr. Cashell, there is something coming through here, too. Leave me alone till I tell you."

"But I thought you'd come to see this wonderful thing—Sir," indignantly at the end.

"Leave me alone till I tell you. Be quiet."

I watched—I waited. Under the blue-veined hand—the dry hand of the consumptive—came away clear, without erasure:

> And my weak spirit fails
> To think how the dead must freeze—

he shivered as he wrote—

> Beneath the churchyard mould.

Then he stopped, laid the pen down, and leaned back.

For an instant, that was half an eternity, the shop spun before me in a rainbow-tinted whirl, in and through which my own soul most dispassionately considered my own soul as that fought with an over-mastering fear. Then I smelt the strong smell of cigarettes from Mr. Shaynor's clothing, and heard, as though it had been the rending of trumpets, the rattle of his breathing. I was still in my place of observation, much as one would watch a rifle-shot at the butts, half-bent, hands on my knees, and head within a few inches of the black, red, and yellow blanket of his shoulder. I was whispering encouragement, evidently to my other self, sounding sentences, such as men pronounce in dreams.

"If he has read Keats, it proves nothing. If he hasn't—like causes *must* beget like effects. There is no escape from this law. *You* ought to be grateful that you know 'St. Agnes Eve' without the book; because, given the circumstances, such as Fanny Brand, who is the key of the enigma, and approximately represents the latitude and longitude of Fanny Brawne; allowing also for the bright red colour of the arterial blood upon the handkerchief, which was just what you were puzzling over in the shop just now; and counting the effect of the professional environment, here almost perfectly duplicated— the result is logical and inevitable. As inevitable as induction."

Still, the other half of my soul refused to be comforted. It was cowering in some minute and inadequate corner—at an immense distance.

Hereafter, I found myself one person again, my hands still gripping my knees, and my eyes glued on the page before Mr. Shaynor. As dreamers accept and explain the upheaval of landscapes and the resurrection of the dead, with excerpts from the evening hymn or the multiplication-table, so I had accepted the facts, whatever they might be, that I should witness, and had devised a theory, sane and plausible to my mind, that explained them all. Nay, I was even in advance of my facts, walking hurriedly before them, assured that they would fit my theory. And all that I now recall of that epoch-making theory are the lofty words: "If he has read Keats it's the chloric-ether. If he hasn't, it's the identical bacillus, or Hertzian wave of tuberculosis, *plus* Fanny Brand and the professional status which, in conjunction with the main-stream of subconscious thought common to all mankind, has thrown up temporarily an induced Keats."

Mr. Shaynor returned to his work, erasing and rewriting as before with swiftness. Two or three blank pages he tossed aside. Then he wrote, muttering:

The little smoke of a candle that goes out.

"No," he muttered. "Little smoke—little smoke—little smoke. What else?" He thrust his chin forward toward the advertisement, whereunder the last of the Blaudett's Cathedral pastilles fumed in its holder. "Ah!" Then with relief:—

The little smoke that dies in moonlight cold.

Evidently he was snared by the rhymes of his first verse, for he wrote and rewrote "gold—cold—mould" many times. Again he sought inspiration from the advertisement, and set down, without erasure, the line I had overheard:

And threw warm gules on Madeleine's young breast.

As I remembered the original it is "fair"—a trite word—instead of "young," and I found myself nodding approval, though I admitted that the attempt to reproduce "its little smoke in pallid moonlight died" was a failure.

Followed without a break ten or fifteen lines of bald prose—the naked soul's confession of its physical yearning for its beloved— unclean as we count uncleanliness; unwholesome, but human exceedingly; the raw material, so it seemed to me in that hour and in that place, whence Keats wove the twenty-sixth, seventh, and eighth stanzas of his poem. Shame I had none in overseeing this revelation; and my fear had gone with the smoke of the pastille.

"That's it," I murmured. "That's how it's blocked out. Go on! Ink it in, man. Ink it in!"

Mr. Shaynor returned to broken verse wherein "loveliness" was made to rhyme with a desire to look upon "her empty dress." He picked up a fold of the gay, soft blanket, spread it over one hand, caressed it with infinite tenderness, thought, muttered, traced some snatches which I could not decipher, shut his eyes drowsily, shook his head, and dropped the stuff. Here I found myself at fault, for I could not then see (as I do now) in what manner a red, black, and yellow Austrian blanket coloured his dreams.

In a few minutes he laid aside his pen, and, chin on hand, considered the shop with thoughtful and intelligent eyes. He threw down the blanket, rose, passed along a line of drug-drawers, and read the names on the labels aloud. Returning, he took from his desk

Christie's *New Commercial Plants* and the old Culpepper that I had given him, opened and laid them side by side with a clerky air, all trace of passion gone from his face, read first in one and then in the other, and paused with pen behind his ear.

"What wonder of Heaven's coming now?" I thought.

"Manna—manna—manna," he said at last, under wrinkled brows. "That's what I wanted. Good! Now then! Now then! Good! Good! Oh, by God, that's good!"

His voice rose and he spoke rightly and fully without a falter:—

> Candied apple, quince and plum and gourd,
> And jellies smoother than the creamy curd,
> And lucent syrups tinct with cinnamon,
> Manna and dates in Argosy transferred
> From Fez; and spiced dainties, every one
> From silken Samarcand to cedared Lebanon.

He repeated it once more, using "blander" for "smoother" in the second line; then wrote it down without erasure, but this time (my set eyes missed no stroke of any word) he substituted "soother" for his atrocious second thought, so that it came away under his hand as it is written in the book—as it is written in the book.

A wind went shouting down the street, and on the heels of the wind followed a spurt and rattle of rain.

After a smiling pause—and good right had he to smile—he began anew, always tossing the last sheet over his shoulder:—

> "The sharp rain falling on the window-pane,
> Rattling sleet—the wind-blown sleet."

Then prose: "It is very cold of mornings when the wind brings rain and sleet with it. I heard the sleet on the window-pane outside, and thought of you, my darling. I am always thinking of you. I wish we could both run away like two lovers into the storm and get that little cottage by the sea which we are always thinking about, my own dear darling. We could sit and watch the sea beneath our windows. It would be a fairyland all of our own—a fairy sea—a fairy sea. . . ."

He stopped, raised his head, and listened. The steady drone of the Channel along the sea-front that had borne us company so long leaped up a note to the sudden fuller surge that signals the change from ebb to flood. It beat in like the change of step throughout an army—this renewed pulse of the sea—and filled our ears till they, accepting it, marked it no longer.

> "A fairyland for you and me
> Across the foam—beyond . . .
> A magic foam, a perilous sea."

He grunted again with effort and bit his underlip. My throat dried, but I dared not gulp to moisten it lest I should break the spell that was drawing him nearer and nearer to the high-water mark but two of the sons of Adam have reached. Remember that in all the millions permitted there are no more than five—five little lines— of which one can say: "These are the pure Magic. These are the clear Vision. The rest is only poetry." And Mr. Shaynor was playing hot and cold with two of them!

I vowed no unconscious thought of mine should influence the blindfold soul, and pinned myself desperately to the other three, repeating and re-repeating:

> A savage spot as holy and enchanted
> As e'er beneath a waning moon was haunted
> By woman wailing for her demon lover

But though I believed my brain thus occupied, my every sense hung upon the writing under the dry, bony hand, all brown-fingered with chemicals and cigarette-smoke.

Our windows fronting on the dangerous foam,

(he wrote, after long, irresolute snatches), and then—

"Our open casements facing desolate seas
Forlorn—forlorn—"

Here again his face grew peaked and anxious with that sense of
loss I had first seen when the Power snatched him. But this time
the agony was tenfold keener. As I watched it mounted like mercury
in the tube. It lighted his face from within till I thought the visibly
scourged soul must leap forth naked between his jaws, unable to
endure. A drop of sweat trickled from my forehead down my nose
and splashed on the back of my hand.

"Our windows facing on the desolate seas
And pearly foam of magic fairyland—"

"Not yet—not yet," he muttered, "wait a minute. *Please* wait a
minute. I shall get it then—"

Our magic windows fronting on the sea,
The dangerous foam of desolate seas . . .
For aye.

"*Ouh,* my God!"
From head to heel he shook—shook from the marrow of his
bones outwards—then leaped to his feet with raised arms, and
slid the chair screeching across the tiled floor where it struck the
drawers behind and fell with a jar. Mechanically, I stooped to
recover it.
As I rose, Mr. Shaynor was stretching and yawning at leisure.
"I've had a bit of a doze," he said. "How did I come to knock
the chair over? You look rather—"

"The chair startled me," I answered. "It was so sudden in this quiet."

Young Mr. Cashell behind his shut door was offendedly silent.

"I suppose I must have been dreaming," said Mr. Shaynor.

"I suppose you must," I said. "Talking of dreams—I—I noticed you writing—before—"

He flushed consciously.

"I meant to ask you if you've ever read anything written by a man called Keats."

"Oh! I haven't much time to read poetry, and I can't say that I remember the name exactly. Is he a popular writer?"

"Middling. I thought you might know him because he's the only poet who was ever a druggist. And he's rather what's called the lover's poet."

"Indeed. I must dip into him. What did he write about?"

"A lot of things. Here's a sample that may interest you."

Then and there, carefully, I repeated the verse he had twice spoken and once written not ten minutes ago.

"Ah. Anybody could see he was a druggist from that line about the tinctures and syrups. It's a fine tribute to our profession."

"I don't know," said young Mr. Cashell, with icy politeness, opening the door one half-inch, "if you still happen to be interested in our trifling experiments. But, should such be the case——"

I drew him aside, whispering, "Shaynor seemed going off into some sort of fit when I spoke to you just now. I thought, even at the risk of being rude, it wouldn't do to take you off your instruments just as the call was coming through. Don't you see?"

"Granted—granted as soon as asked," he said unbending. "I *did* think it a shade odd at the time. So that was why he knocked the chair down?"

"I hope I haven't missed anything," I said. "I'm afraid I can't say that, but you're just in time for the end of a rather curious performance. You can come in, too, Mr. Shaynor. Listen, while I read it off."

The Morse instrument was ticking furiously. Mr. Cashell inter-preted: "*'K.K.V. Can make nothing of your signals.'*" A pause. "*'M.M.V. M.M.V. Signals unintelligible. Purpose anchor Sandown Bay. Examine instruments to-morrow.'* Do you know what that means? It's a couple of men-o'-war working Marconi signals off the Isle of Wight. They are trying to talk to each other. Neither can read the other's messages, but all their messages are being taken in by our receiver here. They've been going on for ever so long. I wish you could have heard it."

"How wonderful!" I said. "Do you mean we're overhearing Portsmouth ships trying to talk to each other—that we're eaves-dropping across half South England?"

"Just that. Their transmitters are all right, but their receivers are out of order, so they only get a dot here and a dash there. Nothing clear."

"Why is that?"

"God knows—and Science will know to-morrow. Perhaps the induction is faulty; perhaps the receivers aren't tuned to receive just the number of vibrations per second that the transmitter sends. Only a word here and there. Just enough to tantalise."

Again the Morse sprang to life.

"That's one of 'em complaining now. Listen: *'Disheartening—most disheartening.'* It's quite pathetic. Have you ever seen a spiritualistic seance? It reminds me of that sometimes—odds and ends of messages coming out of nowhere—a word here and there—no good at all."

"But mediums are all impostors," said Mr. Shaynor, in the door-way, lighting an asthma-cigarette. "They only do it for the money they can make. I've seen 'em."

"Here's Poole, at last—clear as a bell. L.L.L. *Now* we sha'n't be long."

Mr. Cashell rattled the keys merrily. "Anything you'd like to tell 'em?"

"No, I don't think so," I said. "I'll go home and get to bed. I'm feeling a little tired."

Mary E. Wilkins Freeman

(1852–1930)

MARY ELEANOR WILKINS WAS born in Massachusetts, where she worked for decades as private secretary to Oliver Wendell Holmes, Sr. After winning a prize for her own writing as a teenager, she first wrote for children. She sold her first adult story to Mary Louise Booth, the legendary editor of *Harper's Bazaar*. Early in her life she lost both a sister and her parents, and throughout her adult writing she demonstrates a melancholy compassion for lost and hurt children. Her initial writing was for children, after she won a story prize during her own teen years and decided to pursue writing.

"It is natural to suppose that any reader of current English literature would know Miss Wilkins," proclaimed a magazine article at the turn of the twentieth century. Although her star faded during the middle of the century, Freeman received a great deal of distinguished admiration in her day. Mark Twain was a fan. When the American Academy of Arts and Letters created the William Dean Howells Medal for Distinction in Fiction, its first recipient was Freeman. In 1903, the book *Women Authors of Our Day in Their Homes* nicely described her as "the most delicate and appreciative delineator of rural New England characters who has written within a generation."

Freeman was a disciple of the innovative mystery writer Anna Katharine Green, whose 1878 novel, *The Leavenworth Case*, was the first serious detective novel written by a woman. Freeman wrote to Green and emulated some of her techniques in stories such as "The Long Arm." Her disarmingly casual story of a small-town psychic vampire, "Luella Miller," appears in the Connoisseur's Collection volume *Dracula's Guest*.

You will find no haunted mansions, no tormented aristocrats or monks. She wrote about ordinary people living ordinary lives, and the supernatural sneaks up on them through everyday activities. The first words in the story "Luella Miller" are "Close to the village street stood the one-story house. . . ." It's the kind of image for which Mary E. Wilkins Freeman (sometimes referred to by her earlier name Mary Eleanor Wilkins) is remembered, from her stories— whether realistic or supernatural—about unknown lives in undistin-guished places. Her distaste for the suffocating strictures of religious doctrine can be traced to her own Congregationalist upbringing. In her fiction, she portrays the narrow-minded religious orthodoxy that haunted her own childhood, the ties that bind small commu-nities, and a long line of abandoned and abused children.

In one story, "The Vacant Lot," a woman goes out to hang laundry and finds the shadow of another woman hanging the shadows of laundry, but no one is there—only shadows. Freeman wrote especially well, with sensitivity but not sentimentality, about the lives of women and children. She is best known for her stories of lost, abandoned, even spectral children—as in "The Wind in the Rose-Bush," which is sweet and sad but somewhat predictable, and "The Lost Ghost." She explored dreams, with powerful sexual subtexts beyond her era, in stories such as "A Symphony in Lavender" and "The Hall Bedroom," which was first published in 1903 in the March 28 issue of *Collier's* magazine. Its evocation of other dimen-sions succeeds because Freeman wrote with both feet firmly planted in mundane normality but her vision focused beyond it.

The Hall Bedroom

MY NAME IS MRS. Elizabeth Jennings. I am a highly respectable
woman. I may style myself a gentlewoman, for in my youth I
enjoyed advantages. I was well brought up, and I graduated at a
young ladies' seminary. I also married well. My husband was that
most genteel of all merchants, an apothecary. His shop was on the
corner of the main street in Rockton, the town where I was born,
and where I lived until the death of my husband.

My parents had died when I had been married a short time, so I
was left quite alone in the world. I was not competent to carry on
the apothecary business by myself, for I had no knowledge of drugs,
and had a mortal terror of giving poisons instead of medicines.
Therefore I was obliged to sell at a considerable sacrifice, and the
proceeds, some five thousand dollars, were all I had in the world.
The income was not enough to support me in any kind of comfort,
and I saw that I must in some way earn money. I thought at first
of teaching, but I was no longer young, and methods had changed
since my school days. What I was able to teach, nobody wished to
know. I could think of only one thing to do: take boarders. But the
same objection to that business as to teaching held good in Rockton.
Nobody wished to board. My husband had rented a house with a
number of bedrooms, and I advertised, but nobody applied. Finally
my cash was running very low, and I became desperate. I packed

up my furniture, rented a large house in this town and moved here.
It was a venture attended with many risks. In the first place the rent
was exorbitant, in the next I was entirely unknown. However, I am
a person of considerable ingenuity, and have inventive power, and
much enterprise when the occasion presses. I advertised in a very
original manner, although that actually took my last penny, that is,
the last penny of my ready money, and I was forced to draw on my
principal to purchase my first supplies, a thing which I had resolved
never on any account to do. But the great risk met with a reward,
for I had several applicants within two days after my advertisement
appeared in the paper. Within two weeks my boarding-house was
well established, I became very successful, and my success would
have been uninterrupted had it not been for the mysterious and
bewildering occurrences which I am about to relate. I am now
forced to leave the house and rent another. Some of my old boarders
accompany me, some, with the most unreasonable nervousness,
refuse to be longer associated in any way, however indirectly, with
the terrible and uncanny happenings which I have to relate. It
remains to be seen whether my ill luck in this house will follow me
into another, and whether my whole prosperity in life will be forever
shadowed by the Mystery of the Hall Bedroom. Instead of telling
the strange story myself in my own words, I shall present the Journal
of Mr. George H. Wheatcroft. I shall show you the portions beginning on January 18 of the present year, the date when he took up his
residence with me. Here it is:

January 18, 1883. Here I am established in my new boarding-
house. I have, as befits my humble means, the hall bedroom,
even the hall bedroom on the third floor. I have heard all my
life of hall bedrooms, I have seen hall bedrooms, I have been in
them, but never until now, when I am actually established in one,
did I comprehend what, at once, an ignominious and sternly
uncompromising thing a hall bedroom is. It proves the ignominy

of the dweller therein. No man at thirty-six (my age) would be domiciled in a hall bedroom, unless he were himself ignominious, at least comparatively speaking. I am proved by this means incontrovertibly to have been left far behind in the race. I see no reason why I should not live in this hall bedroom for the rest of my life, that is, if I have money enough to pay the landlady, and that seems probable, since my small funds are invested as safely as if I were an orphan-ward in charge of a pillar of a sanctuary. After the valuables have been stolen, I have most carefully locked the stable door. I have experienced the revulsion which comes sooner or later to the adventurous soul who experiences nothing but defeat and so-called ill luck. I have swung to the opposite extreme. I have lost in everything—I have lost in love, I have lost in money, I have lost in the struggle for preferment, I have lost in health and strength. I am now settled down in a hall bedroom to live upon my small income, and regain my health by mild potations of the mineral waters here, if possible; if not, to live here without my health—for mine is not a necessarily fatal malady—until Providence shall take me out of my hall bedroom. There is no one place more than another where I care to live. There is not sufficient motive to take me away, even if the mineral waters do not benefit me. So I am here and to stay in the hall bedroom. The landlady is civil, and even kind, as kind as a woman who has to keep her poor womanly eye upon the main chance can be. The struggle for money always injures the fine grain of a woman; she is too fine a thing to do it; she does not by nature belong with the gold grubbers, and it therefore lowers her; she steps from heights to claw and scrape and dig. But she can not help it oftentimes, poor thing, and her deterioration thereby is to be condoned. The landlady is all she can be, taking her strain of adverse circumstances into consideration, and the table is good, even conscientiously so. It looks to me as if she were foolish enough to strive to give the boarders their money's worth, with the due regard for the main chance which is inevitable. However, that is of minor importance to me, since my diet is restricted.

It is curious what an annoyance a restriction in diet can be even to a man who has considered himself somewhat indifferent to gastronomic delights. There was to-day a pudding for dinner, which I could not taste without penalty, but which I longed for. It was only because it looked unlike any other pudding that I had ever seen, and assumed a mental and spiritual significance. It seemed to me, whimsically no doubt, as if tasting it might give me a new sensation, and consequently a new outlook. Trivial things may lead to large results: why should I not get a new outlook by means of a pudding? Life here stretches before me most monotonously, and I feel like clutching at alleviations, though paradoxically, since I have settled down with the utmost acquiescence. Still one can not immediately overcome and change radically all one's nature. Now I look at myself critically and search for the keynote to my whole self, and my actions, I have always been conscious of a reaching out, an overweening desire for the new, the untried, for the broadness of further horizons, the seas beyond seas, the thought beyond thought. This characteristic has been the primary cause of all my misfortunes. I have the soul of an explorer, and in nine out of ten cases this leads to destruction. If I had possessed capital and sufficient push, I should have been one of the searchers after the North Pole. I have been an eager student of astronomy. I have studied botany with avidity, and have dreamed of new flora in unexplored parts of the world, and the same with animal life and geology. I longed for riches in order to discover the power and sense of possession of the rich. I longed for love in order to discover the possibilities of the emotions. I longed for all that the mind of man could conceive as desirable for man, not so much for purely selfish ends, as from an insatiable thirst for knowledge of a universal trend. But I have limitations, I do not quite understand of what nature—for what mortal ever did quite understand his own limitations, since a knowledge of them would preclude their existence?—but they have prevented my progress to any extent. Therefore behold me in my hall bedroom, settled at last into a groove of fate so deep that I have lost the sight of even my horizons. Just at present, as I write here, my horizon on the left, that is my physical horizon, is a wall covered with cheap paper. The paper is an indeterminate pattern in white and gilt. There are a few photographs of my own hung about, and on the large wall space beside the bed there is a large oil painting which belongs to my landlady. It has a massive tarnished gold frame, and, curiously enough, the painting itself is rather good. I have no idea who the artist could have been. It is of the conventional landscape type in vogue some fifty years since, the type so fondly reproduced in chromos—the winding river with the little boat occupied by a pair of lovers, the cottage nestled among trees on the right shore, the gentle slope of the hills and the church spire in the background—but still it is well done. It gives me the impression of an artist without the slightest originality of design, but much of technique. But for some inexplicable reason the picture frets me. I find myself gazing at it when I do not wish to do so. It seems to compel my attention like some intent face in the room. I shall ask Mrs. Jennings to have it removed. I will hang in its place some photographs which I have in a trunk.

January 26. I do not write regularly in my journal. I never did. I see no reason why I should. I see no reason why any one should have the slightest sense of duty in such a matter. Some days I have nothing which interests me sufficiently to write out, some days I feel either too ill or too indolent. For four days I have not written, from a mixture of all three reasons. Now, to-day I both feel like it and I have something to write. Also I am distinctly better than I have been. Perhaps the waters are benefiting me, or the change of air. Or possibly it is something else more subtle. Possibly my mind has seized upon something new, a discovery which causes it to react upon my failing body and serves as a stimulant. All I know is, I feel distinctly better, and am conscious of an acute interest in doing so, which is of late strange to me. I have been rather indifferent, and sometimes have wondered if that were not the cause rather than the result of my state of health. I have been so continually balked that I have settled into a state of inertia. I lean rather comfortably against my obstacles. After all, the worst of the pain always lies in the struggle. Give up and it is rather pleasant than otherwise. If one did not kick, the pricks would not in the least matter. However, for some reason, for the last few days, I seem to have awakened from my state of quiescence. It means future trouble for me, no doubt, but in the meantime I am not sorry. It began with the picture—the large oil painting. I went to Mrs. Jennings about it yesterday, and she, to my surprise—for I thought it a matter that could be easily arranged—objected to having it removed. Her reasons were two; both simple, both sufficient, especially since I, after all, had no very strong desire either way. It seems that the picture does not belong to her. It hung here when she rented the house. She says if it is removed, a very large and unsightly discoloration of the wall-paper will be exposed, and she does not like to ask for new paper. The owner, an old man, is traveling abroad, the agent is curt, and she has only been in the house a very short time. Then it would mean a sad upheaval of my room, which would disturb me. She also says that there is no place in the house where she can store the picture, and there is not a vacant space in another room for one so large. So I let the picture remain. It really, when I came to think of it, was very immaterial after all. But I got my photographs out of my trunk, and I hung them around the large picture. The wall is almost completely covered. I hung them yesterday afternoon, and last night I repeated a strange experience which I have had in some degree every night since I have been here, but was not sure whether it deserved the name of experience, but was not rather one of those dreams in which one dreams one is awake. But last night it came again, and now I know. There is something very singular about this room. I am very much interested. I will write down for future reference the events of last night. Concerning those of the preceding nights since I have slept in this room, I will simply say that they have been of a similar nature, but, as it were, only the preliminary stages, the prologue to what happened last night.

I am not depending upon the mineral waters here as the one remedy for my malady, which is sometimes of an acute nature, and indeed constantly threatens me with considerable suffering unless by medicine I can keep it in check. I will say that the medicine which I employ is not of the class commonly known as drugs. It is impossible that it can be held responsible for what I am about to transcribe. My mind last night and every night since I have slept in this room was in an absolutely normal state. I take this medicine, prescribed by the specialist in whose charge I was before coming here, regularly every four hours while awake. As I am never a good sleeper, it follows that I am enabled with no inconvenience to take any medicine during the night with the same regularity as during the day. It is my habit, therefore, to place my bottle and spoon where I can put my hand upon them easily without lighting the gas. Since I have been in this room, I have placed the bottle of medicine upon my dresser at the side of the room opposite the bed. I have done this rather than place it nearer, as once I jostled the bottle and spilled most of the contents, and it is not easy for me to replace it, as it is expensive. Therefore I placed it in security on the dresser, and, indeed, that is but three or four steps from my bed, the room being so small. Last night I wakened as usual, and I knew, since I had fallen asleep about eleven, that it must be in the neighborhood of three. I wake with almost clock-like regularity and it is never necessary for me to consult my watch.

I had slept unusually well and without dreams, and I awoke fully at once, with a feeling of refreshment to which I am not accustomed. I immediately got out of bed and began stepping across the room in the direction of my dresser, on which I had set my medicine-bottle and spoon.

To my utter amazement, the steps which had hitherto sufficed to take me across my room did not suffice to do so. I advanced several paces, and my outstretched hands touched nothing. I stopped and went on again. I was sure that I was moving in a straight direction, and even if I had not been I knew it was impossible to advance in any direction in my tiny apartment without coming into collision either with a wall or a piece of furniture. I continued to walk falteringly, as I have seen people on the stage: a step, then a long falter, then a sliding step. I kept my hands extended; they touched nothing. I stopped again. I had not the least sentiment of fear or consternation. It was rather the very stupefaction of surprise. "How is this?" seemed thundering in my ears. "What is this?"

The room was perfectly dark. There was nowhere any glimmer, as is usually the case, even in a so-called dark room, from the walls, picture-frames, looking-glass or white objects. It was absolute gloom. The house stood in a quiet part of the town. There were many trees about; the electric street lights were extinguished at midnight; there was no moon and the sky was cloudy. I could not distinguish my one window, which I thought strange, even on such a dark night. Finally I changed my plan of motion and turned, as nearly as I could estimate, at right angles. Now, I thought, I must reach soon, if I kept on, my writing-table underneath the window; or, if I am going in the opposite direction, the hall door. I reached neither. I am telling the unvarnished truth when I say that I began to count my steps and carefully measure my paces after that, and I traversed a space clear of furniture at least twenty feet by thirty—a very large apartment. And as I walked I was conscious that my naked feet were pressing something which gave rise to sensations the like of which I had never experienced before. As nearly as I can express it, it was as if my feet pressed something as elastic as air or water, which was in this case unyielding to my weight. It gave me a curious sensation of buoyancy and stimulation. At the same time this surface, if surface be the right name, which I trod, felt cool to my feet with the coolness of vapor or fluidity, seeming to overlap the soles. Finally I stood still; my surprise was at last merging into a measure of consternation. "Where am I?" I thought. "What am I going to do?" Stories that I had heard of travelers being taken from their beds and conveyed into strange and dangerous places, Middle Age stories of the Inquisition flashed through my brain. I knew all the time that for a man who had gone to bed in a commonplace hall bedroom in a very commonplace little town such surmises were highly ridiculous, but it is hard for the human mind to grasp anything but a human explanation of phenomena. Almost anything seemed then, and seems now, more rational than an explanation bordering upon the supernatural, as we understand the supernatural. At last I called, though rather softly, "What does this mean?" I said quite aloud, "Where am I? Who is here? Who is doing this? I tell you I will have no such nonsense. Speak, if there is anybody here." But all was dead silence. Then suddenly a light flashed through the open transom of my door. Somebody had heard me—a man who rooms next door, a decent kind of man, also here for his health. He turned on the gas in the hall and called to me. "What's the matter?" he asked, in an agitated, trembling voice. He is a nervous fellow.

Directly, when the light flashed through my transom, I saw that I was in my familiar hall bedroom. I could see everything quite distinctly—my tumbled bed, my writing-table, my dresser, my chair, my little wash-stand, my clothes hanging on a row of pegs, the old picture on the wall. The picture gleamed out with singular distinctness in the light from the transom. The river seemed actually to run and ripple, and the boat to be gliding with the current. I gazed fascinated at it, as I replied to the anxious voice:

"Nothing is the matter with me," said I. "Why?"

"I thought I heard you speak," said the man outside. "I thought maybe you were sick."

"No," I called back. "I am all right. I am trying to find my medicine in the dark, that's all. I can see now you have lighted the gas."

"Nothing is the matter?"

"No; sorry I disturbed you. Good-night."

"Good-night." Then I heard the man's door shut after a minute's pause. He was evidently not quite satisfied. I took a pull at my medicine-bottle, and got into bed. He had left the hall-gas burning. I did not go to sleep again for some time. Just before I did so, some one, probably Mrs. Jennings, came out in the hall and extinguished the gas. This morning when I awoke everything was as usual in my room. I wonder if I shall have any such experience to-night.

January 27. I shall write in my journal every day until this draws to some definite issue. Last night my strange experience deepened, as something tells me it will continue to do. I retired quite early, at half-past ten. I took the precaution, on retiring, to place beside my bed, on a chair, a box of safety matches, that I might not be in the dilemma of the night before. I took my medicine on retiring; that made me due to wake at half-past two. I had not fallen asleep directly, but had had certainly three hours of sound, dreamless slumber when I awoke. I lay a few minutes hesitating whether or not to strike a safety match and light my way to the dresser, whereon stood my medicine-bottle. I hesitated, not because I had the least sensation of fear, but because of the same shrinking from a nerve shock that leads one at times to dread the plunge into an icy bath. It seemed much easier to me to strike that match and cross my hall bedroom to my dresser, take my dose, then return quietly to my bed, than to risk the chance of floundering about in some unknown limbo either of fancy or reality.

At last, however, the spirit of adventure, which has always been such a ruling one for me, conquered. I rose. I took the box of safety matches in my hand, and started on, as I conceived, the straight course for my dresser, about five feet across from my bed. As before, I traveled and traveled and did not reach it. I advanced with groping hands extended, setting one foot cautiously before the other, but I touched nothing except the indefinite, unnameable surface which my feet pressed. All of a sudden, though, I became aware of something. One of my senses was saluted, nay, more than that, hailed, with imperiousness, and that was, strangely enough, my sense of smell, but in a hitherto unknown fashion. It seemed as if the odor reached my mentality first. I reversed the usual process, which is, as I understand it, like this: the odor when encountered strikes first the olfactory nerve, which transmits the intelligence to the brain. It is as if, to put it rudely, my nose met a rose, and then the nerve belonging to the sense said to my brain, "Here is a rose." This time my brain said, "Here is a rose," and my sense then recognized it. I say rose, but it was not a rose, that is, not the fragrance of any rose which I had ever known. It was undoubtedly a flower-odor, and rose came perhaps the nearest to it. My mind realized it first with what seemed a leap of rapture. "What is this delight?" I asked myself. And then the ravishing fragrance smote my sense. I breathed it in and it seemed to feed my thoughts, satisfying some hitherto unknown hunger. Then I took a step further and another fragrance appeared, which I liken to lilies for lack of something better, and then came violets, then mignonette. I can not describe the experience, but it was a sheer delight, a rapture of sublimated sense. I groped further and further, and always into new waves of fragrance. I seemed to be wading breast-high through flower-beds of Paradise, but all the time I touched nothing with my groping hands. At last a sudden giddiness as of surfeit overcame me. I realized that I might be in some unknown peril. I was distinctly afraid. I struck one of my safety matches, and I was in my hall bedroom, midway between my bed and my dresser. I took my dose of medicine and went to bed, and after a while fell asleep and did not wake till morning.

January 28. Last night I did not take my usual dose of medicine. In these days of new remedies and mysterious results upon certain organizations, it occurred to me to wonder if possibly the drug might have, after all, something to do with my strange experience.

I did not take my medicine. I put the bottle as usual on my dresser, since I feared if I interrupted further the customary sequence of affairs I might fail to wake. I placed my box of matches on the chair beside the bed. I fell asleep about quarter past eleven o'clock, and I waked when the clock was striking two—a little earlier than my wont. I did not hesitate this time. I rose at once, took my box of matches and proceeded as formerly. I walked what seemed a great space without coming into collision with anything. I kept sniffing for the wonderful fragrances of the night before, but they did not recur. Instead, I was suddenly aware that I was tasting something, some morsel of sweetness hitherto unknown, and, as in the case of the odor, the usual order seemed reversed, and it was as if I tasted it first in my mental consciousness. Then the sweetness rolled under my tongue. I thought involuntarily of "Sweeter than honey or the honeycomb" of the Scripture. I thought of the Old Testament manna. An ineffable content as of satisfied hunger seized me. I stepped further, and a new savor was upon my palate. And so on. It was never cloying, though of such sharp sweetness that it fairly stung. It was the merging of a material sense into a spiritual one. I said to myself, "I have lived my life and always have I gone hungry until now." I could feel my brain act swiftly under the influence of this heavenly food as under a stimulant. Then suddenly I repeated the experience of the night before. I grew dizzy, and an indefinite fear and shrinking were upon me. I struck my safety match and was back in my hall bedroom. I returned to bed, and soon fell asleep. I did not take my medicine. I am resolved not to do so longer. I am feeling much better.

January 29. Last night to bed as usual, matches in place; fell asleep about eleven and waked at half-past one. I heard the half-hour strike; I am waking earlier and earlier every night. I had not taken my medicine, though it was on the dresser as usual. I again took my match-box in hand and started to cross the room, and, as always, traversed strange spaces, but this night, as seems fated to be the case every night, my experience was different. Last night I neither smelled nor tasted, but I heard—my Lord, I heard! The first sound of which I was conscious was one like the constantly gathering and receding murmur of a river, and it seemed to come from the wall behind my bed where the old picture hangs. Nothing in nature except a river gives that impression of at once advance and retreat. I could not mistake it. On, ever on, came the swelling murmur of the waves, past and ever past they died in the distance. Then I heard above the murmur of the river a song in an unknown tongue which I recognized as being unknown, yet which I understood; but the understanding was in my brain, with no words of interpretation. The song had to do with me, but with me in unknown futures for which I had no images of comparison in the past; yet a sort of ecstasy as of a prophecy of bliss filled my whole consciousness. The song never ceased, but as I moved on I came into new sound-waves. There was the pealing of bells which might have been made of crystal, and might have summoned to the gates of heaven. There was music of strange instruments, great harmonies pierced now and then by small whispers as of love, and it all filled me with a certainty of a future of bliss.

At last I seemed the centre of a mighty orchestra which constantly deepened and increased until I seemed to feel myself being lifted gently but mightily upon the waves of sound as upon the waves of a sea. Then again the terror and the impulse to flee to my own familiar scenes was upon me. I struck my match and was back in my hall bedroom. I do not see how I sleep at all after such wonders, but sleep I do. I slept dreamlessly until daylight this morning.

January 30. I heard yesterday something with regard to my hall bedroom which affected me strangely. I can not for the life of me say whether it intimidated me, filled me with the horror of the abnormal, or rather roused to a greater degree my spirit of adventure and discovery. I was down at the Cure, and was sitting on the veranda sipping idly my mineral water, when somebody spoke my name. "Mr. Wheatcroft?" said the voice politely, inter-rogatively, somewhat apollogetically, as if to provide for a possible mistake in my identity. I turned and saw a gentleman whom I recognized at once. I seldom forget names or faces. He was a Mr. Addison whom I had seen considerable of three years ago at a little summer hotel in the mountains. It was one of those passing acquaintances which signify little one way or the other. If never renewed, you have no regret; if renewed, you accept the renewal with no hesitation. It is in every way negative. But just now, in my feeble, friendless state, the sight of a face which beams with pleased remembrance is rather grateful. I felt distinctly glad to see the man. He sat down beside me. He also had a glass of the water. His health, while not as bad as mine, leaves much to be desired.

Addison had often been in this town before. He had in fact lived here at one time. He had remained at the Cure three years, taking the waters daily. He therefore knows about all there is to be known about the town, which is not very large. He asked me where I was staying, and when I told him the street, rather excitedly inquired the number. When I told him the number, which is 240, he gave a manifest start, and after one sharp glance at me sipped his water in silence for a moment. He had so evidently betrayed some ulterior knowledge with regard to my residence that I questioned him.

"What do you know about 240 Pleasant Street?" said I.

"Oh, nothing," he replied, evasively, sipping his water.

After a little while, however, he inquired, in what he evidently tried to render a casual tone, what room I occupied. "I once lived a few weeks at 240 Pleasant Street myself," he said. "That house always was a boarding-house, I guess."

"It had stood vacant for a term of years before the present occupant rented it, I believe," I remarked. Then I answered his question. "I have the hall bedroom on the third floor," said I. "The quarters are pretty straitened, but comfortable enough as hall bedrooms go."

But Mr. Addison had showed such unmistakable consternation at my reply that then I persisted in my questioning as to the cause, and at last he yielded and told me what he knew. He had hesitated both because he shrank from displaying what I might consider an unmanly superstition, and because he did not wish to influence me beyond what the facts of the case warranted. "Well, I will tell you, Wheatcroft," he said. "Briefly all I know is this: When last I heard of 240 Pleasant Street it was not rented because of foul play which was supposed to have taken place there, though nothing was ever proved. There were two disappearances, and—in each case—of an occupant of the hall bedroom which you now have. The first disappearance was of a very beautiful girl who had come here for her health and was said to be the victim of a profound melancholy, induced by a love disappointment. She obtained board at 240 and occupied the hall bedroom about two weeks; then one morning she was gone, having seemingly vanished into thin air. Her relatives were communicated with; she had not many, nor friends either, poor girl, and a thorough search was made, but the last I knew she had never come to light. There were two or three arrests, but nothing ever came of them. Well, that was before my day here, but the second disappearance took place when I was in the house—a fine young fellow who had overworked in college. He had to pay his own way. He had taken cold, had the grip, and that and the overwork about finished him, and he came on here for a month's rest and recuperation. He had been in that room about two weeks, a little less, when one morning he wasn't there. Then there was a great hullabaloo. It seems that he had let fall some hints to the effect that there was something queer about the room, but, of course, the police did not think much of that. They made arrests right and left, but they never found him, and the arrested were discharged, though some of them are probably under a cloud of suspicion to this day. Then the boarding-house was shut up. Six years ago nobody would have boarded there, much less occupied that hall bedroom, but now I suppose new people have come in and the story has died out. I dare say your landlady will not thank me for reviving it."

I assured him that it would make no possible difference to me. He looked at me sharply, and asked bluntly if I had seen anything wrong or unusual about the room. I replied, guarding myself from falsehood with a quibble, that I had seen nothing in the least unusual about the room, as indeed I had not, and have not now, but that may come. I feel that that will come in due time. Last night I neither saw, nor heard, nor smelled, nor tasted, but I—felt. Last night, having started again on my exploration of, God knows what, I had not advanced a step before I touched something. My first sensation was one of disappointment. "It is the dresser, and I am at the end of it now," I thought. But I soon discovered that it was not the old painted dresser which I touched, but something carved, as nearly as I could discover with my unskilled finger-tips, with winged things. There were certainly long keen curves of wings which seemed to overlay an arabesque of fine leaf and flower work. I do not know what the object was that I touched. It may have been a chest. I may seem to be exaggerating when I say that it somehow failed or exceeded in some mysterious respect of being the shape of anything I had ever touched. I do not know what the material was. It was as smooth as ivory, but it did not feel like ivory; there was a singular warmth about it, as if it had stood long in hot sunlight. I continued, and I encountered other objects I am inclined to think were pieces of furniture of fashions and possibly of uses unknown to me, and about them all was the strange mystery as to shape. At last I came to what was evidently an open window of large area. I distinctly felt a soft, warm wind, yet with a crystal freshness, blow on my face. It was not the window of my hall bedroom, that I know. Looking out, I could see nothing. I only felt the wind blowing on my face.

Then suddenly, without any warning, my groping hands to the right and left touched living beings, beings in the likeness of men and women, palpable creatures in palpable attire. I could feel the soft silken texture of their garments which swept around me, seeming to half infold me in clinging meshes like cobwebs. I was in a crowd of these people, whatever they were, and whoever they were, but, curiously enough, without seeing one of them I had a strong sense of recognition as I passed among them. Now and then a hand that I knew closed softly over mine; once an arm passed around me. Then I began to feel myself gently swept on and impelled by this softly moving throng; their floating garments seemed to fairly wind me about, and again a swift terror overcame me. I struck my match, and was back in my hall bedroom. I wonder if I had not better keep my gas burning to-night? I wonder if it be possible that this is going too far? I wonder what became of those other people, the man and the woman who occupied this room? I wonder if I had better not stop where I am?

January 31. Last night I saw—I saw more than I can describe, more than is lawful to describe. Something which nature has rightly hidden has been revealed to me, but it is not for me to disclose too much of her secret. This much I will say, that doors and windows open into and out-of-doors to which the outdoors which we know is but a vestibule. And there is a river; there is something strange with respect to that picture. There is a river upon which one could sail away. It was flowing silently, for to-night I could only see. I saw that I was right in thinking I recognized some of the people whom I encountered the night before, though some were strange to me. It is true that the girl who disappeared from the hall bedroom was very beautiful. Everything which I saw last night was very beautiful to my one sense that could grasp it. I wonder what it would all be if all my senses together were to grasp it? I wonder if I had better not keep my gas burning to-night? I wonder—

This finishes the journal which Mr. Wheatcroft left in his hall bedroom. The morning after the last entry he was gone. His friend, Mr. Addison, came here, and a search was made. They even tore down the wall behind the picture, and they did find something rather queer for a house that had been used for boarders, where you would think no room would have been let run to waste. They found another room, a long narrow one, the length of the hall bedroom, but narrower, hardly more than a closet. There was no window, nor door, and all there was in it was a sheet of paper covered with figures, as if somebody had been doing sums. They made a lot of talk about those figures, and they tried to make out that the fifth dimension, whatever that is, was proved, but they said afterward they didn't prove anything. They tried to make out then that somebody had murdered poor Mr. Wheatcroft and hid the body, and they arrested poor Mr. Addison, but they couldn't make out anything against him. They proved he was in the Cure all that night and couldn't have done it. They don't know what became of Mr. Wheatcroft, and now they say two more disappeared from that same room before I rented the house.

The agent came and promised to put the new room they discovered into the hall bedroom and have everything new—papered and painted. He took away the picture; folks hinted there was something queer about that, I don't know what. It looked innocent enough, and I guess he burned it up. He said if I would stay he would arrange it with the owner, who everybody says is a very queer man, so I should not have to pay much if any rent. But I told him I couldn't stay if he was to give me the rent. That I wasn't afraid of anything myself, though I must say I wouldn't want to put anybody in that hall bedroom without telling him all about it; but my boarders would leave, and I knew I couldn't get any more. I told him I would rather have had a regular ghost than what seemed to be a way of going out of the house to nowhere and never coming back again. I moved, and, as I said before, it remains to be seen whether my ill luck follows me to this house or not. Anyway, it has no hall bedroom.

❊

E. Nesbit

(1858–1924)

EDITH NESBIT IS BEST known as the author of several novels for
children that appeared in the first decade of the new century but
which feel late Victorian in their voice. She wrote with a free imagination and a delicious literate wit. One series, about a group of
children whose surname is never given, features marvelous creations
such as the mythic, vainglorious bird that cavorts through *The
Phoenix and the Carpet* and the cantankerous wish-granting Psammead or sand fairy of *Five Children and It*. The adventures are less
fantastic but no less entertaining in *The Railway Children* and other
books about the Bastable family.

But the sunny escapades permitted by the era's standards of children's literature could not encompass all of Nesbit's protean imagination. Much of it spilled over into darker visions, ranging from
ghost stories such as "Man Size in Marble" to horrific science fiction
such as "The Five Senses," which was published in the *London Magazine* in December 1909. Nesbit lacked Edith Wharton's light touch;
like M. R. James, she summoned a visceral horror, but without
James's oblique, antiquarian way of sidling up to the monstrous.
Nesbit ran straight toward it and away from it. Often she was
shocking and even vulgar, and few of her stories end happily. It was
mere truth in advertising when she titled her 1893 collection *Grim
Tales*. Yet Nesbit seems to have also had an optimistic side. Along

with her husband, Hubert Nesbit, she founded the Fabian Society in 1884.

Superstitious, a believer in ghosts, intelligent and talented but emotionally troubled, Nesbit recalls the visceral torment of embodiment—the always looming proximity of pain and death—that haunted Mary Shelley. She faces this terror again in her science fiction story "The Five Senses." In her memoir of childhood, *My School Days*, Nesbit devotes an entire chapter, "The Mummies of Bordeaux," to her terrifying visit as a young girl to the crypt under-neath the Basilique Saint-Michel, where she saw many naturally mummified bodies and skeletons displayed after they were unearthed from a nearby cemetery. (This public display did not end until 1990, after which it was replaced with a video history.) In retrospect, she estimated that the vault held about two hundred bodies, but the official number was more like seventy.

A small vault, as my memory serves me, about fifteen feet square, with an arched roof, from the centre of which hung a lamp that burned with a faint blue light, and made the guide's candle look red and lurid. The floor was flagged like the passages, and was as damp and chill. Round three sides of the room ran a railing, and behind it—standing against the wall, with a ghastly look of life in death—were about two hundred skeletons. Not white clean skeletons, hung on wires, like the one yon see at the doctor's, but skeletons with the flesh hardened on their bones, with their long dry hair hanging on each side of their brown faces, where the skin in drying had drawn itself back from their gleaming teeth and empty eye-sockets. Skeletons draped in mouldering shreds of shrouds and grave-clothes, their lean fingers still clothed with dry skin, seemed to reach out towards me. There they stood, men, women, and children, knee-deep in loose bones collected from the other vaults of the church, and heaped round them. On the wall near the door I saw the dried body of a little child hung up by its hair.

I don't think I screamed or cried, or even said a word. I think
I was paralysed with horror.

Nesbit worried that in writing fiction to earn a living she betrayed
her true calling as a poet, but even her most admiring proponents
admit that her poetry seems pallid and insincere alongside her best
novels and stories. Perhaps Nesbit took for granted the unique qualities that inspired her most memorable work. Don Marquis hated
to admit that he would be remembered primarily as creator of Archy,
the vers libre poet reincarnated as a New York City cockroach;
Arthur Conan Doyle resented the way that Sherlock Holmes's
popularity eclipsed his historical novels. As Doris Langley Moore
remarked in her quirky 1966 biography of Nesbit, not a page of a
novel such as *The Treasure Seekers* "lacks the magic vividness only
to be imparted by an original mind." Moore speculated that much
of Nesbit's fanciful but empathetic narration derived from "her
recollection of her poignant feelings to re-create at will those
daydreams of supernatural power by which the vulnerable compensate themselves for their helplessness."

In "The Five Senses," Nesbit daydreams about transcending the
limits of bodily perception, and in doing so creates a character reminiscent of a twentieth-century superhero. The comic book character Peter Parker is bitten by a radioactive spider and turns himself
into Spider-Man; lawyer Matt Murdock is blinded by an encounter
with radioactive material, but in return his other senses grow fantastically acute, and he chooses to exploit them while masked as Daredevil. Nesbit's character Boyd Thompson, in contrast, deliberately
injects himself with a chemical compound that he has spent years
creating. It enhances his bodily senses until he feels the microscopic
roughness of a glass syringe and amplifies the lingering aftertaste of
coffee until he can hardly bear its intensity.

With her usual offhand wit, Nesbit barely nods toward a scientific explanation and adds, "I trust this is clear?"

The Five Senses

Professor Boyd Thompson's services to the cause of science are usually spoken of as inestimable, and so indeed they probably are, since in science, as in the rest of life, one thing leads to another, and you never know where anything is going to stop. At any rate, inestimable or not, they are world-renowned, and he with them. The discoveries which he gave to his time are a matter of common knowledge among biological experts, and the sudden ending of his experimental activities caused a few days' wonder in even lay circles. Quite unintelligent people told each other that it seemed a pity, and persons on omnibuses exchanged commonplaces starred with his name.

But the real meaning and cause of that ending have been studiously hidden, as well as the events which immediately preceded it. A veil has been drawn over all the things that people would have liked to know, and it is only now that circumstances so arrange themselves as to make it possible to tell the whole story. I propose to avail myself of this possibility.

It will serve no purpose for me to explain how the necessary knowledge came into my possession; but I will say that the story was only in part pieced together by me. Another hand is responsible for much of the detail and for a certain occasional emotionalism which is, I believe, wholly foreign to my own style. In my original statement of the following facts I dealt fully, as I am, I may say without immodesty, qualified to do, with all the scientific points of the narrative. But these details were judged, unwisely as I think, to be needless to the expert, and unintelligible to the ordinary reader, and have therefore been struck out; the merest hints have been left as necessary links in the story. This appears to me to destroy most of its interest, but I admit that the elisions are perhaps justified. I have no desire to assist or encourage callow students in such experiments as those by which Professor Boyd Thompson brought his scientific career to an end.

Incredible as it may appear, Professor Boyd Thompson was once a little boy who wore white embroidered frocks and blue sashes; in that state he caught flies and pulled off their wings to find out how they flew. He did not find out, and Lucilla, his little girl-cousin, also in white frocks, cried over the dead, dismembered flies, and buried them in little paper coffins. Later, he wore a holland blouse with a belt of leather, and watched the development of tadpoles in a tin bath in the stable yard. A microscope was, on his eighth birthday, presented to him by an affluent uncle. The uncle showed him how to surprise the secrets of a drop of pond water, which, limpid to the eye, confessed under the microscope to a whole cosmogony of strenuous and undesirable careers. At the age of ten, Arthur Boyd Thompson was sent to a private school, its Headmaster an acolyte of Science, who esteemed himself to be a high priest of Huxley and Tyndal, a devotee of Darwin. Thence to the choice of medicine as a profession was, when the choice was insisted on by the elder Boyd Thompson, a short, plain step. Inorganic chemistry failed to charm, and under the cloak of Medicine and Surgery the growing fever of scientific curiosity could be sated on bodies other than the cloak-wearer's. He became a medical student and an enthusiast for vivisection.

The bow of Apollo was not always bent. In a rest-interval, the summer vacation, to be exact, he met again the cousin—second, once removed—Lucilla, and loved her. They were betrothed. It was a long, bright summer full of sunshine, garden-parties, picnics, archery—a decaying amusement—and croquet, then coming to its own. He exulted in the distinction already crescent in his career, but some half-formed wholly unconscious desire to shine with increased lustre in the eyes of the beloved caused him to invite, for the holiday's ultimate week, a fellow student, one who knew and could testify to the quality of the laurels already encircling the head of the young scientist. The friend came, testified, and in a vibrating interview under the lime-trees of Lucilla's people's garden, Mr. Boyd Thompson learned that Lucilla never could, never would, love or marry a vivisectionist.

The moon hung low and yellow in the spacious calm of the sky; the hour was propitious, the lovers fond. Mr. Boyd Thompson vowed that his scientific research should henceforth deal wholly with departments into which the emotions of the non-scientific cannot enter. He went back to London, and within the week bought four dozen frogs, twelve guinea-pigs, five cats, and a spaniel. His scientific aspirations met his love-longings, and did not fight them. You cannot fight beings of another world. He took part in a debate on "Blood Pressure," which created some little stir in medical circles, spoke eloquently, and distinction surrounded him with a halo.

He wrote to Lucilla three times a week, took his degree, and published that celebrated paper of his which set the whole scientific world by the ears; "The Action of Choline on the Nervous System" I think its name was.

Lucilla surreptitiously subscribed to a press-cutting agency for all snippets of print relating to her lover. Three weeks after the publication of that paper, which really was the beginning of Professor Boyd Thompson's fame, she wrote to him from her home in Kent.

Arthur, you have been doing it again. You know how I love you, and I believe you love me; but you must choose between loving me and torturing

dumb animals. If you don't choose right, then it's goodbye, and God
forgive you.
Your poor Lucilla, who loved you very dearly.

He read the letter, and the human heart in him winced and
whined. Yet not so deeply now, nor so loudly, but that he bethought
himself to seek out a friend and pupil, who would watch certain
experiments, attend to the cutting of certain sections, before he
started for Tenterden, where she lived. There was no station at
Tenterden in those days, but a twelve-mile walk did not dismay
him.

Lucilla's home was one of those houses of brave proportions and
an inalienable bourgeois stateliness, which stand back a little from
the noble High Street of that most beautiful of Kentish towns. He
came there, pleasantly exercised, his boots dusty, and his throat dry,
and stood on the snowy doorstep, beneath the Jacobean lintel. He
looked down the wide, beautiful street, raised eyebrows, and
shrugged uneasy shoulders within his professional frock-coat.

"It's all so difficult," he said to himself.

Lucilla received him in a drawing-room scented with last year's
rose leaves, and fresh with chintz that had been washed a dozen
times. She stood, very pale and frail; her blonde hair was not teased
into fluffiness, and rounded over the chignon of the period but
banded Madonna-wise, crowning her with heavy burnished plaits.
Her gown was of white muslin, and round her neck black velvet
passed, supporting a gold locket. He knew whose picture it held.
The loose bell sleeves fell away from the slender arms with little
black velvet bracelets, and she leaned one hand on a chiffonier of
carved rosewood, on whose marble top stood, under a glass case, a
Chinese pagoda, carved in ivory, and two Bohemian glass vases
with medallions representing young women nursing pigeons. There
were white curtains of darned net, in the fireplace white ravelled
muslin spread a cascade brightened with threads of tinsel. A canary

sang in a green cage, wainscoted with yellow tarlatan, and two red
rosebuds stood in lank specimen glasses on the mantelpiece.

Every article of furniture in the room spoke eloquently of the
sheltered life, the iron obstinacy of the well-brought-up.

It was a scene that invaded his mental vision many a time, in the
laboratory, in the lecture-room. It symbolized many things, all dear,
and all impossible.

They talked awkwardly, miserably. And always it came round to
this same thing.

"But you don't mean it," he said, and at last came close to her.

"I do mean it," she said, very white, very trembling, very
determined.

"But it's my life," he pleaded; "it's the life of thousands. You don't
understand."

"I understand that dogs are tortured. I can't bear it."

He caught at her hand.

"Don't," she said. "When I think what that hand does!"

"Dearest," he said very earnestly, "which is the more important,
a dog or a human being?"

"They're all God's creatures," she flashed, unorthodoxly unorth-
odox. "They're all God's creatures." With much more that he
heard and pitied and smiled at miserably in his heart.

"You don't understand," he kept saying, stemming the flood
of her rhetorical pleadings. "Spencer Wells alone has found out
wonderful things, just with experiments on rabbits."

"Don't tell me," she said. "I don't want to hear."

The conventions of their day forbade that he should tell her
anything plainly. He took refuge in generalities. "Spencer Wells,
that operation he perfected, it's restored thousands of women to
their husbands—saved thousands of women for their children."

"I don't care what he's done—it's wrong if it's done in that way."

It was on that day that they parted, after more than an hour of
mutual misunderstood reiteration. He, she said, was brutal. And,

besides, it was plain that he did not love her. To him she seemed unreasonable, narrow, prejudiced, blind to the high ideals of the new science.

"Then it's goodbye," he said at last. "If I gave way, you'd only despise me, because I should despise myself. It's no good. Goodbye, dear."

"Goodbye," she said. "I know I'm right. You'll know I am, some day."

"Never," he answered, more moved and in a more diffused sense than he had ever believed he could be. "I can't set my pleasure in you against the good of the whole world."

"If that's all you think of me," she said, and her silk and her muslin whirled from the room.

He walked back to Staplehurst, thrilled with the conflict. The thrill died down, went out, and left as ashes a cold resolve.

That was the end of Mr. Boyd Thompson's engagement.

It was quite by accident that he made his greatest discovery. There are those who hold that all great discoveries are accident—or Providence. The terms are, in this connection, interchangeable. He plunged into work to wash away the traces of his soul's wounds, as a man plunges into water to wash off red blood. And he swam there, perhaps, a little blindly. The injection with which he treated that white rabbit was not compounded of the drugs he had intended to use. He could not lay his hand on the thing he wanted, and in that sort of frenzy of experiment, to which no scientific investigator is wholly a stranger, he cast about for a new idea. The thing that came to his hand was a drug that he had never in his normal mind intended to use—an unaccredited, wild, magic medicine obtained by a missionary from some savage South Sea tribe and brought home as an example of the ignorance of the heathen.

And it worked a miracle.

He had been fighting his way through the unbending opposition of known facts, he had been struggling in the shadows, and this discovery was like the blinding light that meets a man's eyes when his pick-axe knocks a hole in a dark cave and he finds himself face to face with the sun. The effect was undoubted. Now it behoved him to make sure of the cause, to eliminate all those other factors to which that effect might have been due. He experimented cautiously, slowly. These things take years, and the years he did not grudge. He was never tired, never impatient; the slightest variations, the least indications, were eagerly observed, faithfully recorded.

His whole soul was in his work. Lucilla was the one beautiful memory of his life. But she was a memory. The reality was this discovery, the accident, the Providence.

Day followed day, all alike, and yet each taking almost unperceived, one little step forward; or stumbling into sudden sloughs, those losses and lapses that take days and weeks to retrieve. He was Professor, and his hair was grey at the temples before his achievement rose before him, beautiful, inevitable, austere in its completed splendour, as before the triumphant artist rises the finished work of his art.

He had found out one of the secrets with which Nature has crammed her dark hiding-places. He had discovered the hidden possibilities of sensation. In plain English, his researches had led him thus far; he had found—by accident or Providence—the way to intensify sensation. Vaguely, incredulously, he had perceived his discovery; the rabbits and guinea-pigs had demonstrated it plainly enough. Then there was a night when he became aware that those results must be checked by something else. He must work out in marble the form he had worked out in clay. He knew that by this drug, which had, so to speak, thrust itself upon him, he could intensify the five senses of any of the inferior animals. Could he intensify those senses in man? If so, worlds beyond the grasp of his tired mind opened themselves before him. If so, he would have achieved a discovery, made a contribution to the science he had loved so well and followed at such a cost, a discovery equal to any that any man had ever made.

Ferrier, and Leo, and Horsley; those he would outshine. Galileo, Newton, Harvey; he would rank with these.

Could he find a human rabbit to submit to the test?

The soul of the man Lucilla had loved, turned and revolted. No: he had experimented on guinea-pigs and rabbits, but when it came to experimenting on men, there was only one man on whom he chose to use his new-found powers. Himself.

At least she would not have it to say that he was a coward, or unfair, when it came to the point of what a man could do and dare, could suffer and endure.

His big laboratory was silent and deserted. His assistants were gone, his private pupils dispersed. He was alone with the tools of his trade. Shelf on shelf of smooth stoppered bottles, drugs and stains, the long bench gleaming with beakers, test tubes, and the glass mansions of costly apparatus. In the shadows at the far end of the room, where the last going assistant had turned off the electric lights, strange shapes lurked: wicker-covered carboys, kinographs, galvanometers, the faintly threatening aspect of delicate complex machines all wires and coils and springs, the gaunt form of the pendulum myographs, and certain well-worn tables and copper troughs, which for the moment had no use.

He knew that this drug with others, diversely compounded and applied, produced in animals an abnormal intensification of the senses; that it increased—nay, as it were, magnified a thousandfold, the hearing, the sight, the touch—and, he was almost sure, the senses of taste and smell. But of the extent of the increase he could form no exact estimate.

Should he tonight put himself in the position of one able to speak on these points with authority? Or should he go to the Royal Society's meeting and hear that ass Netherby maunder yet once again about the secretion of lymph?

He pulled out his notebook and laid it open on the bench. He went to the locked cupboard, unfastened it with the bright key that hung instead of seal or charm at his watch-chain. He unfolded a paper and laid it on the bench where no one coming in could fail to see it. Then he took out little bottles, three, four, five, polished a graduated glass and dropped into it slow, heavy drops. A larger bottle yielded a medium in which all mingled. He hardly hesitated at all before turning up his sleeve and slipping the tiny needle into his arm. He pressed the end of the syringe. The injection was made.

Its effect, though not immediate, was sudden. He had to close his eyes, staggered indeed and was glad of the stool near him, for the drug coursed through him as a hunt in full cry might sweep over untrodden plains. Then suddenly everything seemed to settle; he was no longer helpless but was once again Professor Boyd Thompson, who had injected a mixture of certain drugs and was experiencing their effect.

His fingers, still holding the glass syringe, sent swift messages to his brain. When he looked down at his fingers, he saw that what they grasped was the smooth, slender tube of clear glass. What he felt that they held was a tremendous cylinder, rough to the touch. He wondered, even at the moment, why, if his sense of touch were indeed magnified to this degree, everything did not appear enormous— his ring, his collar. He examined the new phenomenon with cold care. It seemed that only that was enlarged on which his attention, his mind, was fixed. He kept his hand on the glass syringe, and thought of his ring, got his mind away from the tube, back again in time to feel it small between his fingers, grow, increase, and become big once more.

"So *that's* a success," he said, and saw himself lay the thing down. It lay just in front of the rack of test tubes, to the eye, just that little glass cylinder. To the touch it was like a water-pipe on a house side, and the test tubes, when he touched them, like the pipes of a great organ.

"Success," he said again, and mixed the antidote. For he had found the antidote in one of those flashes of intuition, imagination, genius, that light the ways of science as stars light the way of a ship in dark waters. The action of the antidote was enough for one night.

He locked the cupboard, and, after all, was glad to listen to the maunderings of Netherby. It had been lonely there, in the atmosphere of complete success.

One by one, day by day, he tested the action of his drugs on his other senses. Without being technical, I had perhaps better explain that the compelling drug was, in each case, one and the same. Its action was directed to this set of nerves or that by means of the other drugs mixed with it. I trust this is clear?

The sense of smell was tested, and its laboratory, with its mingled odours, became abominable to him. Hardly could he stay himself from rushing forth into the outer air to wash his nostrils in the clear coolness of Hampstead Heath. The sense of taste gave him, magnified a thousand times, the flavour of his after-dinner coffee, and other tastes, distasteful almost beyond the bearing point.

But "Success," he said, rinsing his mouth at the laboratory sink after the drinking of the antidote, "all along the line, success."

Then he tested the action of his discovery on the sense of hearing. And the sound of London came like the roar of a giant, yet when he fixed his attention on the movements of a fly all other sounds ceased, and he heard the sound of the fly's feet on the shelf when it walked. Thus, in turn, he heard the creak of boards expanding in the heat, the movement of the glass stoppers that kept imprisoned in the proper bottles the giants of acid and alkali.

"Success!" he cried aloud, and his voice sounded in his ears like the shout of a monster overcoming primeval forces. "Success! Success!"

There remained only the eyes, and here, strangely enough, the Professor hesitated, faint with a sudden heart-sickness. Following a intensification there must be reaction. What if the reaction exceeded that from which it reacted, what if the wave of tremendous sight stemmed by the antidote ebbing, left him blind? But the spirit of the explorer in science is the spirit that explores African rivers, and sail amid white bergs to seek the undiscovered Pole.

He held the syringe with a firm hand, made the required

puncture, and braced himself for the result. His eyes seemed to swell to great globes, to dwindle to microscopic globules, to swim in a flood of fire, to shrivel high and dry on a beach of hot sand. Then he saw and the glass fell from his hand. For the whole of the stable earth seemed to be suddenly set in movement, even the air grew thick with vast overlapping shapeless shapes. He opined later that these were the microbes and bacilli that cover and fill all things in this world that looks so clean and bright.

Concentrating his vision, he saw in the one day's little dust on the bottles myriads of creatures, crawling and writhing, alive. The proportions of the laboratory seemed but little altered. Its large lines and forms remained practically unchanged. It was the little things that were no longer little, the invisible things that were now invisible no longer. And he felt grateful for the first time in his life for the limits set by Nature to the powers of the human body. He had increased those powers. If he let his eye stray idly about, as one does in the waltz, for example, all was much as it used to be. But the moment he looked steadily at any one thing it became enormous.

He closed his eyes. Success here had gone beyond his wildest dreams. Indeed he could not but feel that success, taking the bit between its teeth, had perhaps gone just the least little bit too far.

And on the next day he decided to examine the drug in all its aspects, to court the intensification of all his senses, which should set him in the position of supreme power over men and things, transform him from a Professor into a demi-god.

The great question was, of course, how the five preparations of his drug would act on or against each other. Would it be intensification, or would they neutralize each other? Like all imaginative scientists, he was working with stuff perilously like the spells of magic, and certain things were not possible to be foretold. Besides, this drug came from a land of mystery and the knowledge of secrets which we call magic. He did not anticipate any increase in the danger of the experiment. Nevertheless he spent some hours in arranging and destroying papers, among others certain pages of the yellow notebook. After dinner he detained his man as, laden with the last tray, he was leaving the room.

"I may as well tell you, Parker," the Professor said, moved by some impulse he had not expected, "that you will benefit to some extent by my will. On conditions. If any accident should cut short my life, you will at once communicate with my solicitor, whose name you will now write down."

The model man, trained by fifteen years of close personal service, drew forth a notebook neat as the Professor's own, wrote in it neatly the address the Professor gave.

"Anything more, sir?" he asked, looking up, pencil in hand.

"No," said the Professor, "nothing more. Goodnight, Parker."

"Goodnight, sir," said the model man.

THE NEXT WORDS THE model man opened his lips to speak were breathed into the night tube of the nearest doctor.

"My master, Professor Boyd Thompson; could you come round at once, sir. I'm afraid it's very serious."

It was half past six when the nearest doctor—Jones was his unimportant name—stooped over the lifeless body of the Professor.

He shook his head as he stood up and looked round the private laboratory on whose floor the body lay.

"His researches are over," he said. "Yes, he's dead. Been dead some hours. When did you find him?"

"I went to call my master as usual," said Parker; "he rises at six, summer and winter, sir. He was not in his room, and the bed had not been slept in. So I came in here, sir. It is not unusual for my master to work all night when he has been very interested in his experiments, and then he likes his coffee at six."

"I see," said Doctor Jones. "Well, you'd better rouse the house and fetch his own doctor. It's heart failure, of course, but I daresay he'd like to sign the certificate himself."

"Can nothing be done?" said Parker, much affected.

"Nothing," said Dr. Jones. "It's the common lot. You'll have to look out for another situation."

"Yes, sir," said Parker; "he told me only last night what I was to do in case of anything happening to him. I wonder if he had any idea?"

"Some premonition, perhaps," the doctor corrected.

The funeral was a very quiet one. So the late Professor Boyd Thompson had decreed in his will. He had arranged all details. The body was to be clothed in flannel, placed in an open coffin covered only with a linen sheet, and laid in the family mausoleum, a moss-grown building in the midst of a little park which surrounded Boyd Grange, the birthplace of the Boyd Thompsons. A little property in Sussex it was. The Professor sometimes went there for weekends. He had left this property to Lucilla, with a last love-letter, in which he begged her to give his body the hospitality of the death-house, now hers with the rest of the estate. To Parker he left an annuity of two hundred pounds, on the condition that he should visit and enter the mausoleum once in every twenty-four hours for fourteen days after the funeral.

To this end the late Professor's solicitor decided that Parker had better reside at Boyd Grange for the said fortnight, and Parker, whose nerves seemed to be shaken, petitioned for company. This made easy the arrangement which the solicitor desired to make—of a witness to the carrying out by Parker of the provisions of the dead man's will. The solicitor's clerk was quite good company, and arm in arm with him Parker paid his first visit to the mausoleum. The little building stands in a glade of evergreen oaks. The trees are old and thick, and the narrow door is deep in shadow even on the sunniest day. Parker went to the mausoleum, peered through its square grating, but he did not go in. Instead, he listened, and his ears were full of silence.

"He's dead, right enough," he said, with a doubtful glance at his companion.

"You ought to go in, oughtn't you?" said the solicitor's clerk;

"Go in yourself if you like, Mr. Pollack," said Parker, suddenly angry; "anyone who likes can go in, but it won't be me. If he was alive, it 'ud be different. I'd have done anything for him. But I ain't going in among all them dead and mouldering Thompsons. See? If we both say I did, it'll be just the same as me doing it."

"So it will," said the solicitor's clerk; "but where do I come in?"

Parker explained to him where he came in, to their mutual consent.

"Right you are," said the clerk; "on those terms I'm fly. And if we both say you did it, we needn't come to the beastly place again," he added, shivering and glancing over his shoulder at the door with the grating.

"No more we need," said Parker.

Behind the bars of the narrow door lay deeper shadows than those of the ilexes outside. And in the blackest of the shadow lay a man whose every sense was intensified as though by a magic potion. For when the Professor swallowed the five variants of his great discovery, each acted as he had expected it to act. But the union of the five vehicles conveying the drug to the nerves, which served his five senses, had paralysed every muscle. His hearing, taste, touch, scent, and sight were intensified a thousandfold—as they had been in the individual experiments—but the man who felt all this exaggerated increase of sensation was powerless as a cat under kurali. He could not raise a finger, stir an eyelash. More, he could not breathe, nor did his body advise him of any need of breathing. And he had lain thus immobile and felt his body slowly grow cold, had heard in thunder the voices of Parker and the doctor, had felt the enormous hands of those who made his death-toilet, had smelt intolerably the camphor and lavender that they laid round him in the narrow, black bed; had tasted the mingled flavours of the drug and its five mediums; and, in an ecstasy of magnified sensation, had made the lonely train journey which coffins make, and known himself carried into the mausoleum and left there alone. And every sense was intensified, even his sense of time, so that it seemed to him that he had lain there for many years. And the effect of the drugs showed no sign of any diminution or reaction. Why had he not left directions for the injection of the antidote? It was one of those slips which wreck campaigns, cause the discovery of hidden crimes. It was a slip, and he had made it. He had thought of death, but in all the results he had anticipated death's semblance had found no place. Well, he had made his bed, and he must lie on it. This narrow bed, whose scent of clean oak and French polish was distinct among the musty, intolerable odours of the charnel house.

It was perhaps twenty hours that he had lain there, powerless, immobile, listening to the sounds of unexplained movements about him, when he felt with joy, almost like delirium, a faint quivering in the eyelids.

They had closed his eyes, and till now, they had remained closed. Now, with an effort as of one who lifts a grave-stone, he raised his eyelids. They closed again quickly, for the roof of the vault, at which he gazed earnestly, was alive with monsters; spiders, earwigs, crawling beetles, and flies, far too small to have been perceived by normal eyes, spread giant forms over him. He closed his eyes and shuddered. It felt like a shudder, but no one who had stood beside him could have noted any movement.

It was then that Parker came—and went.

Professor Boyd Thompson heard Parker's words, and lay listening to the thunder of Parker's retreating feet. He tried to move—to call out. But he could not. He lay there helpless, and somehow he thought of the dark end of the laboratory, where the assistant before leaving had turned out the electric lights.

He had nothing but his thoughts. He thought how he would lie there, and die there. The place was sequestered; no one passed that way. Parker had failed him, and the end was not hard to picture. He might recover all his faculties, might be able to get up, able to scream, to shout, to tear at the bars. The bars were strong, and Parker would not come again. Well, he would try to face with a decent bravery whatever had to be faced.

Time, measureless, spread round. It seemed as though someone had stopped all the clocks in the world, as though he were not in time but in eternity. Only by the waxing and waning light he knew of the night and the day.

His brain was weary with the effort to move, to speak, to cry out. He lay, informed with something like despair—or fortitude. And then Parker came again. And this time a key grated in the lock. The Professor noted with rapture that it sounded no louder than a key should sound, turned in a lock that was rusty. Nor was the voice other than he had been used to hear it, when he was man alive and Parker's master. And—

"You can go in, of course, if you wish it, miss," said Parker disapprovingly; "but it's not what I should advise myself. For me it's different," he added, on a sudden instinct of self-preservation; "I've got to go in. Every day for a fortnight," he added, pitying himself.

"I will go in, thank you," said a voice. "Yes, give me the candle, please. And you need not wait. I will lock the door when I come out." Thus the voice spoke. And the voice was Lucilla's.

In all his life the Professor had never feared death or its trappings. Neither its physical repulsiveness, nor the supernatural terrors which cling about it, had he either understood or tolerated. But now, in one little instant, he did understand.

He heard Lucilla come in. A light held near him shone warm and red through his closed eyelids. And he knew that he had only to unclose those eyelids to see her face bending over him. And he could unclose them. Yet he would not. He lay there, still and straight in his coffin, and life swept through him in waves of returning power. Yet he lay like death. For he said, or something in him said:

"She believes me dead. If I open my eyes it will be like a dead man looking at her. If I move it will be a dead man moving under her eyes. People have gone mad for less. Lie still, lie still," he told himself; "take any risks yourself. There must be none for her."

She had taken the candle away, set it down somewhere at a distance, and now she was kneeling beside him and her hand was under his head. He knew he could raise his arm and clasp her—and Parker would come back perhaps, when she did not return to the house, come back to find a man in grave-clothes, clasping a mad woman. He lay still. Then her kisses and tears fell on his face, and she murmured broken words of love and longing. But he lay still. At any cost he must lie still. Even at the cost of his own sanity, his own life. And the warmth of her hand under his head, her face against his, her kisses, her tears, set his blood flowing evenly and strongly. Her other arm lay on his breast, softly pressing over his heart. He would not move. He would be strong. If he were to be saved, it must be by some other way, not this.

Suddenly tears and kisses ceased; her every breath seemed to have stopped with these. She had drawn away from him. She spoke. Her voice came from above him. She was standing up.

"Arthur!" she said. "Arthur!" Then he opened his eyes, the narrowest chink. But he could not see her. Only he knew she was moving towards the door. There had been a new quality in her tone, a thrill of fear, or hope was it? or at least of uncertainty? Should he move; should he speak? He dared not. He knew too well the fear that the normal human being has of death and the grave, the fear transcending love, transcending reason. Her voice was further away now. She was by the door. She was leaving him. If he let her go, it was an end of hope for him. If he did not let her go, an end, perhaps, of reason, for her. No.

"Arthur," she said, "I don't believe . . . I believe you can hear me. I'm going to get a doctor. If you *can* speak, speak to me."

Her speaking ended, cut off short as a cord is cut by a knife. He did not speak. He lay in conscious, forced rigidity.

"Speak if you can," she implored, "just one word!"

Then he said, very faintly, very distinctly, in a voice that seemed to come from a great way off, "Lucilla!"

And at the word she screamed aloud pitifully, and leaped for the entrance; and he heard the rustle of her crape in the narrow door. Then he opened his eyes wide, and raised himself on his elbow. Very weak he was, and trembling exceedingly. To his ears her scream held the note of madness. Vainly he had refrained. Selfishly he had yielded. The cold band of a mortal faintness clutched at his heart.

"I don't want to live now," he told himself, and fell back in the straight bed.

Her arms were round him.

"I'm going to get help," she said, her lips to his ear; "brandy and things. Only I came back. I didn't want you to think I was frightened. Oh, my dear! Thank God, thank God!" He felt her kisses even through the swooning mist that swirled about him. Had she really fled in terror? He never knew. He knew that she had come back to him.

That is the real, true, and authentic narrative of the events which caused Professor Boyd Thompson to abandon a brilliant career, to promise anything that Lucilla might demand, and to devote himself entirely to a gentlemanly and unprofitable farming, and to his wife. From the point of view of the scientific world it is a sad ending to much promise, but at any rate there are two happy people hand in hand at the story's ending.

There is no doubt that for several years Professor Boyd Thompson had had enough of science, and, by a natural revulsion, flung himself into the full tide of commonplace sentiment. But genius, like youth, cannot be denied. And I, for one, am doubtful whether the Professor's renunciation of research will be a lasting one. Already I have heard whispers of a laboratory which is being built on the house, beyond the billiard-room.

But I am inclined to believe the rumours which assert that, for the future, his research will take the form of extending paths already well trodden; that he will refrain from experiments with unknown drugs, and those dreadful researches which tend to merge the chemist and biologist in the alchemist and the magician. And he certainly does not intend to experiment further on the nerves of any living thing, even his own. The Professor had already done enough work to make the reputation of half-a-dozen ordinary scientists. He may be pardoned if he rests on his laurels, entwining them, to some extent, with roses.

The bottle containing the drug from the South Seas was knocked down on the day of his death and swept up in bits by the laboratory boy. It is a curious fact that the Professor has wholly forgotten the formulae of his experiment, which so nearly was his last. This is a great satisfaction to his wife, and possibly to the Professor. But of this I cannot be sure; the scientific spirit survives much.

To the unscientific reader the strangest part of this story will perhaps be the fact that Parker is still with his old master, a wonderful example of the perfect butler. Professor Boyd Thompson was able to forgive Parker because he understood him. And he learned to understand Parker in those moments of agony, when his keen intellect and his awakened heart taught him, through his love for Lucilla, the depth of that gulf of fear which lies between the quick and the dead.

Arthur Conan Doyle

(1859–1930)

DURING THE SECOND QUARTER of the twentieth century, Harold Ross, the founder of the *New Yorker*, whimsically instructed his writers to be specific in identifying allusions by reminding them that only two figures were known to everyone in Western culture at that time. One was real and the other fictional: Harry Houdini and Sherlock Holmes. Even Houdini has faded over time into a silent movie montage, but Holmes remains as vivid as ever.

Arthur Conan Doyle complained that his fictional detective's popularity kept the author from scaling nobler heights in literature. Whatever his other books' virtues, however, relatively few people today are reading *Micah Clarke* and *The White Company* instead of "The Adventure of the Speckled Band" and *The Hound of the Baskervilles.* Neither Conan Doyle's work as a missionary for spiritualism nor as a defender of the British Empire—not his work as physician, historical novelist, patriot, journalist, celebrity, or occasionally even sleuth asked to solve real-life crimes—can rival his creation of the immortal consulting detective.

After several years of writing short stories of adventure and horror—some of them rejected, some published anonymously, as usual at the time—Doyle created Sherlock Holmes during off hours waiting for patients to wander into his new medical office in Southsea, Portsmouth. He moved there in 1882, after medical school at the University of Edinburgh, and he wrote the first Holmes book, *A Study in Scarlet*, in only a few weeks in early 1886. Not until December of the following year, in *Beeton's Christmas Annual*, did the world meet Holmes. The first novel received modest but respectable reviews, and in 1889 an editor with the U.S.-based *Lippincott's Magazine* invited Doyle to write a novella, which became *The Sign of the Four*, the second Holmes novel. More positive reviews followed. Then, in the summer of 1891, *The Adventures of Sherlock Holmes*—the first dozen short stories, beginning with "A Scandal in Bohemia"—launched in the newly minted *Strand Magazine*, and thus began the astonishing rise and international popularity of Holmes and the assured success of his creator.

Throughout his career, whatever the popularity of Holmes and his other creations—such as the rousing and atmospheric science fiction novel *The Lost World*, which influenced everyone from Edgar Rice Burroughs to Michael Crichton—Doyle continued to write stories rooted in his love of ghosts, inventions, monsters, and heroic adventure. "The Horror of the Heights" combines various ideas in a mix reminiscent of Jules Verne, whose books Doyle had admired since childhood. "There are jungles in the upper air," says the author of the blood-stained manuscript that appears within the following story. "Jungle" was still an exotic, imperial term in the British imagination, one rich in danger, and Doyle transposed it from the land to the air above. After centuries of brilliant, optimistic advances in our ancient dream of flying, it had been only a decade since Orville and Wilbur Wright had performed the first sustained heavier-than-air flight at Kitty Hawk, North Carolina. There were enough lacunae in knowledge about the upper atmosphere to permit an enterprising writer to populate them with terrifying creatures, as if scribbling "Here there be monsters" on the unexplored corners of a medieval map.

"The Horror of the Heights" was published in the November

1913 issue of the *Strand Magazine*. It was soon reprinted in the Philadelphia-based *Everybody's Magazine* and elsewhere, including (as a mark of Doyle's popularity at the time) in an immediate Russian translation. Five years after its first appearance, Doyle included it in his collection *Danger! and Other Stories*.

The Horror of the Heights

THE IDEA THAT THE extraordinary narrative which has been called the Joyce-Armstrong Fragment is an elaborate practical joke evolved by some unknown person, cursed by a perverted and sinister sense of humour, has now been abandoned by all who have examined the matter. The most *macabre* and imaginative of plotters would hesitate before linking his morbid fancies with the unquestioned and tragic facts which reinforce the statement. Though the assertions contained in it are amazing and even monstrous, it is none the less forcing itself upon the general intelligence that they are true, and that we must readjust our ideas to the new situation. This world of ours appears to be separated by a slight and precarious margin of safety from a most singular and unexpected danger. I will endeavour in this narrative, which reproduces the original document in its necessarily somewhat fragmentary form, to lay before the reader the whole of the facts up to date, prefacing my statement by saying that, if there be any who doubt the narrative of Joyce-Armstrong, there can be no question at all as to the facts concerning Lieutenant Myrtle, R.N., and Mr. Hay Connor, who undoubtedly met their end in the manner described.

The Joyce-Armstrong Fragment was found in the field which is called Lower Haycock, lying one mile to the westward of the village of Withyham, upon the Kent and Sussex border. It was on the fifteenth of September last that an agricultural labourer, James Flynn, in the employment of Mathew Dodd, farmer, of the Chauntry Farm, Withyham, perceived a briar pipe lying near the footpath which skirts the hedge in Lower Haycock. A few paces farther on he picked up a pair of broken binocular glasses. Finally, among some nettles in the ditch, he caught sight of a flat, canvas-backed book, which proved to be a note-book with detachable leaves, some of which had come loose and were fluttering along the base of the hedge. These he collected, but some, including the first, were never recovered, and leave a deplorable hiatus in this all-important statement. The notebook was taken by the labourer to his master, who in turn showed it to Dr. J. H. Atherton, of Hartfield. This gentleman at once recognized the need for an expert examination, and the manuscript was forwarded to the Aero Club in London, where it now lies.

The first two pages of the manuscript are missing. There is also one torn away at the end of the narrative, though none of these affect the general coherence of the story. It is conjectured that the missing opening is concerned with the record of Mr. Joyce-Armstrong's qualifications as an aeronaut, which can be gathered from other sources and are admitted to be unsurpassed among the air pilots of England. For many years he has been looked upon as among the most daring and the most intellectual of flying men, a combination which has enabled him to both invent and test several new devices, including the common gyroscopic attachment which is known by his name. The main body of the manuscript is written neatly in ink, but the last few lines are in pencil and are so ragged as to be hardly legible exactly, in fact, as they might be expected to appear if they were scribbled off hurriedly from the seat of a moving aeroplane. There are, it may be added, several stains, both on the last page and on the outside cover which have been pronounced by the Home Office experts to be blood—probably human and certainly mammalian. The fact that something closely resembling the organism of malaria was discovered in this blood, and that Joyce-Armstrong is known to have suffered from intermittent fever, is a remarkable example of the new weapons which modern science has placed in the hands of our detectives.

And now a word as to the personality of the author of this epoch-making statement. Joyce-Armstrong, according to the few friends who really knew something of the man, was a poet and a dreamer, as well as a mechanic and an inventor. He was a man of considerable wealth, much of which he had spent in the pursuit of his aeronautical hobby. He had four private aeroplanes in his hangars near Devizes, and is said to have made no fewer than one hundred and seventy ascents in the course of last year. He was a retiring man with dark moods, in which he would avoid the society of his fellows. Captain Dangerfield, who knew him better than anyone, says that there were times when his eccentricity threatened to develop into something more serious. His habit of carrying a shot-gun with him in his aeroplane was one manifestation of it.

Another was the morbid effect which the fall of Lieutenant Myrtle had upon his mind. Myrtle, who was attempting the height record, fell from an altitude of something over thirty thousand feet. Horrible to narrate, his head was entirely obliterated, though his body and limbs preserved their configuration. At every gathering of airmen, Joyce-Armstrong, according to Dangerfield, would ask, with an enigmatic smile: "And where, pray, is Myrtle's head?"

On another occasion after dinner, at the mess of the Flying School on Salisbury Plain, he started a debate as to what will be the most permanent danger which airmen will have to encounter. Having listened to successive opinions as to air-pockets, faulty construction, and over-banking, he ended by shrugging his shoulders and refusing to put forward his own views, though he gave the impression that they differed from any advanced by his companions.

It is worth remarking that after his own complete disappearance it was found that his private affairs were arranged with a precision which may show that he had a strong premonition of disaster. With these essential explanations I will now give the narrative exactly as it stands, beginning at page three of the blood soaked notebook:—

Nevertheless, when I dined at Rheims with Coselli and Gustav Raymond I found that neither of them was aware of any particular danger in the higher layers of the atmosphere. I did not actually say what was in my thoughts, but I got so near to it that if they had any corresponding idea they could not have failed to express it. But then they are two empty, vainglorious fellows with no thought beyond seeing their silly names in the newspaper. It is interesting to note that neither of them had ever been much beyond the twenty-thousand-foot level. Of course, men have been higher than this both in balloons and in the ascent of mountains. It must be well above that point that the aeroplane enters the danger zone—always presuming that my premonitions are correct.

Aeroplaning has been with us now for more than twenty years, and one might well ask: Why should this peril be only revealing itself in our day? The answer is obvious. In the old days of weak engines, when a hundred horse-power Gnome or Green was considered ample for every need, the flights were very restricted. Now that three hundred horse-power is the rule rather than the exception, visits to the upper layers have become easier and more common. Some of us can remember how, in our youth, Garros made a world-wide reputation by attaining nineteen thousand feet, and it was considered a remarkable achievement to fly over the Alps. Our standard now has been immeasurably raised, and there are twenty high flights for one in former years. Many of them have been undertaken with impunity. The thirty-thousand-foot level has been reached time after time with no discomfort beyond cold and asthma. What does this prove? A visitor might descend upon this planet a thousand times and never see a tiger. Yet tigers exist, and if he chanced to come down into a jungle he might be devoured. There are jungles of the upper air, and there are worse things than tigers which inhabit them. I believe in time they will map these jungles accurately out. Even at the present moment I could name two of them. One of them lies over the Pau–Biarritz district of France. Another is just over my head as I write here in my house in Wiltshire. I rather think there is a third in the Homburg–Wiesbaden district.

It was the disappearance of the airmen that first set me thinking. Of course, every one said that they had fallen into the sea, but that did not satisfy me at all. First, there was Verrier in France; his machine was found near Bayonne, but they never got his body.

There was the case of Baxter also, who vanished, though his engine and some of the iron fixings were found in a wood in Leicestershire. In that case, Dr. Middleton, of Amesbury, who was watching the flight with a telescope, declares that just before the clouds obscured the view he saw the machine, which was at an enormous height, suddenly rise perpendicularly upwards in a succession of jerks in a manner that he would have thought to be impossible. That was the last seen of Baxter. There was a correspondence in the papers, but it never led to anything. There were several other similar cases, and then there was the death of Hay Connor. What a cackle there was about an unsolved mystery of the air, and what columns in the halfpenny papers, and yet how little was ever done to get to the bottom of the business! He came down in a tremendous vol-plané from an unknown height. He never got off his machine and died in his pilot's seat. Died of what? "Heart disease," said the doctors. Rubbish! Hay Connor's heart was as sound as mine is. What did Venables say? Venables was the only man who was at his side when he died. He said that he was shivering and looked like a man who had been badly scared. "Died of fright," said Venables, but could not imagine what he was frightened about. Only said one word to Venables, which sounded like "Monstrous." They could make nothing of that at the inquest. But I could make something of it. Monsters! That was the last word of poor Harry Hay Connor. And he *did* die of fright, just as Venables thought.

And then there was Myrtle's head. Do you really believe—does anybody really believe—that a man's head could be driven clean into his body by the force of a fall? Well, perhaps it may be possible, but I, for one, have never believed that it was so with Myrtle. And the grease upon his clothes—"all slimy with grease," said somebody at the inquest. Queer that nobody got thinking after that! I did—but, then, I had been thinking for a good long time. I've made three ascents—how Dangerfield used to chafe me about my shot-gun—but I've never been high enough. Now, with this new light Paul Veroner machine and its one hundred and seventy-five Robur, I should easily touch the thirty thousand to-morrow. I'll have a shot at the record. Maybe I shall have a shot at something else as well. Of course, it's dangerous. If a fellow wants to avoid danger he had best keep out of flying altogether and subside finally into flannel slippers and a dressing-gown. But I'll visit the air-jungle tomorrow—and if there's anything there I shall know it. If I return, I'll find myself a bit of a celebrity. If I don't, this note-book may explain what I am trying to do, and how I lost my life in doing it. But no drivel about accidents or mysteries, if *you* please.

I chose my Paul Veroner monoplane for the job. There's nothing like a monoplane when real work is to be done. Beaumont found that out in very early days. For one thing, it doesn't mind damp, and the weather looks as if we should be in the clouds all the time. It's a bonny little model and answers my hand like a tender-mouthed horse. The engine is a ten-cylinder rotary Robur working up to one hundred and seventy-five. It has all the modern improvements; enclosed fuselage, high-curved landing skids, brakes, gyroscopic steadiers, and three speeds, worked by an alteration of the angle of the planes upon the Venetian-blind principle. I took a shot-gun with me and a dozen cartridges filled with buck-shot. You should have seen the face of Perkins, my old mechanic, when I directed him to put them in. I was dressed like an Arctic explorer, with two jerseys under my overalls, thick socks inside my padded boots, a storm-cap with flaps, and my talc goggles. It was stifling outside the hangars, but I was going for the summit of the Himalayas, and had to dress for the part. Perkins knew there was something on and implored me to take him with me. Perhaps I should if I were using the biplane, but a monoplane is a one-man show—if you want to get the last foot of lift out of it. Of course, I took an oxygen bag; the man who goes for the altitude record without one will either be frozen or smothered—or both.

I had a good look at the planes, the rudder-bar, and the elevating lever before I got in. Everything was in order so far as I could see. Then I switched on my engine and found that she was running sweetly. When they let her go she rose almost at once upon the lowest speed. I circled my home field once or twice just to warm her up, and then, with a wave to Perkins and the others, I flattened out my planes and put her on her highest. She skimmed like a swallow down wind for eight or ten miles until I turned her nose up a little and she began to climb in a great spiral for the cloud-bank above me. It's all-important to rise slowly and adapt yourself to the pressure as you go.

It was a close, warm day for an English September, and there was the hush and heaviness of impending rain. Now and then there came sudden puffs of wind from the south-west—one of them so gusty and unexpected that it caught me napping and turned me half-round for an instant. I remember the time when gusts and whirls and air-pockets used to be things of danger before we learned to put an overmastering power into our engines. Just as I reached the cloud-banks, with the altimeter marking three thousand, down came the rain. My word, how it poured! It drummed upon my wings and lashed against my face, blurring my glasses so that I could hardly see. I got down on to a low speed, for it was painful to travel against it. As I got higher it became hail, and I had to turn tail to it. One of my cylinders was out of action—a dirty plug, I should imagine, but still I was rising steadily with plenty of power. After a bit the trouble passed, whatever it was, and I heard the full deep-throated purr—the ten singing as one. That's where the beauty of our modern silencers comes in. We can at last control our engines by ear. How they squeal and squeak and sob when they are in trouble! All those cries for help were wasted in the old days, when every sound was swallowed up by the monstrous racket of the machine. If only the early aviators could come back to see the beauty and perfection of the mechanism which have been bought at the cost of their lives!

About nine-thirty I was nearing the clouds. Down below me, all blurred and shadowed with rain, lay the vast expanse of Salisbury Plain. Half-a-dozen flying machines were doing hackwork at the thousand-foot level, looking like little black swallows against the green background. I dare say they were wondering what I was doing up in cloud-land. Suddenly a grey curtain drew across beneath me and the wet folds of vapour were swirling round my face. It was clammily cold and miserable. But I was above the hail-storm, and that was something gained. The cloud was as dark and thick as a London fog. In my anxiety to get clear, I cocked her nose up until the automatic alarm-bell rang, and I actually began to slide backwards. My sopped and dripping wings had made me heavier than I thought, but presently I was in lighter cloud, and soon had cleared the layer. There was a second—opal coloured and fleecy—at a great height above my head, a white unbroken ceiling above, and a dark unbroken floor below, with the monoplane labouring upwards upon a vast spiral between them. It is deadly lonely in these cloud-spaces. Once a great flight of some small water-birds went past me, flying very fast to the westwards. The quick whirr of their wing and their musical cry were cheery to my ear. I fancy that they were teal, but I am a wretched zoologist. Now that we humans have become birds we must really learn to know our brethren by sight.

The wind down beneath me whirled and swayed the broad cloud-plain. Once a great eddy formed in it, a whirlpool of vapour, and through it, as down a funnel, I caught sight of the distant world. A large white biplane was passing at a vast depth beneath me. I fancy it was the morning mail service betwixt Bristol and London. Then the drift swirled inwards again and the great solitude was unbroken.

Just after ten I touched the lower edge of the upper cloud-stratum. It consisted of fine diaphanous vapour drifting swiftly from the westward. The wind had been steadily rising all this time and it was now blowing a sharp breeze—twenty-eight an hour by my gauge. Already it was very cold, though my altimeter only marked nine thousand. The engines were working beautifully, and we went droning steadily upwards. The cloud-bank was thicker than I had expected, but at last it thinned out into a golden mist before me, and then in an instant I had shot out from it, and there was an unclouded sky and a brilliant sun above my head—all blue and gold above, all shining silver below, one vast glimmering plain as far as my eyes could reach. It was a quarter past ten o'clock, and the barograph needle pointed to twelve thousand eight hundred. Up I went and up, my ears concentrated upon the deep purring of my motor, my eyes busy always with the watch, the revolution indicator, the petrol lever, and the oil pump. No wonder aviators are said to be a fearless race. With so many things to think of there is no time to trouble about oneself. About this time I noted how unreliable is the compass when above a certain height from earth. At fifteen thousand feet mine was pointing east and a point south. The sun and the wind gave me my true bearings.

I had hoped to reach an eternal stillness in these high altitudes, but with every thousand feet of ascent the gale grew stronger. My machine groaned and trembled in every joint and rivet as she faced it, and swept away like a sheet of paper when I banked her on the turn, skimming down wind at a greater pace, perhaps, than ever mortal man has moved. Yet I had always to turn again and tack up in the wind's eye, for it was not merely a height record that I was after. By all my calculations it was above little Wiltshire that my air-jungle lay, and all my labour might be lost if I struck the outer layers at some farther point.

When I reached the nineteen-thousand foot level, which was about midday, the wind was so severe that I looked with some anxiety to the stays of my wings, expecting momentarily to see them snap or slacken. I even cast loose the parachute behind me, and fastened its hook into the ring of my leathern belt, so as to be ready for the worst. Now was the time when a bit of scamped work by the mechanic is paid for by the life of the aeronaut. But she held together bravely. Every cord and strut was humping and vibrating like so many harp strings, but it was glorious to see how, for all the beating and buffeting, she was still the conqueror of Nature and the mistress of the sky. There is surely something divine in man himself that he should rise so superior to the limitations which Creation seemed to impose—rise, too, by such unselfish heroic devotion as this air-conquest has shown. Talk of human degeneration! When has such as story as this been written in the annals of our race?

These were the thoughts in my head as I climbed that monstrous inclined plane with the wind sometimes beating in my face and sometimes whistling behind my ears, while the cloud-land beneath me fell away to such a distance that the folds and hummocks of silver had all smoothed out into one flat, shining plain. But suddenly I had a horrible and unprecedented experience. I have known before what it is to be in what our neighbours have called a *tourbillon*, but never on such a scale as this. That huge, sweeping river of wind of which I have spoken had, as it appears, whirlpools within it which were as monstrous as itself. Without a moment's warning I was dragged suddenly into the heart of one. I spun round for a minute or two with such velocity that I almost lost my senses, and then fell suddenly, left wing foremost, down the vacuum funnel in the centre. I dropped like a stone, and lost nearly a thousand feet. It was only my belt that kept me in my seat, and the shock and breathlessness left me hanging half-insensible over the side of the fuselage. But I am always capable of a supreme effort—it is my one great merit as an aviator. I was conscious that the descent was slower. The whirlpool was a cone rather than a funnel, and I had come to the apex. With a terrific wrench, throwing my weight all to one side, I levelled my planes and brought her head away from the wind. In an instant I had shot out of the eddies and was skimming down the sky. Then, shaken but victorious, I turned her nose up and began once more my steady grind on the upward spiral. I took a large sweep to avoid the danger-spot of the whirlpool, and soon I was safely above it. Just after one o'clock I was twenty-one thousand feet above the sea-level. To my great joy I had topped the gale, and with every hundred feet of ascent the air grew stiller. On the other hand, it was very cold, and I was conscious of that peculiar nausea which goes with rarefaction of the air. For the first time I unscrewed the mouth of my oxygen bag and took an occasional whiff of the glorious gas. I could feel it running like a cordial through my veins, and I was exhilarated almost to the point of drunkenness. I shouted and sang as I soared upwards into the cold, still outer world.

It is very clear to me that the insensibility which came upon Glaisher, and in a lesser degree upon Coxwell, when, in 1862, they ascended in a balloon to the height of thirty thousand feet, was due to the extreme speed with which a perpendicular ascent is made. Doing it at an easy gradient and accustoming oneself to the lessened barometric pressure by slow degrees, there are no such dreadful symptoms. At the same great height I found that even without my oxygen inhaler I could breathe without undue distress. It was bitterly cold, however, and my thermometer was at zero, Fahrenheit. At one-thirty I was nearly seven miles above the surface of the earth, and still ascending steadily. I found, however, that the rarefied air was giving markedly less support to my planes, and that my angle of ascent had to be considerably lowered in consequence. It was already clear that even with my light weight and strong engine-power there was a point in front of me where I should be held. To make matters worse, one of my sparking-plugs was in trouble again and there was intermittent misfiring in the engine. My heart was heavy with the fear of failure.

It was about that time that I had a most extraordinary experience. Something whizzed past me in a trail of smoke and exploded with a loud, hissing sound, sending forth a cloud of steam. For the instant I could not imagine what had happened. Then I remembered that the earth is for ever being bombarded by meteor stone, and would be hardly inhabitable were they not in nearly every case turned to vapour in the outer layers of the atmosphere. Here is a new danger for the high-altitude man, for two others passed me when I was nearing the forty thousand-foot mark. I cannot doubt that at the edge of the earth's envelope the risk would be a very real one.

My barograph needle marked forty-one thousand three hundred when I became aware that I could go no farther. Physically, the strain was not as yet greater than I could bear, but my machine had reached its limit. The attenuated air gave no firm support to the wings, and the least tilt developed into side-slip, while she seemed sluggish on her controls. Possibly, had the engine been at its best, another thousand feet might have been within our capacity, but it was still misfiring, and two out of the ten cylinders appeared to be out of action. If I had not already reached the zone for which I was searching then I should never see it upon this journey. But was it not possible that I had attained it? Soaring in circles like a monstrous hawk upon the forty-thousand-foot level I let the monoplane guide herself, and with my Mannheim glass I made a careful observation of my surroundings. The heavens were perfectly clear; there was no indication of those dangers which I had imagined.

I have said that I was soaring in circles. It struck me suddenly that I would do well to take a wider sweep and open up a new air-tract. If the hunter entered an earth-jungle he would drive through it if he wished to find his game. My reasoning had led me to believe that the air-jungle which I had imagined lay somewhere over Wiltshire. This should be to the south and west of me. I took my bearings from the sun, for the compass was hopeless and no trace of earth was to be seen—nothing but the distant silver cloud-plain. However, I got my direction as best I might and kept her head straight to the mark. I reckoned that my petrol supply would not last for more than another hour or so, but I could afford to use it to the last drop, since a single magnificent vol-plané could at any time take me to the earth.

Suddenly I was aware of something new. The air in front of me had lost its crystal clearness. It was full of long, ragged wisps of something which I can only compare to very fine cigarette-smoke. It hung about in wreaths and coils, turning and twisting slowly in the sunlight. As the monoplane shot through it, I was aware of a faint taste of oil upon my lips, and there was a greasy scum upon the woodwork of the machine. Some infinitely fine organic matter appeared to be suspended in the atmosphere. There was no life there. It was inchoate and diffuse, extending for many square acres and then fringing off into the void. No, it was not life. But might it not be the remains of life? Above all, might it not be the food of life, of monstrous life, even as the humble grease of the ocean is the food for the mighty whale? The thought was in my mind when my eyes looked upwards and I saw the most wonderful vision that ever man has seen. Can I hope to convey it to you even as I saw it myself last Thursday?

Conceive a jelly-fish such as sails in our summer seas, bell-shaped and of enormous size far larger, I should judge, than the dome of St. Paul's. It was of a light pink colour veined with a delicate green, but the whole huge fabric so tenuous that it was but a fairy outline against the dark blue sky. It pulsated with a delicate and regular rhythm. From it there depended two long, drooping green tentacles, which swayed slowly backward and forwards. This gorgeous vision passed gently with noiseless dignity over my head, as light and fragile as a soap-bubble, and drifted upon its stately way.

I had half-turned my monoplane, that I might look after this beautiful creature, when, in a moment, I found myself amidst a perfect fleet of them, of all sizes, but none so large as the first. Some were quite small, but the majority about as big as an average balloon, and with much the same curvature at the top. There was in them a delicacy of texture and colouring which reminded me of the finest Venetian glass. Pale shades of pink and green were the prevailing tints, but all had a lovely iridescence where the sun shimmered through their dainty form. Some hundred of them drifted past me, a wonderful fairy squadron of strange, unknown argosies of the sky—creatures whose forms and substance were attuned to these pure heights that one could not conceive anything so delicate within actual sight or sound of earth.

But soon my attention was drawn to a new phenomenon—the serpents of the outer air. These were long, thin, fantastic coils of vapour like material, which turned and twisted with great speed, flying round and round at such a pace that the eyes could hardly follow them. Some of these ghost-like creatures were twenty or thirty feet long, but it was difficult to tell their girth, for their outline was so hazy that it seemed to fade away into the air around them. These air-snakes were of a very light grey or smoke colour, with some darker lines within, which gave the impression of a definite organism. One of them whisked past my very face, and I was conscious of a cold, clammy contact, but their composition was so unsubstantial that I could not connect them with any thought of physical danger, any more than the beautiful bell-like creatures which had preceded them. There was no more solidity in their frames than in the floating spume from a broken wave.

But a more terrible experience was in store for me. Floating downwards from a great height there came a purplish patch of vapour, small as I saw it first, but rapidly enlarging as it approached me, until it appeared to be hundreds of square feet in size. Though fashioned of some transparent, jelly-like substance, it was none the less of much more definite outline and solid consistence than anything which I had seen before. There were more traces, too, of a physical organisation, especially two vast shadowy, circular plates upon either side, which may have been eyes, and a perfectly solid white projection between them which was as curved and cruel as the beak of a vulture.

The whole aspect of this monster was formidable and threatening, and it kept changing its colour from a very light mauve to a dark, angry purple so thick that it cast a shadow as it drifted between my monoplane and the sun.

On the upper curve of its huge body there were three great projections which I can only describe as enormous bubbles, and I was convinced as I looked at them that they were charged with some extremely light gas which served to buoy up the misshapen and semi-solid mass in the rarefied air. The creature moved swiftly along, keeping pace easily with the monoplane, and for twenty miles or more it formed my horrible escort, hovering over me like a bird of prey which is waiting to pounce. Its method of progression—done so swiftly that it was not easy to follow—was to throw out a long, glutinous streamer in front of it, which in turn seemed to draw forward the rest of the writhing body. So elastic and gelatinous was it that never for two successive minutes was it the same shape, and yet each change made it more threatening and loathsome than the last.

I knew that it meant mischief. Every purple flush of its hideous body told me so. The vague, goggling eyes which were turned always upon me were cold and merciless in their viscid hatred. I dipped the nose of my monoplane downwards to escape it. As I did so, as quick as a flash there shot out a long tentacle from this mass of floating blubber, and it fell as light and sinuous as a whip-lash across the front of my machine. There was a loud hiss as it lay for a moment across the hot engine, and it whisked itself into the air again, while the huge flat body drew itself together as if in sudden pain. I dipped to a vol-piqué, but again a tentacle fell over the monoplane and was shorn off by the propeller as easily as it might have cut through a smoke wreath. A long, gliding, sticky, serpent-like coil came from behind and caught me round the waist, dragging me out of the fuselage. I tore at it, my fingers sinking into the smooth, glue-like surface, and for an instant I disengaged myself, but only to be caught round the boot by another coil, which gave me a jerk that tilted me almost on to my back.

As I fell over I blazed off both barrels of my gun, though, indeed, it was like attacking an elephant with a pea-shooter to imagine that any human weapon could cripple that mighty bulk. And yet I aimed better than I knew, for, with a loud report, one of the great blisters upon the creature's back exploded with the puncture of the buck-shot. It was very clear that my conjecture was right, and that these vast clear bladders were distended with some lifting gas, for in an instant the huge cloud-like body turned sideways, writhing desperately to find its balance, while the white beak snapped and gaped in horrible fury. But already I had shot away on the steepest glide that I dared to attempt, my engine still full on, the flying propeller and the force of gravity shooting me downwards like an aerolite. Far behind me I saw a dull, purplish smudge growing swiftly smaller and merging into the blue sky behind it. I was safe out of the deadly jungle of the outer air.

Once out of danger I throttled my engine, for nothing tears a machine to pieces quicker than running on full power from a height. It was a glorious spiral vol-plané from nearly eight miles of altitude—first, to the level of the silver cloud-bank, then to that of the storm cloud beneath it, and finally, in beating rain, to the surface of the earth. I saw the Bristol Channel beneath me as I broke from the clouds, but, having still some petrol in my tank, I got twenty miles inland before I found myself stranded in a field half a mile from the village of Ashcombe. There I got three tins of petrol from a passing motor-car, and at ten minutes past six that evening I alighted gently in my own home meadow at Devizes, after such a journey as no mortal upon earth has ever yet taken and lived to tell the tale. I have seen the beauty and I have seen the horror of the heights—and greater beauty or greater horror than that is not within the ken of man.

And now it is my plan to go once again before I give my results to the world. My reason for this is that I must surely have something to show by way of proof before I lay such a tale before my fellow-men. It is true that others will soon follow and will confirm what I have said, and yet I should wish to carry conviction from the first. Those lovely iridescent bubbles of the air should not be hard to capture. They drift slowly upon their way, and the swift monoplane could intercept their leisurely course. It is likely enough that they would dissolve in the heavier layers of the atmosphere, and that some small heap of amorphous jelly might be all that I should bring to earth with me. And yet something there would surely be by which I could substantiate my story. Yes, I will go, even if I run a risk by doing so. These purple horrors would not seem to be numerous. It is probable that I shall not see one. If I do I shall dive at once. At the worst there is always the shot-gun and my knowledge of. . . .

Here a page of the manuscript is unfortunately missing. On the next page is written, in large, straggling writing:—

Forty-three thousand feet. I shall never see earth again. They are beneath me, three of them. God help me; it is a dreadful death to die!

Such in its entirety is the Joyce-Armstrong Statement. Of the man nothing has since been seen. Pieces of his shattered monoplane have been picked up in the preserves of Mr. Budd-Lushington, upon the borders of Kent and Sussex, within a few miles of the spot where the note-book was discovered. If the unfortunate aviator's theory is correct that this air-jungle, as he called it, existed only over the South-west of England, then it would seem that he had fled from it at the full speed of his monoplane, but had been overtaken and devoured by these horrible creatures at some spot in the outer atmosphere above the place where the grim relics were found. The picture of that monoplane skimming down the sky, with the nameless terrors flying as swiftly beneath it and cutting it off always from the earth while they gradually closed in upon their victim, is one upon which a man who valued his sanity would prefer not to dwell. There are many, as I am aware, who still jeer at the facts which I have here set down, but even they must admit that Joyce-Armstrong has disappeared, and I would commend to them his own words:

This note-book may explain what I am trying to do, and how I lost my life in doing it. But no drivel about accidents or mysteries, if *you* please.

❖

Acknowledgments

THANKS FIRST TO MY tireless four-year-old son, Vance, whose love of books and nature already bodes well. Many thanks to my agent, Heide Lange, who has been guarding my career for two decades, and to her assistants Stephanie Delman and Samantha Isman. George Gibson, my editor at Bloomsbury through seven books, advised and patiently edited. Thanks also to the rest of the crew at Bloomsbury USA: assistant editor Grace McNamee, art director Patti Ratchford, production editor Carrie Hsieh, and publicist Sarah New. Thank you to the invaluable crew at the Greensburg and Hempfield Area Library, who track down obscure tomes: Sara Deegan, Jessica Kiefer, Christine Lee, and Aurea Lucas. Also many thanks to library director Linda Matey and to Diane Ciabattoni and Donna Davis. Perpetual gratitude to the former director and ongoing pal, Cesare Muccari. John Spurlock and Jon Erickson were essential, as usual. Jerry Felton, Robert Majcher, and Katherine Neely keep yours truly typing.

Bibliography and Suggested Further Reading

THIS BIBLIOGRAPHY INCLUDES SOURCES cited in, or useful in the writing of, this book's introductory essay or its individual story introductions. It also includes selected biographies, general introductions to the topics of science fiction stories up to the Edwardian era, and essays and articles of particular relevance. It excludes works by those authors whose stories appear in this anthology and thus receive attention in the biographical note that introduces their contribution. For further information about many of the authors whose stories are included in this volume, see the other volumes of my Connoisseur's Collection series for Bloomsbury, cited below under Sims.

Aldiss, Brian. *Billion Year Spree: The True History of Science Fiction.* New York: Doubleday, 1973.

Ashley, Mike, ed. *The Dreaming Sex: Early Tales of Scientific Imagination by Women.* London: Peter Owen, 2011.

Beckson, Karl. *London in the 1890s: A Cultural History.* New York: W. W. Norton & Company, 1992.

Bentley, Nicolas. *The Victorian Scene: 1837–1901.* London: Weidenfeld and Nicolson, 1968.

Bleiler, Everett F. *Science-Fiction: The Early Years.* Kent, OH: Kent State University Press, 1990.

Buckland, Adelene. *Novel Science: Fiction and the Invention of Nineteenth-Century Geology*. Chicago: University of Chicago Press, 2013.

Conan Doyle, Arthur. *Arthur Conan Doyle: A Life in Letters*, edited by Jon Lellenberg, Daniel Stashower, and Charles Foley. New York: Penguin Press, 2007.

———. *Memories and Adventures*. London: Hodder and Stoughton, 1924.

Crain, Caleb. "The Monarch of Dreams." Review of *The Magnificent Activist: The Writings of Thomas Wentworth Higginson, 1823–1911*, edited by Howard N. Meyer. *The New Republic*, May 28, 2001.

Davidson, Cathy N. *The Experimental Fictions of Ambrose Bierce: Structuring the Ineffable*. Lincoln, NE: University of Nebraska Press, 1984.

Ensor, Sir Robert. *England 1870–1914*. London: Oxford University Press, 1936.

Hopkins, Lisa. "Jane C. Loudon's 'The Mummy!': Mary Shelley Meets George Orwell and They Go in a Balloon to Egypt." *Cardiff Corvey: Reading the Romantic Text* 10 (June 2003).

Jarrell, Randall. *Kipling, Auden & Co.: Essays and Reviews, 1935–1964*. New York: Farrar, Straus and Giroux, 1980. See especially Jarrell's essays "On Preparing to Read Kipling," "In the Vernacular," and "The English in England."

Lottman, Herbert R. *Jules Verne: An Exploratory Biography*. New York: St. Martin's Press, 1996.

Maugham, W. Somerset. "Introduction." *Maugham's Choice of Kipling's Best*. New York: Doubleday, 1953.

Mitchell, Sally. *Frances Power Cobbe: Victorian Feminist, Journalist, Reformer*. Charlottesville: University of Virginia Press, 2004.

Moore, Doris Langley. *E. Nesbit: A Biography*. Philadelphia: Chilton Books, 1966.

Morris, Roy, Jr. *Ambrose Bierce: Alone in Bad Company*. New York: Oxford University Press, 1995.

Moskowitz, Sam, ed. *The Crystal Man: Stories by Edward Page Mitchell.* New York: Doubleday, 1973.

Peithman, Stephen, ed. *The Annotated Tales of Edgar Allan Poe.* New York: Doubleday, 1981.

Ricketts, Harry. *Rudyard Kipling: A Life.* New York: Carroll & Graf, 2000.

Seed, David. *Anticipations: Essays on Early Science Fiction and Its Precursors.* Liverpool: Liverpool University Press, 1995.

Sims, Michael, ed. *Dracula's Guest: A Connoisseur's Collection of Victorian Vampire Stories.* New York and London: Walker/Bloomsbury, 2009.

Wineapple, Brenda. *White Heat: The Friendship of Emily Dickinson and Thomas Wentworth Higginson.* New York: Knopf Publishing Group, 2008.

A Note on the Author

Michael Sims is the author of *The Story of Charlotte's Web*, which the *Washington Post*, *Boston Globe*, and other venues chose as a best book of the year; *The Adventures of Henry Thoreau*; and *Arthur and Sherlock*, among other books. His book *Adam's Navel* was a *New York Times* Notable Book and a *Library Journal* Best Science Book. He edits the Connoisseur's Collection series of Victorian anthologies, including *Dracula's Guest*, *The Dead Witness*, and *The Phantom Coach*. He lives in western Pennsylvania.